D1332969

Standing in the Shadows

PETER ROBINSON

Standing in the Shadows

HODDER &
STOUGHTON

First published in Great Britain in 2023 by Hodder & Stoughton
An Hachette UK company

1

Copyright © Peter Robinson 2023

A CIP catalogue record for this title is available from the British Library

Hardback ISBN 978 1 529 34316 8
Trade Paperback ISBN 978 1 529 34317 5
eBook ISBN 978 1 529 34319 9

Typeset in Plantin light by Manipal Technologies Limited

Printed and bound in Great Britain by Clays Ltd, Elcograf S.p.A.

Hodder & Stoughton policy is to use papers that are natural, renewable
and recyclable products and made from wood grown in sustainable forests.
The logging and manufacturing processes are expected to conform
to the environmental regulations of the country of origin.

Hodder & Stoughton Ltd
Carmelite House
50 Victoria Embankment
London EC4Y 0DZ

www.hodder.co.uk

Standing in the Shadows

I

28 November 1980

Let me start at the beginning. The first sign that something was wrong was the police patrol car parked outside the house, along with a black Ford Capri. The next thing I noticed was that the front door was wide open, and people I didn't recognise stood talking in the hallway, one of them a uniformed police officer.

I flew up the front steps two at a time and went in. Or tried to. Before I got far, the uniformed officer held out his arm to bar my way.

'Oy, you can't go in there,' he said. 'It's a possible crime scene.'

'What do you mean? I live here.'

He consulted his clipboard.

'Name?'

'Nicholas Hartley.'

He screwed up his eyes and ran his finger down the list. It can't have been that hard to find my name; there are two bedsits on the ground floor, two in the basement, two on the first floor and a one-bedroom flat at the top. Seven of us altogether. It was student accommodation.

'Nicholas Hartley. First floor?'

'That's me.'

One of the men he had been talking to was peering over the officer's shoulder at the clipboard. 'It's OK, Glen,' he said. 'Let him through.' Then he looked at me. 'Come on, son, show me where you live.'

'What's going on?' I asked, but he just gestured for me to get going.

The stairs creaked as we walked up, but other than that, the house seemed quite silent. I opened the door to my lowly bedsit, and the man followed me inside. Within moments he was joined by a colleague, and the room felt overcrowded. Both men were burly, like rugby players, one only slightly shorter than the other. But what he lacked in height he made up for in girth. He was balding and had a nose that had clearly been broken more than once. The other, who had led me up, was younger and slimmer, with cropped ginger hair and freckles. Both wore navy overcoats open over baggy suits, and their well-shined shoes were crusted with mud. I took off my parka and tossed it on the bed, along with my satchel. It was cold in my room, but I didn't really have the presence of mind to bung a coin in the meter and turn on the gas heater that occupied the large, disused fireplace. I was discombobulated. No doubt that was their intention. They kept their overcoats on.

'Mind if we come in, Nick?' asked Baldy.

I was about to say that it didn't look as if I had much choice, seeing as they were both already over the threshold, but I stopped myself in time. Somehow, I got the impression they wouldn't have much of a sense of humour. Not on the job, at any rate, and they certainly acted as if they were on the job.

'Do you mind telling me who you are and showing some identification?' I asked, shutting the door behind them.

'Not at all.' Baldy took a wallet from his pocket and flipped it open. 'DI Glassco, and my colleague here is DC Marley. Like him.' He pointed to a poster of Bob Marley I had on my wall.

'A fan of his, are you?' asked DC Marley.

'I like his music,' I answered.

'Hmph. Give me the Beatles any day. Student, are you?'

As Marley spoke, DI Glassco started conducting a casual search of my room, poking around in drawers, on top of the wardrobe, peeking behind the moth-eaten curtain that hid the kitchenette with its hotplate and sink. His movements made me nervous.

'Yes,' I said. 'I've just started my final year. What are you doing here? Have you got a search warrant?'

'No, but if you like,' said DI Glassco, 'I'll stay here with you while DC Marley runs out and gets one.' They both stared at me, blank expressions on their faces.

'Forget it,' I said. 'Just hurry up.'

'Why?' asked Glassco, lifting the edge of the mattress. 'Got somewhere you have to be? Something you have to do?'

'An essay to write,' I said.

'Mind if I sit down?' Marley asked. 'My feet are killing me.' There were only two small armchairs in the room, res-cued from a local bonfire a year ago. Marley eased into one of them and gestured for me to take the other. 'We won't bite,' he said.

I sat. Glassco leaned against the fireplace, tapped an Embassy Regal from a packet of twenty and lit it. I took my tin of tobacco from my pocket and started to roll an Old Holborn. I heard a thud from upstairs. Alice's room.

'What's happening up there?' I asked, remembering the patrol cars outside.

'Never you mind about that,' said Glassco. 'We're taking care of things. The uniforms are searching and protecting the scene till the SOCOs come.'

'Scene? SOCOs?'

'Scenes-of-crime officers.'

'What scene? What crime?'

'You know the lass who lived up there?'

'Alice? Yes.' I noticed that he used the past tense, but the significance didn't really dawn on me fully until later. At the moment, I was simply confused and stunned to find myself being questioned by the police. I had never had any sort of contact with the law before.

'Know her well?' Glassco asked.

I paused. 'Her name's Alice Poole. She's a social sciences and politics student. Parents are quite well off. Own a brewery in Lincolnshire. That's why she can afford the Penthouse.'

'Penthouse?'

'What we call it. The upstairs flat.'

'Oh, I see,' said Glassco. 'A joke, eh?'

'That's right.'

'When did you last see Alice?'

'Yesterday evening.'

'What time?'

'Around seven. I was just getting back from the chippy and she was on her way out.'

'Off where?'

'She didn't say, but it seemed pretty obvious to me that she was going to her boyfriend's place. Mark. They were supposed to be heading down to London for a demo this weekend. She was carrying a smallish rucksack. The weather was terrible, though. It was pissing down and the wind was blowing even worse than today. The roads were bad. Flash floods. I don't know if they got off this morning or not. I don't even know if they were planning on driving or taking the train.'

'Owns a car, does he, this Mark?'

'Yes. A Morris Marina. Dark blue.'

'What demo were they going to?'

'Does it matter? Ban the Bomb. Reclaim the Night. Out with Thatcher. You name it.'

'Bit of a commie, this Alice? A Bennite?'

'She's just very political. Socialist. Marxist.'

'CND, women's lib and all that?'

'All of the above. And then some.'

'Red Brigade? IRA? Baader-Meinhof Gang? Weathermen?'

'I wouldn't go that far. No. Alice is pro-peace, against violence.'

'You?'

'I'm apolitical.'

'A political what?'

'No. I mean, I'm not really interested.'

'Did they often go away to demos and suchlike?'

'I suppose so. They've been down to London before, a couple of times. I think Mark has friends there.'

'Did she say anything to you when you saw her?'

'Just something about it being a miserable night.'

'That's all?'

'Yes. Neither of us wanted to stand around in the street talking.'

'How did she seem?'

'What do you mean?'

'Was she upset about anything? Did she seem worried, angry, frightened?'

'No, nothing like that. Not that I noticed. Just normal, I suppose. If anything, she seemed in a hurry. It might have been the weather.'

Glassco squinted down at me. 'Sure that was the last time you saw her?'

'Yes. I told you. Why would I . . . ? What's wrong? Has something happened to Alice?'

'Why would you think that?' Marley asked.

'Just the way you're behaving. What you're not telling me. You're not here for no reason.'

'Ah. I can tell why they let you into university,' said Marley. He glanced up towards Glassco, who gave him a curt nod. 'Where have you been?'

'When?'

'Let's start with today,' Marley asked.

'The university; I had lectures.'

'What lectures?'

'Nineteenth-Century Novel, and a Shakespeare tutorial.'

'And last night, after you saw Alice Poole?'

'I was here.'

'Alone?'

'Yes.'

'Doing what?'

'Working on an essay I had due for today's tutorial.'

'Essay about what?'

'Shakespeare's use of silence.'

'What *silent* plays would those be, then?' Marley asked.

'*The Tempest. Measure for Measure. Hamlet.*'

'I thought Shakespeare's plays were full of people talking.'

I said nothing. I knew he was baiting me.

'So, you were here all night? In this room? Working on this essay?'

'And reading. Yes. Mostly.'

'*Mostly?* You did go out, then?'

'I finished my essay earlier than I thought I would, so I went to the pub for last orders. The Hyde Park. Just up the road, on the corner.'

'Who with?'

'I met some mates there. It was nothing arranged. Just casual, like.'

'What time?'

'It would have been about a quarter to ten, something like that. I had two pints, then came home.'

'Is that what you usually do on an evening?'

'Sometimes. If I've got any money in my pocket.'

'You'd be able to give us the names of these mates you were drinking with, would you? They'd vouch for you?'

'If they had to, yes. I'm not lying.'

'No one said you were, son,' said Glassco, smoothly taking over from Marley. 'We just have to cross all the t's and dot all the i's in our job. We'll be asking everyone else here the same questions. What's the boyfriend's second name?'

'Woodcroft. Mark Woodcroft.'

'You sound as if you don't approve.'

'I can't imagine why you'd think that. You're reading things into what I say. Anyway, what about him?'

'We'd like to find him, that's all, ask him a few questions. Know where he lives?'

'St John's Terrace,' I said. 'Just across the park. But I told you, they were planning on going away. Maybe they went despite the weather.'

'*He* might have gone to a demo in London,' Glassco said. 'The boyfriend. But *she* definitely hasn't. Did you see them go?'

I felt my blood turning to ice water. 'No. Of course not. What do you mean, *she* hasn't gone anywhere?'

'Is it likely they changed their minds?'

'Alice could be impulsive. I don't know about Mark. And like I said, the weather was bad, though it did stop raining later.'

'Do you own a car?'

'Me? Good Lord, no. Can't afford one. I never even learned to drive. Besides, I hardly need one here. The university's in easy walking distance.'

'We can check, you know. The driving and all.'

'Go ahead.'

'What about Alice?'

'No. She could afford one, but she hasn't learned to drive yet, either.'

'Can you help us find the boyfriend?'

'I'm afraid I can't. I've told you all I know. I don't know much about him. He's not a student, so he won't be in a lecture or anything.'

'What does he do? Where does he work?'

'I don't know. I don't even know if he does. Work, that is.'

'But he's got a car, you said. He must have a bob or two. Any idea where he might have got it from?'

'No. Maybe he did have a job. I don't know. Maybe he's unemployed now. Just because I live in the same house as his girlfriend, it doesn't mean we're mates or anything. We don't live in one another's pockets.'

'You must see him around the place.'

'Occasionally. He spends some time here with Alice. They split their time between his place and hers.'

'So you *don't* like him?' said Marley.

I gave him a sharp glance. 'I didn't say that.'

'It's just the impression I get from your tone, the expression on your face whenever his name comes up.'

I let the silence stretch for a moment, then said, 'I don't think he's right for her, that's all.'

'Why not?'

'I just don't trust him. There's something about him. Something a bit off.'

'"A bit off"?' Glassco repeated. 'What does that mean? Alice Poole obviously didn't feel the same way.'

I shrugged. 'I don't particularly like him, now that you mention it. I'm sure there are people you don't like, too. But what I'm saying is that I don't keep track of him. I don't have any idea what he does or where he goes.'

'How long has he been living with her?'

'They're not technically living together, but they've been going out since the beginning of term, maybe even longer. The summer. I don't know.'

'Couple of months, at least, then,' said Glassco. 'When was the last time he stopped over?'

'I don't know. I don't keep tabs on them.'

'Days, weeks, months?'

'It was earlier this week sometime. Maybe Monday.'

'How did they seem together?'

'I don't know. I don't have her flat bugged. I didn't see them together.'

'What can you tell us about her?'

'Alice? Like I said, she's a student.'

'Bright lass, then, is she?'

'She takes her studies seriously. Works hard. She's just like anyone else, really. Perhaps more radical than most.'

'Good-looking?'

I glanced away, down at the threadbare carpet. 'I suppose so.'

'Fancy her yourself, did you, Nick? You're not queer, are you?'

'No, I'm not,' I said. 'Not that there'd be anything wrong with it if I was.' I felt myself flushing and knew my anger must be obvious to Glassco and Marley. Maybe that's what they had been trying to do, make me lose my temper in the hope I'd give something away. But about *what*? They exchanged glances, then Glassco stubbed out his cigarette in the ashtray on my work table – pinched from the local pub – and they both just stared at me.

'Sorry,' said Marley finally. 'Didn't mean to embarrass you or upset you. If you really *did* like her, I'm afraid we've got some bad news.'

'What? Has something happened to her? A car crash or something? Has he hurt her?' Though I had a terrible inkling of just what was coming.

'Worse than that,' said Glassco. 'I'm sorry to be the one telling you this, son, but Alice Poole was found dead this morning.'

24 November 2019

Time was of the essence, Grace Hutchinson knew as she arrived at the dig early that bright Sunday morning in November. Soon the field she was standing in would be a shopping centre, and its priceless artefacts lost for ever under Tommy Hilfiger, BOSS, Adidas and McDonald's. She knew that the grid the site boss, Malcolm, had assigned her was not one of the most promising. She also knew that he done this not because he didn't like her, but because he *did* like her, too much, and she had turned down his request for a date. Still, she would do her best without complaining. She reminded herself what she had learned from past experience: there was no predicting what she might find under the earth, even at the far end of a neglected field by a drystone wall. The landscape would have appeared completely different in Roman times.

It was cold enough that she could see her breath, but the ground wasn't frozen yet, and the slightly damp soil was still loose, so it didn't prove too difficult to make a good start. The mechanical digger had cleared away the sod and topsoil during the week.

After she had worked for a while, Grace leaned on her spade to catch her breath and felt the cold breeze ruffle her hair and chill the sweat on her brow. She looked out over the fields towards the traffic on the A1, almost a mile away to the east. Before work was due to begin on the giant new shopping centre and access roads, the archaeologists were allowed their turn. Highways England, along with the construction company, had managed to negotiate a deal for the Northern Archaeological Associates to get in there first and see what they could find.

An earlier dig, further up the A1, had yielded a great deal of information about the Roman occupation of the north. People already knew quite a lot about settlements at Catterick and Bainesse, and they knew that the A1 followed the old Roman road, Dere Street, from York up to Hadrian's Wall. But they'd had no idea what a wealth of pottery, leather shoes, bracelets, rings and human remains lay beneath the earth, not to mention traces of old boundaries and buildings, walls, bridges and so on. Grace had been on that dig. She remembered well the surge of excitement at each new discovery – unusual beads indicating trade with the Balkans, Spain and North Africa, an amphora with an exotic design, a discarded spur or marble figurine – after hours of hard work and boring sieving or brushing. They had found evidence of Iron Age presence, too – coins and coin-making facilities – so the meeting of the modern A1, running north and south, and the A66, running east and west, had clearly been an important centre of commerce and settlement for many centuries.

Only now were the experts beginning to piece things together. That was why this dig was important. It lay on the eastern outskirts of Eastvale, a few miles south of the Scotch Corner dig, over which the new motorway access roads now ran, and all the signs and preliminary scans suggested this one might also provide a wealth of riches. But not Grace's particular grid, she thought.

Grace tucked her hair behind her ears and got back to work again, but before she had dug much further down, her shovel scraped against something more solid than the soil. She stopped immediately. At about three feet, she was nowhere near deep enough for Roman remains, but something was clearly there, blocking her way, just beneath the earth. She picked up her trowel and light brush and carefully stepped into the trench. Then she knelt and gently scooped soil away with her trowel, using the brush with her other hand. It was slow and painstaking work, but before long she came to a halt, certain of what she had found, even before the whole object had been uncovered. She stood up, feeling a little shaky, and called out to Malcolm. He came striding over the field in that authoritative male way he had and peered sternly over the lip of the trench at what she had partially unearthed.

'Bloody hell,' he said. 'What have you gone and done now?'

Grace shook her head. 'What should we do?'

'Leave it,' Malcolm said. 'You've hardly disturbed it any more than you needed to see what it is. Best stop now and call the police.'

Grace joined him up on the edge of the hole and they both stared down at what was clearly a human skull.

24 November 2019

When Banks assessed the damage the following morning, he realised that he didn't feel too bad, despite the large Highland Park he had drunk out in the conservatory before going to bed. It had seemed like a good idea at the time. He had been to the Dog and Gun to hear Penny Cartwright sing. It was a rare local performance, as these days she was much in demand in halls and folk clubs around the country. There seemed to be a folk revival lately, and Penny was reaping some of the benefits of it. Well-deserved, Banks thought, as she had certainly paid her dues for long enough. He had hoped to spend some time with her over a drink or two after the performance, but there were a bunch of other folkies in attendance, friends and hangers-on, and he had felt excluded, so he had wandered off home alone. Then came the Highland Park and Richard Thompson's *Acoustic Classics*.

Now it was Sunday morning, and time to relax. First, he put the kettle on, then he headed down the hallway and through the small anteroom he used as his study to the front door, where he bent to pick up the papers. Sunday meant movie, music and book reviews. He always seemed to end up buying or streaming something. He felt vaguely guilty about the streaming, but if there were any record shops left, he would certainly frequent them; nor would he complain if the recording artists got their way and took a fairer share of the streaming profits. He had never minded paying for his books or records. Fortunately, Eastvale had both a Waterstones and an independent bookshop, and between them he could usually get what he wanted quickly enough. And he had to confess to using Amazon on occasion.

The kettle boiled, and he made a cup of tea, then slipped a slice of white bread in the toaster as he prepared his spot at the breakfast nook. 'White bread for toast,' his father had always maintained. 'How can you tell when it's done if it's brown to start with?' Banks smiled at the thought of his father, now only about forty miles or so away near the Northumbrian border in a private care home, edging towards his nineties along with Banks's mother. They were still basically healthy, though, despite numerous minor ailments that plagued everyone as they got older.

The toast popped up and he was just reaching for the marmalade when his mobile rang. Wondering who the hell would be calling at such an hour on a Sunday morning, he answered.

'Sorry to bother you, sir,' came DC Gerry Masterson's voice, 'but we've got a situation here, and I think you'd better come.'

'One thing at a time,' said Banks. 'What situation, and where's "here"?'

'It's still a mystery.'

'Well, I suppose mysteries are our business. Start with where this one might be?'

'In a field just east of town, about a mile from the A1. You know, where they're going to widen the road and put up that new shopping centre. To get here, you need to take that lane that runs parallel, just—'

'I think I know the one you mean,' said Banks. 'But what are *you* doing there?'

'I caught the call. I'm on duty today.'

'Weren't you on duty last Sunday?'

'I was. Yes. But it's difficult, sir. I don't mind. I've nothing else to do today. We're short-staffed. DS Jackman's on that refresher course, and she won't be back until Monday. And DI Cabbot . . . well . . . you know.'

Banks did know. Annie Cabbot hadn't been quite on the ball since her father Ray had died the previous month, and she had taken a leave of absence to sort out his affairs. Hardly surprising, Banks thought, as her mother had died when Annie was very young, and Ray had brought her up almost single-handedly.

'OK,' he said, biting back the career-killing urge to tell Gerry that an attractive young woman like her ought to have a lot more to do on a Sunday morning than hang about in muddy fields looking at . . . well, he didn't know that yet. 'What's it all about?'

'A skull.'

'Human?'

'The archaeologist says so.'

'Archaeologist?'

'She dug it up,' Gerry said. 'You know they found all that Roman stuff up the A1 when the motorway work was going on there?'

'Yes.'

'Well, they think there may be a hoard here, too, further south, and they've got permission to dig in this field before work starts on that new designer village.'

'And this archaeologist . . . ?'

'Grace, sir. Grace Hutchinson.'

'This Grace Hutchinson. What else does she say?'

'She came across it when she'd just started digging in the field this morning.'

'Any particular reason she doesn't think it's one of her Romans? They found a whole burial ground last time they went out on a dig around these parts.'

'Not deep enough. This one was under only about three feet of soil.'

'And the field?'

'Not exactly prime farmland. More like a stretch of waste ground, really. Grace says she doesn't think it's been used for years. Not big enough to be worth planting cash crops, for a start, and the soil's not particularly good. Too acidic, apparently. Besides, the highways department and the property developers have got their hands on it.'

'Any signs of cause of death?'

'Not yet. But Grace has been very careful. She only uncovered the skull, and brushed enough soil off to make sure that's what it was. Then she stopped.'

'Anything buried with it?'

'Grace thinks it appears very much as if the rest of the skeleton was present, but she didn't want to disturb anything.

I took the liberty of brushing more soil away, and that seems to be the case. What should we do now? Should I call the CSIs? Do you want to come out and have a look first?'

Banks thought for a moment. On the one hand, he could hardly neglect his duty and leave Gerry, still a mere detective constable, to deal with the situation by herself, but on the other, he had a slice of toast fast growing cold in one hand, the culture section of the *Sunday Times* open on the table in front of him, and a cup of Yorkshire Gold tea steaming beside it. And the kitchen was nice and warm. He sighed. 'Stay put,' he said. 'Don't call in the team just yet. I'll be with you as fast as I can.'

28 November 1980

Alice? Dead? When Glassco and Marley left, I was sick in my tiny sink. I cleaned myself up, made a cup of tea and rolled another cigarette. I was still shaking. I'd had the remnants of a quid deal in my pocket throughout the police visit, so I'd been nervous as Marley poked about my drawers, worried he would want to search my person. Luckily, I had nothing else stashed in the room, and the visit obviously wasn't about drugs. As I slumped back in my armchair, I could hear thuds and muffled voices coming from upstairs. They were turning over Alice's flat. Outside, car doors slammed and footsteps sounded up and down the front steps. What the hell had happened? I had asked how, why, but they wouldn't give me any more details. Only that she was dead.

Then I realised.

Though the Yorkshire Ripper had been inactive for about fifteen months, and was thought either to have retired or died, he had recently struck again. It was now just over a week since poor Jacqueline Hill had been murdered – by the Ripper, the police thought – in Headingley, not more than a mile or so up Otley Road from here. Jacqueline was a second-year English student at the university, just like me. I knew her by sight from various lectures, and to say hello to, but we didn't share any tutorial groups, and we obviously moved in different circles. Still, it was bloody close to home, and we were all devastated. Since then, the sense of panic and fear had returned to the north with a vengeance. Nobody felt safe. Despite the overwhelming police presence on the streets, women stayed indoors, or ventured out at night only in groups of two or more. The pubs and university area went quiet after seven o'clock, and the city centre emptied out.

Alice and her friends had organised another 'Reclaim the Night' walk just days after Jacqueline's murder. Along with two hundred other women, she had marched on the Plaza Cinema in the city centre, which, in its wisdom, was showing a double bill of *The Beasts* and *Climax*, and then down to the Odeon, on the Headrow, which was featuring Michael Caine and Angie Dickinson in Brian de Palma's *Dressed to Kill*.

Alice had also spoken at a conference on sexual violence in all its forms – in the workplace, on the streets, at home. She argued that the more power women asked for, the more men used sexual violence as a means of control. I couldn't argue with that. Hundreds of women also marched to defy the curfew, arguing that they shouldn't be the ones to have to hide away and limit their freedom because of male sexual violence. I couldn't argue with that, either. Nor with their contention that the police hadn't taken as much notice when the Ripper was killing prostitutes as they did now there were decent, innocent women among his victims. If Alice had still been with me, we would have been in agreement about it all. But none of the anger and the passion with which it was delivered diminished the atmosphere of fear that permeated the streets of Leeds in those times.

The police wouldn't give any details away about Alice's death, but they probably thought it was also the work of the Ripper. Why else wouldn't they tell me anything?

But, my God, could it really be Alice? All Glassco had said was that she was dead, not murdered or anything. But would they be making such a fuss if she had died in a car crash, for example? And if that had been the case, wouldn't Mark have been killed, too, or at least badly injured? Yet they implied they didn't know where he was. Did they suspect him?

Maybe it hadn't been the Ripper, but I was becoming convinced that somebody had killed Alice. And *where* had she died? When? I imagined her body lying broken and pale, maybe even bloody, in some bushes or on some waste ground somewhere. As far as I knew, she had stopped at Mark's last night, then they would have set off early this morning to London. She didn't have any lectures on a Friday, though she never minded missing one or two if they got in the way of a good cause, so I hadn't expected to see her back here until maybe Tuesday or Wednesday next week.

I tried to remember exactly what she had said when she passed me on her way out. As I'd told Glassco, she had been in a hurry, and she had seemed brusque and keen to get away. But I'd thought nothing of that. For one thing, I was her ex, and we'd hardly been talking much lately, even in comfortable surroundings, and, as I remembered, Alice had never been much of a one for street-corner conversations. It was also raining hard.

She had, I remembered, hardly stopped walking, just muttered something about the miserable weather and having to get along. There had been a sense of purpose about her, though. She was walking with that stiff, determined, clipped gait – her *clickety-clack* walk, I always called it – that she always walked with when she had somewhere important to go or something to do. Or when she was pissed off with someone. An impatient walk. I had thought little of it at the time, more concerned with getting in out of the rain before my fish and chips went cold and got soggy, but when I thought about it now, there was definitely a sense of urgency about her. Was she not going to Mark's, as I had assumed? Or perhaps not immediately? Had she somewhere else to go first? Something to do? Something to say to someone? Could that have been the reason for what had happened? I told myself not to let my imagination run away with me, but as usual, it was more a matter of me running away with my imagination, which was hard to stop.

Alice. I couldn't believe it. Didn't want to believe it. It was true that we had split up, and that for a while I had hated her. But that passed. Then Mark entered the scene. She had seemed happy with him. That was the main thing, I told myself. And almost convinced myself. But I *couldn't* keep on hating her; I loved her too much. And now she was dead, and the police were all over her life. I kept imagining how she had died. Did she suffer? Was she raped? Strangled? Beaten? Stabbed? Was it slow and drawn-out or mercifully quick? Did it hurt?

I stayed where I was and listened to the footsteps coming and going. The SOCOs, if that was who turned up in the minivan, certainly made plenty of noise. I knew that Glassco and Marley, or others just like them, would be back knocking on my door again before long. They would talk to all the tenants in the house, to Geoff, Dave, Sally, Anton and Maria as well. But they would certainly be back at my door. I could tell by the way Glassco had stared at me when he told me Alice was dead. It sounded impossible, I know, but I couldn't help thinking that he suspected maybe *I* was the one who had killed her. Did that mean he also thought *I* was the Yorkshire Ripper?

24 November 2019

Banks stood on the edge of the trench with DC Gerry Masterson and the supervisor, Malcolm Briers, looking down at the skull and the patches of bone Grace had uncovered with her light brushing. This wasn't his first skeleton. Some years ago, a young boy had discovered one in a dried-up reservoir, and that had resulted in a case that took Banks right back to events of the Second World War. He discovered then that putting a timeline to such things was often a long and difficult process, with no guarantee of success. Just *how* long was a job for the forensics team, the pathologist and the lab technicians to work out.

As he stared at the dirt-streaked skull, he thought of Webster's line about the skull beneath the skin and about the way skulls had been used over the centuries as *memento mori*, something the Romans who had lived in the area would certainly have known a lot about.

He found himself having too many uninvited morbid thoughts these days, as he got older. According to his doctor, he was in good health, with blood pressure and cholesterol under control, albeit through medication. He was also trim and in fairly good physical shape, more through good luck than good habits. Most people said he looked hardly a day over fifty. On his last check-up, the doctor had mentioned a 'slightly worrisome' liver enzyme that he would like to keep an eye on, and added that it may have something to do with alcohol consumption. As he assumed most people did, Banks halved the true number of drinks he had per week when his doctor asked. He hadn't yet started thinking in units and hoped he never would.

'I do hope you can wrap this up quickly,' Malcolm Briers said. 'We have limited time to do our job here as it is, before the heavy equipment comes in.'

'It's hard to say,' Banks told him, turning his gaze away from the skull and his mind from thoughts of death. 'Too many variables. But we'll do our best. Wouldn't want trying to find a murderer to interfere with digging up a few old coins and baubles, would we?'

Briers reddened. 'I wouldn't exactly call . . . er . . . well, no, I suppose not, if you put it like that. But how do you know this person was murdered? And isn't it likely the perpetrator is long dead, too?'

'Those are both questions we have to answer in our investigation, and neither one is as easy as you may think. First off, who owns the land?'

'It belonged to a local farmer. I'm sorry, but I don't know his name.'

'You say belonged. Did he sell up?'

'Compulsory purchase order. This is the last field to the west of the road. That lane just over the wall there marks the border of his land. This place was more of a scrag-end than anything else.'

'I see. When was this?'

'About two years ago. Highways England decided they needed to widen this section of the A1, turn it into another stretch of motorway. And build a shopping centre, of course.'

'That wouldn't be Highways England, though? The shopping centre?'

'No. A private developer. Or a consortium. In league with them. Luckily, we – that's the Northern Archaeological Associates – get first dibs before the heavy work begins.'

'Know where this farmer is now?'

'No idea. He moved away, of course. Probably living it up on the Costa del Packet or some such place.'

Banks turned to Gerry. 'Make a note,' he said. 'Find out who owned the land before the compulsory purchase order, and where he lives now.'

Gerry made a jotting in her notebook.

'Who found the skull?' Banks asked Briers. 'DC Masterson mentioned someone called Grace Hutchinson.'

'That's Grace, over there,' Gerry said, pointing.

Briers nodded. 'Yes. Grace is one of our best archaeologists. She's beads.'

Banks glanced over at Grace and the three of them started walking towards where she sat on a picnic hamper, a red plastic cup from the top of a vacuum flask held in both hands. 'Beads?' Banks said.

'Yes,' said Briers. 'Her speciality. You've no idea how much beads can tell us about migratory patterns and trade relations in the ancient world. Grace, you've already met DC Masterson. This is Detective Superintendent Banks. He wants to ask you a few questions, if you would be so kind.' Then Briers stalked off, slipping his mobile from his pocket and keying in a number as he did so. Banks thought of calling out to ask him not to tell anyone about what they had found, but he decided not to bother. People would find out soon enough, and it was hardly a race against time. Despite the sunshine, it was a cool day, and every once in a while, a brief gust of frigid air blew in from the east.

Grace glanced up at Banks's approach. She had nice eyes, he noticed: sea-green behind her black-framed glasses, under dark, well-groomed eyebrows. No make-up, cheeks a little red with the cold. Like the rest of the archaeological team, she was wearing a baseball cap, high-vis orange jacket and jeans.

'Hello,' she said, standing and shaking his hand. 'I'm afraid I can't tell you anything more than I've already told DC Masterson.'

'Just humour me,' said Banks. 'Did you disturb or move the bones in any way?'

'No. We're trained to be especially careful in this job, of course. Much of what we find is incredibly fragile.'

'Done much of this sort of thing?'

'I've been on quite a few digs, yes. Here and overseas.'

'Still, it must have come as a shock to you?'

'Well, I'm quite used to finding skeletons, but it's not every day I find a fresh one, so to speak. I'm all right.'

'Haven't you done some sort of preliminary tests? To find out if it was worth digging here, for example?'

'Yes, of course. Though we knew there was something here because of other finds nearby. It's all linked. But we certainly weren't expecting a Roman burial ground. This is what we call a "rescue excavation". Soon it's going to be buried for ever. Well, at least until shopping malls become archaeological finds themselves. If you know what I mean.'

'I do,' Banks said. 'I can just imagine some lucky blighters digging up a Marks & Spencer outlet a thousand years in the future. I wonder what they'll make of it?'

'Perhaps that they're not that much different from the people who came before them. The Romans had markets, their version of the shopping mall, I suppose.'

'The closest I've come to a Roman shopping mall is the one in Caesar's Palace,' said Banks, remembering a brief side trip to Las Vegas on his California holiday some years ago – the life-size replica of Michelangelo's *David* and the 'Forum Shops'.

Grace laughed. 'Anyway, we drew up a project design about exactly what we're going to do, and why.'

'What about X-rays and so on? Or detectorists?'

'The latter can be an occupational hazard, though they have on occasion proved valuable. Not this time, though. And we used ground-penetrating radar on certain areas, but we couldn't cover everything, of course.'

'And nothing showed up?'

'Not this. We didn't get this far back.'

'We'll probably have to bring in cadaver dogs, at least to cover the immediate area.'

'Can they sniff out Roman remains, too?'

'Actually, they're quite remarkable, though I'm not sure their talents go that far.' Banks paused. 'But you said you weren't expecting a Roman burial ground.'

'We're not. Not just here. But you never know your luck.'

'What were your first thoughts when you found the skull?'

'That three feet was too shallow to be uncovering anything ancient, and that somebody must have dumped it there recently. I mean, if you end up dead under two or three feet of earth, it's pretty obvious somebody put you there, isn't it?' She gave a brief shudder.

'I'd say so. But we still need to know cause of death before we can begin any full investigation. It's not rare for someone to bury a relative who died a natural death, for example. Not everyone's as rational as we'd like to think. I know it's probably impossible to answer, but I have to ask: any idea how long ago?'

'That's for the scientists to figure out,' Grace said. 'I'm an archaeologist, not an anthropologist.'

'We need both on a case like this. Can you have a stab at it?'

Grace glanced down at the skull, then back at Banks and Gerry. 'I'm sorry,' she said. 'Lacking any kind of external evidence, I can't say. I mean, if it was like Vesuvius or something, timing is relatively easy, as long as you know when the eruption took place and covered everything and everyone in lava, of course, but without . . . Well, you'd need to know the soil composition, pH balance, insect activity and so on. I don't know much about all that. Also, how long the layer above took to form. There's no simple formula, as far as I know. Even your experts must have told you it's near impossible to gauge how long a relatively recent skeleton has been lying there?'

'It was worth a try. I'm no anthropologist, either, and believe it or not, it's not every day I come across a human skeleton.'

'It's my first,' Gerry announced. 'What about carbon dating?'

Banks had been caught out on that one before, and he jumped in before Grace had time to answer. 'That's only useful for true archaeological finds, really old ones. It only works on something over five hundred years old or thereabouts, and I certainly wouldn't say our friend has been here that long.'

Grace gave Banks a nod of approval. 'Your superintendent is right on both counts,' she said.

'Ah,' said Gerry. 'Pity.'

Grace smiled. 'Yes. I stopped as soon as I knew what it was. I know enough not to disturb the scene. I suppose you'll want your experts in to dig the whole thing up now?'

'Yes. And we might have to dig up a larger area.'

'Why?'

'If this is a murder victim,' Banks said, pointing over at the trench, 'then there's always the possibility there might be other victims buried nearby.'

'You mean a serial killer?'

'Something like that. We'll start with the radar, too, of course,' said Banks, 'but as you remarked, it's not always a hundred per cent reliable. I'd still value your help. I doubt my men could do a better job than a trained archaeologist in clearing up the earth around a skeleton and searching for

anything of interest, anything that might help us answer a few
basic questions, so I'd appreciate it if you would stick around
and help out. I need our official forensic team on it for legal
reasons as much as anything. Chain of evidence and so on.
But when they're here, I think you should carry on doing
what you were doing and work with them. Stefan Nowak's
our Crime Scene Manager. He's a good bloke. You'll get along
fine with him. We'll take care of the procedural stuff and the
lab analysis. Gerry here will act as liaison.'

'You want *me* to work for you?'

'Well, we could bring some other, outside archaeologist,
someone we've worked with before, but as you're here, and
you did uncover the corpse, I think your input could be
valuable.'

Grace gave Banks a crooked smile. 'So, I'm sort of depu-
tised, am I?'

'Well, I don't have a sheriff's star to give you, but yes, you
can consider yourself a fully paid-up member of the posse.'
Banks glanced over at Briers, who was now chatting with one
of the other diggers. 'Your boss seems worried about us taking
over the scene.'

'Don't worry about Malcolm,' Grace said. 'I can handle
him. He tends to be a bit of a worrywart. And he's not exactly
my "boss". It's true we're on a tight deadline, depending on
the construction company. They can be impatient. Bullies.
But, even so, he's got no real reason to get his knickers in a
twist. They'll wait. They'll have to. Especially now.'

Banks stepped into the trench and felt his knees crack as
he squatted to get a closer look at the remains. The front of
the skull and jaw were completely free of dirt, and the bone
had turned a dull yellow. Chemicals in the soil composition,
he guessed. The right side, around the temple, was broken.
He could see no more structural damage – no more cracks

or splits or holes – but one other thing did catch his attention. When he got up, he turned to Grace and said, 'See the exposed teeth there?'

Grace nodded.

'I could be wrong,' Banks went on, 'but as far as I know, the Romans didn't use gold fillings in their teeth, did they?'

'As a matter of fact, they did, but I very much doubt they'd be as well fitted as that one, and probably not on one of the grunts posted to the northern provinces.'

'Ha,' said Banks, straightening up and smiling back. 'Now I can see I made the right decision in deputising you.'

2

One of the many problems with November weather was how early it got dark. By three o'clock, visibility was starting to wane for the delicate work Grace and the forensic team had to do. When Nowak and his CSIs had arrived later in the morning, most of the other archaeologists had been sent home, except two students Grace had chosen to help her. Someone drove up to the Burger King at Scotch Corner and fetched lunch for those remaining, then DC Masterson went back to Eastvale HQ to talk to AC Gervaise and get the technicalities of the investigation rolling. As no cause of death had been established yet, they wouldn't be rolling out a full murder investigation, bringing in the arc lamps for night work, but Banks had a feeling that might not be far off.

The CSIs had erected a makeshift tent around and above the scene in case of rain, and Grace and her colleagues busied themselves with covering the hole with heavy-duty polythene, just to be on the safe side, weighing it down with heavy stones around the edges. Several CSIs had checked the surrounding area with ground-piercing radar but found nothing. Even so, they had dug a little deeper, to approximately the same depth Grace had reached, but still found nothing. Perhaps *not* a serial killer, then, Banks thought.

The CSIs and archaeologists had managed to move the skeleton on to a stretcher without much trouble, keeping it in one piece, and a forensic anthropologist colleague of

Dr Karen Galway's, the Home Office pathologist, would be along in a day or two to examine it. Lacking any better alternative, they had transported the bones to Dr Galway's autopsy suite in the basement of Eastvale General Infirmary. It was a dead body, after all.

Everyone knew that the first twenty-four hours in a fresh murder investigation were the most important, but that was not necessarily true in a case like this. Until they had some idea of *who* the victim was, *when* the corpse had been buried, and *what* the cause of death had been, there wasn't a great deal more anyone could do. As Grace had said, though, people don't die of natural causes then bury themselves three feet under the ground.

When they had moved the skeleton, they had found some buttons, scraps of clothing, pieces of metal, and what looked like the remains of a leather belt and shoes. These had all been carefully placed in evidence bags and logged. They might be able to provide some information about how long the body had lain there and who it was. Banks was disappointed that they had found neither *terminus ante quem* nor *terminus post quem*. As Grace had also pointed out, not even a forensic anthropologist could pin down the exact time a body had been buried, but sometimes they got lucky and found it had been buried just above electricity cables laid in 1987 and under a patio not built until 1990. That told them the body had been buried there between 1987 and 1990. It was what Grace had meant when she mentioned Vesuvius earlier. Vesuvius was probably the best-known marker of time of death. Once they knew the date and time Vesuvius erupted, it was easy enough to figure out the rest. Until that date changed in the light of new discoveries, of course.

'I never asked you what you're doing here on a Sunday in November,' Banks said as Grace packed away her trowel, brush and sieve.

'We work all year round and every day of the week,' Grace answered, gesturing to her colleagues. 'Unless the ground's frozen or covered in snow, of course. And we tend not to get much done during periods of heavy rain, which, as you can imagine, occur quite often up here in North Yorkshire. But several of the diggers are students, volunteers, and they have classes during the week, so they're helping us in their spare time.'

'You?'

'I finished my PhD three years ago. Since then, I've been working in the field. Or should I say "fields"?'

'Well, thanks for your help today.'

'I didn't do anything, really.'

'You'll come back tomorrow?'

'Yes, of course. Remember, I'm a deputy now.'

Banks handed her his card. 'Just give me a ring when you're ready. I'll make sure Stefan or one of his team is here. And we can arrange transport for you, if you like. We'll be leaving PC Morton here as nightwatchman, so don't be surprised when you see him in the morning. I very much doubt he'll have anything to do – there's unlikely to be anyone disturbing things – but we have to follow procedures. After all, the dig is a crime scene now, even though we aren't sure *what* the crime is or how long ago it was committed.'

'What a job,' Grace said, glancing at Morton. 'I hope you've got a torch and a good book.'

Banks glanced at PC Morton, who merely shrugged. 'It's all right, ma'am,' he said. 'And I'm dressed warm enough.'

'Can I give you a lift anywhere?' Banks asked Grace.

'No, thanks. My car's just up the lane. And I'll drive in tomorrow, too. No need to make any special arrangements.'

They left PC Morton and climbed over the stile over the drystone wall to the lane. Dark grey clouds threatened low on the horizon, turned almost black by the setting sun silhouetting them from behind and beneath.

Banks smiled at a sudden memory of his daughter, Tracy, when she was very young, ignoring the stile the rest of the family was using and clambering over the wall itself. 'That's *my* style,' she had said with a flourish, and broke them all up. A smart-mouthed little girl she was, and she had grown into a smart-mouthed young woman.

The tree-lined lane was narrow and unpaved, with hedge-rows growing around the ditches on both sides. There was no way two cars could pass one another, not without one getting stuck in a ditch, so every now and then there was a passing place. Bad luck if you were the one who had to back up. Banks imagined they had probably caused many a fight over the years, especially between irate local farmers and the army of tourists who descended on the Dales every summer in caravans and campers.

That said, though, most of the time the lane was probably unused, as it led from nowhere to nowhere and mostly provided access to the occasional remote farmhouse. This was hardly wild Dales country, so close to the A1, but as soon as you stepped even a few yards away from a major road, things changed quickly. He could hear the rumble of traffic in the distance, but the trees blocked out the view now he was on the other side of the wall. They were odd-looking trees, not majestic and wide-spreading, but squat, black, knotty and gnarled, with thick trunks and branches twisted into strange shapes, like headless torsos with their arms stretched out, strongmen flexing their muscles or Prometheus trying to break free from his chains. Most still had a few leaves left clinging to their branches and twigs. Banks thought they seemed creepy in the louring twilight and half expected one of them to start moving like the Ents in *Lord of the Rings*.

He waved farewell to Grace, who drove off in a dark blue Mini, then leaned against the wall to contemplate the scene. There was no immediate access to or from the motorway, but it wouldn't have been too difficult for whoever had dumped the body to do so from the lane where Banks was standing. The hardest part would have been getting the dead weight over the stile. It was a quiet, deserted area, and there wasn't a farmstead in sight. It was unlikely anyone would have been around to interrupt the disposal, especially if it had taken place late at night, or in the small hours. This part of the landscape probably hadn't changed much over the centuries, except for deforestation and the encroachment of the widened road to the east. Banks remembered a line from one of Linda Palmer's poems about Roman outposts in Yorkshire: 'Our Empire's heart is strained. / There's no blood left to nourish us here at the extremities. / Slowly, we all go numb.' Was that what it had felt like for the Romans stationed up here? Or was it just poetic licence on Linda's part?

Banks was beginning to feel a bit numb himself, now that darkness had fallen and what little, weak sunlight that remained had vanished behind low clouds. Drawing his collar up, he set off down the lane to his car. Just time to nip home for a quick shower and a change of clothing before dinner in town with Dirty Dick Burgess.

28 November 1980

As the afternoon wore on and the grey light turned to darkness, I put money in the gas meter and remained in my room playing old records, mostly things Alice and I had enjoyed when we were together – which meant plenty of Bowie, Elvis Costello and Joy Division. Later in the evening, I started to get really depressed midway through 'She's Lost Control' so I headed for the stairs.

One of the things about a large house divided into student bedsits is that turnover is pretty high, and as soon as you get to know someone, they're gone. Sometimes you don't even get to meet the other tenants at all, especially if they're not in your department and your schedules are different. Also, because of the student year, a lot of tenants would move out at the end of term, and their rooms might remain empty all summer if the landlord couldn't find a summer school student to rent to.

But the one constant in this house was Geoff.

Geoff was always there. He was the only one in the building who *wasn't* a student. Geoff actually had a *real job*. Why he stayed, I don't know. But he did. He worked as a librarian at the central library in the city centre. He was also the only tenant with a television set, and he was generous enough to invite me and Anton, my best friend since we met in a tutorial group in our first year, to watch a few favourite programmes, such as *Quatermass*, *Fawlty Towers* and *Not the Nine O'Clock News*. Sometimes, if we were settled for an evening's viewing, he would fry up some bacon butties and I'd bring along a few tins of beer. He lived in the ground-floor bedsit with the bay window looking out over the front garden. In summer, we'd go up to my room and climb out of my window to sit on top of the bay and smoke joints and watch the world go by. From there we could see all the way over Hyde Park to the university buildings.

The location was ideal for a student, just a short walk across the park from the university, and the canny owner had converted the property into reasonably priced bedsits some years ago. He didn't do much in the way of maintenance, though. The brown lino was cracked and discoloured, and the fading cream wallpaper was peeling off where it joined the high ceiling with cobwebs in its ornate mouldings and cornices. A single bare bulb lit the entire dingy staircase.

When I knocked on Geoff's door, he opened it and said, 'Fancy a pint?'

That was exactly what I wanted. A pint. Or two. Or three.

There was no police officer on the front door to demand where we were going. They seemed to have all gone home. After all, wherever Alice had died, it hadn't been in this building. This wasn't a crime scene. But no doubt they would be back tomorrow.

We walked up to the Hyde Park, on the main road, and found an empty table next to the central island. It wasn't a typical student pub like the Original Oak, up in Headingley, or the Eldon and the Fenton, both practically on university property, but it was close. The air was usually thick with smoke and the ceiling was stained a dull amber from so many years of nicotine. I got in a couple of pints at the long bar and Geoff offered me one of his Craven A. We lit up. I sat with my back to the island and Geoff sat on a stool, lank hair hanging over his ears and glasses perched on the end of his rather long nose. As usual, he wore a scuffed leather jacket over his sweatshirt, and jeans, though for work he always wore a suit.

'So what's going on?' he asked.

'Have they talked to you yet?' I asked. 'The police.'

'Soon as I got home from work. I must say they were bloody rude, and poking and prodding all over the place. It's not a police state yet. At least it wasn't last time I heard.'

'Might be before long, if our new PM gets her way.'

'Now you're sounding just like Alice.'

I looked away.

'What's happened, Nick?' Geoff went on. 'They wouldn't tell me anything, but it's serious, isn't it?'

I nodded. 'All I know is that Alice's dead. That's all they told me.'

'Dead? Fuck me. I can't . . . I'm really sorry, mate.'

'Did you watch the news? Wasn't there anything about her?'

'I missed it tonight. Too late.'

'I'm assuming she must have been murdered. I mean, you wouldn't have so many coppers around asking me for an alibi if she'd just been run over or dropped dead of an aneurism or something, would you?'

'I suppose not,' Geoff said. 'Didn't they give you any details, either?'

'None at all. They were pretty interested in my movements, though.'

'Well, they would be, wouldn't they?'

'Why do you say that?'

'You know. You and Alice. You were pretty close.'

'*Were* being the operative word.'

'Oh, come on, Nick. You were still carrying a torch for her. You know you were. You were crying on my shoulder half the summer.'

I stiffened. 'I didn't realise I'd been such a burden.'

'Calm down, mate. I didn't say you were a burden. You were fucking broken-hearted, is all.'

'We'd been together nearly two years,' I said, in little more than a whisper. 'You're right, though. I was still in love with her.'

I remembered the night Alice and I met at a department party in the first week of our first term at the university. I was taken with her slender figure and blonde good looks, her full lips, high Nordic cheekbones and dark, dark blue eyes. Her laugh was infectious, and when we had been chatting for half an hour, I felt as if I had known her for ever, and I wanted to be with her just as long. I asked if I could walk her home – even then the Ripper was active, and it was dangerous for women out alone at night – and she said OK. She lived on Brudenell Road then, and she asked me in for a coffee. We stayed up all night talking – just talking – about music and books and life, the universe and everything, and when I left for my flat the following morning, I finally knew what it felt like to be walking on air.

But that was then. I was already living on Kensington Terrace, and when the student renting the Penthouse had a breakdown and left partway through the first term, Alice moved in. She liked her creature comforts, and I couldn't picture her living happily in a cramped bedsit like mine. Up there, she had her own bathroom, a small kitchenette, bedroom and living room. Besides, we had only been going out just over a month then, and we hadn't considered living together. As it turned out, we never did, though we rarely spent a night apart.

'What did you tell them?' I asked Geoff.

'About what?'

'You know. Alice and me.'

'Nothing,' said Geoff.

'Did you tell them how upset I was over the break-up?'

'Well, yeah. You must have given them some indication earlier. They let on that you'd already told them you'd had a relationship with her and that you weren't happy about her seeing Mark.'

'I told them no such thing. But it doesn't matter. I think they suspect me.'

'Oh, come on! No way.'

'Seriously. I think they do. They might even think . . . you know . . . that I'm the Ripper.'

'That's bloody ridiculous, mate. You should just listen to yourself. You're getting paranoid.'

I drank some beer. 'Maybe.'

'Where were you?'

'When?'

'Last night.'

I glanced around the large lounge bar. 'Here,' I said. 'Steve and Chris from the film society were here. They'd just been to see some Jean-Luc Godard film or other and were raving about it. I told them I thought Godard was pretentious drivel. They'll remember me.'

'Well, then. There's your alibi.'

'I don't even know what time . . . you know . . . it happened. I was only here for about an hour towards the end of the evening. Before that, I was in my room working. Alone. Same after.'

'I dunno, mate,' Geoff said. 'Surely if they really thought it was you, they'd have taken you in for questioning?'

'They'll be searching for more evidence. A weak alibi isn't enough. And maybe they want to let me stew for a while.'

'They should know if you were going to kill anyone, it would have been Mark, not Alice.'

I stared at him.

'Sorry,' he went on, reddening. 'Just . . . you know . . . saying.'

'It's true I didn't like the bastard,' I admitted. 'But I didn't kill anyone.'

'I believe you, mate. Honest. Another pint?'

I started to get to my feet. 'Sure.'

Geoff put his hand on my shoulder and gently pushed me back into my seat. 'My shout,' he said, and headed off. I rolled a cigarette and sat back on the bench. There was a fair crowd at the bar as everyone knew last orders was coming up soon and old Maurice would be trotting around the tables collecting glasses and telling us it was time, gentlemen, please, and hadn't we got no homes to go to.

While Geoff was gone, Jill, a girl from my tutorial group, stopped by on her way back from the bar and leaned over me. 'Have you heard about the murder?' she asked.

'What murder?'

'I don't know the details,' she said, 'but according to what I heard from a friend of mine earlier, someone found a girl's body in the bushes in Burley Park this morning. A dog walker, I think. Who found it, I mean.'

'Burley Park? Did they say who the girl was?'

'No. But everyone's guessing it was the Ripper who did it. It's so close to home. We're all scared. Again. So soon.'

'Are you OK? I can walk—'

'Oh, no, I'm fine, thanks. With friends.' She gestured to a table in the far corner. 'Liz and Russ and Martin. We share a house, so we'll be walking home together. Thanks a lot for the offer, though. See you later. You should come over sometime.'

'Yeah, I will. See you.'

Geoff came back with the drinks, saw my expression and said, 'You all right?'

'What? Oh, yeah.' I picked up the pint. 'Cheers. Thanks.'

'Cheers.' Geoff leaned forward. 'Guess what I heard waiting at the bar.'

'What?'

'Just a couple of blokes talking about the murder, that's all. Alice.'

'What did they say?'

'They didn't know who it was, of course, just that a student had been murdered and her body dumped in Burley Park. They're saying the Ripper did it.'

And for a split second, an image of Alice naked in my arms flashed through my mind. It only lasted a moment, but in that moment, I could feel her, hear her breathing, see her perfect skin, *smell* her as vividly as if she were right beside me. All these things no longer existed, except in my memory. And in Mark's memory, of course. The bastard. I felt an anger surge in me and noticed my hand shaking as I picked up my pint glass to drink. I wasn't so sure about the Ripper business, not so sure at all. Because if it *was* Alice's body they had found in the park, where the hell was Mark, and why wasn't he here? And what the hell was Alice doing in Burley Park? I felt like crying into my beer.

24 November 2019

Banks was ten minutes late for his dinner with Dirty Dick Burgess at Provençale, a tiny bistro tucked away between the market square and the river gardens. He hadn't bothered texting, and Burgess seemed happy enough sitting at the rickety wooden table with a pint of lager in front of him and his mobile in his hand.

'What you reading?' Banks asked. 'Proust? Dostoevsky?'

Burgess grunted. 'Texas Hold 'Em. And I just lost with a full house. Bastard had a straight flush. Can you believe it?'

Banks, who had never bothered to find out which hand beat which in poker, said, 'Just as well the stakes aren't real. Or are they?'

Burgess gave him a look of disgust. 'I'm not that stupid. It's just an app.'

Banks had discovered Provençale shortly after falling in love with all things French on a recent trip to Paris and had become a regular customer. It wasn't quite up to the standards of Marcel McGuignan's Le Coq d'Or, Eastvale's own two-Michelin-star establishment, but then neither were the prices. The food was good, and it made a change from takeaways.

The lights were dim, supplemented by candles wedged in old wine bottles, and the air was scented with fresh-baked baguettes, garlic and herbes de Provence. Someone had wedged a folded-up beermat under one of the table legs to stop it from wobbling too much on the uneven stone-flagged floor. Impressionist posters hung on the walls and French chanteuses warbled softly in the background – Edith Piaf, Juliette Gréco, Françoise Hardy – along with the occasional Serge Gainsbourg or Jacques Brel number. The conversations from the nearby tables were muted, and even though the tiny space was full, the bistro didn't feel crowded. Their table stood next to the whitewashed wall, just below a Toulouse-Lautrec poster for the Moulin Rouge. A basket of fresh, warm bread already sat before them on the blue and white checked tablecloth.

'Nice,' said Burgess, glancing around. 'Kind of place you might take a date if you want to get laid.'

'Don't get any ideas.'

'As if.' Burgess slugged some beer. A waiter appeared beside them. She looked young, probably a student from the local college, catering or culinary arts programme. She offered them printed menus and asked Banks if he'd like a drink. He ordered a large Chateau Guyot. Two glasses over the course of the evening would be his limit.

'Talking about getting laid,' said Burgess, 'whatever happened to that Croatian bint you were seeing a while back? You know, the—'

'She wasn't Croatian,' Banks said. 'Nelia's Moldovan. And I wasn't *seeing* her. She was Ray Cabbot's partner.'

'The chap who died? Annie's father? The artist?'

'Yes.'

'Lucky devil, from what I heard. Probably died with a smile on his face. And look on the bright side: she's a free agent now.'

'Ray died alone, of a heart attack. And he was a mate of mine.'

'Sorry. What became of her?'

'No idea,' Banks lied. 'She just disappeared.' He knew that the police were searching for Nelia, or Zelda, and though he'd known Burgess long enough to call him a friend, he wouldn't trust anyone, especially a fellow copper, with her whereabouts.

'Fair enough,' Burgess said, holding up the menu. 'What do you recommend?'

'I'm going to be really boring and order steak frites,' said Banks. 'But the lamb shank is good, if that's what you fancy, the seafood dishes are usually reliable, and the duck confit goes down a treat.'

The waiter returned with the wine and they both ordered.

'Sorry I was late,' Banks said. 'Something came up.'

'A case?'

'Not sure what it is yet, except someone unearthed a skeleton at an archaeological dig, and it sure as hell isn't Marcus Aurelius.'

'I hate fucking skeletons,' Burgess said. 'No matter how much the boffins bugger about, you never find out how long they've been there. It's all about bloody insects, rates of decay and pH balances and what have you.'

'I'm with you on that,' Banks said. 'But that skeleton was a living person once and if someone took that life, it's up to us to find out who.'

'Probably dead by now.'

'Maybe so. That'll cut down on the paperwork if we ever find out who did it. We've closed the site up for the night, left a uniform on guard duty. No need to bring out the arc lamps and heavy artillery on this just yet. The experts can get back to work out there bright and early tomorrow. What brings you up here? What have you been up to?'

'Nothing very interesting,' Burgess said. 'At the moment, I'm up to my neck in this inquiry into undercover policing. You know, the SDS, as it was at first – Special Demonstration Squad – and they weren't demonstrating washing-up liquid.'

'Weren't they disbanded?'

'That's right. 2008. "Lost their moral compass", according to one of them. As if they ever had one. But they just changed the name to the National Public Order Intelligence Unit and carried on as before. Never did find that moral compass. Theresa May called for an inquiry in March 2015, when she was Home Secretary, and it started up officially in March of the following year. The damn thing's set to go on until 2023, at least.'

'What's your role?'

'General dogsbody. Interviews. Timelines. They call me "Investigations Manager". *Manager.* I ask you. If I wanted to be a "manager", I'd have gone to fucking business school. That's why I'm up here. Have to go to Durham first thing tomorrow to talk to a young woman who claims she had a kid by one of the undercover officers, so I thought I'd stop off and see my old mate on the way.'

Their meals came, along with another pint of lager. 'Looks good,' Burgess said of the duck confit.

Banks speared a few frites, was tempted to make a chip butty with the baguette, then decided against it. 'Did you ever work undercover?' he asked, when the waiter had gone.

'No, I never did have that pleasure,' said Burgess. 'You?'

'Once.'

'How long?'

'About a year. Nearly did for my marriage.'

'When was this?'

'Mid-seventies.'

'And where were you assigned?'

'Notting Hill.'

'Investigating?'

'Drugs, mostly. And some peripheral political organisations.'

'Like what?'

'Young Liberals. You might well laugh, but they were a hotbed of revolutionaries back then.'

'Young Liberals?' Burgess waved his wrist loosely. 'I'll bet they were a terrifying bunch.'

Banks laughed. 'Well, hardly that. But look at Jeremy Thorpe. It's not every day a leader of a political party gets put on trial for conspiracy to murder. Not here, at any rate. And the Liberal party was on the rise at that time. They might not have won an election, but they were hoping to gain seats and some power. Enough to get the Labour government worried, at any rate.'

'Did you get involved in the scandal?'

'Only in a small way. I mean, I heard things at meetings. Loose talk. The homosexual relationship, the cover-up, and so on. The rumours started around 1975, but the trial wasn't until '79. I knew nothing that required me to testify in court.'

'Find anything else out back then?'

'Not much. Certainly not enough to offset the time and money spent on me. I went to a few demos, just to stay in character, people handing out rotten eggs and tomatoes to throw at Margaret Thatcher.'

'She wasn't PM in the mid-seventies.'

'No. That was Callaghan at the time. Maggie was leader of the opposition. But she'd also been Education Secretary under Heath until 1974. Stopped free milk in schools. Don't you remember "Thatcher, Thatcher, milk-snatcher"?'

'Christ, that's right. I'd forgotten about that. I was probably too busy cracking students' heads and beating up innocent suspects. That must have stuck in your craw, though, saving Thatcher from rotten eggs and tomatoes.'

'I didn't say I managed to save her from every last one.'

Burgess chuckled. 'Better watch what you say. It's all coming home to roost, as these things do. The way it works these days, if you did anything out of line in the last fifty years or so, you can expect it to come back and bite you on the arse any day now.'

'If only someone had told me that fifty years ago,' said Banks.

'Why? You didn't . . . ? Don't tell me I'm going to come across your name in this inquiry.'

'No. I'm only joking.' But as Banks spoke, he cast his mind back. There was *something*, he remembered, something he deeply regretted, something that still caused him the occasional sleepless night, but surely no one could know about it?

'We're lucky there was no Twitter or Facebook back then, or we'd probably all be in deep doo-doo,' Burgess said, reverting to one of his favourite Americanisms.

'Speak for yourself. That's one reason I stay away from the antisocial media. Even without them, it's amazing the trails and evidence people left behind. I suppose it's lucky for our jobs that people feel such a compelling need to write things down, or take photographs and post them on Instagram, TikTok or whatever. Sometimes it seems to me some people almost *want* to get caught.'

'I know,' said Burgess. 'Or they feel they're somehow above the law. But I'm sure you've lived an exemplary life, except for the Thatcher incident. Yes, I'll have another,' he said to the passing waiter. Banks gestured for a second glass of wine, too.

'I'll bet there was plenty of free pussy, too,' Burgess said.

'I won't dignify that with an answer.'

'It wasn't a question.'

'It was there for those who wanted it.'

'But you didn't?'

'I'm not saying I was never tempted. But I was a married man. A *newly* married man at that. Just a kid, really.'

'That never stopped anyone before. And as far as I can remember, you're at your randiest when you're just a kid.'

Banks took a deep breath. 'What can I say? I'm not trying to make out I was better or morally superior to anyone else. I just didn't, that's all. You have to understand what it was like. It wasn't difficult to lose yourself in your fake identity, convince yourself that you were who you said you were, even if that person didn't really exist. And if you didn't really exist, there could be no consequences for what you did. In retrospect, I suppose it was a kind of Stockholm syndrome of the self.'

'So how did you stay sane?'

'I'm not entirely sure I did,' Banks said. 'It was weird, one of the strangest and most disturbing periods in my life. Like I was acting all the time. Sometimes I even forgot who I really was. But a lot of the time I was two people at once, standing in the shadows watching myself pretend to be someone else, do things *I* wouldn't do. But it *was* me . . . It's not surprising, some of the things that happened. I did things . . .' Banks shook his head. 'I mean, when you're no longer yourself and you've got carte blanche, you can *really* plumb the depths and get into trouble. Unless you're extremely self-determined and have an unerring sense of morality, of right and wrong. Or you believe so passionately in the absolute rightness and necessity of what you're doing that you accept the end justifies the means.'

'But you didn't?'

'It was a job. I know that's no excuse, but I was a young copper and I was supposed to be gathering intelligence about possible criminal acts, past and future. Somehow, I managed to hang on to my sense of who I really was, and perhaps that's why I didn't stray. I just pretended I was a Cold War spy.'

'James Bond?'

'Not exactly. There were girls, and sometimes they'd throw themselves at you, but mostly they were wasted and burned-out on drugs, or fanatical about some extreme political cause or other, and somehow that didn't appeal to me. I was dealing with drugs-related stuff most of the time, except when it intersected with political groups, passing myself off as a small-time dealer and so on, and I know I helped put a few bad guys away, but, like I said, politics did come into it. You'd be surprised how many Young Liberals enjoyed a toke or a snort every now and then. I didn't see myself as working for Callaghan, in a political job, though I will say that the Home Secretary Roy Jenkins was a decent bloke, especially compared to what we've got today. And you probably know I was never a great fan of Thatcher.'

'Hence the eggs and tomatoes.'

'So I was derelict in my duty. Bite me.'

'I don't think it's a sacking offence, but I'll see what I can do for you if your name does come up in my brief. Why did you get out of it?'

Banks took a sip of wine, 'a beaker full of the warm South'. 'My term of duty ended. I suppose I could have carried on – renewed my contract, so to speak – but I wanted to get as far away from it as I could and move on to real detective work. Not to mention save my marriage. It was a struggle when it ended, getting back to normal. Or what I thought was normal – I wasn't even sure about that any more. It changed me.'

'See a shrink?'

'No way. I wouldn't want that on my record, especially as I was just starting out. You know as well as I do, you suck it up. I just worked through it as best I could. It certainly put a strain on my marriage. That's when I almost lost Sandra. I wouldn't have blamed her. She said she didn't know who she was living with any more. It was like she didn't even know the scruffy, long-haired, foul-mouthed bastard I'd become. She didn't like him much, either. And nor did I. Pudding? The crème brûlée's good.'

Burgess patted his stomach. 'No, it'll spoil my figure. I'll have another pint and then I'm off to bed.'

'Where you staying?'

'That little boutique hotel up on Castle Hill.'

'Nice.'

'It's only because you don't have a Premier Inn or Travelodge in Eastvale. That's the sort of place they usually put me.'

Banks caught the waiter's attention and ordered another lager for Burgess and a black coffee for himself.

'That was a fine meal,' Burgess said, when he had his pint in his hand. 'I do love French food. It almost makes me sorry we've left the EU.'

'Oh, that wasn't such a bad decision,' said Banks.

'What happened to the old leftie liberal elitist Banks I used to know? The Remainer?'

'Maybe it's the ageing process, but I can't really say any of that stuff interests me any more. What's the point? What's done is done. Who knows, maybe the Leave people were right about getting out of Europe after all. We should leave the poor buggers over there alone. Haven't we done them enough damage already? It started with fish and chips and Watney's Draught Red Barrel and football hooligans, and now it's villas in Tuscany, fixer-uppers in the Dordogne and timeshares on the Costa del Sol. Not to mention easyJet, Ryanair, Tui, cheap lager and "Genuine British Food" everywhere. It's like that old Monty Python sketch. The one about the travel agent.

Torremolinos, Torremolinos. No. I think it's time to give our European neighbours some peace and quiet, let them lick their wounds and sort out their union while we concentrate on boosting our sense of *Englishness* and wrecking ours.'

Burgess laughed. 'Watch it, mate. That's sedition. Besides, I like cheap lager and fish and chips as well.'

'Me, too. Fish and chips, anyway. But if I were in Portugal, I might try *caldo verde* or *sardinhas assadas*.'

'Sardines and chips?'

'If you must.'

'You might be getting cynical in your old age, Banksy, but you're still a bloody liberal elitist commie at heart.'

3

25 November 2019

When Banks arrived for the post-mortem late on Monday morning, the hospital volunteers were putting up Christmas decorations in the corridors of Eastvale Infirmary's basement: twisting concertinas of green and red streamers hanging from the ceiling, an occasional cut-out Santa head, complete with cotton-wool beard and red hat, stuck to the wall, a large tree at the far end hung with blinking lights and tinsel, a crooked angel astride its top. Somehow it seemed out of place. Banks could understand why such cheerful decorations might be useful in the wards and A & E, but the basement was the realm of the dead, the home of Eastvale's mortuary and post-mortem suite. Banks also imagined, with no evidence whatsoever, that all the stuff no civilians ever saw in hospitals ended up in bins down there somewhere, too: plastic bags full of blood-soaked cotton wool and rags, along with wheely bins of amputated limbs, abandoned livers and kidneys, tumorous spleens, pancreases and lungs, severed breasts and broken hearts. One of the doors, he imagined, led to a cellar with a huge furnace, and some poor sod had the job of feeding all this human detritus to the flames.

Dr Galway and her forensic anthropologist were already present, as well as Grace Hutchinson. Grace wouldn't have anything to do with the practical matters of the post-mortem, but she might be able to answer any questions that came up about the discovery and transportation of the skeleton that lay on the slab before them, assembled like a jigsaw puzzle. The smaller bones were crusted with soil here and there, and the rest appeared to have been cleaned, though they were stained like neglected teeth by the minerals and deposits in the soil. Banks could see that most of the bones were unconnected, and the skull was detached from the spine. A few strands of reddish hair still clung to it in places, a sign of faded pigment, Banks knew, rather than an indication they were dealing with a redhead.

'Late as usual, Superintendent Banks,' said Dr Galway. She wasn't wearing her usual scrubs today, he noticed, but was casually dressed in faded jeans and a bottle-green blouse. It made her seem far younger and much less severe than her official outfit. The forensic anthropologist was a doctor from Newcastle called Francis Runcorn. In his early forties, Banks guessed, he sported fashionably trimmed light brown hair, a gym-freak's body and a pair of red Nike trainers below his designer jeans. He looked as if he had just completed a ten-mile run without a drop of sweat or a gasp for breath. Grace was impressed; Banks could tell by the way she hung on his every word. For a moment, an image of Dr Ioan Williams, who had carried out his previous skeleton post-mortem, flashed before his eyes – the wire-rimmed glasses and gobstopper Adam's apple. Williams had been a prize creep, ogling Annie Cabbot as he ran his hand over the skeleton's sciatic notch. You'd never get away with that nowadays, Banks thought. Good at his job, though.

'Sorry,' he said. 'Started without me?'

'We've just taken some measurements,' said Grace Hutchinson. 'Dr Runcorn says he's between 177 and 178 centimetres.'

'That's around five foot ten for you dinosaurs,' said Dr Galway, with a glance towards Banks. 'How are you?' she asked, her voice softening.

'Fine, thanks.'

'No more ill effects from the concussion?'

'None at all. Though given the way my memory's going these days, I wouldn't know.'

'Happens with age,' she said, and turned back to the skeleton. There was no need for the hose to sluice blood away, or for the scalpels, probes and other instruments she used on fleshed corpses, but the microphone still hung over the table and their observations were all being recorded.

Banks turned to Dr Runcorn. 'Grace said "he" when she referred to the body. Was that just general usage or have you determined the sex?'

'It's a "he",' Dr Runcorn said. 'At least, that's the pronoun I'd use. Dr Galway had already figured that out from the thickness of bones in the skull, and that lump of bone mass that's more developed in males.'

'That and the pelvis,' Dr Galway added. 'It's usually wider and lower in females. There are other signs, the sciatic notch and pubic curve, for example, but I think you can take our word for it that we're dealing with a male skeleton.'

'Caucasian, too,' Dr Runcorn added. 'You can see from the shape of the skull, the face and nose.'

'Any ideas of his age when he died?' Banks asked the room in general.

'Hard to say,' said Dr Runcorn. 'I'd like to do some tests – X-rays of ossification centres – the centres that actually produce the bones – spectrograph analysis and so on, to deter-mine bone mineral density and other presences. I'd also like to bring in a forensic odontologist to help narrow things down, but I'd estimate, from the condition of the bones – epiphyseal union, cranial sutures and so on – that what we have here are the remains of a male between the ages of fifty and sixty, and error is most likely to be on the side of his being older rather than younger.'

'Eighty? Ninety?'

'There's not that much degeneration,' Dr Runcorn said. 'And there are no immediate indications of any bone disease, serious deterioration or significant trauma. Not even a healed fracture in any of the ribs, limbs or joints. All in all, I'd say he was pretty healthy until he died, but we did notice this,' he said, dramatically turning the skull.

Banks stared at the right temple, the broken area he had noticed at the grave site. The others had clearly seen it, too, and knew its implications. It looked like a fracture pattern, as if someone had taken a hammer or some other blunt object to the man's head.

'Cause of death?' Banks asked.

'Can't say,' Dr Galway answered. 'But a blow that powerful would most likely have killed him if he'd been alive when it was inflicted. You can see where bone fragments have been driven into where the brain matter would have been. The temple is quite a fragile area.'

'Any way of telling for sure?'

'Whether he was alive when this happened?'

'Yes.'

'A closer examination of the edges of the fractures,' Dr Galway said. 'If a blunt object was used, you can sometimes find traces of metal or wood in the bone long after death occurred. What do you think, Dr Runcorn?'

'I agree. You can also graph the way the fracture lines run. There were definitely two hard blows, hard enough to splinter the bone, as Dr Galway said. But as yet we have no way of knowing exactly *how* or with what those blows were delivered. We'll need more tests, I'm afraid. A full analysis could take a while.'

'Take your time,' said Banks. 'I just need to know whether it's likely we're dealing with a murder, and how long ago it might have happened. Then we can initiate a full, official investigation and start trying to find out who he was.'

'In my opinion,' said Dr Runcorn, 'I'd get that investigation up and running now. Blows like this don't usually happen by accident, whether ante- or post-mortem. Not this shape and in this form. I'm not saying the person couldn't have tripped and fallen on a conveniently bifurcated blunt object and someone panicked and buried the body for some reason, but it's doubtful. Dr Galway?'

'I agree. And taking into account the wounds and the fact the body was buried in a remote field, I'd say you're after a murderer. The weapon used was probably a poker, or something very similar. If you want to wait, we'll get started on the necessary tests.'

'Including DNA?'

'Yes,' said Dr Galway. 'But, as you know, we can only get mitochondrial DNA from bones, and that's only useful if it matches a sample in your databases.'

'Which means only if he was a cop, a convicted criminal or in the military. Yes, I know.' He glanced at Grace. 'Notice anything else around the site that might help us identify him?'

'There were a few small objects,' Grace said. 'A ring. No inscription, unfortunately.'

'Wedding ring?'

'Looks more like a signet ring now we've got it cleaned up.'

'Anything else?'

'Buttons, zipper, fragments of an old leather belt and buckle. Shoe leather. Leather is always well preserved in acidic soils. We've even found Roman sandals dating back to . . . well, to Roman times. Not here, of course, not yet, but at the previous dig. Also something that may be scraps of fabric – perhaps a bedsheet – but we can't say yet if they're natural or synthetic. It looks as if there might be some sort of writing on the belt's inside surface. Manufacturer's name or tailor's, for example. But your CSIs said they'd need to clean everything up and conduct further examinations. Stefan has taken it all to the lab. He's having someone called Kim Lee examine it.'

'Probably an M & S off-the-peg suit,' said Dr Runcorn. 'But you never know. There may be bespoke belt makers still around. Savile Row, perhaps?'

'We'll get it all checked out at the lab,' said Banks. 'Can we get any reasonable idea of when chummy here was buried? I know that's the question you all hate, but I have to ask. If we can pin down the time of death, even the year, it narrows our workload immensely.'

'Well,' Dr Runcorn said, 'there's the dental work. That gold filling, for a start. It may give us some clues. I know dental records are usually a dead loss – I mean, you can hardly canvass every dentist in the country – but maybe a few local enquiries might bear fruit. Sadly, there's no bridge work or implants with serial numbers to help us.'

'And the bones are discoloured, but not a great deal,' added Dr Galway. 'They take their colour from the surrounding earth, so the longer they're down there, the more they absorb. There's no soft tissue or pigment left, but the bone is still in good condition. It hasn't started flaking or crumbling.'

'So how long?' Banks asked.

'Less than ten years, I'd estimate,' said Dr Runcorn. 'But the rate at which skeletons deteriorate is highly unpredictable. It depends so much on—'

'I know,' said Banks. 'Soil, pH balances, dampness, temperature, insect activity.'

'Yes,' said Dr Runcorn. 'All of the above. You *have* been doing your homework. Anyway, the soil is quite acidic, pH 5.5 – lower around the actual skeleton, as it should be – and I'm sure you know there's plenty of rainfall in this part of the world, also acidic if we listen to the environmentalists. And though us northerners often complain of the cold and damp, it's generally a fairly temperate climate, and we get very few days per year below freezing. I've taken all that into account.' He glanced at Grace. 'I'm afraid the acidity doesn't bode well for your Roman remains. The bones might well have dissolved completely by now.'

'So we're down to sometime after 2009,' Banks said. 'That's a good start. Anything else?'

'Again, it's an estimate – a body can take anywhere from one month to several years to skeletonise, depending on many factors – but I'd say not much later than early 2016, based on the overall state of the climate, the remains, the bone colour, and the absence of ligaments and soft tissue. Again, there are more tests I can run to narrow things down somewhat, but not by much. Carbonate testing, for example, ultraviolet fluorescence and an Uhlenhut reaction. But even then, it probably won't be as close as you'd like.'

'If you can give me a five-year range, I'd be eternally grateful. Seven years is a pretty good start. At least we know what we're dealing with, to some extent. That's a fairly recent crime. Same if you can narrow the age of the victim to within five or ten years.'

'Well, I'll do my best, Superintendent. As I say, there are many tests that can be done. Give me a few days?'

'As long as you need. And we'll start working it from our end as of now. There's one important thing you've given us already.'

'Oh? What's that?' Dr Runcorn asked.

'If our victim here was killed between 2009 and 2016, there's a very good chance his killer is still alive.'

'True enough,' said Dr Runcorn. 'There are a few more things I need before I can get started: more information on soil composition, mineral and bacterial content, a more accurate idea of temperature variation, rainfall and so on.' He glanced at Grace. 'If there's a convenient time, I may visit the site with you?'

'Of course. Whenever you like. Just let me know. Or Superintendent Banks.'

'I'll leave you two to make the arrangements,' said Banks. 'How are things going at the dig, Grace?'

'Your team is still working on the rest of the field,' Grace said. 'They finished with the ground-piercing radar early this morning and found nothing significant. When I left, they'd brought in the cadaver dogs, and some of your men and some of our volunteers were doing more digging in designated spots. But I honestly don't think there are more bodies buried there.'

'Thanks for your help,' Banks said. Then to the doctors, 'Keep at it. I'll get back to the station and set a few actions in motion, starting with missing persons. If he's local, someone might have missed him.' He glanced at his watch. 'Drink, anyone? It's a tradition to head to the Unicorn over the road after a post-mortem. And as it's about lunchtime . . .'

'You never told me,' said Dr Galway with a smile.

'Well, you're usually up to your elbows in blood.'

Dr Galway waved her arms in the air. 'Not today,' she said. 'Count me in.'

'Me, too,' said Grace.

'I'll bow out, if I may,' said Dr Runcorn. 'I'm anxious to get started.'

And so the three of them, Banks, Grace and Dr Galway, left the building.

29 November 1980

The first time Alice and I kissed, my legs actually turned weak at the knees and started shaking. I could hardly stand. I had been wanting her, dreaming of her, consumed by her for about two weeks, but had been too afraid to make a move, too afraid of rejection, I suppose, despite nights spent talking and listening to music together. Then one evening, in my room, she stood at the sink in the little kitchenette pouring water into the kettle, her hip at a sexy angle and the curve of her waist never more inviting, and I couldn't help but walk up behind her and put my arms around her waist. I expected her to freeze, to give me some reason why this couldn't happen, but she didn't. She turned in my arms, and before we knew it, we were kissing and edging our way back towards the mattress on the floor that acted as my bed. The rest went by in a blur of ecstasy.

A week later, Alice moved into the Penthouse. She had been sharing a house with three other girls, and they weren't getting along very well together, so she jumped at the chance to move into a one-bedroom flat and, or so I liked to think, be closer to me. I kept my own bedsit, but to all intents and purposes we were living together. We even spent the following summer, at the end of our first year, travelling around Europe on a rail pass – from Amsterdam to Zurich to Venice, Florence, Rome, the French Riviera, Barcelona, Cordova, Madrid and, finally, three wonderful days in Paris.

In the second year, perhaps I should have seen the signs, noticed the cracks appearing. After Margaret Thatcher came to power, in May towards the end of our first year, after the Winter of Discontent. Alice became more political, edged further to the left in that odd but predictable way the well-off often do. I was no fan of Thatcher, either, but I was more inclined to let politics be than Alice was.

I buried myself more in my literary studies. I wanted to be a writer, and I wrote mostly poetry back then. Alice wanted to change the world; I wanted to understand it and describe its intricacies and hidden corners. We started spending more time apart, me in my bedsit and her in her flat, at meetings or out distributing pamphlets in the city centre. I confess that there were one or two one-night stands followed by guilt-wracked days. Then things came to a head at the end of the second year, only about six months ago, when we had planned to head for Ireland, to a lovely cottage in Galway we had rented for the summer. When the time came, she said that she wasn't coming with me, even though we would lose our deposit. It was over.

Our final argument lasted almost as long as the ecstatic talking on our first night. Alice said I just wasn't engaged enough for her. That I had no real political passions or beliefs. That I was a bourgeois fantasist. A dreamer. An individualist. A romantic. I'd read all the requisite books – Fanon, Marx, *The Female Eunuch*, Simone de Beauvoir, Engels, Foucault, even the Marxist literary critics like Lukas – and I'd even watched *Battle for Algiers* with her, but it wasn't enough, she said. I still preferred Sartre and Camus to Foucault and Fanon, and Li Po and Tu Fu to Mao's Little Red Book. Sure, I believed in a fairer society, knew all the anti-capitalist arguments by heart, but I didn't believe them, according to Alice. I was merely chanting by rote. Workers unite. Power to the people. All I really cared about were my precious reactionary Romantic poets – Keats, Shelley, Wordsworth, Coleridge. I even tried to convince her that young Wordsworth and Shelley were hardly reactionary, but it got me nowhere.

Perhaps she was right about me. All I knew was that I couldn't come up with any decent counter-arguments to persuade her to stay, though in all fairness, I'd say she had already set out her stall, and any cogent argument I used to attempt to prove my leftie credentials would be dismissed as mere lip service. I did try to argue back, but she just dismissed me as a 'phoney'. I accused her of appropriating the infantile insult from *Catcher in the Rye,* and she simply folded her arms, smiled down at me and said it was typical of me to say something like that. Point proven.

The problem was that I liked poetry and fiction too much. They were frivolous to her and would be no help in the coming revolutionary upheaval that would be necessary to change society for the better. I clung too much to the status quo. When it came right down to it, she said, I was a *Conservative,* perhaps the greatest insult of all.

And so the night from hell went on. In the end, when she stormed back up to the Penthouse, I can't say I wasn't relieved. I was exhausted by the struggle and had even started to wonder whether I wanted to hang on to this woman who had become, it seemed to me, a humourless robotic sloganeering firebrand.

Of course, it wasn't until she was gone, truly gone, that I missed her. That was when I moped around the bedsit all day, ignoring my work, writing lousy love poems and doing badly in my exams, when I watched TV most evenings with Geoff or sat in Anton's bedsit listening to weird free jazz and electronic music and smoking joints. I didn't actually cry on Geoff's shoulder, or Anton's, or even in the presence of either, but I know I was very bad company indeed. All summer.

Instead of going with me to Galway, Alice went home to her parents in Lincolnshire for the summer. One immediate result of our break-up was that I lost a good deal of money I couldn't afford on the summer cottage rental, so overseas travel was out of the question. Alice was wealthy enough not to worry about little things like paying her debts, and I was too angry and too ashamed to ask for her share, so I simply stayed put. I suppose I could have gone home. Maybe I should have. But my parents lived in Portsmouth, a long way, and there was nothing left for me down there. All my old school friends had left, as I had, and my parents were preoccupied with their own lives, friends and jobs. I just didn't fit. My two married sisters also lived close to home and dumped their bratty kids on my parents as often as possible. Another reason to stay away.

When the new term began, my third and final year, Alice came back. I hadn't seen her all summer, although her parents had kept up the rent on the Penthouse for her because she liked it so much, and suitable places were hard to come by (another foible of the well-off leftie). My heart leaped when I saw her for the first time. She'd had her beautiful blonde hair cut fairly short, in a sort of pixie style, but she looked just as wonderful as she always had to me. Maybe time had done its healing best? I couldn't help but hope that the past was behind us. It was, but not in the way I hoped. Silly me.

Though she was polite about it, she made it quite clear from the start that I was the last person she wanted to pass the time of day with, and that she already had a new boyfriend, someone *copacetic* she had met at a political meeting towards the end of the previous academic year, someone who shared her views and her *commitment to the cause*. That got me thinking perhaps they had met and bonded *before* she split up with me, that her criticisms of me and her newfound political zealousness towards the end of the previous academic year were, in fact, *his*. It made sense. She had become far more hard-left since the end of our second year. I'd put it down to the fact that Margaret Thatcher was establishing herself as the Iron Lady, hammering the unions, but perhaps there were other reasons.

Whatever the truth of it was, the new boyfriend soon made his presence felt.

25 November 2019

Lunch at the Unicorn had been enjoyable, though the food was at best passable, and Banks's chicken was dry, his chips cold. The landlord kept a good cellar, though, and the Black Sheep was in excellent condition. Conversation had quickly drifted away from freshly dug-up skeletons to Roman burial rituals, travel plans for the following year and England's prospects in the summer's Euros.

Late in the afternoon, the core team, such as it was, held their first meeting about the case in Banks's spacious office, which they were using as a makeshift murder room until things escalated – if they did. Banks, DC Gerry Masterson and DS Winsome Jackman sat around the low glass table, notepads and pens scattered before them beside half-full coffee mugs. A whiteboard stood against the back wall with a few pictures of the scene and skeleton tacked to it, but little else. As the case progressed, the photos would be joined by names, details of the post-mortem, X-rays, dates and anything that seemed relevant. It was a visual refresher that anyone on the team could study at any time in the hope of some sort of epiphany.

'First off,' said Banks, 'welcome back, Winsome. Everything OK?'

Winsome beamed. 'Just fine, sir. Couldn't be better.'

'And Terry? How's he bearing up?'

'If you mean how does he feel about being a stay-at-home dad, he's over the moon. Just as I am to be back at work. Not that I don't love motherhood. I mean . . . I dote on little Joshua, but . . .'

Gerry patted Winsome's shoulder. 'It's all right,' she said. 'We know what you mean. And we're happy to have you back, too, sarge.'

'Where's Annie?' Winsome asked. 'DI Cabbot . . . ?'

'Annie's taking care of her father's affairs,' Banks said. 'He left a will, but the cottage is a bit of a rummage box, it seems. Mostly artworks. You know what Ray was like.'

'Poor Annie,' said Winsome. 'No time to say goodbye.'

Annie's relationship with her father Ray had ended on a sour note, Banks could have added, but didn't. That was for Annie to explain, or not. But Banks knew that she felt guilty he had died while they were at loggerheads about his relationship with a beautiful younger woman, Zelda, who had disappeared, and whose loss, Annie was convinced, had precipitated her father's heart attack.

Banks knew where Zelda was, but it was complicated. That was why he had evaded Burgess's questions at dinner the previous evening. She was wanted for questioning by the police, and Banks had crossed the line, broken just about every rule in the book to help her. Why, he wasn't sure. Perhaps he was a bit in love with her, but that wasn't the reason. He wouldn't have tried to sleep with his best friend's partner anyway, even if he had been in with a chance. No, it went deeper and was, if possible, more complex than that. One day, perhaps, he would understand it. But for the present, things were as they were.

Banks had found Ray's body at the top of the stairs, and the image still haunted him. It also turned out that Ray had bequeathed him a collection of almost 2,000 LPs – vinyl as they called them these days – along with a top-of-the-line Marantz turntable to link to his sound system. At home, he was engaged in rearranging his entertainment room to install racks along one wall to house the LPs, along with his own small collection, the precious few that had survived his various moves over the years. There were some duplicates, of course, but he would sort that out later. Nobody needed two copies of *Trout Mask Replica* or The Fugs' *Golden Filth*. He was, however, grateful for Gong and the 13th Floor Elevators, missing from his collection for too long. To be fair to Ray, though, it wasn't all sixties rock, psychedelia and prog; there were a few jazz LPs, from Bechet to Bird.

'Down to business, such as it is,' Banks said. He told Gerry and Winsome about the post-mortem and how they were still awaiting more accurate results.

'In the meantime, though,' Gerry said, 'it sounds as if we're after identifying a healthy white male between the ages of fifty and sixty, who was killed by two blows to the head sometime between 2009 and 2016. *Possibly*. Am I right?'

Banks scratched his head. 'When you put it like that,' he said, 'it does sound daunting. But that's about all we've got so far. As I said, Dr Runcorn and Dr Galway may be able to narrow the numbers down after they've carried out their various tests, and if the team finds any other evidence at the scene, we might get a lead. The items found in the grave might help, too, but I wouldn't get your hopes too high. We've got our work cut out for us.'

'You can say that again,' said Winsome. 'Couldn't you have found an easier case for me on my return? I may be rusty, you know, despite the quick refresher course.'

'I doubt that, Winsome,' said Banks. 'As the case develops – if it does – we'll naturally bring in more officers and civilian personnel as required. The first thing to do is to find out who he was.'

'How about a reconstruction?' Winsome asked. 'From the skull?'

Banks shook his head. 'Too expensive,' he said. 'Not to mention it takes for ever and is often wildly inaccurate.'

'We don't even know if he was local,' Gerry said.

'Agreed. But we do know that someone buried him locally, in a remote field – he certainly didn't do that himself – and how far would you be willing to drive with a body in the boot of your car?'

'Not too far,' Winsome said. 'Especially with cameras everywhere and the possibility of being stopped for the slightest traffic infringement.'

'Right,' said Banks. 'So, local or not, I'd guess he wasn't killed too far away from where he was buried.'

'There's another thing, too,' said Gerry.

'Yes?'

'Given the time frame, there's a good chance our killer is still alive.'

'Yes,' said Banks, 'I thought of that, too. And it raises another problem. We need to keep this business as quiet as we can for the time being. If it gets out that we've found the body, the killer might go to ground, if he hasn't already. It's to our advantage that he doesn't know his identity may become known to us before long.'

'You can depend on us,' said Winsome.

Banks smiled. 'I bloody well hope so. I'm pretty sure I can count on Drs Galway and Runcorn, too, along with Grace Hutchinson. But I'm not too sure about all the others working on the dig. One of them may have already talked to the press. Already. People do.'

'So how do we proceed, guv?' Winsome asked.

'Softly, softly. And we try to keep it as quiet as we can. But there's nothing we can do to make sure everyone keeps schtum, so we'd be better off expecting unwanted publicity at some point soon and thinking of ways we might turn it to our advantage. Maybe in terms of identifying the victim. Obviously, someone knows who he is.'

'I've got the details of the farm's previous owner,' said Gerry, shuffling her papers. 'His name is Harold Gillespie, and he lives in Lytham.'

'Hmm, posh,' said Banks. 'Can you head over there tomorrow and have a chat with him?'

'Of course.' Gerry made a note.

'You've spoken with him already? This Gillespie?'

'Only briefly, to make sure he was the right one, and that he was likely to be in tomorrow. I mean, I assumed you'd want me to go and talk to him. I didn't tell him . . . you know . . . about the skeleton. He sounded OK.'

'Still, he'll know you're coming. He'll be prepared.'

'I'm sorry, sir. I didn't think. Is he a suspect?'

'At this stage, just about everyone's a suspect. But no, I very much doubt that he was stupid enough to bury someone he killed on his own land.'

'He might not have known what was going to happen,' Gerry said. 'The compulsory purchase order, the dig.'

'True enough. He could hardly have known about that so far back. But when he did find out, he would have had time to move the body if he felt it necessary. Either way, I'd say it was maybe a bit *too* close to home to be worth the risk in the first place. No need to go at him hard, but use your subtle wiles, follow your instinct. You'll know what to ask, where to push. Mostly, at this point, we're interested in dates, anything that might us help pin down *who* we're dealing with. So you don't want to scare him off.'

'I think I can manage it.'

'Good. Also, I was just in touch briefly with Grace Hutchinson at the scene and she tells me the ground-piercing radar and cadaver dog search have turned up no other bodies. They've only a little more left to do, but so far so good.'

'That's good news, right?' Gerry said.

'It is. Though another body might have given us more to go on. Still, we can hardly complain that no one else has been murdered and buried there, can we? After you've seen Harold Gillespie, I'd like you both to get stuck into the missing persons files for the years in question. That's 2009 to 2016, remember, unless we hear different. Sorry for the tedious work, but the powers that be are not exactly overpopulating our case with personnel. There'll be a lot of names, but you'll also be able to eliminate most of them by sex, ethnicity and age. Also, lots of them probably turned up again, or have already been found. Fortunately, we're not interested in missing teens.'

'What kind of area should we cover?' Winsome asked.

'Given what we were saying earlier, I think we'll start with North Yorkshire, then if you have no success there, move out to the rest of the county. And if you get lucky with any of these, remember, we'll have dental records for comparison. If we can track down the dentist. Also DNA, though Dr Galway tells me that might not be quite as useful as we'd like to think, unless he was in an occupation like ours that requires DNA records, or we find a possible close relative.'

'What about the family tree and ancestry sites?' Gerry asked. 'Some forces have had success with DNA matches through them. You know, tracking down a brother or cousin or some other relative.'

'We'll keep that in mind. I'm pretty sure they can identify a common ancestor through mitochondrial DNA, though I could be wrong. It's worth checking into.' He stood up. 'OK, I'm heading home now. I should be around here most of the day tomorrow, so keep in touch. And Winsome, let me say again, what a pleasure it is to see you back. Say hello to Terry and wee Joshua from me.'

'Thanks, sir. Will do.' Winsome followed Gerry out of the office.

29 November 1980

The first time I saw Alice and Mark together was about a month before her murder, at a departmental welcome-back party. It was my final year, and I knew I had a lot to catch up on if I wanted to get a first and go on to do postgraduate work at Cambridge. But the summer's depression had continued even beyond the start of term. I had been low on energy since the beginning of classes, and I didn't seem to be picking up any steam. I had also been avoiding social contact as much as possible, which is why I made myself go to the party. Besides, Jill was there, an attractive girl – a fellow English literature student, too – and I thought she had shown more than a little interest in me. At the risk of sounding unfeeling, I will admit that perhaps she might present a welcome distraction. I had no idea that Alice and Mark would be there, too.

Alice introduced me to Mark in the narrow passage between the kitchen and the living room. I'm not sure what I had expected but it wasn't what I saw. He was tall and handsome, with his dark hair over his forehead in a fringe and almost down to the collar of his maroon, open-neck shirt. He wore the shirt untucked over straight-leg jeans, along with low-top white trainers, and everything about him seemed crisp and clean, not like most of the scruffy Marxists I'd seen around the place – or students, for that matter. But, then, Mark wasn't a student. He had a cool, detached air about him and looked like a front man in one of the punk or new wave bands I'd seen. Or that singer from the Doors. Jim Morrison. A rock star, anyway. Of course, Alice was quite the clothes horse herself, with her model's figure, Nordic cheekbones and pixie cut. That night she was wearing a short denim dress – showing off her long, tapered legs – and block-heeled white mules. I had to admit, though it made me feel quite sick to do so, that they made a handsome couple.

People kept brushing past us on their way to or from the drinks, and I spilled more than a few drops of my beer after someone or other jogged my elbow. It was clear that none of us wanted to hang around at such close quarters making small talk, so Alice led Mark off to introduce him to someone else. I can't say it was my finest moment, but the rest of the evening I spent mostly cuddling up to Jill, in the hopes that it would make Alice jealous. It didn't, and I felt like a prick later when I snuck out and went home early. Alone.

It was later that same night that I *heard* them for the first time. I hadn't been sleeping well, for obvious reasons, and when their footsteps on the stairs woke me at about 2 a.m., I couldn't get back to sleep. A short while later, I heard Alice's familiar gasps of pleasure, and I realised they were making love. It was faint, but it was more than loud enough for me.

The bedsprings creaked faster and faster, and the brass bedstead clanged against the wall. Alice's gasps built slowly to a series of gasps and cries, then a climax, which culminated in a grunt from Mark, harmonising strangely with Alice's long, loud scream. Then they went silent.

I was biting my fist and fighting back the tears by then, curled up in the foetal position, shaking, my imagination running wild with pictures of the two of them naked together, what he was doing to her, how she was enjoying it. About a quarter of an hour later, it started up again and went on even longer. The rattling and yelping were more pronounced this time, and the scream of climax seemed never-ending. The images proliferated.

I clamped my hands over my ears as tightly as I could and gritted my teeth. But still the sounds got through. It seemed ages before I managed to pull myself together. I lay there waiting, breath held, for it to start again, but time went by and it didn't. I heard the bedsprings creak, and someone walked across the floor, then the toilet flushed. After that came silence. Finally, I let out my breath.

By then I knew sleep would be impossible. I got up and made myself a cup of tea and rolled a joint, then I searched through my records for something that suited my mood and finally picked Leonard Cohen's first album. Cohen was out of fashion these days, what with punk and new wave and whatever, but nobody did break-up songs for students of literature like he did. I played it a little more loudly than I should have done at that time in the morning – 'So Long, Marianne', 'Hey, That's No Way to Say Goodbye' – perhaps in the hopes that Alice would hear the strains in her post-coital bliss, and that it would make her feel guilty, or even better, make her realise the error of her ways. But I heard nothing more from upstairs. No doubt the night's exertions had assured them both of a deep sleep.

That was the first of many such nights. It would probably have been like that every night if Mark hadn't had such a nice flat down on St John's Terrace, according to Alice, where they sometimes stayed and granted me a night's peace. But I still didn't sleep. And my work still suffered. Sometimes I thought I was living all the clichés. I had once been walking on air, but now there were times when I actually felt as if my heart were breaking. As if something as soft and squishy as my heart *could* break. And I never did get over the niggling feeling that, somehow, Alice *knew* I could hear, and that she pumped up the volume precisely for that reason.

25 November 2019

It had been a long day. Or at least it had felt like one when Banks got home just after seven o'clock. The front door of Newhope Cottage opened directly into the little anteroom Banks had used as his study earlier. There was an old desktop computer, a filing cabinet and a battered sofa next to a standard lamp where he sometimes sat to read, though these days he preferred the conservatory, with its sunsets and view of the fields sloping up to Tetchley Fell out back.

He first picked up the late post, which consisted mostly of junk, and which he consigned to the recycling basket beside his desk, then he walked down the hall to the kitchen. As he hadn't finished his lunch at the Unicorn, he had picked up some Thai beef curry and chicken fried rice down in Helmthorpe on his way home. He poured himself a glass of wine, selected some Haydn string quartets and sat down at the breakfast nook – just a small pine table with a couple of benches wedged in a corner, with enough room for four at the most – and poured some low sodium soy sauce on the rice.

The Seamus Heaney book he had bought the previous week was still on the table, and he picked it up when he had finished his food. He enjoyed the first poem, 'Digging', and read on, taking the book and his wine through to the conservatory, where he sat in his favourite wicker chair. The world outside was in almost total darkness – no moon, no stars – and all that was visible was the undulating line the top of Tetchley Fell cut against the night sky, separating black from dark blue. Other than that, Banks could see nothing but his own reflection and the glow of the orange-shaded table lamp beside him. He let the rhythms and images of Heaney's verse transport him far away as he sipped the wine, and soon he felt a heavy weariness struggle with the need to finish his work in the entertainment room.

Tiredness almost won out, but before pouring a second glass of wine, Banks dragged himself to his feet and went into the room, which stretched the length of the house on the eastern side and housed his music and movie collections, along with the means of enjoying them – decent video and audio equipment, surround sound and comfortable seating. Most of his recent purchases consisted of box sets – Bruckner's symphonies, Shostakovich quartets and Blu-ray sets of Hitchcock, Truffaut and Kubrick classics, along with a collection of film noir. But he still kept all his old CDs, even though he had downloaded most of them to the computer, and from there to a couple of iPods, before streaming came along and iPods were phased out.

Once again, he studied the space on the wall he had marked out for Ray's vinyl collection. There were just short of 2,000 LPs, and he had worked out, judging an album to be about 3 mm thick, that he would require about twenty feet of shelf space, which could be achieved, he estimated, by shifting a few pieces of furniture around and moving a small bookcase into the study. That would give him seven clear feet of wall to work with. To accommodate the collection, then, he would need three levels of sturdy shelving, or perhaps four if he were to include his own old vinyl albums, as well as some double albums and box sets, and have room for any he might buy in the future. Streaming was all very well, and instant gratification was a definite plus, but there was nothing like a solid disc of music, be it silver and small or black and large. He still had a small collection of 45s, too, both singles and EPs, going all the way back to Elvis's 'Good Luck Charm' from 1962.

The first task was to empty the allotted space, and he began by carrying piles of books through to the study, followed by the bookcase itself. Luckily, it was quite flimsy – a cheap flat-box purchase – and didn't give him a hernia, but it did exhaust his patience with physical activity for the evening.

He returned to the conservatory, where he poured another glass of wine. He had already decided that he was not the person to build the bookshelves. He had never been much good at woodwork, even back at school, when the tasks had been relatively easy. It made much more sense, he had decided, to employ someone who knew how to do such jobs, and who enjoyed doing them. That way, he would also be providing work and adding to someone's income. Much better than being selfish and doing it himself. He would only swear a lot. He knew a carpenter in Eastvale, Liam, a regular at the Queen's Arms, and they had agreed on a fair price for the job, which he hoped could be finished by the following weekend. Then he could arrange for the discs to be brought over from Ray's cottage. Annie had already asked him if he would meet her there the following afternoon to help her make a start on sorting things out.

Back in the conservatory, he found himself thinking about the skeleton that Grace Hutchinson had discovered the previous day. Grace had reported that the cadaver dogs had finished their work and found no more recent remains. In fact, they hadn't been very excited about anything at all buried in the field, which didn't bode too well for Grace and her team digging for Roman remains. Still, though they might not find any bodies, they could possibly unearth a villa and a hoard of treasure. Archaeology sounded like an interesting job, and not entirely different from being a detective. Banks wondered if he should have pursued a career in that field.

Most skeletal remains were unearthed, he knew, relatively close to where the victim had been killed. That usually meant a cellar in a house, where it may be discovered during renovations or demolition, or a garden dug up by new owners. Some murderers seemed to think their sins would remain buried for ever. But in this case, it appeared as if the body had been transported to its burial place, though how far was anyone's guess. The immediate assumption they had made was that it was likely somewhere close, and that the killer had chosen to bury the body in the field because he thought it would be safe from discovery. And it would have been, had it not been for the vagaries of Highways England and the Northern Archaeological Associates.

But the killer might have travelled some distance, and this might have been the first likely-looking burial spot he had chanced upon. That would make Banks's job even more difficult than it seemed already. All he could do was wait for the results of missing persons checks and hope that something in there offered a clue as to the identity of the victim. At least they had a possible time frame, 2009–2016. It was more than long enough, but it could have been a hell of a lot longer.

It would be useful to know when the compulsory purchase order was issued. Malcolm Briers had said it was about two years ago, but a more accurate date might be more useful. Harold Gillespie should know when it was. Banks made a mental note to tell Gerry, before she headed off the following morning, to ask him, though he was sure it was a question she would have on her list. Still, no harm in ticking all the boxes.

He could hear sheep bleating out on the hillside and somewhere in the distance a nightbird cried out. When it came to a decision between a third glass of wine and an early night, bed won out.

4

1 December 1980

On Monday I was sitting in the MJ Lounge enjoying a quick coffee between lectures when Gary Kirk, a guy from the Marxist Society Alice used to hang around with, approached me.

'Mind if I join you?' he asked.

'It's a free world.' I was well brought up, and I'm normally quite nice to people, but I didn't especially like Gary Kirk. Not that I ever thought there was anything other than political partisanship between him and Alice. With his thinning hair combed back from a high forehead and plastered to his skull, and his steel-rimmed glasses over grey eyes that probably wouldn't change expression when he sentenced you to a lifetime's hard labour in the Gulag, he was a hard-line ideologue with impeccable working-class credentials he never let anyone forget. The Kirks of this world I could do without. I called him 'Pasha', after the Tom Courtenay character in *Doctor Zhivago*. Alice hadn't liked that, had told me it was reductive and counterproductive, or some such thing. I told her she'd lost her sense of humour. She didn't find that funny.

Kirk spilled a little coffee down the front of his shirt and tried to rub it off after he sat down. 'Damn,' he said.

'You'll only make it worse,' I told him.

'It's just that shirts are so expensive these days. We can't all afford to be shopping at Burton's.'

'For Christ's sake, there's a charity shop in the Merrion Centre. Try that. Or some stain-remover.'

'Not necessary,' Kirk said. 'Besides, half the city centre is given over to charity shops or moneylenders these days, or hadn't you noticed?' He settled back. 'Look,' he went on, 'tell me to fuck off if you want, but I know you were a friend of Alice's – Alice Poole – and I just want you to know I'm sorry to hear about what happened to her.'

By then, we all knew the bare details from the papers and TV news. Alice's body had been found in Burley Park early Friday morning by a woman walking her dog. Her rucksack had been found nearby, which was how the police had learned her identity so quickly. There were no details about *how* she had died, of course, only that there were 'similarities' to the Ripper case. Police were still searching for her boyfriend, who had disappeared, along with his Morris Marina. They gave the car's colour and licence number and asked anyone with any information to come forward and . . . blah, blah, blah.

'Allowed to feel sorrow, are you?' I said. 'I thought that might be one of your forbidden bourgeois emotions.'

He gave me a sad but forgiving smile. Poor sinner, me. 'I'm not here to talk politics,' he said. 'But I liked Alice, and I just wanted to say, you know, first off, that I'm sorry.'

'OK,' I said, feeling suitably humbled. 'I apologise. I'm just a bit touchy about the subject, that's all.'

'Understandable. You were together, I understand? A couple.'

'Ha! You could say that. First two years. Before she caught politics.'

'She always had "politics", as you put it. We just helped her shape it and bring it to the forefront. You can't blame us for that.'

But I could. 'I'm not interested in blaming anyone,' I said. 'I don't really want to talk about it. OK?'

'Fine with me. That's why I'm here.'

'Oh?'

'Well, with you two still being close and all, I'm wondering if you can tell me whether she managed to resolve her little problem.'

'What problem would that be?'

'I don't know. She wasn't that forthcoming. But a day or so before . . . you know . . . I tried to engage her in conversation about the demo, but she cut me off. She said she was having boyfriend problems and she'd get back to me as soon as it was resolved.'

'Boyfriend problems? First I've heard it. Wait a minute. You don't think that meant me, do you?'

'No. Not at all. I know she'd finished with you. No. This was about the new boyfriend. Mark Woodcroft.'

'I thought he was an old friend of yours?'

'No. I met him over the summer at a Socialist Workers Party conference. He'd just come up here from London and was wanting to make new contacts. I told him we had a good group right here in Leeds. He said he wasn't a student, but I told him that didn't matter. There was nothing to stop him attending our lectures. We have the Socialist Workers Party here, too. And we welcome members from all walks of life. We can always use people to help distribute pamphlets and publicise events.'

'Before or after Alice?'

'Oh, after. She joined towards the end of last year. At least, she started attending meetings and discussions around that time.'

So there went my theory of Alice and Mark getting together while she was still with me. I don't know how that made me feel. Maybe there was, somewhere deep inside, a sense of relief, but it was so deep as to almost not exist. More than anything, though, the thought that she *hadn't* been unfaithful gave me a feeling of love and a rush of desire for her.

'Well, did she?' Kirk asked.

'Did she what?'

'Resolve her little problem.'

'I've no idea. She never mentioned it to me. My guess would be no.' I thought again of that last time I had seen her, hurrying off in the rain. Her urgency, edginess. That *clickety-clack* walk. 'Did *you* go to the demo?'

'No. I was planning on it, but something came up.'

'Have you seen Mark recently?' I asked.

'Not for a while, no.'

'Can you remember the last time?'

'Last week sometime.'

'What does he do?'

'What do you mean?'

'For a living. If he isn't a student.'

'As far as I know, he's on the dole. There'll be a lot more of that now Thatcher's starting to go full throttle.'

'Right. What else do you know about him?'

'Nothing, really. He never talks much about his life or his parents or anything. I got the impression he's from London or somewhere not far away, and that he'd worked at a number of jobs, mostly manual labour. He's twenty-five, a few years older than the rest of us, and largely self-educated. He has a sharp mind, though, quick in argument, but I sometimes get the impression he's a bit . . . how should I put it . . . not insincere, exactly, but maybe a touch superficial. And I'm not sure I'd trust him.'

'Do you mean he lacks conviction?'

'No. He seemed convicted enough.'

'Just too full of passionate intensity?'

'What?'

'Yeats. Never mind.'

'Right. Well, what I mean is it's sometimes as if he learned it by rote – the right responses, arguments. Not heartfelt.'

'A phoney?'

'Yes. Exactly. But don't quote me on it.'

'I didn't think you lot were interested in the devices and desires of the human heart.'

'There's a lot you don't know about us.'

'Who does he hang out with, apart from you?'

'I don't know. And he doesn't hang out with me. I can't say I'm particularly close to him. I get the impression he's a bit of a loner. He did OK at our social, though. Friendly enough.'

'You have socials? What do you do, sing the "Internationale" and do a few Cossack dances?'

'Very funny.' He eyed me sideways. 'Are you always so cynical?'

'Only when the mood takes me.'

'That's what Alice said once. That you just didn't take her interest in socialism seriously. You felt the constant need to belittle it, make fun of what she believed, and so belittle her.'

It enraged me that Alice had talked to this twat about me. 'I had no idea she shared her feelings so freely.'

'And with someone like me? I suppose not. But she seemed depressed sometimes. We had a couple of heart-to-hearts. She was still very fond of you, you know. She regretted some of the things she said to you.'

'What things?'

'She didn't say, not specifically. Just that she felt she'd over-stepped the mark. If you ask me, I'd say she sometimes seemed to regret you'd split up, though I can't imagine why.'

I felt a lump in my throat. 'What about Mark? Wasn't she in love with him?'

'I don't think they were in love. No. That's not what I would call it.' Kirk stood up. 'If it means anything at all to you now, I don't think they would have lasted much longer. I'm sorry. Perhaps I didn't put that very well. What I meant was, had things turned out differently, you two might have got together again.'

'Despite my cynicism and lack of conviction?'

'Maybe *because* of them. Alice was a lot more complex than even you seem to think. Anyway, I'd better be off now.'

'Peasants to liberate from the yoke of capitalist imperialism?'

'Something like that.'

'Tell me, were *you* interested in Alice? Did you try to get her into bed?'

'No,' Kirk said. 'My sexual interests lie in another direction entirely. But I liked her. Bye.' He turned away and walked off.

That went well, Hartley, I told myself, as I reeled from the idea that Alice and I might have got back together. I wasn't going to show any emotion in front of Kirk, but I had to admit that statement choked me up inside. Though I had barely admitted it to myself, I *had* harboured the hope that Alice and I would get back together again, that our estrangement and Mark's presence in her life were nothing but minor ephemeral distractions that would soon fade.

I also had to admit that Kirk was a lot more emotionally sharp than I thought he was. Did Alice really think I was a cynic? I always believed I was a romantic, and that was why she dumped me, because of my penchant for bourgeois individualism.

At least I knew a little more about Mark now, though it didn't help me very much. According to all reports, he had disappeared. What the hell had happened to him? Where could he be? Had he been killed along with Alice? That didn't make sense. The Ripper only attacked women walking alone. So what if it *wasn't* the Ripper? Who might have a motive for wanting Alice and Mark dead? Was the motive political? Terrorists, or something? Or *Conservatives*? That seemed very far-fetched. All I knew was that his car was gone and hadn't been found yet. Maybe it would yield some answers when it was. If it was.

Interesting, though, what Kirk had said about Alice's little boyfriend problem. Could it be that Mark himself had killed her? I finished my coffee and hurried off to the Coleridge lecture.

26 November 2019

There are few sights more dismal than an English seaside resort in the late November drizzle, but Lytham St Annes managed to go against the grain, Gerry thought, as she drove slowly along the coast road waiting for the satnav to resume giving directions. At least there were no amusement arcades, as far as she could see, or busy piers lined with gift shops and rides, like Blackpool, just a few miles up the coast. Only the quaint Victorian St Annes Pier, which stretched across the sand to the water's edge close by a row of colourful beach huts. There certainly seemed to be plenty of golf courses, and the area had a general air of affluence.

Winsome sighed as she gazed over the expanse of the Irish Sea. Gerry followed her gaze. The water was calm, almost glass-like, and a few small fishing boats were visible out to sea, along with an oil tanker heading south. It was a scene Annie Cabbot's father, Ray, might have liked to paint, Gerry thought, feeling a sudden pang of loss. Ray had teased her mercilessly about her 'pre-Raphaelite looks' and suggested that he'd like to paint her in the nude, but she had grown used to that and managed to laugh it off. There was hardly any point making a fuss, even if she had wanted to. Ray wasn't her boss or a co-worker. He was just a friend, an acquaintance, really. And she didn't mind the teasing so much. In return, she just called him a dirty old man and enjoyed his guffaws.

But the thing that won her heart absolutely was that shortly after she had almost been killed in a flood, Ray had presented her with a beautiful head and shoulders sketch of herself. She had framed it and hung it on her living-room wall. And that was what she would always remember Ray for.

'Peaceful, isn't it?' Winsome said. 'I'd almost forgotten what the seaside's like.'

'It's a beautiful stretch of coastline,' Gerry agreed.

'Of course, you come from around here, don't you?'

'A bit further south. The other side of the estuary. Formby. We didn't live right by the sea, but I spent plenty of time out playing in the dunes when I was a young girl. It's all National Trust land.'

'I envy you.'

Gerry's eyes widened. 'What? It wasn't exactly Montego Bay. Many people would envy you that for a childhood.'

Winsome smiled. 'I suppose so. Though we were up in the mountains, inland, and it could get pretty lonely up there.'

'Your dad was a police officer, wasn't he?'

'Yes. Spring Mount. He's retired now.'

'Will you be heading back to visit the family and show off young Joshua?'

'Eventually. Though I hope they'll manage to get over here first. It will certainly be great to see them again. It's been a long time. Over five years.'

'You came over by yourself, right?'

'That's right. To go to university. I wanted a new life, a sense of adventure.'

'It must have been hard.'

'At first, yes. I was very lonely, stuck away in my little student bedsit, too shy to venture out and try to make friends. And everything was so different, so strange. And so cold.'

'But you got over it?'

'I must have done, though I can't say I remember any specific moment when things started to change. I met people in lectures and tutorials, got to know them better. They invited me to parties and pub nights. All of a sudden, I had friends and a life.'

'What about being . . . you know . . . Jamaican?'

'Being Black, you mean?'

'Yes. I mean, did you encounter any racism?'

Winsome snorted. 'Of course I did. Almost every day, in one form or another. Oh, it wasn't always obvious, like racial insults and slurs. Often it was just little things – a glance, a word, a cold shoulder. I can't say my parents didn't warn me, though they had never been here at that time. They'd heard. Everyone in the community knew someone who'd gone to England.'

'Didn't it upset you?'

'Absolutely. But I wasn't going to let anyone see that. Sometimes I cried myself to sleep when I was alone in my bedsit at night, but I wasn't going to let their ignorance and cruelty get me down. Besides, it was a pretty mixed crowd I hung out with. African, Indian, Pakistani, Korean, as well as white. That helped. There were people I could talk to, people who understood how I felt. And later, when I joined the police, a lot of it was just being a woman, you know that as well as I do. Being a Black woman made it more difficult, of course, but just being a woman in the first place meant you had to work much harder, take all their stupid little jokes and insults with a smile. You must have experienced that?'

'Well, I do get a bit of stick over my posh accent and red hair.'

Winsome laughed.

They passed an ornate white church with a high tower resembling a lighthouse, then on past a sign to another golf course.

'Ever played golf?' Gerry asked.

'Me? No. I honestly don't have time.'

'Not now, I suppose,' said Gerry. 'I just thought . . .'

'No. Never. I always thought it was a rich old white man's game. I'm not sure they even let Black people on the courses. Or women. Don't tell me you play?'

'What about Tiger Woods? Or the LPGA? Anyway, I'm getting into it. You probably don't know about this, having been away for a while, but I've been seeing Jared Lyall from tech support over at County HQ, and he's been giving me a few lessons, like. He's very keen. I seem to be quite good at it.'

'Good for you,' said Winsome. 'Aha. East Beach. Is this it?'

Gerry checked the satnav and nodded. 'One of these houses.'

They drove by a long terrace of mixed hotels and houses, either real Victorian or in the Victorian style. Varying sizes, but mostly high and narrow with plenty of bay windows. They knew that Gillespie lived in a ground-floor flat and soon found the right place and a parking spot right outside. Before heading up the path, they turned to admire the view and smell the salt air. Seagulls screeched overhead. Beyond a broad swathe of grass lay the sea, stretching as far as the eye could see. Gerry wondered if the speck of land she could see out in the distance was the Isle of Man or just a nameless lump of rock. She knew that just south of the Ribble Estuary lay Formby, where her parents still lived, then Crosby, Liverpool, and the Wirral, but she couldn't see them.

They walked up a steep flight of steps and Gerry rang the doorbell. In short order, a dog started barking, then a man answered. Gerry's first thought was that he didn't look like a farmer. For some reason she had an image of a big, burly man with a red face and hairs growing out of his ears, but Gillespie didn't seem outdoorsy at all. He was slight and wiry, a little frail and completely bald. She guessed he was in his early seventies. He was wearing brown cords and a V-necked cricket jumper over a pale green shirt. When he answered the door, he was holding a Labrador retriever by its collar. 'Be quiet, Jasper,' he said.

'Mr Gillespie?' Gerry asked.

'The very same. Are you the one I talked to on the telephone? Do come in.' He stood aside, holding the door and the dog, as Winsome and Gerry edged in. The door led directly into a large, warm living room. Gerry could see no fire in the fireplace, so she assumed the flat must be centrally heated. Wherever it came from, the heat was welcome. She'd had the heater in the car turned up high all the way, but it hadn't done much to alleviate the chill that seemed to permeate everything on days like this.

But Gillespie's living room was an oasis of warmth.

'Don't mind Jasper,' Gillespie said, as the dog started sniffing crotches. 'He's very friendly. He likes visitors. He'll soon calm down.'

Jasper didn't show much sign of doing that, Gerry thought as she stroked the dog's head, at the same time gently pushing it away from where it wanted to put its nose.

After they had all made themselves comfortable on the sofa and armchairs – and Jasper, disappointed in his failed assaults, had gone off to curl up and sulk by the empty hearth, licking his balls – Gillespie rubbed his hands together and offered tea or coffee. They both said yes to tea, and he ambled off into the kitchen. The view through the large picture window was magnificent, the same as they had enjoyed before coming in, only from a little higher up. They could still hear the seagulls and watch them swoop over the shallows, searching for fish.

Gillespie walked back in with teapot, cups, saucers and bis-cuits on a silver tray, which he set down on the low pine table. It fitted with the rest of the place, Gerry thought. Everything was light in colour, from the off-white walls to the pale blue three-piece suite and light brown parquet floor. Gerry noticed a slight tremor in Gillespie's hands as he put down the tray. Jasper glanced over but appeared uninterested.

'Give it a few minutes to mash,' Gillespie said, then settled back in his armchair. 'Now, what can I do for you two lovely young ladies? You didn't give much away when we spoke on the telephone.'

Gerry thought of taking him to task on the 'lovely', but she realised it would alter the dynamics of the entire interview, so she swallowed it with a smile. Winsome just looked at him with a neutral expression on her face.

'You used to own Wilveston Farm, near Eastvale, is that right?' she asked.

'Yes.'

'When did you leave?'

'You might say I was forced out. Compulsory purchase order. March 13th, 2017.'

'How long had you been there?'

'In spirit, all my life, I suppose. I was born there. My father farmed the land, and his father before him. I took over in 1994, when Dad fell ill, but my children spent much of their childhoods there. Go back a bit further and you'll find us Gil-lespies as farm labourers and shepherds over the centuries.'

'So you must have been hit especially hard when the CPO came through?' Gerry asked.

'I won't deny it. It hurt, but it was bound to happen sometime.'

'Oh?'

'What I mean is, when I could no longer keep it up, or when I died, whichever came first.'

'What about your children?'

Gillespie snorted. 'Two boys, both grown up, married and moved away. Couldn't get away fast enough. I'm a granddad, too, now, you know, though you wouldn't know it from how often I see my grandchildren.'

'Pity,' said Winsome.

'Yes. There was no chance of passing the farm on. They weren't interested. One works with computers in San Francisco, and the other's on an oil rig off the coast of Africa somewhere. Not a farmer among them.'

'So what were your plans for the future?'

Gillespie shrugged. 'I don't really know that I had any. Work the farm as long as I could, then sell it, I suppose. I was employing too many labourers even then, as I couldn't do all the heavy lifting myself. Bad back. Maybe the CPO came at the right time. And it was generous enough. At least to buy this flat. Even so, no one likes being forced to do something by the government. I can't see why any of this is of interest to you. Surely you—'

'Do you know about the dig?' Winsome asked.

'Dig?'

'Yes, on what used to be your land.'

'I can't say I've paid much attention to developments over there lately. I did hear about some Roman remains found up near Scotch Corner. Is that what you mean?'

'Not quite,' said Gerry. 'The experts from the Scotch Corner dig got the idea there might be other sites of interest further south, so when the road widening and the new shopping centre were approved, and you were served with the CPO, they got permission to get in first and check out the area.'

'Including my old farm?'

'Yes.'

'But I still don't see where you're going with this.'

'One of the archaeologists was working specifically on the westernmost field, the one near the lane.'

'That scraggly old wasteland?'

'Did you ever use it?'

Gillespie shook his head. 'It wasn't good for anything. Even the grass there gave the sheep bellyache. And you couldn't grow anything. Not anything you could sell, at any rate. Unless you like swedes and turnips, and it wasn't big enough to make a profit from even growing them. Why?'

Gerry glanced at Winsome and said, 'It seems there was a Roman settlement around there. During the early stages of the digging, a young woman uncovered a skeleton.'

'Well, you'd expect that, wouldn't you?'

'It wasn't Roman. It hadn't been there that long.'

'Since when, then?'

'Our best estimate is between 2009 and 2016.'

Gillespie's jaw dropped. 'Bloody hell. And I left in 2017.'

'That's right.' Gerry paused. 'There's still a margin of error on the dates at the moment, but it's certainly possible the body was buried while you were still running the farm. Do you know anything about it?'

'Jesus Christ. No, nothing at all. Like I said, I never had call to go over there – it was the far end of the property, more than a mile away from the farmhouse, and the field was just waste ground. Except . . . wait a minute . . .'

'What, Mr Gillespie?'

Gillespie got to his feet. 'Can you show me exactly where this skeleton was buried?'

Gerry took out a plan of the field from her briefcase and unfolded it. She pointed to a spot just over the wall from the lane, at the farthest end of the property from the A1. Gillespie slid his hand inside his jumper and took some wire-rimmed reading glasses from the top pocket of his shirt. He peered over Gerry's shoulder.

'Hmm,' he said. 'Well, I might be able to help you narrow down the timeline.'

'How can you help us?'

'Just a minute,' Gillespie said. 'I need to check my old records. Won't be a sec.'

He disappeared towards the kitchen, and they heard foot-steps going up wooden stairs. So it was a two-level flat. Nice. Gerry and Winsome took the opportunity to finish their tea and sample one of the custard creams Gillespie had put out.

He came back empty-handed. 'Sorry. I got rid of a lot of that stuff when I left the farm.' Gillespie sat down again and Jasper stirred, stood and wagged his tail a few times but soon curled up again.

'What were you looking for?' Winsome asked.

'That section of the farm, though virtually unused, was susceptible to occasional periods of flooding. Flash floods, I guess you'd call them, usually causing problems in the lane. Something to do with the drainage. It's not much used, as it links only local villages and isolated farms, but of course enough people need it for access to their homes and work that they made a fuss to the local council. The long and the short of it is that we had to get some work done, which included taking apart the wall and digging up part of that field, along with the lane on the other side, to clear it. The council main-tained that there had to be some sort of blockage there that disrupted natural drainage of the land around. Either that or some ancient underground irrigation pipes that burst every year. I told them that was pure poppycock, of course, but they insisted we get the diggers in. In the end, we had the drains cleaned out and ditches dug on both sides of the wall.'

Gerry picked up the plan again and pointed to where the skeleton had been found. 'And that was where they did the digging?'

'Yes. All around there. Had half the bloody field up.'

'When was this?'

'That's what I was looking for. The old accounts. A receipt or something.'

'But you couldn't find it?'

'Afraid not.'

'Can you remember anything about when this work took place?' Gerry asked.

'Not exactly. It's one of the things that goes as you get older, you know. Your memory.'

'Could you make a guess at the year?'

'It was a while ago. Early teens, I think. And one thing I do remember, it was in the spring. April or May, sometime around then. You can probably find out from the company that did the work.'

'You remember their name?'

'Eastvale Drainage Solutions. We always used them for plumbing or drainage problems. Whenever it was, as far as I know, they didn't find any evidence of a skeleton or Roman remains, or I'm sure they would have let me know.'

'Obviously they didn't,' said Winsome. 'But they would certainly have unearthed this skeleton if it had been there then. Thanks, Mr Gillespie. That's a big help.'

And it might save us a pile of work, Gerry thought, making a note of the company name, if it knocks even a couple of years off the missing persons search list. She realised there was a possibility that whoever had been buried there may have been missing for some time before the murder and burial. Such cases happened and made the headlines. But they were rare. People wrote books about them. Or made documentaries and thrillers. She remembered a film she had seen about a weirdo who kidnapped girls and kept them in some sort of underground complex until Morgan Freeman came along and set them free. If they drew a blank at first, then they would have to go back and extend the search even further, in both place and time, but it often made sense to search in the most obvious place first.

They got to their feet and edged towards the door as Jasper uncurled again and padded towards them. This time Winsome bent and stroked him and he stopped jumping up at her.

'He obviously likes you more than he does me,' Gerry said.

'Now there's an epitaph: "She was much loved by dogs."'

She thanked Gillespie again for his cooperation, and they went out to the car. As Gerry started it up, Winsome glanced at her watch and said, 'I'm getting a bit peckish. I know it's out of season, but do you think we might stop off in Blackpool on the way back and see if there are any fish and chip shops open?'

2 December 1980

As I had no lectures on Tuesday afternoon, and I also had the house to myself, I crept up the stairs to Alice's flat. I had already made sure there were no police still lurking either inside or outside the house. There was no one. There hadn't even been anyone left on guard the first night. They had finished their search, and no doubt found nothing relevant to her murder, and they clearly thought they had no reason to guard the flat. After all, it wasn't a crime scene. So, what was I hoping to find?

Fortunately, I still had a key. Alice could be very forgetful about practical matters like that, and after we split up, she had never asked for it back. There was one moment when I was on the verge of throwing it back at her, but I thought better of it. I had never needed to use it before, had almost forgotten I still had it.

Don't get me wrong, I'm not a panty-sniffer or anything like that. That's not the reason I went up there. Though the police had released no more details of the murder, and had made no substantial connections with the Ripper as far as I was aware, I had got the impression that they were less interested in Mark as a suspect than I thought they ought to be. True, I had no evidence of any wrongdoing on his part, but even so. Alice had been on edge about something when I met her in the street that night, and Gary Kirk from the Marxist Society had told me that she had said something about boyfriend problems, and that she would let him know as soon as things were resolved. Maybe they never were resolved, or were resolved by her murder. It certainly seemed that nobody had seen Mark since that night. I had no idea what I expected to find in her flat, but it was worth a look.

What would happen to her stuff? I wondered, as I closed the door softly behind me and saw the familiar Lowry print on the wall over the bookcase. I supposed her parents would come and collect it all. I hadn't even heard anything about the funeral yet, though I supposed the police would keep hold of the body for a post-mortem. And who was going to tell me about the arrangements?

Besides, Alice didn't have a lot of possessions. Though she could probably afford one, she had no television set. Opium of the masses, along with religion, no doubt. The only furniture in the living room, apart from a sofa and a couple of armchairs, was an antique coffee table, the bookcase and a new stereo system her parents had bought her for her last birthday. Beside it stood a stack of LPs, Alice's favourites I was familiar with: the Clash, the Jam, the Damned and the Ramones. She always did like punk more than I did, though we both agreed it had pretty much died a couple of years ago, and the Clash had really moved on with *London Calling*. But the hard punk records were still around. I preferred new wave artists like Talking Heads, Patti Smith and Television.

On the coffee table lay a copy of *Marxism Today* featuring an interview with Lech Walesa, and a flyer for forthcoming gigs in the refectory, along with a bottle of gin, half-full. Alice had circled Siouxsie and the Banshees and Gang of Four in red, with exclamation marks. Had we still been a couple, had she still been alive, we would have been going to those gigs together.

Though I had been in the room many times, I still felt like a stranger, an interloper. I also didn't know what I had come for, what I expected to find. The living room was much the same as it had been during our time together, except for the addition of one new framed print – Brueghel's *Landscape with the Fall of Icarus* – which told me that underneath all her revolutionary politics, Alice had retained a degree of discerning artistic sensibility. We had seen and admired it in the Museum of Fine Arts in Brussels on our European odyssey, and I had later read her the Auden and William Carlos Williams poems about it. She said she liked the Williams best as it sounded less public-school stuffy.

From what I could see, the place hadn't been given any real going-over at all. There was nothing strewn on the floor, no drawers gaping open and picture frames askew. Perhaps the police were tidier than the movies would have us believe, though I doubted it. Whatever search they had made must have been cursory indeed, I concluded. Which obviously meant they thought the answers to her murder lay elsewhere. Mark's flat, perhaps?

I sat down on the sofa and fingered the patchwork wool afghan Alice sometimes used for warmth on winter nights when we would snuggle up and listen to music together. She had told me her grandmother had knitted it for her when she was much younger, and it had evolved from a childish fixation, like a treasured teddy bear or something, into a sort of talisman, a source of comfort and security. Perhaps it should be buried with her as a kind of shroud.

I thought once again of what Kirk told me, that he didn't think Mark and Alice had been in love. How he knew, I had no idea, but maybe he was right. After all, how can two people who think love is a romantic indulgence, a bourgeois obsession that impedes social progress, be in love?

Perhaps Alice had been on her way to tell Mark that it was over and she was coming back to me. But I couldn't have it both ways, I realised. If she rejected love as a bourgeois emotion, why would she come back to me? And if he had no great passion for her, why had he killed her? Not a crime of passion, then? Some other reason? On the other hand, maybe Mark was the kind of person who couldn't bear to lose something he thought of as *his*? Maybe Alice had underestimated the depth of his feelings, his sense of entitlement and possession. If there was one thing I had learned from studying great literature, it was that human passion often has a power far greater than reason or political ideology. Tolstoy knew that.

There was no sense sitting around getting gloomy, so I started a search of my own. Her study desk held nothing but stationery items, books and notes for an essay she appeared to be writing on the historical significance of E. P. Thompson's *The Making of the English Working Class* and Richard Hoggart's *The Uses of Literacy,* both of which I had introduced her to in our early days. Not that they got me any credit when it came to her dumping me over my lack of political engagement.

I already knew that Alice didn't keep any diaries or journals, so I hadn't expected to find a written narrative leading up to her murder, full of clues and signposts. I suppose if there had been such a thing, the police would have already taken it. She had owned an address book, I remember, and that was nowhere to be found.

I did find a pocked-size ringed notebook, the kind you could buy cheaply at WHSmith. Alice had clearly used it for random inconsequential pencil jottings. Many of them were indecipherable – her handwriting was mostly an illegible scrawl – but seemed to consist of shopping lists, brand names of fashionable clothing she had read about in Sunday colour supplements, or the occasional must-have book or LP. Everything was set down there willy-nilly on each lined page, dozens of circled jottings, many sideways or upside down, as if she simply grabbed the pad when she needed it. As far as I could tell, there were no personal confessions, nothing approaching a diary or a journal. I put it back in her desk drawer.

I almost baulked at entering the bedroom, scene of our most intimate encounters, and some of the most upsetting in the final days. Nothing had changed. The same colourful duvet covered the double bed, decorated with images of butterflies. I remember identifying the chalkhill blue, dark green fritillary and the Duke of Burgundy, among others, and she had been amazed I knew their names. And me a Portsmouth city boy. I didn't tell her that my fascination with Nabokov had begotten a fascination with collecting butterflies in my mid-teens. I doubt very much that Alice would have approved of my admiration for the author of *Lolita* or my habit of patiently gassing and pinning such beautiful creatures.

The wardrobe was still full of her dresses, skirts and jackets, and, yes, the bedroom drawers were stuffed with her underwear as well as T-shirts and blouses. I will admit to a certain frisson at touching the smooth silk and soft cotton as I felt about for anything hidden beneath. I was disgusted with myself for that, and found nothing there, anyway. And I certainly never sniffed anything. Knowing Alice, it was all clean and fresh.

The dressing table was littered with creams and potions. Though Alice didn't usually wear much make-up, she did love, on occasion, to get dressed up to the nines, applying lipstick, eyeshadow and mascara and Lord knows what else. Though she was serious in her politics and disdained frivolity, there was definitely a girlish side to her nature, not to mention a more than passing interest in fashion.

A Wedgwood jewellery box sat beside a phial of Chanel No 5 (had Mark bought her that, the bastard?) and it was filled with the familiar chains, rings, necklaces, bracelets and earrings I had seen her wear over the time we were together. I felt a lump in my throat when I picked up a simple gold heart on a chain I had bought her the previous Christmas.

By now, I was starting to feel as if I couldn't take any more. Tears pricked at my eyes. The flat was becoming claustrophobic, sucking all the air out of me, and I began to feel dizzy. I flopped down on the bed. It was as if I was realising for the first time the full horror of what had happened. Alice was dead. We hadn't just split up. She was *dead*, and I would never, ever see her again, hear her laughter, touch her lips, run my hand over the smooth skin of her belly. And it wasn't just because we had split up as a couple – hadn't Gary Kirk told me he thought there was a chance we might have got back together? – but because she was dead. Because someone – the Ripper or Mark or some other maniac – had cut, bludgeoned or strangled the life out of her, and it was a truth I could barely live with.

The room was spinning as I staggered to my feet and made it through to the living room. There, I managed to steady myself a little before dashing out of the door and back down the stairs to my own flat, already dark in the fading light of a December afternoon. I rolled a cigarette with shaking hands. I felt like a drink, but the pubs were closed, and I didn't have anything in the flat. I remembered Alice's half bottle of gin upstairs but couldn't bring myself to go back up and get it. I would do without. Instead, I threw on my leather jacket and headed out, hands thrust deep in my pockets, and walked and walked, oblivious to where I was going, until my feet hurt, then I took a bus back home.

26 November 2019

Wraiths of mist stretched and twisted in ghostly tentacles over the moors. Banks remembered the night when he and Ray had gone wandering about searching for Zelda in the dark. People got lost easily out there. The moor was dangerous, especially in darkness or bad weather. Its wild craggy surface, covered in gorse and heather, hid many treacherous bogs and steep, unexpected gullies.

Windlee Farm, Ray's house, stood on a rise, and the moorland stretched out to the west below and beyond it. To the east, about half a mile away, stood the village of Lyndgarth. The mist swirled about six or seven feet above the rough terrain, like clouds seen from an aeroplane. A mile or so to the south-west, the dark crumbling towers of Devraulx Abbey poked through like rotten teeth. The air was cold and damp. Banks gave a shudder and went indoors. Annie called out from upstairs, and he found her sitting on the floor in Ray's studio, which hadn't changed since the last time he had been there and found Ray's body at the top of the stairs. Standing in that same spot again brought the memory back with a jolt.

Annie gave him a crooked smile. He could see that she had been crying. 'Thanks for coming.'

'You're welcome. What are you up to?'

Annie held out the sketchbook she was holding. Banks took it and looked at the drawing of a young woman bearing a remarkable resemblance to Annie, an unreadable expression on her face: distant, apprehensive, but also almost beatific. It sent a shiver up his spine.

'My mother,' she said. 'Just before she went into hospital to have me. Don't you think it's amazing?'

'I do,' said Banks. It made him think of a Hockney drawing he'd seen at a National Portrait Gallery exhibition that had a similar effect on him: a drawing of Hockney's mother, as she sat in her best coat and hat, waiting for the car to come and take them to his father's funeral. 'Ray had a remarkable talent.'

Banks handed back the sketchbook and Annie set it down with a pile of others on the floor. 'Ray didn't approve of photographs,' she said. 'He said they had no emotion, no soul. We had arguments about that.'

Banks and Ray had argued the merits of photography, too. 'Those who can, paint,' said Ray, 'and those who can't, take photographs.' Banks had argued that photography was, or could be, an art in its own right, and backed up his argument with famous names – Henri Cartier-Bresson, Ansel Adams – but all to no avail. There was no way you could get the heart involved in setting a few knobs and pushing a button, Ray had argued.

'Mum and some of the others in the commune took photos, though,' Annie went on, 'so there are a few old albums lying around, but better than a family album of snapshots, we have Ray's sketchbooks. Every major occasion is in there, in some form or another. My first steps, communion, a family holiday in Provence, even my mother's funeral.'

'That's original,' Banks said. 'Typical of Ray.'

Annie gave him a sharp glance. 'There was nothing typical about Ray.'

'I meant . . . Oh, never mind. You said you'd appreciate a helping hand. What with?'

'The Witch's things.'

Annie had taken to calling Zelda 'the Witch'. In her mind, Zelda was to blame for Ray's death. Banks had tried to explain that Zelda couldn't help being abducted by old enemies, no matter how much her disappearance had upset Ray. But Annie argued that she shouldn't have had such enemies in the first place. That she was a disturbed young woman who had beguiled and seduced Ray for his money, and eventually caused his death. There was no winning this war, or even a battle, Banks knew, so he generally shied away from the subject. There was no doubt that Zelda was trouble, but then, so was Ray. He had smoked too much, drunk too much, worked too hard and never took any exercise.

'What kind of help?' Banks said.

'I'd like you to deal with it.'

'What do you mean?'

'What I say. Deal with it. Get rid of it. Her stuff. All of it. Clothes, artworks, personal effects. I don't want to see, hear or smell any traces that woman was ever in this house. Do it any way you like. Fire would probably work best.'

'That's quite a job,' Banks said.

'Will you help me, or should I get someone else? No doubt I'd find a few willing arsonists on our books.'

Banks sighed. 'I'll help you,' he said.

'And you're welcome to keep anything of hers you want. Even the nude drawings and paintings Ray did of her. Especially them. I can't bear to look at them.'

Banks noticed a sheet covering some paintings in the corner, ones of Zelda he remembered from his last visit. He guessed that Annie would have also removed the charcoal sketches from the walls in the kitchen and dining area, some of them nudes that had made him feel a little uncomfortable when he and Annie first had dinner with Ray and Zelda. Was that really only about a year ago?

'That's crazy,' Banks said. 'They must be worth a fortune. Why don't you just sell them?'

'I'd rather burn them than profit from them,' Annie said. 'And if you won't take them, that's exactly what I'll do. I don't want a trace of her remaining. I might even burn down that wooden hut she used for a studio in the garden.'

'Are you thinking of moving in here?' Banks asked. 'It's yours now. And it's a lot bigger than where you're living at the moment. Closer to work, too.'

Annie's house was tiny – 'bijou' would have been a kind word to describe it – and it also suffered from being in the centre of a higgledy-piggledy network of ginnels and snickets. Banks called the area 'the labyrinth' because it was almost impossible to find your way through without a length of string to follow.

'I don't know,' Annie said. 'I might. I'll have to think about it.'

'You don't need the money from selling it,' Banks said. 'I'm sure Ray left you well provided for.'

'What do you mean by that?'

'Ray was a very wealthy man, Annie. You know that. His paintings sold. Have done for years. He's famous.'

'What about the Witch?'

'You know as well as I do that he left something to provide for her, too. He loved her, Annie. Take it or leave it. It was a heart attack that killed Ray, not her. Years of living without a thought for tomorrow. He had a good life, and he was happy towards the end, with Zelda. True, he was heartbroken when she was abducted, but who wouldn't be? You need to accept that.'

Annie gave him a withering glance, then turned away. 'No doubt she'll come crawling out from under her rock now she knows she can get her hands on his money.'

Zelda had made it clear she had no interest in any inheritance. Perhaps the money could somehow be put into trust, Banks thought, and she would be in a position to claim it one day, if she changed her mind, or at least give it to charity. But for now, she needed to be left alone. Besides, all that was for the lawyers to sort out.

'Any LPs you want?' he asked.

'You must be joking. I don't even have a hi-fi.'

'A turntable's what you need.'

'Whatever. Take them. They're yours. Ray left them specifically to you.'

'It'll take me a couple of trips to move out everything you want rid of,' he said. 'There's not all that much room in my boot. Besides, I have to get some shelves built back home.'

'Take your time,' Annie said, searching in her shoulder bag and tossing him a key. 'But don't take too long. Maybe rent a van. I'm going away for a while before making my mind up about what to do.'

'Probably a good idea,' Banks said. 'Have a nice holiday. Where are you thinking of going?'

'I don't know yet. I think I'll just drive to the airport and take the first flight out.'

'Better hope it's not just going to East Midlands.'

Annie didn't laugh.

3 December 1980

Baldy and Ginger were there to meet me when I got off the paternoster lift after my Milton lecture on Wednesday morning. That meant they must have been to the department administrator's office to find out where I was. So now everyone would know I was a person of interest to the police. Soon the whole university would start to think I was the Yorkshire Ripper.

People watched as I walked away between the burly, balding DI Glassco and slighter, ginger-haired DC Marley. One of the watchers was Jill, to whom I had been talking as we came down in the lift. At least they hadn't handcuffed me. The wind was up and I had to wrap my scarf around my neck to stop it flapping about. Despite the weather, we could have easily walked to Millgarth, just off the Headrow, in far less time than it took to walk to their car, parked on Willow Terrace Road, and drive around the fiendish city centre one-way system until we pulled up outside the police headquarters, which looked more like a prison, with its rows of narrow slit windows. 'Fortress' Millgarth certainly deserved its nickname. It was as unwelcoming a building as ever could be, a squat four or five storeys – it was hard to tell which, as there were no windows at all for the first twenty feet or so – of pure brutalist monstrosity.

I must confess I was still in somewhat of a daze as they ushered me inside, through their various security protocols and into a corridor lined with noticeboards between office doors badly in need of a fresh coat of paint. The place smelled too. Cigarette smoke mostly, of course, but other, less obvious odours – a whiff of urine, sweat and fear. I knew from reading the papers that Millgarth housed the famous 'Ripper Room', centre of activities for the ongoing hunt for the killer, and I certainly saw plenty of activity in the corridors on my way to the interview room. I doubt that everyone rushing about carrying file folders and shouting out greetings was part of the Ripper inquiry – naturally, there were other cases to deal with, too – but the sense of urgent activity was overpowering.

The interview room provided a relatively quiet haven, despite smelling of mould and stale tobacco smoke. I was left alone there, no doubt with a guard outside the door, for a good hour or so, while Glassco and Marley probably enjoyed a cup of tea and three or four fags. The metal table was bolted to the floor and the chairs were uncomfortable. Mine had a wobbly leg at the front, so I spent a bit of time rocking back and forth on it. But the room was so bland I couldn't even describe the colour of the walls. They hadn't searched me or confiscated my possessions, and I still had my books with me, so I suppose I could have read some of *Paradise Lost*, but it's hard to concentrate on Milton when you're sitting in a police interview room suspected of being the Yorkshire Ripper, awaiting a grilling. Would they hit me, use the rubber hose-pipe, or apply some more discreet and undetectable form of torture I couldn't run screaming to the press about? I'm just not that cool a customer, so I smoked a couple of roll-ups and passed the time gnawing at my fingernails, shifting about in my hard chair and worrying about what they would ask me and how unlikely my answers might seem.

Finally, the door opened and DI Glassco came in, closely followed by a forbidding but attractive WPC in uniform, who sat next to him with a pad in front of her and pen in her hand.

'This is WPC Raglan,' said Glassco. 'We won't be taping this interview, so she'll be taking notes.' He rolled up his shirt-sleeves and loosened his tie. Strands of Brylcreemed black hair lay plastered to his skull in a comb-over.

I wiggled in my chair. 'Is this how you usually do things? Is that legal?'

'In this case, yes. This is just an informal chat, Nick. It's what we call an "intelligence interview". You haven't been arrested or charged with anything. No caution necessary. It *is* voluntary, isn't it?'

'Does that mean I'm free to leave?'

'Any time you want.'

'I suppose so, then. What about a solicitor? Do I need one?'

Glassco smiled sideways at WPC Raglan, then turned back to me. 'Too much telly,' he said. 'I've already told you you're not being arrested or charged with anything. Sure, you can have your solicitor if you want. Have you even got one? Most people don't. But if you do, we'll probably have to caution you and things can get awkward after that. Detention and so on. We've got cells downstairs. Not big ones, but big enough. Can't you just have a chat with me? Help us out. If you've done nothing, you've nothing to be afraid of. As far as we've been able to ascertain, you have no criminal record and have never been in trouble with the police. Is that true?'

'Yes.'

He spread his hands. 'Then . . .'

'OK,' I said. 'But why bring me here? Why not just come and see me at home again?'

Glassco glanced around the room. 'I'll agree this is a disagreeable environment – it could probably do with a lick of paint and a few colourful posters – but we have facilities here we lack in the home.'

I wondered what those facilities might be – that aforementioned rubber hosepipe, for example? – but kept my mouth shut. Best just get this over with as quickly as possible, I thought.

'So can we start?' Glassco asked.

I nodded.

He referred to his notebook, open on the table before him. 'The last time we talked, you told me you'd seen Alice Poole on the night she disappeared.'

'That's right. She was going out as I was coming in.'

'And there was nothing unusual in her manner, nothing to indicate there was anything wrong, that she was afraid of anything? Or anyone?'

'No. I . . .'

'You were what, Nick?'

'Nothing.'

'Go on. You were going to say something. It doesn't matter how unimportant *you* think it was.'

'Why won't you tell me anything? I still don't know what happened to Alice, except you think someone killed her. Did the Ripper do this or not?'

'We can't divulge specifics of the investigation to you. Surely you must be aware of that?'

'But the papers . . . I mean, they just said her body had been found in Burley Park and there were "similarities" to the Ripper killings. What similarities? What happened to her? How did she get there? Did she suffer?'

'We don't know whether she suffered,' said Glassco. 'And we're still trying to find out what happened to her. All I can tell you is that if we're right about this so far, it was quick.'

'That's something, I suppose,' I muttered.

Glassco took an Embassy Regal from his packet and offered one to WPC Raglan. She accepted and he lit them both with a gold lighter. He didn't offer me one so I rolled my own.

'Can I continue with my questions?' Glassco asked.

I took a long drag. 'Yes. Sorry.'

'I want you to tell me what you were going to say.'

'It was nothing, really, but I got the impression that Alice seemed preoccupied.'

Glassco frowned. 'In what way?'

'It's hard to say. That's why I didn't . . . but I bumped into a friend of hers from the Marxist Society in the coffee lounge a couple of days ago, and he asked me if Alice had settled her problems with her boyfriend.'

'This would be Mark Woodcroft?'

'Yes.'

'And this friend – her name?'

'His. Gary Kirk.'

'What exactly did this Kirk say to you?'

'He asked me if I knew whether she'd resolved her "little problem".'

'What problem would this be?'

'I've no idea. I didn't know she had one.'

'Go on.'

'I asked him about it, and he said she'd given him to believe that she was having boyfriend problems.'

'Meaning Mark Woodcroft?'

'Of course.'

'But she could have meant you, couldn't she? You were her boyfriend at one time, weren't you? You didn't tell us about that.'

'Yes, but not then. Not since May. And it didn't seem relevant. Besides, I wondered the same, who he meant, so I asked him. Gary Kirk. He said she specifically meant Mark.'

'How could he be so sure?'

'I don't know. But he was.'

'Anything else?'

'No.'

'So neither of you ever found out what this problem was and whether it was resolved?'

'That's right. I never saw her again.'

'So what was it about her when you passed each other that evening? What disturbed you?'

'I told you. It was nothing. Just the way she walked, and her voice.'

'What about her voice?'

'It was clipped, tight. She just said something about the weather being bad and that she had to go. She was in a hurry. I thought she didn't want to stand around in the rain. I didn't blame her. My fish and chips were getting wet. But she was more businesslike than usual.'

'What do you mean?'

'It was more the sort of walk she had. When she meant business. You didn't get in her way when she walked like that. I called it her *clickety-clack* walk, but she didn't like it when I said that. Thought I was making fun of her.'

'Did it happen often?'

'No. Not often at all. That's why it struck me as odd.'

'Why didn't you tell us this the last time we talked to you?'

'I told you. It was nothing, just a passing impression, that's all. Gone as fast as it came.'

'And you thought she was angry with Mark Woodcroft, not you?'

'Of course. I knew I'd done nothing to upset her. She had no reason to be mad at me. Believe me, I know what that feels like. But I hadn't talked to her in days, and that last time we met, everything had been amicable enough.'

'Didn't you feel just a little pleased that Mark was in for a good talking-to?'

'Maybe a little. But why don't you ask him what happened? Where is he? You can ask him about all this. Have you found him yet?'

'We're still looking,' said Glassco. 'Do *you* have any idea where he might be?'

'Me? No, of course not.'

'Can you remember anything else about Alice that evening? What was she wearing, for example?'

'Jeans, a light blue puffer jacket, ankle boots.'

'And you mentioned an overnight bag last time. Are you sure about that?'

'Yes. Not a bag really. A sort of rucksack.'

'The sort of thing you use to go camping?'

'Yes. But maybe not as big. And you'd never catch Alice camping.'

'Strictly three-star hotels?'

'As many stars as she could get.'

'Was money a problem between you two?'

'Money's always a problem when you're a student. But no, I wouldn't say it was an issue with us. Her parents were generous. I mean, they paid her rent to keep the Penthouse on over the summer, even though she was mostly at home in Lincolnshire. But we were both on a pretty similar student budget. It wasn't as if she had to pay for me when we went to the pictures or anything.'

'And the hotels?'

'A bit of a joke between us. We went around Europe the summer before this one and stayed at some pretty ropey places, even youth hostels. It didn't bother her, but it was clear she'd rather have been in the Ritz. Certainly not in a tent.'

'OK,' said Glassco, glancing at his watch. 'Like a cup of tea?'

'Tea would be nice,' I said. 'How long is this going to go on?'

'Not long. Just a few more questions. Need the toilet or anything?'

'No, thanks.'

'Cathy, love, get us a couple of teas, will you?' Glassco glanced at me again. 'Milk and two sugars?'

'Fine,' I said.

WPC Raglan blew out a long plume of smoke, stubbed out her cigarette and left the room, with a sharp glance back at Glassco. While she was gone, Glassco amused himself by shifting around the papers on the table. When WPC Raglan returned with the tea on a tray, she was accompanied by a tall, slim man, a few years older than Glassco, but with more hair. He wore a dark brown suit, mauve shirt and a striped tie with little silver shields on it that probably denoted membership of some local rugby or cricket club. A gold tie clip held it in place. Neither Glassco nor Raglan introduced him, and he simply leaned back on the doorjamb and stood there, arms folded, as Glassco picked up the questioning again.

'Let's go back to the night in question,' he said. 'We've checked with your friends and they confirm that you met them in the Hyde Park pub for a couple of pints, and that you seemed in reasonably good spirits, and then they say you all walked back down Hyde Park Road, and you turned off and went home.'

'That's right.'

'This would be about ten to eleven?'

'They don't give you a lot of drinking-up time at the Hyde Park.'

'What did you do then?'

'What do you mean?'

'When you got home at ten to eleven. What did you do?'

'I stayed up for a while, played a couple of records, read for a bit, then I went to bed.'

'What time?'

'About half past twelve.'

'Is that your usual bedtime?'

'I don't have a usual bedtime. It all depends.'

'On what?'

'How tired I am. Whether I have work to do, what time in the morning lectures begin, whether I've been to a party, have a girl with me, if there's any beer in the house—'

'All right, all right. I get it,' Glassco snapped.

Was he trying to impress the man by the door? I wondered. And did he think I was trying to make a fool of him? I couldn't tell.

'You didn't go out again?' he asked.

'I told you. I went to bed.'

'Alone?'

'Sadly, yes.'

'You say you don't own a car?'

'I don't just *say* it. It's true.'

'Do you have a licence?'

'No. I told you before. I never even took a driving lesson, never mind a test.'

I got the feeling he didn't believe me about not driving. No doubt he would be asking around.

'Let's move on,' he said. 'Can you tell me where you were and what you were doing on November 17th?'

'What night of the week was that?'

'It was a Monday.'

'Mondays I sometimes go to the Original Oak.'

'With friends?'

'Yes.'

'Did you go that Monday?'

'I think so. Yes.'

'The Oak's in Headingley, isn't it?'

'Yes. Top of St Michael's Road.'

'Not far from the Arndale Centre, Alma Road?'

The penny dropped. 'Now, wait a minute—'

'Did you know Jacqueline Hill? You were both students at the university, after all. Same department, as far as I remember.'

'Yes, but I didn't know her. It's a big department, you know. There are hundreds of students. And she's the year below me.'

'See her around, did you?'

'At lectures, occasionally. But I didn't know her socially. I never even spoke a word to her.'

'All right, Nick. Don't get too upset.'

'I'm not—'

'What about September 1st, 1979?'

'How can you expect me to remember back that far. But hang on a minute. September 1st, you say?'

'That's right.'

I folded my arms. 'I was in Paris. With Alice. You can check with the authorities.'

'Hotel?'

'I can't remember the name, but I can find out. They must have some record. We signed a register.'

'January 31st, 1978?'

'Well that, I *can* tell you. I was at school in Portsmouth, the sixth form, studying for my mock A-levels. I assume they have attendance records. How long are you going to continue with this farce? I know where you're going with this, you know. But no matter what you say, I am not the fucking Yorkshire Ripper.'

Glassco glanced over at the man by the door. I turned in time to catch him giving a quick shake of his head before leaving the room and closing the door behind him.

'What just happened?' I asked. 'Who is he?'

'Nothing you need concern yourself about.'

'He's from the Ripper Squad, isn't he?'

'I'm afraid I can't—'

'You really did think I was the fucking Yorkshire Ripper.'

'There's no need to swear,' said Glassco. 'Especially with a lady present.'

'I disagree,' I said. 'There's *every* fucking reason to swear. My apologies, Miss Raglan. But seriously, you must be crazy. I was fifteen when all that stuff started. A schoolboy. And living about three hundred miles from here.'

'All right,' Glassco said. 'Calm down, Nick. This Ripper business has got us all on edge. You haven't had to deal with it. See the bodies. Talk to the families.'

'And you have?'

His silence said it all.

'Do you seriously believe that Alice was a victim of the Yorkshire Ripper? So soon after poor Jacqueline Hill?'

'It doesn't look like it, but we don't rule anything out these days. As the papers said, there are "similarities". Anyway, I'm done with you for the time being.' Glassco stood up and WPC Raglan followed suit. 'We might need to talk to you again,' he went on. 'So don't leave town, as they say in the movies. Show Mr Hartley out, please, Cathy.'

And as I followed the silent WPC Raglan down the corridor, I realised that while Glassco probably didn't think I was the Yorkshire Ripper any more, he sure as hell suspected that I'd killed Alice and Mark, then driven off in Mark's car, dumped her in Burley Park and buried his body where I thought no one would find it.

5

27 November 2019

Winsome felt as if she were going through airlocks, like the ones in those sci-fi films her husband Terry loved so much. But when the second set of sliding glass doors hissed shut behind her, she was finally standing in the forensics lab. As the building adjoined police HQ, and there were always people coming and going, it needed an air-cleansing system between the two, so that as little foreign material as possible was transferred, thus avoiding possible contamination of valuable evidence.

The lab was buzzing with activity, not to mention the humming, ticking, rattling and clacking of the various machines. People in lab coats mingled with those in jeans and open-neck shirts, as well as some in suits. Winsome herself was casually dressed in black trousers and a white blouse. The overall impression of the place was one of pristine whiteness and brushed-steel grey, but colourful posters dotted here and there on the walls broke up the monotony, and one of the technicians bent over a microscope was wearing a tie-dyed bandana.

'Winsome. Wonderful to see you again.' Jazz Singh greeted her with a hug. 'How's little Josh?'

'He's fine. But I've told you, Jazz, it's *Joshua*. There'll no doubt be plenty of time for Josh when he gets older.'

Jazz held her hands up. 'OK, OK, sorry. Little Joshua.'

Truth be told, little Joshua was becoming hard to handle, though Winsome kept that to herself. She hadn't mentioned it to Banks or Gerry and didn't intend to tell Jazz, either. The baby didn't sleep well and made sure the rest of the household joined him in his noisy insomnia. Even Peaches, their usually well-behaved Jack Russell. Winsome loved Joshua to bits, but sometimes she longed for one of the old remedies – a drop of laudanum, say, or at the very least a tot of whisky – to help him sleep. The kind of things perhaps her grandparents might have resorted to. She wouldn't do it, of course. But so far as she knew, you couldn't be arrested for your thoughts yet.

Winsome had been on a brief refresher course before returning to active duty and already found that when she was away from Joshua, she couldn't wait to get back to him again, hold him in her arms to rock him and smell that baby smell of mingled milk, nappies, vomit and talcum powder. It was all very confusing, but at least she knew she wasn't suffering from postpartum depression. Everyone told her that her feelings were normal. And Terry was a rock, though even he couldn't do anything about their interrupted sleep patterns. As a consequence, Winsome felt tired most of the day, and worried it would affect her work performance.

'Anyway,' Jazz went on, 'what brings you over here?'

Winsome glanced around the large open-space lab. Jazz specialised in blood and DNA, she knew, which weren't especially relevant to the case she was working on – at least not yet. 'I'm on the skeleton case,' she said. 'Is Stefan around?'

'Should be here somewhere,' Jazz said. 'The last time I saw him, he was talking with Vic Manson over by the coffee machine.'

'Thanks. See you later.'

'Sure. And remember, if you need a babysitter . . .'

Winsome thanked Jazz, then threaded her way through the benches to the coffee machine, saying hello here and there to the staff she knew. She found Stefan Nowak sitting on Vic Manson's desk poring over a sheet of fingerprints.

Not her case. Skeletons don't have fingerprints. Vic was nowhere to be seen.

Stefan was Crime Scene Manager, and when he wasn't organising his team at the scene, he could usually be found in the lab tracking down the various items submitted for forensic analysis. Some things they could handle on the premises, but others – ballistics, for example – had to be sent out to one of the forensic service providers for analysis. At a charge, of course.

Stefan greeted Winsome with a big smile and an outstretched hand. He was a handsome man, regarded as quite a dish around the station. He was originally from Poland, with a fine head of wavy chestnut hair. Women seemed to fall all over him, and even Winsome sometimes got tongue-tied in his presence, but nobody knew very much about his personal life. There were no scandals, no hints of office romances. Some said he was gay, though that wasn't the vibe Winsome got from him. Not that he ever overstepped any boundaries with her, or with anyone else as far as she was aware.

'The skeleton,' she said. Not having put a name to the victim made it awkward, so they just called it 'the skeleton case' for the time being. Maybe they should give it a name, like Herman or Sammy. Sammy the Skeleton.

Stefan put the fingerprint sheet down on the table. 'Ah, yes. The skeleton. I don't think there are any developments yet, but our findings from the scene are all with Kim. Come on.'

Kim Lee was the Scientific Support Coordinator, main liaison between the lab and the evidence found at the scene. She was a short, curly-haired woman of indeterminate age – late thirties, Winsome would guess – with an astonishing range of knowledge, from the properties of different bleaches to the complex operating systems of mobile phones. Kim worked with the experts in various specialised fields, as well as with Dr Galway. Hers was an exacting job, Winsome guessed. When they found her, she was sitting on a high stool at a lab bench strewn with objects in a state of advanced decay. None of them was recognisable to Winsome.

'I'm sorry I don't have much for you yet,' Kim said. 'I've just been trying to sort out what might be of some use and what's just rubbish.' She gestured to another bench. 'They're over here.'

Winsome followed her. 'What have you got?'

'Well, it was fairly obvious that chummy wasn't naked when he was tipped into the grave.' She pointed to what looked to Winsome like a burned sheet of paper. 'There are some possible scraps of clothing that survived because they were protected by the belt. They need further analysis, but on first examination, the fabric seems high-end natural. I'll be doing close fabric analysis later today, if there's enough of it, see what it's made of. It also appears as if the body was wrapped in a cotton bedsheet, a few scraps of which survived.' She gestured to include the other items on the tray. 'We also found two horn buttons, probably from a suit, the remains of a zip, most likely the fly from his trousers, and a partial belt and pair of shoes. Leather is very well preserved in acidic soil. The belt is most likely calfskin, and it had a metal buckle like a T on its side. The shoes are good Italian leather, maybe even handmade. Again, I need to examine them in more detail, see if I can find a name or symbol of some kind. They're definitely not your cheap high street footwear. But all I can really tell you so far is that he was probably a snazzy dresser, and he didn't mind spending a bob or two on his gear. Handmade leather shoes don't come cheap.'

'No wallet, keys or notebook?'

'No such luck. I would hazard a guess that any identification he was carrying was either taken from his pockets by his killer before the body was dumped, or it disintegrated along with everything else. But don't quote me on that. Keys and fragments of leather would most certainly have survived, but I very much doubt that a notebook, for example, would have tolerated this length of time underground, unless it was leather-bound.'

'How long was he under, can you tell? Does six or seven years seem right?'

'So I'm told,' Lee said. 'And who am I to say any different. Generally speaking, a body takes eight to twelve years to decompose completely when buried without a coffin or any sort of embalming process. The flies can't get at it to lay their eggs, so decomposition due to maggot activity is eliminated, or at least limited. However, there are other insects under the surface, beetles and so on, and the soil in the field is acidic, so that would have speeded up the process. And as you know, Yorkshire can be quite damp, so that would also speed things up.'

Winsome laughed. 'Quite damp? There's understatement for you.'

'Shall we say very wet, then?' Kim paused. 'I've pretty much given you the complete list. It's possible there are some tooling marks on the inside of the belt. Something embossed. Maybe a manufacturer's name or retailer.' She used pincers to hold up some shreds of burned cloth. Winsome could see the marks but that was all. 'It'll take me a while,' Kim went on, 'but I might be able to make some sense out of it. And these are the buttons.' She picked up a plastic bag in which lay two misshapen lumps.

'You said they're horn,' Winsome said. 'Isn't that illegal?'

'Immoral perhaps, but not illegal. At least not in this case, I shouldn't think. I'll need further analysis to be certain, but I very much doubt that they're rhino horn – most of that goes for aphrodisiacs – but probably water buffalo, which isn't illegal.'

'What about the ring?'

'Ah, yes.' Kim reached for another plastic bag, this one with a chunky gold signet ring inside. 'As far as I can tell, it's eighteen karats.'

'I'm no gold expert – sadly,' said Winsome with a smile. 'Is that good?'

'Pretty good. The best you can get is twenty-four karats, which isn't much use for jewellery, as well as being prohibitively expensive. It's mostly the kind of gold you buy as an investment, and it has some medical and electrical uses. This is a step below, but still good quality.'

'Any markings?'

'None. If there were any, they've been erased over time. Sorry. But we do possibly have a man between fifty and sixty in a high-end suit wearing an eighteen-karat signet ring, a calfskin belt and fine, possibly bespoke, leather shoes.'

'He had a gold filling, too,' said Winsome.

'Hmm. Well, that about sums it up. Though I've still got quite a lot of work to do before I can confirm or elaborate on any of this. Which means—'

Winsome held out her palm and backed away. 'OK, OK. I get the hint. I'm going.'

Kim smiled. 'See you later,' she said. 'And don't keep bugging me. I'll give you a ring when I have anything more.'

4 December 1980

It was the day after the police interview, a dismal afternoon, when I found myself standing outside Mark's house on St John's Terrace in the rain. I had purposely taken this route back home from the university, where I'd just sat through a dull lecture on Thomson's 'The Seasons'. I don't know why I came by way of Mark Woodcroft's old dwelling, but I suspect I wanted to talk to someone there. After all, the last time I saw Alice, I thought she was on her way there with something on her mind, walking her *clickety-clack* walk, and Gary Kirk had asked me if she had managed to resolve her 'boyfriend problem'. Now Alice was dead and Mark Woodcroft was . . . well, that was the problem: nobody really knew what or where Mark Woodcroft was.

Like the other houses on the street, it was a tall, narrow Victorian terrace built of dark stone and brick, with a high-pitched slate roof. There was no gate, and from where I stood by the low wall and hedge, I could see that the garden was overgrown with shrubs and weeds. A large tree spread its bare, dark branches over the scene, and the house seemed to loom over me. Lights were already showing in two of the upstairs windows and in the bay window.

As I was trying to pluck up the courage to go and ring the doorbell, I noticed a curtain twitch in the bay window. Then the front door opened and a slight figure stood there, a girl, I thought, though I couldn't be certain, as she was silhouetted by the bright hall light. Behind her, I could see the beginning of the carpeted staircase to the first floor and the little table where the first person down probably put the post in a morning, just like the house where I had my bedsit.

'What do you want?' she asked in a high-pitched, shaky voice. Definitely a girl, a student, most likely. She gestured towards the inside of the house. 'Why are you hanging about? My flatmate's in there with her hand on the phone. Any funny business, all I have to do is shout and she'll call the police.'

I saw the curtain twitch again and thought I could glimpse a partial face. Whether she was holding a telephone or not, I had no idea. Probably not. Most students' bedsits or flats don't have phones. But it didn't matter. I held my hand up and started walking up the flagged garden path. 'No, please. I'm not . . . I mean, I'm sorry if I frightened you.'

'Don't come any closer,' she said, when I was about halfway to the door.

I heard a voice from behind her shout, 'Is everything OK, Lucy?'

'Yes,' she called back over her shoulder. 'Don't worry, I'm all right.'

I stopped. 'I'm not a . . . Lucy, I'm a friend of Alice Poole's, that's all. Isn't this where Mark Woodcroft lived? Her boy-friend.'

It might have been my imagination, but the girl seemed to relax a little, though her hand was still on the doorknob and she remained ready to retreat at any moment.

'Are you Nick, then? The one they're all talking about?'

'Who?'

'Everyone. After lectures this morning. I'm first-year English. Even I've heard of you. They say the police picked you up yesterday and took you away. What do you want here?'

'Did you know Mark and Alice?'

'No.'

'But Mark does live here, doesn't he?'

'Upstairs. He did, at any rate. I don't know where he is now. I haven't seen him since . . . well . . . you know. But we don't know him. Not really. Susie and I keep to ourselves. He's older than us, anyway.'

'Wasn't he friendly?'

'He was polite enough. Always said hello, smiled and so on. But that was as far as it went.'

'It's just that this is the last place I think Alice came before she was killed.'

'They're saying you did it, you know. Some are even saying you must be the Ripper. I shouldn't be standing here talking to you.'

'I didn't do anything. They let me go, didn't they? Would they have done that if they thought I'd done anything? And as for being the Ripper, I was in school in Portsmouth when he started. I just wanted . . . I mean, do you know anything about what happened that night?'

'Like I said, Susie and me keep to ourselves.'

'Didn't you hear anything, see anyone? Anything at all unusual.'

'I've told you, I . . .'

'What?'

'I heard them arguing earlier that evening. That's all.'

'When was this?'

'After he came back with the takeaway.'

'Mark went out for a takeaway?'

'Yes. About eight o'clock.'

'How long was he gone?'

'About twenty minutes, maybe half an hour. He took the car; I heard him start it up.'

'How do you know he went for a takeaway?'

'I could smell it in the hall, after he got back. Curry.'

'And that's when they started arguing?'

'Not long after.'

'Did they argue often?'

'I don't think so. I didn't notice it if they did.'

'And you would have?'

'Mark's flat is on the first floor. Not directly above us, but we sometimes heard things.'

'So you would have noticed any arguments?'

'Probably. I could hear them talking sometimes. Not arguing, like. Just talking.'

'But that night they were rowing?'

'That's what it sounded like. But I couldn't tell what they were saying.'

'Did you hear sounds of a struggle, a fight, of anything physical?'

'Good Lord, no. Nothing like that.'

'What happened?'

'They stopped. At least, they started talking more quietly.'

'Did you hear anything else, later on?'

'They went out. At least I think it was them. Woke me up.'

'What time?'

'It must have been around two o'clock in the morning. Why do you want to know all this?' Lucy stamped from foot to foot and hugged herself. 'I'm getting cold. I'm going inside. And you must be soaked. Go home. I can't tell you anything else.'

I was soaked. My jeans were sticking to my legs, my trainers were letting in water, and the rain was dripping down the back of my neck.

'Wait. Just a minute, Lucy. Please. What did you hear?'

Lucy relented and leaned her hip against the doorjamb. 'Just footsteps on the stairs, the front door opening and closing. A car starting, driving off. Then I must have drifted off to sleep again.'

'Two sets of footsteps?'

'I don't know. I was half asleep. Heavy footsteps. Loud enough to wake me up, at any rate. It was pretty weird, I suppose, when I thought about it later, them going out at that time of night in such bad weather. There'd be nothing open. Even the clubs would be shut by then. But my mind wasn't really working properly at the time, you know, so I wasn't thinking right.'

'Were they still arguing then?'

'They weren't saying anything at all. Not that I heard.'

'Did anything happen after that?'

'I slept.' Lucy paused, then said, 'Do you think *he* did it? Mark Woodcroft? Are you thinking she was dead before they left the house? That he was carrying her? Did we have a murderer living here in our house?'

'Could he have been? Carrying her, that is.'

'I don't know. How would I know that?'

'You said you heard "heavy footsteps". Is that what you were getting at?'

'I'm not getting at anything,' she said. 'Please go away.'

'I'm sorry I bothered you. OK? I suppose you told the police all this?'

'Police? No. What police?'

'They must have been around asking questions, surely?'

'The police never talked to us at all. Not like you. At least not when me or Susie was in.'

'But they'd have come back, surely, if you were out? Left a card?'

'Well, they didn't leave anything. *If* they came. Apart from a couple of blokes who came around the day after and went through the flat up there, we haven't seen any police at all. At least, I assume they were police. I just supposed they hadn't found anything that made them suspicious of Mark. Or that they thought he was dead as well. None of it makes any sense.'

'That must be it,' I said, turning away. 'Thanks for your time. And again, I'm sorry for frightening you.'

'That's OK,' Lucy said, closing the door. 'You can't be too careful these days, though, can you, not with you-know-who on the prowl?'

27 November 2019

When Gerry first looked at the latest numbers to get a general idea of the task ahead, she despaired. In the year ending the previous March, 35,489 people had been reported missing in Yorkshire and Humberside alone, one person every fifteen minutes. Admittedly, 22,779 of them were children – a staggering number – but that still left 12,710 adults. If that was representative of recent years, how on earth was she going to get through checking all those who fitted the time frame for the skeleton, even with Winsome's help? It was the kind of job you might expect an office full of civilian clerks to help with, but there was no chance of anything like that with the present budget constraints.

The best she could do was hope for an early break. True, there were likely to be more cases closed since then, as more people were found, returned home of their own accord, or were discovered to have died. But that would still leave a large number of unexplained disappearances, as Gerry knew from past experience. Most people who go missing are found relatively quickly, and there were only 255 people still missing from the year starting March 2018 and ending March 2019, 74 of them children. It was still a disturbing number, and Gerry was ready to despair again when she realised that if she was expected to sift through at least four years of statistics from the whole of Yorkshire, she could expect to be dealing with upward of a thousand people. Even after she had eliminated the children and those under fifty, it would still be a struggle.

And, of course, the victim might well not have been from Yorkshire at all, but transported there from, say, Lancashire, County Durham, or even Northumberland. There were some big cities there, including Manchester, Carlisle and Newcastle, and therefore there was bound to be a much higher number of missing persons. Not to mention the West Yorkshire cities such as Leeds, Bradford, Huddersfield and so on. It was beginning to feel like a nightmare.

Gerry started to feel her breath locking in her throat as she contemplated the task ahead. She took a few deep breaths, followed by a sip of green tea from the mug beside her. Calm down, she told herself, keep it simple to start with. She began scratching notes on the yellow legal pad she always kept beside her computer. The first thing she had to do was get the actual reports from the various county forces. Names. Ages. Then she could start to whittle things down. If the forensic anthropologist came up with an even closer age range for the victim, and Kim Lee in the lab managed to obtain some sort of narrative of the man from the fragments left behind in his grave, then she might be able to refine the search even more. First of all, though, the reports. And the first number to call on a case like this was the NCA's UK National Missing Persons Bureau. They had been helpful in the past, and she hoped they would be again. She reached for the phone.

8 December 1980

Glassco and Marley didn't return the following day, nor did they lie in wait for me outside the English Department. Over the weekend, life went on, and the early December gloom suited the city perfectly. There were more candlelight demonstrations, and the general mood remained tense. Mostly, women still stayed indoors, fearing the Ripper lurked in every shadowy doorway or on every patch of wasteland. The police were saying nothing. While the Ripper case dominated the news, there were no real developments, nothing specific, no revelations.

The pressure on the police was growing, though, and the chief constable, Ronald Gregory, came up with a 'think tank' of senior officers from outside the local force – fresh eyes, so to speak. The papers called it the 'Super Squad'. Gregory didn't say as much, but everyone knew his own men were exhausted and demoralised by now, after the Ripper tape debacle and the well-publicised interventions of various soothsayers and clairvoyants. They must have been at the end of their tether. George Oldfield, who had been running the case for some time, was quietly dropped due to ill health. The rest of the news was all about the recession and how Thatcher's policy of monetarism was to blame. Alice and I would have agreed on that.

After my 'interview' with Glassco at Millgarth, I soon began to feel something of a pariah. Even the day after my public humiliation, Lucy had been afraid at first and had told me that everyone was talking about me as if *I* had murdered Alice. Others were more subtle, though, especially my friends. It wasn't as if anyone accused me or sent me to Coventry, but I was definitely persona non grata in the places I used to haunt. It was a general feeling of loss of membership to the club, whatever that club was; the house I lived in, Jill and her friends, the MJ Lounge, the Hyde Park, the university community in general.

Everyone managed a weak smile and a hello before discreetly edging away, but never much more. Even Geoff from downstairs, whom I regarded a close friend. We usually got together on a Friday night to watch *To Serve Them All My Days*, which was up to about the eighth episode, but when I went down and knocked on his door, I got no reply. Thinking he was out, I went back upstairs for a while, then decided to go to the pub. As I passed his door, I could hear the TV, and from outside on the street I could see the glow of the screen behind his closed curtains. Well, I told myself, maybe he'd just nipped out to the local offie when I called, but I wasn't convinced.

The only person who stuck by me was Anton. He wasn't someone you talked to about your feelings or asked for emotional advice. As far as I remember, we never discussed the murder. He knew Alice, of course, through me, and expressed his sorrow that she was dead. But that was it. In fact, the first time I saw him after Alice's murder he gave me a book of haiku and we sat in almost total silence for the evening, smoking dope and drinking wine and listening to Nico's *Desertshore*. I can't say the music did a great deal for my spirits. But that was Anton.

On Saturday evening, when I tried to join Jill and her mates in the Hyde Park, the atmosphere was frosty. Jill didn't quite cringe when I sat next to her, but she almost did. I could feel her drawing in on herself, putting her shutters up, closing herself in a protective shell against my presence.

I went home early.

Over the next couple of days, my moods shifted from anger, to melancholy and self-pity, then back to anger again. On Sunday I kept my door shut, saw no one, and no one came to see me. On Monday I skipped lectures and stayed in.

Fuck them, I thought. If they really believe that I'd killed Alice, or that I was the Yorkshire Ripper or something, then *fuck them*.

27 November 2019

Eastvale Drainage Solutions had their offices at a small business park on the southern edge of town, just beyond the big roundabout. Banks manoeuvred into a slot in the small car park, between a green van with the company's logo on it – a cartoon of a smiling man holding a large spanner aloft – and a silver Honda hatchback. It was late afternoon and already the darkness was closing in, helped by a thick grey cloud cover. There would be rain before the night was over, Banks guessed, perhaps a heavy enough rain to keep Eastvale Drainage Solutions busy for a few days. Floods were so common these days.

It was pretty much a routine call to pin down the exact date of the work done on Wilveston Farm some years ago. Normally, it would be a job for Gerry or Winsome, not for the senior investigating officer, but Banks wanted to keep Gerry working on the missing persons angle, and he had spent a while in Chief Superintendent Gervaise's office that afternoon making a case for at least two or three extra personnel to help her. He was told that his request was 'under consideration', which meant 'don't hold your breath'. Winsome would have done it, but Banks sensed that she was tired, and he knew she had baby Joshua waiting for her, so he told her to head home, and set off for the drainage specialists himself. Winsome put a brave face on it all, but Banks remembered what Sandra had been like when their children were born, especially Brian, the first. Every moment away from him was a moment of agony for her, even though every moment *with* him could feel much the same.

It felt good to get out of the office, where he had spent most of the day on paperwork and the technicalities of setting up a new investigation. The one drawback to his high rank was less time on the streets, the nitty-gritty of an investigation, so he took every opportunity he could to get out there, even on a straightforward follow-up interview like this one, something he could probably have done over the phone. The company that had carried out the work might also be able to tell him more about the land they had drained, and its owner.

Eastvale Drainage Solutions was housed in a two-storey red-brick building crammed between a high-end furniture showroom and a glazier. The front door opened into a reception area with chairs and a table littered with recent magazines, like the old doctor's or dentist's waiting room. The flowery scent of air freshener made Banks's nose itch.

He had telephoned earlier and arranged to see the boss, Leonard Farrier, and the young man on the reception desk said he could go straight up. It wasn't the kind of office complex where you needed key cards and buzzing intercoms to pass from one place to another; in Eastvale Drainage Solutions, it seemed you could walk pretty much anywhere you wanted. Nor was it big enough to get lost in. Banks followed directions down the corridor then up some stairs to a slightly nicer, carpeted corridor and knocked on the door marked 'Leonard Farrier, Head Supervisor'.

Farrier turned out to be an amicable fellow in his late fifties or early sixties, with a few wisps of grey hair still clinging to his shiny scalp. He wore a tweed jacket, despite the heat in the office, and an open-neck shirt. His desk was cluttered with bits and pieces, from notepads and pens to sections of copper tubing and deconstructed valves. The filing cabinets and bookshelves were crammed with loose-leaf binders and stacks of invoices and work orders held together by rubber bands. Banks felt that if he breathed too heavily, the whole lot would come tumbling down and bury the two of them.

'You're in luck,' said Farrier, when Banks had made himself as comfortable as possible in the hard-backed, and hard-bottomed, chair.

Banks raised an eyebrow.

'That job you told me about over the phone. The one you want to talk to me about.'

'Yes?'

'Well, I did it. At least, I was one of the team that Steve sent out there. Steve Mallory. He was the boss back then. Retired two years ago. But first off, let's have some refreshments. Tea? Coffee? Something stronger?'

Banks fancied a glass of whisky, but he quelled the urge. 'A cup of tea would be great, thank you. No milk or sugar.'

'Coming right up.'

Farrier spoke to someone over the phone, then leaned back in his chair and linked his hands behind his head. 'In fact,' he said, 'I've done quite a lot of work for the Gillespies over the years.'

'The farm had drainage problems?'

'Not especially, no. It just comes with the territory. You know the amount of rain we get up here, but you might not notice the periods of drought so much. Farmers ideally need a constant, measured and reliable source of irrigation. In addition to the basic services, such as drain surveys and repairs, leak detection, excavation, flood pumping and so on, we also handle irrigation systems. And we don't just install and run. We have a maintenance plan. Jack Gillespie – that's Harold's father, who used to run the farm – made arrangements with our company years ago, before I was even working here, and Harold kept them up when he was running the place.'

'When did you start?'

'I started as an apprentice, straight from school. I was sixteen. 1975. Worked my way up, and here I am today. Lord of all I survey.'

He spread his arms, which came dangerously close to dislodging a pile of bulging file folders from the shelf behind him. At that moment, a silver-haired woman in thick spectacles, jeans and a pink polo-neck sweater came in with the tea on a tray, set it on the desk in front of Farrier, and left.

'You must excuse Daisy,' he said when the door had closed. 'She's a woman of few words, and most of them you could do without. But don't get me wrong, I wouldn't be without her for the world. It's Daisy keeps this place running.' He passed Banks a mug of tea. It had the firm's name and logo on it. The cartoon character brandishing a spanner.

'So you've known the Gillespie family a long time?'

'Indeed.'

'What sort of work did you do for them?'

'All sorts. Domestic and commercial. Mostly domestic the last few years. It was sad to see the old place get bulldozed to make way for a new shopping centre.'

'I'll bet. Lost business, too.'

Farrier glanced sharply at him. 'It wasn't the money. Not so much. You get comfortable with folks you've been working with for years. And I can't say as I see there's much value in another bloody shopping centre.'

'They'll probably need your services, too.'

'No doubt. Even so . . .'

'So, did you say you were actually working on the team that dealt with the far field?'

'That's right.' Farrier took a slurp of tea. It was still too hot for Banks to sip. 'Team leader. I had three men working for me on that job. Three days, it took us.'

'What was the problem?'

'Basically, it came down to blocked drains. Over time, a lot of muck gets carried into drainage systems – dirt, fallen leaves, grass, twigs and so on. It builds up slowly and eventually causes problems. In this case, whenever it rained heavily, the lane and the far end of the field, by the wall, flooded. The field didn't matter so much as nobody used it, but a couple of locals complained about the lane, so Mr Gillespie asked us if we could do anything.'

'Do you remember their names, these locals?'

'I'm afraid not. I didn't deal with the complaint, only the solution.'

'Did you fix the problem?'

'Oh, aye.'

'And none of you noticed anything odd while you were working.'

'Such as?'

Banks hadn't told Farrier over the telephone *why* he wanted to know about the field repairs. 'A dead body, perhaps.'

Farrier put his cup down quickly enough to slop a little tea on the papers in front of him. 'A dead body, you say?'

'Yes. Though, actually, I'm more interested in the absence of a dead body.'

'Well, there you're in luck again, because I can tell you, absolutely and categorically, that there were no dead bodies buried at the far end of that field. I think we might have let you know at the time if there had been.'

'I would hope so,' Banks said. 'First off, can you tell me the dates when the work was done?'

'I thought you might ask me that,' Farrier said. 'That's why I got out the order before you arrived. Now if only . . .' He started shifting sheets of paper, bulky folders and lumps of metal around on his desk, muttering to himself. As he watched, Banks was reminded of those arcade machines where you slide 2p down a slot into a pile of coins teetering on a cliff edge moving back and forth, and hope yours will be the one that dislodges the money.

Eventually, Farrier held up a few stapled sheets of paper in triumph, without dislodging anything. 'Aha!' he said. 'Knew it was here somewhere.' He ran down the sheet with his forefinger. 'Right, yes, here it is.' He held up the sheet for Banks to see. 'May 2012. The 8th to the 11th, to be exact.'

'Is that long- or short-term in your field?'

'Average for a job like that. There's a lot of digging, then clearing out, creating new drainage.'

Banks pulled the farm plan from his briefcase and turned it around so that Farrier could see. 'What sort of area did you cover?'

Farrier scrutinised the plan, half standing and using his forefinger again to trace the lines. 'I'd say we went about eight or ten feet inside the wall that boundaries the field. Most of the work we did was on the ditches outside, both sides of the road, but the blockage had backed things up. As I remember, we even had to replace some ancient pipes.'

'Ten feet,' Banks said. The body had been buried only about three feet from the wall. Banks guessed that whoever was doing it didn't want to have to drag his load any further. Also, the wall would act as cover if any other motorist should happen to drive by. 'How deep?' he asked.

'Four to five feet, for the most part.'

'And you finished this work on May the eleventh, 2012?'

'So it says here.'

'Can you do me a photocopy?'

'Certainly.' Farrier picked up the phone again and Daisy came to take the order away. 'It'll be waiting for you at reception when you leave,' he told Banks.

'Thanks very much.' This would help Gerry narrow down her search by three years. It also sounded as if the Eastvale Drainage team had done a thorough job that had necessitated digging up ground under which a skeleton was discovered seven years later. 'You say you did all the maintenance work for the Gillespies. Was there ever anything of interest? Anything odd or unusual?'

Farrier scratched his temple. 'Like a dead body, you mean?'

'Whatever. Roman remains, perhaps?'

'No. Nothing like that. Not that I can remember. But you do come across a few odd finds in our line of work. We once discovered an unexploded bomb at a farm out Richmond way. What it was doing there, I have no idea. I mean, nobody bombed Richmond.'

'Dumping it on the way back from bombing Glasgow shipyards, or Liverpool docks,' Banks suggested.

'I suppose so.'

'But nothing on Gillespie's land?'

'No. Have you talked to him about all this? Harold, I mean. He might remember more than I do.'

'Two of my officers talked to him yesterday,' Banks said.

'I don't mean to be nosy,' Farrier said, 'but is this about that skeleton they found?'

'Yes,' said Banks.

'I thought so. I read about it in the paper. They didn't say exactly where it had been found, though. Anyway,' he went on, 'I would have thought Harold Gillespie would be able to help you with that.'

'Why do you say that?'

Farrier leaned back and locked his hands behind his head again. 'Didn't you know? He used to be a copper, himself, Harold Gillespie did.'

Well, there's something I might not have learned if I'd simply made a phone call, Banks thought as he left.

9 December 1980

On Tuesday morning, completely out of the blue, came news that floored me, along with the rest of the world, and knocked even the Yorkshire Ripper off the front page.

John Lennon had been shot to death in New York City the night before.

It was Anton who told me. He tapped on my door at the ungodly hour (for him) of nine o'clock, pale-faced and red-eyed behind his granny glasses and simply said, 'Someone shot John Lennon, man. Shot him and killed him.' I put the radio on, and we heard the official news, both still stunned. I made tea and after we'd drunk it, mostly in silence, Anton drifted back down to his own bedsit. 'I can't really handle any company right now, man,' he said as he left. 'I need to be alone.'

That was all right with me. I knew he loved John Lennon in particular. He even looked a bit like him.

I had been too young to appreciate the Beatles growing up, though my mother had once told me I used to sing along with 'She Loves You' and 'I Want to Hold Your Hand' when I was three or four. Of course, I heard them often throughout my childhood – my parents were great fans – but by the time I was starting to take notice of popular music, as a teenager, the Beatles had split up, and the pop charts seemed lacklustre to me – Gary Glitter, the Osmonds, the Bay City Rollers – until I discovered the joys of Bowie and Roxy Music. But though they had broken up, the Beatles remained a major presence. I still had some of their LPs I'd bought back then in my collection: *Rubber Soul*, *Revolver*, *Abbey Road*. I also had Paul McCartney's first couple of solo albums, as well as George Harrison's *All Things Must Pass*.

It seems strange that so soon after such a personal loss – Alice, the woman I had loved, shared my dreams with – I should be so stunned by the death of a pop icon, but I was. What can I say? It's hard to explain. In a way I was more affected by the death of John Lennon than I was when Ian Curtis committed suicide back in May, when I played *Closer* over and over again. Maybe it was some weird form of escapism from one misery to another, a more remote, less painful misery. I smoked a couple of joints and listened to old Beatles and Lennon songs all day and evening on the radio.

Alice had loved *Some Time in New York City*, I remembered. It had suited her political inclinations. She had never had much time for the 'war-is-over-all-you-need-is-love shit', as she called it. It was the only solo Lennon record I owned, and that was because of her. Perhaps my two griefs mingled, bled into one another, but it seemed that day as if my whole childhood, in all its innocence, and my times of young love with Alice reared up from my memory and drowned me. Perhaps it was a loss of innocence. I'm not sure. Maybe there are many ends to innocence. I didn't have much money, so I took an empty bottle to the offie round the corner and got it filled with sherry from the barrel for a quid. I thought of dropping in on Anton but decided against it. As I listened to the songs, and memories of the things I'd lost flooded through my mind, I drank all the sherry and became quite maudlin, not to mention sick. I think I even cried when they played 'In My Life' and 'Norwegian Wood'.

I can't remember falling asleep, but when I woke early the following morning with a cheap sherry hangover and a sore throat from smoking too much, I found another shock waiting for me when I went downstairs.

6

For their second meeting, on Thursday morning, the team took over the old boardroom, as usual. The case was now on full steam ahead, and Chief Superintendent Gervaise had also drafted in a young DC from County HQ and promised to try and prise one or two more detectives out of Assistant Chief Constable Ron McLaughlin, though his fingers grasped the purse strings tightly.

DC William Collins was twenty-four years old and hotly tipped for the fast-track programme. He had submitted his application in October and was waiting for the result. In the meantime, his supervisor wanted to give him as broad an experience of the job as possible. Collins, who had thus far been granted the nickname 'Wilkie', had a law degree from the University of Manchester, and he still looked very much the student, with his sandy hair flopping over one eye, old-style NHS glasses, rumpled jacket and skinny jeans. He seemed unhurried and deliberate in his movements and comfortable in his skin, economic in his gestures. He spoke softly with a slight Liverpudlian accent. He was also rumoured to be a whizz with computers. Gerry had brought him up to speed as best she could over the morning. As for Collins himself, he still seemed a little shy and quite star-struck by his temporary new position on the Homicide and Major Crimes Squad, not to mention his attractive new mentor.

And so the three of them – Winsome, Gerry and Wilkie Collins – took their places at the polished oval table, overseen by a gallery of gilt-framed oil paintings of the wool barons who gave Eastvale its status: old men with roast beef complexions, significant whiskers, bulbous noses and stiff, high collars, for the most part. Eastvale had once been a great centre for wool and sheep trade all over the Yorkshire Dales, moors and wolds, being central to the area and close to the A1, the 'Great North Road', its main artery. But these canny old merchants were long gone now, replaced by tourism and various service industries, though farming still remained of great importance to the region.

Banks walked to the front of the room, where a large whiteboard stood in front of the grand old fireplace. The board was already dotted with a few more photos and scribbles, arrows connecting various linked names or dates, but it still didn't add up to much so far.

'As you probably know,' Banks began, 'we've got a revised date on our missing person. Instead of 2009, we now know he can't have been dumped where he was until after May 2012. That doesn't mean he wasn't buried somewhere before and moved later, but that doesn't seem likely unless anyone can think of a good reason why.'

'I suppose if the killer found out that the spot where the body was originally buried was going to be dug up, as this one was later, that might have been a good reason,' said Gerry.

'Fair enough,' said Banks. 'But I still think we'd be best advised to stick to the most obvious course first. That is now between 2012 and 2016, which gives us four years to examine. Yes, our man could have gone missing, been killed before then, but if we chuck away all the parameters, we'll end up with overload. Gerry, you and DC Collins here will have more than enough to work on already. By the way,

DC Collins, welcome to Eastvale Homicide and Major Crimes. I've heard good things about you. I hope they're true.'

Collins glanced at Gerry, lowered his head and blushed. 'Thank you, sir.'

'And let me apologise that this hardly looks like the murder room on a typical TV crime drama, bursting at the seams with eager coppers sitting on the edges of their desks just dying to get at it. There're four of us in all, so we share the work. I think those who know me will know I'm not afraid to get my hands dirty.'

Winsome nudged Gerry and whispered something. Gerry laughed.

'Enough of that,' said Banks, 'or I'll send you both to the headmaster's office.' He tapped the board. 'Let's hope Kim from the lab and Dr Runcorn, our forensic anthropologist, will be coming in with more information soon. If we knew something about what the victim was like – the clothes he wore and so on – we'd have a better idea of what we're after in the missing persons files. And until we know who he was, what he did, we don't have much hope of finding out who wanted him dead. Gerry's already been on to the National Missing Persons Bureau and they're proving helpful. I'm also hoping that Dr Runcorn can give us a more accurate age.' He gestured towards Gerry and Wilkie Collins. 'That would help your search enormously. Any questions or comments so far?'

'What about the media?' asked Winsome. 'How shall we handle them?'

'Same as usual. Actually, they've shown very little interest since the initial excitement of "modern skeleton discovered at Roman excavation site" headlines. According to Grace Hutchinson, there's been a few photographers and local reporters hanging around the field, but not many, and no real national interest. I think we're lucky there's an election coming up.

Not to mention the Hillsborough trial. That keeps them busy. Anyway,' Banks went on, 'we do have one more piece of useful information. I discovered yesterday evening, from a visit to Eastvale Drainage Solutions, that the last owner of Wilveston Farm, on whose property the body was found, was at one time a serving police officer. I don't know if this has any relevance or not, but I think we should find out more about him.'

'Right, sir,' said Gerry. 'I'll get right on it.'

'No, let Winsome do it. You stick with the missing persons.'

'Yes, sir.'

Banks added a question mark beside Gillespie's name on the board. 'Given the job we do,' he said, 'it's more than possible that a retired cop may have enemies who would want to see him out of the way or, in this case, maybe, enemies *he* would like to see out of the way. So when you two are searching through the possible missing persons, bear in mind that any connection with police matters merits an asterisk by the name. And perhaps this is one piece of information we shouldn't pass on to our friendly local media hounds.' Banks took a sip of his coffee. 'How would you describe Gillespie's reaction when you told him about the skeleton?' he asked.

'I'd say he was taken aback, sir,' said Winsome. 'Pretty gobsmacked, truth be told.' She glanced towards Gerry, who agreed.

'Genuine?'

'I think so,' Winsome said. 'I mean, I'd like to think I have pretty good radar for detecting lies and evasions, and it didn't sound any warning bells.'

'I agree,' said Gerry. 'Not that my radar is as good as the sarge's, but I'd swear when we told him it was news to him.'

'OK,' said Banks. 'It's good to have your reactions.'

'Besides,' Winsome added, 'he would hardly bury a body on his own land, would he?'

'Why not?' Banks said. 'According to what we know, it was an unused field next to what was almost an unused lane. Not much chance of a body being dug up there.'

'But what about when he got the CPO?' said Gerry. 'He must have known it would mean them digging up some of his land.'

'But he might have thought by then the body would be unrecognisable, which it pretty much is.'

'But wouldn't he have moved it when he found out about the order?'

'Maybe,' said Banks. 'Or maybe he didn't want to risk it.'

'It still makes more sense that he didn't know it was there,' said Winsome.

'Fair point,' said Banks. 'And we'll keep it in mind.'

'What happens next?' asked Gerry. 'I mean once we've got a list of possibles. I mean, it could be a *really* long list. I've seen some of the numbers.'

'I know it might seem overwhelming,' said Banks, 'and I'm not saying it won't be, but remember, you'll be able to eliminate a lot of candidates right from the get-go, through age, sex, race, health, circumstances and so on. That winnowing is as important a part of the job as the rest, if you don't want to end up wasting time. We're also assuming first off that the killer didn't transport the body the length of the country. Perhaps it was someone who knew the area, knew the neglected field? So start with a circle, say a five-mile radius around the burial site. That shouldn't produce very many possibles, if any. Unless you get *really* lucky. Then move out in five-mile increments as you go. Concentric circles.'

'Until we reach the length of the country?' said Gerry.

Banks laughed. 'Yes. Afraid so. But I'm sure you'll have something long before then. And that's where the hard work starts. TIE. Trace, interview and eliminate. I know you've all heard that more times than you'd care to remember, but after the trace comes the interview. Unless we get a really lucky break, there's going to be a lot of phoning and traipsing around, talking to families, friends, witnesses and so on. Remember, the possibilities will have been missing for some time. Sometime after May 2012.'

'Gillespie left the farm in 2017, sir,' said Winsome.

'Yes, but we have to assume the body was dumped while he was still living there. Dr Runcorn, our forensic anthropologist, gives us a cut-off date of roughly early 2016. But why would Gillespie need to have known anything about it? The farmhouse itself is more than a mile from the outlying field. If he's telling the truth, he never went there. And as you pointed out yourself, it's unlikely he would bury a body on his own land, or that he wouldn't remove it when he heard his land was going to be redeveloped for a new road widening system and shopping centre.'

'Fair enough, sir,' said Winsome.

'It's recent enough that emotions may still be raw, though,' Banks went on, 'that families may still be convinced their loved ones will turn up. And if someone's been missing for a few years and still hasn't been found, it's unlikely anyone you talk to is going to be able to tell you anything that hasn't been uncovered already. Your job will be to act as fresh eyes. Something that didn't seem to mean anything at the time might mean a lot now we have a body. But be sensitive. Play it carefully. And once you've eliminated most of your possibles, we'll see what we've got left. But first comes the trace. Best get to it.'

The three stood up, picked up their pens and pads and made for the door. 'Gerry,' said Banks. 'A word, please.'

Gerry turned back. She bit her lip and stood before him, contrite. 'I know what you're going to say, sir,' she said when the others had left, 'and I'm sorry. I should have run a background check on Gillespie before Winsome and I went to talk to him yesterday. No excuses. I know I'm due for a bollocking.'

'Well, I didn't want to say it in front of the others, but knowing you've made a mistake is a good place to start.'

'I appreciate that, sir. And it won't happen again.'

'I don't think it will. Consider the matter closed. And I didn't ask Winsome to do the background check because I don't think you can do it. I asked her because you and your young lad have got enough on your plate already. By the way, what do you think of young Collins? Does he seem OK to you?'

'Yes, sir. From what little I've seen. He doesn't say much, but he's quick on the uptake.'

'Good. I got the impression from the way he was looking at you just now that he's rather sweet on you.'

Gerry blushed. 'Puppy love, sir. Don't worry, I'll soon disabuse him of any such notions.'

Banks didn't envy the young man his chances, or lack of them.

10 December 1980

Our landlord had placed a small wooden table close to the front door, like the one I had seen behind Lucy at St John's Terrace, and whoever got down first in a morning placed the post there. It wasn't in any particular order, so you had to search through the stack to find out if anything was for you. I was rarely first down, but because of the sherry and not having eaten, I couldn't get back to sleep that morning, even though it was barely light outside. I picked up the small heap from the lino beneath the letterbox and quickly leafed through. I wasn't expecting anything, so was hardly surprised when nothing was exactly what I got, but one item hit me right between the eyes.

It was a simple, cheap postcard with a photo of the Eiffel Tower on front, and when I turned it over, I saw it was addressed in small block capitals to Alice Poole. The message was short and to the point:

Alice,
I'm sorry.

Adieu, —
Mark.

The signature was so large and sprawling, it took up the bottom half of the card. I felt the hairs prickle at the back of my neck, and a wave of nausea lurched up from my stomach. Clutching the postcard, I dashed upstairs and just made it to the toilet in time. Luckily, it was early enough that no one else was up and about.

Back in my room, I washed my mouth out and put the kettle on, then dropped a couple of Alka-Seltzers in some water and drank the fizzy liquid. When I had a mug of sweet tea in my hand, I picked up the postcard again and flopped down in my armchair.

There was no mistaking the message, the signature or the addressee. It was from Mark to Alice. I couldn't make out the postmark because it was slightly blurred, but the stamp was definitely French. So that was where he'd gone. Was the card a kiss-off? It seemed to be. The abrupt apology and 'Adieu' at the end certainly read that way to me. *The bastard.* How could he do that? How could he dump a woman like Alice just like that, as if he were swatting aside a troublesome insect?

But what did it mean in terms of what had happened and what I'd been thinking? Whether I had been constantly aware of it or not, I realised that my mind had been edging ever closer to the idea that perhaps Mark had killed Alice. But this seemed to turn everything topsy-turvy. Unless, of course, it was a ploy to help establish his innocence. But why bother? Or maybe it wasn't from Mark at all. I had no idea what his handwriting or signature were like, so anyone could have written it. But again, why? What would be the point? A bad joke?

If it was genuine, then Mark didn't know what had happened, that Alice had been murdered, and he was somewhere in France enjoying himself, perhaps with another woman. I decided that, either way, he needed to be brought back to face the music. Some music, at any rate, even if it wasn't a fully fledged charge of murder. At the very least he needed to account for his actions and whereabouts on the night Alice was killed, as I had been made to do.

As I sipped the tea and turned things over in my mind, I also started to think, or rethink, what might have happened on the night of the murder, the night I had seen Alice briefly on her way to Mark's to have things out with him. Gary Kirk had implied that there was some issue between them that needed resolving. Maybe that issue had something to do with another woman.

But what about Lucy? Hadn't she heard someone coming down the stairs and driving off late that night? 'Heavy footsteps'. It could have been Mark carrying Alice's body. She was slightly built and wouldn't be too heavy for him. But Lucy hadn't *seen* anything, and she hadn't heard them talking. Earlier, yes, but not then. Perhaps Alice had already left after they had their row, while Lucy had been asleep, gone somewhere else alone and been waylaid by the killer, whether it was the Ripper or not. Then what Lucy heard was nothing more than Mark going noisily down the stairs on his own at about two in the morning and driving off. Or maybe it wasn't even Mark. If it was, though, perhaps he was upset and needed to go for a late-night drive to clear his head, like Americans always seemed to do in the movies. Or was he leaving Alice for this other woman, picking her up and driving off to Paris with her, where some days later he would send Alice this postcard?

Was he planning on coming back to his flat? Lucy had told me that two plainclothes men – police officers, she assumed – had searched Mark's room the day after Alice's body was discovered. Why? They had apparently not questioned Lucy and her flatmate Susie. Why not? Did they know something that the rest of us didn't? The police usually did.

It was almost light outside, though the typical December cloud cover hardly made for welcoming daylight. I rolled a cigarette, lit it and coughed. The postcard had made me more confused than ever, and my head was beginning to pound. For want of a better idea, I took two aspirins and went back to bed, where I tossed and turned with disturbing dreams of Mark and Alice, just beyond my grasp, but vivid enough to keep me in a state of semi-wakefulness until blissful unconsciousness finally kicked in.

28 November 2019

Banks took Winsome to lunch over at the Queen's Arms for Cumberland sausage and mash. Breaking his recent rule about not drinking during the work day, he ordered a pint of Black Sheep along with Winsome's Slimline Tonic.

The pub was busy with office workers and shop assistants from the market square, some of whom said hello as Banks and Winsome walked past their tables. One of the landlord's seemingly endless supply of playlists was streaming Sandy Nelson's 'Let There Be Drums', fortunately not too loud to hinder conversation.

After they had put in their food order, Winsome asked, 'So what *is* going on with Annie? Why isn't she working the case with us? I haven't seen much of her this past while. We haven't had a good chat in ages. She's seemed distant, and I suppose I've been preoccupied with Joshua.'

'Ray's death hit her very hard, and she doesn't seem to be handling it well. You know about her background?'

'That her mother died young, and Annie was brought up in an artists' commune? Yes.'

'It meant that she was especially close to Ray, and he wasn't . . . how should I put it . . . he wasn't one of the most consistent, the most reliable, of parents. I'm not saying he didn't love Annie and wasn't there for her. He was. But he could be unpredictable. He led a bohemian lifestyle, after all.'

'I suppose that's a good word for it,' said Winsome.

'And then there was Zelda,' said Banks.

'I was wondering where she fitted in.'

'She and Ray had a very close relationship, and I think that rattled Annie, made her feel like an outsider. Especially as Zelda was even younger than her. Ray was very successful, you know, and quite well off—'

'So Annie thought that Zelda was some young sexy gold-digger who got her claws into Daddy?'

'Basically, yes.'

'And you?'

'Me? No, of course not. I— Oh, I see what you mean. What do I think?'

Winsome frowned. 'That's all I meant.'

'I can understand Annie's feelings,' Banks rushed on, 'but I tried to tell her that it wasn't like that. Ray and Zelda. It was genuine. The real thing. And it wasn't any sort of personal slight against her. You know something about Zelda's life?'

'She was an orphan kidnapped and sold into sexual slavery, wasn't she? The stuff of nightmares.'

'Indeed. Well, maybe Ray provided one way out of those nightmares. At least he gave her a shot at a normal life. Well, as normal as any life could be with him. And Ray . . . well, he'd had girlfriends since Annie's mother died, of course, but I think when it came right down to it, he'd been very lonely. Zelda was vulnerable, and he took care of her, and in return, she brought a new source of joy into his life. Annie was supposed to be a part of that, but she couldn't make the leap. Too many conflicting emotions. And, of course, her attitude only drove Ray further away. So, the long and the short of it is that Annie's taking a short break from the job to get herself sorted. She was very vague about where she's going or what her plans are, and I didn't push her.'

Banks took a long draught of Black Sheep. Their food arrived, and after a short silence, Winsome looked up from her plate and said, 'By the way, you don't have to treat me any different from the rest, you know, just because of Joshua. I might tire out faster than I used to, but I'm still on the ball. I'm still up to the job.'

'I know you are,' said Banks. 'And I promise I'll work you just as hard as the rest of the team.'

'It's just that you made that call yourself yesterday. Eastvale Drainage Solutions. I could have done it. I *should* have, as it was my fault we didn't do a background check on Gillespie before the interview.'

'I know you could. As for "should", I'm not too sure. Yes, one of you should have checked out Gillespie's background, but Gerry's already apologised and I told her the matter was closed. It's not a big deal. Besides, I had no idea Farrier was going to tell me Gillespie was ex-Job. It came out of the blue. So don't beat yourself up. We'll probably want to talk to Gillespie again, anyway. This way we have some leverage if we need it.'

'And now? Is he a suspect?'

'Let's just say he's more interesting.'

'I'm the senior officer. Not checking was an oversight. The blame's mine.'

'What do you want me to do, Winsome, give you a slap on the wrist?'

Winsome smiled. 'I'd report you straight to the chief super if you did anything like that.'

Banks laughed. 'I suppose I had mixed motives for going. I wanted to get out of the station, myself. I don't get out much.'

'Lonely at the top?'

'Something like that.' He took a bite of sausage and washed it down with Black Sheep. Helen Shapiro's 'Little Miss Lonely' was playing over the system. When they had both emptied their plates, Banks asked, 'I know you haven't had much time, but have you got anywhere with Gillespie's background yet?'

'I've made a start. I must say I've learned quite a lot in a short time – and not just about Gillespie. He joined up in 1964, when he was eighteen, and retired in 1994. That makes him seventy-three right now.'

'So he did his thirty and got out?'

'That's right.'

'Illustrious career?'

'He did all right. Made it to CID quite early on, passed his sergeant's exam in 1970, made inspector five years after that. When he retired, he was a detective superintendent, so I'd say he did all right, if not spectacularly. I mean, he was only forty-eight when he retired.'

'Good point. It took me a hell of a lot longer than that to make superintendent.'

'If you don't mind me saying so, sir, I don't think you exactly toed the line throughout your career, did you?'

'Winsome! What an insinuation.' Banks drank some beer and scratched his head. 'But maybe you've got a point. And 1994 is when he went to live at Wilveston Farm?'

'Around then, yes. And that squares with what he told us. I also got the impression that Gillespie was more of a desk jockey – policy, meetings, committees, mission statements, organisation, that sort of thing. He was also deeply involved with the law and technology. He worked on setting out the PACE regulations and helped write the HOLMES programme. Came to computers early, apparently, and became quite good at it. He did a few spells teaching at Hendon and Coventry, gave a few university lectures to prospective coppers on policing and the law. It's just an impression, but I don't think he got out there and got stuck in as often as you like to do. No real street presence.'

'They also serve . . .' said Banks. 'So nothing stands out? Nothing that might connect him with a skeleton buried on what used to be *his* land?'

'Not as far as I could tell, sir.'

'How many different forces did he serve in?'

'He moved around a fair bit. He started out locally – remember, he was brought up on the farm. It was called the North Riding of Yorkshire Constabulary when Gillespie joined in 1964, but became York and North East Yorkshire Police in 1968. It gets quite complicated around that time. The Police Act came into force in 1964, and a lot more town forces and county forces merged. We went from a hundred and seventeen to only forty-seven forces in England and Wales.

Gillespie transferred to Dorset and Bournemouth when he passed his sergeant's exam in 1970, and worked mostly on Traffic there for five years, after which he went on to work as a detective inspector at the Met, where he served in a variety of departments, some of them classified, again mostly in an administrative capacity, until 1981, when he went to the Cumbria Constabulary. He did eight years there, Traffic again, and on his promotion to superintendent had his final transfer to South Yorkshire, which is where he retired in June 1994.'

'Not so far from home, then?'

'That's when his father became ill, and he decided to go back to Wilveston Farm and keep it going.'

'Right. I suppose he thought he was still young enough for that.'

'Fit enough, too,' Winsome added. 'And they do say farming's in the blood.'

'No on-the-job injuries?'

'None. And very few sick days.'

'Complaints, disciplinary issues?'

'None. Model officer, if a little bland. Of course, he was involved in a number of cases over the years – quite a variety, including drugs – so I can't say for certain there's nothing dodgy buried there. Most of the information I got was easily available. I'd have to dig deeper to find anything like that. Do you want me to keep digging, check out the case files, classified jobs and so on?'

'Why not? And a drugs angle is always worth pursuing. The Met would be interesting, too. It's my bet "classified" means either Special Branch or Counterterrorism. I'll trust you to stay alert for any alarm bells. And maybe when we get some information from Gerry on the missing persons angle, we can look more closely for possible links to Gillespie's police career. In the meantime, though, let's not get blinkered. Gillespie's of interest, yes, but I wouldn't put him on the suspect list yet. I know, I know, we don't even have a bloody suspect list. Let's keep the big picture in view, keep our minds open.'

'Right, sir. Should I go and talk to Gillespie again?'

'Why don't we do that together in a few days' time, when we know a bit more? It would be nice to go armed with a few disturbing questions.'

Winsome smiled. 'Sounds like fun.'

10 December 1980

One disadvantage of a big old house divided into student bedsits is that there's no telephone. Perhaps some of the more expensive residences had better facilities, but not the place where I lived. Even Alice, in her penthouse flat, didn't have a phone.

Most of the time, I didn't miss it at all. My parents finally had one installed at home in Portsmouth just before I came up to university, but my dad complained if I used it to phone my mate Tony down the street to see if he wanted to head out for a pint. Phone calls, even local ones, cost money, he said, and why couldn't I simply walk the hundred yards or so and knock on Tony's door? He had a point.

The nearest phone box was at the corner of Hyde Park Road and Woodhouse Lane and, fortunately for me, it hadn't been vandalised recently. The police had left me a card when they first visited, and I still had it on my mantelpiece. It gave the number at Millgarth and I dutifully dialled it as I stood in the booth, which stank of urine, and watched the traffic speeding by on the main road. Runnels of rain distorted the images like funfair mirrors.

I got through to a switchboard and asked for DI Glassco or DC Marley. The woman on the other end asked my name then told me to hang on. I heard various clicks and buzzes and the murmuring of several voices in the background until, just a couple of minutes later, she came back on the line to tell me that neither officer was available at the moment. I asked if she meant they couldn't come to the phone or they weren't in the building, but she just repeated that neither was available at the moment. I asked her to let them know that I had called, but the line went dead and buzzed before I had even finished. So much for that.

I was starving, but I had no food in the house, so I wandered down Woodhouse Lane, which split the moor into an open space used for circuses and fairgrounds on one side and the pleasant, tree-lined Hyde Park on the other, with its footpaths and children's playground. In a greasy spoon close to the university, I ordered eggs, sausage and chips. Everyone in the cafe seemed to be talking about John Lennon's murder. Apparently, he'd been shot in the back from close range on his way into the Dakota Building, where he and Yoko lived, by a deranged fan called Mark Chapman who, it seemed, had earlier asked him to sign a copy of *Double Fantasy*. Christ, what a world.

After a quick pint at the Fenton, which was already full of its usual mix of punks and art students – and lecturers – I carried on down Woodhouse Lane past the Poly, then cut through the Merrion Centre down to the Headrow. I went to the same entrance to Millgarth that Glassco and Marley had taken me a week ago and got as far as the reception area. Everything beyond the door there was accessible only to authorised personnel. I waited at the desk until a ruddy-faced sergeant with hairs growing out of his nose detached himself from a group of fellow officers, one of whom appeared to be telling a joke, and came over to see what I wanted.

'I'd like to see DI Glassco or DC Marley,' I said.

'And your name is?'

'Nicholas Hartley.'

'What's the purpose of your visit?'

'I want to talk to them about a murder case.'

'Would this be about a murder you've already committed or one you're about to commit?'

'What? No, of course not. They came to interview me at home, then they brought me here last week. I knew the victim. Alice Poole. She was a friend of mine. I have some more information. Just tell them.' I realised that I probably looked bleary-eyed and scruffy, and he probably thought I was one of the crazies they no doubt get from time to time.

'What would this new information be?'

I showed him the postcard. 'This. It's from the man I think they're trying to find. The boyfriend, Mark Woodcroft.'

The sergeant deftly plucked the postcard from my hand and inspected it.

'I brought it to show them, DI Glassco and DC Marley,' I said. 'It could be important.'

'In what way?'

'That's something I need to explain to them.'

'I see. Well, we're all very busy here at the moment, as you can imagine. Not a spare moment with the Ripper still on the prowl.'

'But it might concern that investigation. She was—'

'Stay here.' The sergeant rolled his eyes and picked up the phone. When he'd finished talking, he went back to his paperwork, pointed to a bench and said, 'Wait.'

I sat and waited. Moments later, a tall, slim man I vaguely recognised appeared behind the sergeant and glanced over at me. He tapped the sergeant on the shoulder, bent and whispered something in his ear, then went away. I realised who he was: the man who had appeared by the door in the interview, when Glassco and WPC Raglan had talked to me. Probably from the Ripper Squad, he was the one who had listened while they questioned me about my past movements, who had shaken his head and left when he heard my alibis for dates of the Ripper's murders because he realised I had been too young and too far away to be the killer they were searching for.

'I'll see that DI Glassco gets this,' the sergeant said, waving the postcard.

'No,' I said. 'I want to give it to him myself and explain. Just tell him I'm here.'

'I told you: DI Glassco's busy. I'll see he gets it. Or DC Marley. Give me your phone number, and I'll ask one of them to call you. How about that?'

'I don't have a phone. But I can wait. I—'

'A number you can be contacted through, then?'

'I suppose the English Department at the university. But it would be much better if—'

He waved his hand. 'Just piss off, sonny, there's a good lad.'

1 December 2019

By the time the weekend came around, Gerry and DC Wilkie Collins were still stuck deep in their missing persons search, and both Kim Lee from the lab and the forensic anthropologist Dr Runcorn begged a couple more days to finish their examinations. There was no need for Banks to be present at the station, so he made sure everyone concerned had his mobile number and knew they could get in touch if anything came up.

On Saturday night, he went to the Dog and Gun to hear an up-and-coming folk singer called Emily Hinds, a young protégé of Penny Cartwright's. She looked like an English rose and sang some moving versions of 'Once I Had a Sweetheart' and 'The Trees They Grow So High'. The only drawback, to Banks's mind, was that she didn't seem old enough to have experienced the heartbreak and desolation the songs expressed, so there was a certain degree of authenticity lacking. Her voice was also perhaps straining to be too pure and piercing. Not many could get away with the clarity of tone you heard in Judy Collins and Joan Baez, but that would also sort itself out over time.

During the break, Banks got chatting with Noel Pullman, a local bookseller who also did some roadie work for Penny Cartwright and friends, and when the subject turned to the contents of Ray's LP collection, Noel offered Banks the use not only of his van, but also of his person. All he asked in return was Ray's copy of Jan Dukes de Grey's *Mice and Rats in the Loft,* which Banks was happy to let him have, providing he got a chance to rip it first.

And so, on a grey but so far dry Sunday morning in early December, the two of them drove off along the bouncy, winding, unfenced road to Lyndgarth, and beyond to Windlee Farm. They should be able to make the move in one trip, including Zelda's stuff, Banks thought, and with any luck, it would leave them time for a late pub lunch. The thought of roast beef and Yorkshire pudding was already making his mouth water.

Noel pulled up outside Windlee Farm and gave a shiver as he stepped out of the van. 'Brass monkey weather up here, isn't it?' he said. Then he opened the back doors, ready to receive their treasure. Annie had left the heat on low, so it was more comfortable inside, and the first thing they did was shift the piles of LPs from Ray's shelves into the back of the van, trying to keep them in the order Ray had left them. Noel oohed and aahed about a title every now and then – Ruth White's *Flowers of Evil,* Sagittarius's *Present Tense,* Sandy Bull's *Inventions.* Though he was quite a few years younger than Banks, he was probably even more knowledgeable about sixties and seventies music. 'There's a lifetime's worth of listening here, mate,' he said. 'If you're ever interested in selling it off . . .'

'I doubt I'll be doing that,' said Banks, carrying a stack of LPs, 'but you're welcome to come and have a listen whenever you fancy it.' Just seeing the garish sixties album covers made Banks smile, and at the same, gave him a pang of loss that Ray was no longer around. Perhaps having them in his entertainment room would keep the memory of his friend alive, though he didn't think it would disappear fast, no matter what. Though Noel would probably play them all if he got the chance, Banks wouldn't. He knew from visits to Ray's that a lot of this music was actually pretty bad, despite the occasional unknown gem, and he wasn't a sixties fanatic. Most of the music of the period that he really liked he already had on LP, CD or download. But he also liked lots of other music – classical, jazz, blues – and this collection would stand mostly in memory of Ray. Maybe it was a waste, but that was how he felt. Ray had, after all, bequeathed it specifically to him.

Ray's paintings and drawings of Zelda, that Annie also wanted to be removed, posed a small problem. Banks didn't want Noel to see them – it somehow seemed sleazy, and too much of a liberty – so he left him to finish off the LPs and found more bedsheets to cover the artworks with before he carried them down from Ray's studio. Fortunately, there weren't many, and most were unframed sketches, so they didn't cause him back strain. He worried a little that Noel might ask what they were, but he didn't. Ray had also bequeathed Banks a couple of local landscapes, which Annie had left behind, and two preliminary sketches for the final one he had given to

Gerry shortly after she had almost been killed at the end of a case, which Banks also took to give to her.

After that, Banks found some bin liners in the kitchen and used one for Zelda's clothes. She didn't have an extensive wardrobe – mostly jeans, T-shirts, sweaters and so on – so it didn't take him long. He felt creepy handling her underwear, so tossed it in with the rest of the clothes as quickly as he could. A few pairs of shoes and trainers, and that was it. Another, smaller bin liner took care of toiletries, what little make-up she had and the contents of her bedside drawers. That was where he found the few personal items she owned – worry beads, pens and an empty notebook, an old hair slide, along with a French passport. In the photo, she looked like a rabbit caught in the headlights. In another drawer, photographs of Zelda and Ray, which had clearly been printed from a digital source on poor quality photo paper. On the bedside table lay her mobile and the book she was reading when she was taken, Kazuo Ishiguro's *An Artist of the Floating World*, a bookmark stuck about three-quarters of the way through. There wasn't much. The life Zelda had led didn't give her the opportunity to collect possessions and carry them around with her. As a result, there was nothing she was especially attached to. When he had finished, the room was empty of her presence, as if she had never been there. That, too, made him feel sad. He reminded himself that Zelda wasn't dead, like Ray, and if she wanted to, she could buy another copy of *An Artist of the Floating World* and finish it. Maybe he should send her a copy?

'Anything else?' Noel asked as Banks dumped the bin liners.

'Just her studio,' Banks said. 'There's not a lot in there. It shouldn't take me long. Take a break if you like. I can handle it.'

'You sure? I wouldn't mind a smoke.'

'No. Go ahead.'

Zelda's studio was exactly as it had been the last time he had been there, on the night she was abducted. Apart from one or two fixed tools of her jewellery-making trade – a potter's wheel, a vice here and a buffing machine there – it was mostly a matter of half-finished earrings, necklaces and some of the tools she used for finely detailed work. He would sort it all out later and probably chuck a lot of it. There was also a stack of Zelda's paintings, copies of famous artworks for the most part, and few sketchbooks full of ideas for jewellery designs and future projects. He carried out the easel and painting gear next. There were a few books on the shelves that could go to the Oxfam shop, and a small pile of magazines, mostly about art and politics, that could go into his recycling bin. When he had finished, he closed the door behind him and carried the last bin liner to the van. If Annie really wanted to burn the shed down, she could do it.

Noel was leaning against the side of the van gazing out over the moors to the west, smoking a cigarette. 'All done?' he asked, checking his watch.

'All done.'

'Reckon we've got time to make it to the Hare and Hounds before they stop serving?'

'If we hurry,' said Banks. The Hare and Hounds was one of Helmthorpe's three pubs, and the one that served the best food. The Bridge was a drinker's haunt and the Dog and Gun didn't do the full Sunday lunch.

They made it, and just after they had sat down, Noel with a Coke and Banks with a pint of Timothy Taylor Landlord, his mobile went. Gerry.

Banks excused himself and answered. 'Gerry. What is it?'

'Nothing, sir. I mean, don't get your hopes up. We haven't found our man yet.'

'Then . . . ?'

'I was talking to Kim in the lab and she says she's finished. She's been in touch with Dr Runcorn, too. And he says he's done about as many tests as he can. They're ready to report.'

'Now?'

'Not exactly. They've both been burning the midnight oil, and they'd like a little more time to formalise their findings. They thought maybe we could organise a meeting for tomorrow morning.'

'Excellent,' said Banks. 'Boardroom. First thing. And ask young Wilkie Collins to nip over to the bakery and pick up some croissants, would you?'

Banks could almost hear Gerry smile. It was the kind of task she was usually asked to do, being the most junior team member.

'Will do, sir,' she said. 'Good weekend?'

Banks thought of the paintings and stack of LPs and the desolation of Windlee Farm without Ray and Zelda there. 'I've had worse,' he said, realising as he spoke that it was a typical 'Yorkshire' response.

7

10 December 1980

It was about eight o'clock that Wednesday evening, and I was struggling through James Thomson's 'Autumn' when I heard footsteps outside my door. Dave was the only other person on my floor, and his bedsit was on the other side of the landing. But Dave hardly ever came out of his room. Anyone who passed my door had to be heading for the stairs up to Alice's flat. And sure enough, up they went. Two of them as far as I could tell, and most likely police. Perhaps now I could seize the opportunity to ask them about the postcard and tell them my ideas of what might have happened. I wished that sergeant at Millgarth hadn't snatched the card from me. I didn't trust him to pass it on to Glassco or Marley.

Curious, I waited until I heard footsteps overhead – *definitely* two people – before heading upstairs myself. I knocked on Alice's door.

When it opened, I saw it wasn't the police – at least not like any detective I had ever seen – but a man in his early fifties, perhaps, with grey hair and a neatly trimmed matching beard, still wearing his winter coat, a herringbone pattern with a fur collar.

'Yes?' he said.

I stared at him. He looked familiar.

Then I realised, but before I opened my mouth, he said, 'Just a minute – aren't you Alice's friend? Mick? Is that right?'

'Nick.'

'Sorry. Nick.'

'No problem, Mr Poole. Yes, it's me.'

'Of course, you live in the flat below, don't you?'

'That's right.'

By then an elegant, attractive woman had appeared behind him. She had long, wavy blonde hair and wore a red woollen cape-style overcoat with armholes. Mrs Poole. It wasn't hard to see where Alice got her beauty from. 'Who is it, Reginald?'

He turned to her. 'It's that lad came to visit us with Alice last Christmas. Nick. You remember?'

'Yes, of course. Well, ask him in, won't you?'

'Of course.'

They both stood aside and I walked inside and followed them into the living room. It was no different from the time I had visited just over a week ago: *Marxism Today* on the low glass table, the new Brueghel print on the wall, the colourful afghan draped over the back of the sofa. Mr Poole had already turned on the standard lamp and its warm orange glow cast a soft light on the fabric surfaces.

'Please, sit down,' he said.

I sat. I remembered last Christmas with Alice and her parents at the rambling mansion in the middle of Lincolnshire. I was going home for Christmas itself, but I stopped by there, sort of on my way, just for a couple of days before Christmas Eve. We were given separate rooms, of course, but Alice told me where hers was, and I remember holding my breath as I tiptoed along the wainscotted corridor lined with gilt-framed oil paintings, candelabras that seemed to reach out and impede my progress, and the occasional full set of armour. Well, no, it's not exactly true about the armour, but it felt like a stately home to me. I made it to her room without incident. I felt a little guilty now, as I sat with them. And more than a little sad. They both seemed tired and drawn, which was hardly surprising given what they must have been through over the past week or so.

'I suppose you're wondering what we're doing here,' Mr Poole said.

'Not really,' I answered. 'I mean, it's none of my business. I just wondered who was coming up the stairs, that's all. It's been silent since . . .' I stopped, realising my faux pas. 'Well . . . you know.'

'Yes, I suppose it has,' Mr Poole said.

'You've probably had a long drive,' I said. 'Would you like to come down to my room and have a cup of tea before you do what you've come to do here?'

They both looked at me as if a change of venue would definitely be welcome, and we trooped down to my bedsit, which, I explained on the way, was hardly as grand as Alice's flat.

'No matter,' said Mr Poole, as he sat on the battered and threadbare armchair. His wife sat on the other one, though she seemed unable to relax, as if she were trying to float at least an inch or two above the old cushions, sitting there without really committing herself to the act. I'd had the gas fire on low all evening, but neither took off their coats. I put on the kettle and took the hard-backed chair from my desk.

'We need to make a list of her belongings,' Mr Poole said. 'Before we get someone to come and . . . you know . . . remove them. The landlord gave us a key. The front door was open.'

'It usually is,' I said.

'Not very secure,' Mrs Poole said. 'Anyone could walk in.'

'I suppose so,' I said. 'But we all have locks on our doors. As far as I know, there's never been any sort of problem.' I didn't know how much they knew about Alice's murder, so I wasn't going to go into details about how it hadn't happened here, in the house. I was sure they probably knew that much.

I served the tea, lucky to find that the small amount of milk left in my bottle hadn't gone sour. Then I sat down again and rolled a cigarette. Mrs Poole watched me with a sort of fascinated disgust, as if she'd never seen anyone do such a thing before, and she probably hadn't. I couldn't suppress the thought that if only she knew what her daughter and I were doing down the corridor last Christmas . . . but the memory was a pyrrhic victory. All it did was make me feel even worse about what had happened to Alice. Even so, I had no reason to try to impress the Pooles, or care what they thought about me now, and it was my room, so I lit the cigarette.

'I'm really sorry about Alice,' I said. 'She was . . . she's a great loss.'

'Yes . . . yes,' Mrs Poole said. 'Thank you. Reginald and I are quite desolate. Alice was our only child, you know.'

Alice had told me all about it, and about her mother's miscarriages. 'I can't imagine how terrible it must be for you.'

'And what about you, lad?' Mr Poole said. 'How are you coping?'

'Me?' Did they know that Alice had dumped me for someone else? If not, was there a way I could let them know, subtly, that we had been no longer together? 'I . . . well, I'm devastated, of course. Though Alice and I didn't . . . I mean, I didn't see as much of her . . .'

'We know, son,' Mr Poole said. 'And we were sad to hear it. We told her you seemed like a nice lad.'

I smiled. 'Thanks.' But I managed to hold my tongue before saying it was a pity that Alice had no longer been interested in a 'nice lad'.

'We met Mark,' said Mrs Poole.

'Oh.'

'Yes, they came down over the summer. I must say we had a most pleasant time. Did you know he's quite a fine horseman?'

'No, I didn't.' I knew Alice was a keen equestrian, but had never for a moment thought it was a passion she shared with Mark. Somehow, it changed things, forged a stronger bond between them in my mind. I didn't like that. I also didn't like the idea of him going with her to the Lincolnshire mansion. Had she played the same bedroom game with him as she had with me?

'Yes,' she went on. 'I must say I was rather taken with him. I'm not sure Reginald felt the same way, though.' She gave her husband a pointed glance.

'Now, now, Joyce, don't go telling tales out of school. I liked him well enough. All I said was I thought he could be rather overbearing, that's all. I thought our Alice seemed a bit too much under his spell, always deferring to him in her opinions and so on. She'd always been such a strong-minded lass. Headstrong, you might even say.'

'You know you're only saying that because you disapproved of his political opinions. All I'm saying is that he had an aura of authority about him, a bit of charisma. The kind of boy who could get things done. A good future ahead of him. What do you think, Nick?'

I think he killed her. But did I, after the postcard? I didn't know any more. What I did know was that I remained suspicious of Mark. 'I didn't really know him,' I said. Then I glanced at Mr Poole. 'Though I'm not sure his political views would go down well at the local Conservative Club.'

'Now, now, lad, don't judge a book by its cover.'

'Sorry. But I did get the impression that Mark is very left wing.'

'True enough,' said Mr Poole. 'Our Alice always was full of enthusiasm for helping people and making the world a better place. Not that there's anything wrong with that. I always voted Liberal myself. And I suppose he managed to convince her that his way would work in the best interests of the people. Still, you know what they say: if you're not a communist when you're young, you have no heart, and if you're not a Conservative when you're older, you have no brains. Not completely true, of course, like most sayings, but it makes a point. Youth is a time for idealism, before life knocks it out of you.'

I had been thinking about Alice's politics ever since our final row and decided that when it came right down to it, despite her practical communism, she was far more idealistic than I was. Hers was the true dream. She wanted a fair deal for everyone and a world where no one starved or suffered. Though she accused me of being a romantic dreamer, perhaps I was the more realistic of the two of us. At least I had learned from reading literature that people don't naturally incline to equality and fairness, they have to be *made* to accept them, and therein lies the rub.

'Enough of that, Reginald,' Mrs Poole snapped. 'Honestly, as if things aren't bad enough already without bringing world suffering into it.' She turned to me. 'Where is Mark?' she asked. 'No one mentioned his whereabouts when they talked to us.'

'He's in France,' I said. 'Paris, I think.'

'*Paris?*' Mrs Poole repeated. It sounded remarkably alike in tone to 'A *handbag?*' from a production of *The Importance of Being Earnest* I had seen not too long ago. 'How strange.'

'Yes, it is, isn't it?'

'It's just that we were thinking we'd invite him to the funeral,' Mr Poole said, 'if we could get in touch, like. But if he's in France . . . well . . .'

'Sorry I can't be any more help,' I said. 'I don't have an address. Or even his exact whereabouts, for that matter. He disappeared the same night Alice . . . well, you know . . .'

'How odd,' said Mr Poole. 'Nobody mentioned that to us, either.'

'They probably don't think it's relevant.'

'The police do work in mysterious ways, I'm sure. But now we're here, perhaps *you* would consider attending Alice's funeral, Nick?' he said.

'Me?' I swallowed. I hated funerals, but I knew how important they were to the living. 'Yes,' I said. 'Yes, thank you very much. When is it?'

'In a week's time. We hope. The police . . . they need to keep hold of the . . . er . . . the body. Lord knows what they're doing, but apparently, they're not finished yet. I'd hazard a guess they're trying to link it to this Ripper fellow you've had prowling about these parts. They promised, but . . .'

Mrs Poole gave a long shudder. 'Reginald, please!'

'Sorry, love. But it's true, isn't it, Nick?'

'I wouldn't be surprised,' I said. 'It does seem a coincidence.'

'They said it wouldn't be long, and they'll let us know. We can give you a ring to let you know for certain?'

'I'm afraid I don't have a telephone.'

'Ah, well, the post will have to do, then. It will be short notice.'

'That's OK. Please do let me know, and I'll do my best to come. You know my address.'

Mr Poole stood up and put his empty tea mug on the mantelpiece. 'Right. Well. That's settled.' He turned to his wife. 'Come on, love, we'd better get back upstairs and start making a list of the items we need to take away. I take it the furniture, such as it . . .'

'Yes, it's a furnished flat,' I said. 'Except for the writing desk and chair. They were Alice's. There may be one or two other small items, too. If you have any questions, I'll be here. Just ask.'

'Righty-ho. And thank you, Nick.'

Mrs Poole inclined her head slightly as she passed me on her way out. I wasn't sure whether I was supposed to kiss her hand, but as she still had her gloves on, I didn't bother trying. And that was that. After they had left, I heard them wandering about upstairs, and I put on *All Things Must Pass* as a distraction.

2 December 2019

It wasn't quite light when Banks drove into work on Monday morning. The sky was that strange shade it turns in the blue hour when the night is nearly over and the sun is about to rise. The stars had almost all faded, and there was no moon visible. It seemed to Banks as if it was going to be one of those rarities, a sunny December day. He hoped it was a good omen.

He drove on, Crow Scar towering to his left, over the river, passed the drumlin with the six trees bent over by the wind, went through Fortford, with its excavated Roman ruins and thought again of the dig where Grace Hutchinson had found the mysterious skeleton that now occupied their days.

He arrived at the boardroom ten minutes early and found Wilkie Collins already there, poring over some papers, and a basket of croissants on the table. Collins had also rustled up a carafe of fresh-brewed coffee. At that time in the morning, especially a Monday morning, there couldn't be enough coffee. There was a cupboard in the boardroom and in it were several cups and mugs for visiting personnel. Banks set them on the table next to the carafe, sugar and jug of milk. He took his black, but he knew that not everyone did likewise.

'Go ahead,' he said to DC Collins. 'No need to stand on ceremony.'

Collins poured himself a mug. Black.

Within five minutes, everyone was present, seated and enjoying the treat. In addition to Dr Runcorn, Dr Galway, Winsome, Gerry, Kim Lee and Stefan Nowak, Banks had also invited Grace Hutchinson. After all, she had found the skeleton. She might remember something important. Banks kicked off the meeting by asking Dr Runcorn if he had any better idea of the age the victim had been when he was killed.

'I've done just about all I can,' said Runcorn. 'I've X-rayed the ossification centres, run the spectrographic analysis and talked with the forensic odontologist. He agrees we can narrow down the age about five years, between fifty-five and sixty, maybe a year or two on the plus side, at most. I doubt very much we could do better than that. Luckily, he was a healthy specimen. If there had been fractures and signs of disease to muddy the waters, it would have been an almost impossible task.'

'That's a big help,' said Banks, glancing at Gerry. 'It narrows down our number of possibilities significantly. You say there were no signs of disease?'

'Not even an old fracture, and just as much deterioration as you'd expect in someone of the age I've described. Of course, there are many significant diseases that wouldn't show up, even on the tests I've done. What's your thinking?'

'A remote possibility, that's all,' said Banks. 'That he was terminally ill and we're dealing with some sort of mercy killing.'

Runcorn raised an eyebrow. 'I must say you exhibit a remarkable degree of imagination, Superintendent.'

'When you've been in the job as long as I have,' said Banks, 'not much surprises you.'

'Well, I couldn't say for certain whether he was suffering from a terminal illness, only that I can find no traces on the evidence I have to examine.'

'Like I said, it was a remote possibility.'

'It doesn't quite square with the blows to the skull, either, sir,' chipped in DC Collins, reddening when everyone looked at him. 'I mean, if you were going in for a mercy killing, you probably wouldn't smash the poor sod's brains in, would you? More likely you'd use pills, or a pillow over the face.'

'Good point,' said Banks. 'Anything more on the weapon?'

It was Dr Galway who answered. 'I'd stick with my original assessment. A poker or metal rod of some kind. I've graphed the fracture lines, and they indicate a cylindrical object of the dimensions you would expect if a poker were used. There's no metal in the bone, but that was a long shot. If there ever was, it could have leached away underground.'

'Could be a domestic crime, then,' said Gerry. 'A poker's close to hand.'

'It certainly points in the direction of an unpremeditated assault,' Banks said. 'I've not come across many cases where a killer carries a poker to the scene with him.'

'But how many households even have pokers these days?' said Dr Runcorn.

Banks glanced at Winsome. 'You'd have to live in Yorkshire, doctor,' she said. 'Especially at this time of year. Many of these older rural houses have fireplaces, and they're often much in use. Both Detective Superintendent Banks and my own house have them. Not so sure about Gerry, as she lives in a flat.'

'Mine, too,' said Dr Galway. 'And I have a very sturdy poker on my hearth.'

Runcorn held his hands up. 'I stand corrected,' he said. 'What do we mere city dwellers know?'

'But it does tell us two things, doesn't it?' said Banks. 'That the crime was impulsive and that it might have been local – or at least committed in a house that had a poker. Therefore, most likely somewhere with a functioning fireplace.'

'That probably doesn't help a lot,' Gerry said, 'given what we've already heard about Yorkshire heating systems, but I see what you mean.'

'It's just worth bearing in mind, that's all,' said Banks. 'It might be useful in your search for a missing person, but don't let it lead you and DC Collins away from your other considerations.'

'Not to worry, sir. We're keeping an open mind so far.'

Banks took a moment to nibble on his croissant, which tasted good and buttery, and crisp where it should be. It brought back a sudden memory of his visit to Paris only a couple of months ago. Like Proust and the madeleine, he thought, remembering the outdoor cafe and the girl with the long-stemmed roses who resembled a young Françoise Hardy.

'By the way,' Runcorn said, 'I understand you've narrowed down the time the victim was dumped, to after 2012?'

'Yes. After May. How does that compute?'

'I've no problem with it. I've spent some time at the scene with Grace here, and from the samples I've taken and tests I've done – carbonate, ultraviolet fluorescence – I'd say it's possible that even three years in that damp acidic soil could produce the effect we have, especially if there was significant insect activity.'

'I can vouch for that,' said Grace Hutchinson. 'Creepy crawlies all over the place.'

Runcorn laughed. 'True. I doubt the flies go down that far to lay their eggs, but they're far from the only insects interested in the taste of decaying human flesh.'

'So, we stick at between 2012 and 2016?' said Banks.

'It's unlikely to be later,' said Dr Runcorn, 'and it apparently can't be any earlier. So yes.'

'Thanks, doctor,' said Banks. Then he turned to Kim Lee. 'And what do you have for us, Kim?' he asked.

'Well, I can tell you how he was dressed, where he bought his clothes and what kind of shoes he wore, if that's any help,' she said innocently.

15 December 1980

Needless to say, I had heard nothing from Glassco or Marley about the postcard, even though I had made a point of checking with the departmental secretary every day, despite the suspicious looks she gave me and the clipped tone she used when she had to talk to me. In the end I gave up. Mysterious ways, indeed. As far as I could tell, they were interested in one thing and one thing only: the Yorkshire Ripper. Anything else got put on the back burner until it turned cold. Fair enough; the Ripper had done a lot of damage to a lot of women, and his existence terrorised entire communities. But surely poor Alice deserved justice, too?

One good thing was that, after John Lennon's murder, people started to talk to me again, and a couple of days after, Geoff even invited me down to watch a TV special on Lennon. I mentioned the night of *To Serve Them All My Days* episode when I had knocked on his door and got no answer, and he said he'd just had to nip out to the shop for some bread. He was puzzled, he added, when I didn't turn up, but thought perhaps I just wasn't in the mood. And so, slowly, life started to return closer to normal, though Jill and her crowd still seemed to be avoiding me in the pub.

Anton was still in mourning for his hero, and I saw little of him before the holidays. I decided to leave him to his own devices. Though he was probably my best friend throughout university, in some ways he was practically a hermit and often disappeared for days on end. He seemed quite happy in his room reading a volume of Van Gogh's letters or the poetry of some obscure Roman in the original by candlelight. He was more comfortable with his own company than anyone I've ever known.

We had met in a shared tutorial during our first year and soon became friends. He had found the empty bedsit for me in the same house he was already living in. Anton was a strange character, definitely one of a kind. He dressed in an old sixties way – worn cords, loose-fitting shirts, leather waistcoats. His hair was long and sometimes tied back in a ponytail, and he wore John Lennon glasses and had a wispy beard. He was the only person I've ever known who listened to composers such as Stockhausen, Ligeti and John Cage and really seemed to know and appreciate what they were doing. He also liked weird jazz – Ornette Coleman, Roland Kirk, Don Cherry – and oddball rock, the likes of Soft Machine, John Cale, Nico and so on. In literature, he loved the Beats, especially Burroughs and Gary Snyder, along with the Liverpool poets, and he was a fount of information on all things zen.

When almost a week had gone by since I had handed over the postcard – or, rather, had it snatched from me – I went up to the corner and phoned Millgarth again. This time the person who answered told me that Detective Inspector Glassco and Detective Constable Marley had been reassigned. I asked her who had been assigned to Alice's case in their place, but she just said she couldn't give out that kind of information over the telephone and hung up. I didn't bother calling again.

I had briefly thought of going to the press. A few stories about Alice's murder had appeared in the local paper, and I noted the name of the reporter. Though he came out with no startling revelations, he obviously had a more direct link to the police investigating the matter than I did. But in the end, I decided against the idea. I reasoned that he was not only unlikely to want to give me any information, but would instead pump me for what I knew about Alice and Mark, and it would end up in the paper, perhaps twisted in the lurid way some reporters have. And it would introduce my name into the issue publicly. It had been bad enough suffering the cold shoulders and icy glances daily at lectures and in the MJ Lounge, but if the entire local population thought I was involved, life would be even more unbearable.

So I carried on, working on my end-of-term essay on Coleridge's *Biographia Literaria*, trying to put Alice out of my mind and concentrate on my work, taking a little time off to do some Christmas shopping. It was a lonely time in the house, as most of the others had already gone home for the holidays before the official end of term. Even Geoff had headed down to Bristol to spend Christmas with his folks. Who knew where Anton was? I was going home soon, too. A break would do me good.

Finally, the end of term came, and with it a written invitation to the funeral of Alice Victoria Poole at 1.00 p.m. on Thursday, 18 December. I looked up the village on the map and found it was just west of the Lincolnshire Wolds, off the A631.

2 December 2019

With an impish grin, Kim leaned forward and picked up the last croissant from the basket, dunked it in her coffee, took a bite and sat back.

The others all glanced at her, then at one another.

'Please, go ahead,' said Banks.

'Maybe I exaggerate,' said Kim, 'but not much. Do you mind?' She put the wooden case she had been carrying on the table and opened it. Inside were the fragments and objects that had been found attached to or close to the skeleton in its grave. She laid them out neatly on the table in front of her, each in its own transparent envelope. 'Perhaps,' she said, 'I should begin with the shoes.' She held up a twisted and gnarled object that Banks could vaguely tell might have once been a shoe. 'I'm afraid I drew a blank with the maker's name.

That's too far gone to be rescued by any means at my disposal. It's clear, however, from what remains, that this was a handmade shoe, most likely in the Italian style.'

'So our man likes posh shoes?' Banks said.

'Exactly. And posh shoes – shoes of this quality – do not come cheap.'

'How much?' Gerry asked.

'Somewhere between twelve hundred and five thousand pounds. Possibly more. It all depends on the shoemaker.'

Banks whistled. He bought his shoes at Clarks and rarely paid above fifty pounds. 'And this pair?' he asked.

'Hard to say. I know it's not apparent to the naked eye after however many years underground, but the leather is top quality and the craftsmanship top notch. I'd say, for a pair like this, you'd pay about three or four thousand, less if it's a second or third pair from your last.'

'Sorry?' said Banks. 'Your last what?'

'No. When you have a pair of bespoke shoes made, they make a last of your feet. They use this to make subsequent pairs, so the cost is a little lower and the delivery time quicker. You'll pay more for your first pair, then once the last is made, subsequent pairs will be less expensive.'

'What is the delivery time?' Gerry asked.

'Anywhere between ten weeks and a year. Again, it depends on the manufacturer, the size of the operation.'

'And how many of these shoemakers are there?'

'Far more than you'd care to hear. And it's quite possible that a pair like this was ordered online, or made directly at a small factory in Italy. And I'm afraid with what little we have left, I doubt that any particular shoemaker would be able to give you the information you want – that, I assume, being who bought them.'

'So they're a dead end,' Banks said.

'Except for the fact that they were certainly expensive,' said Kim. 'It's not every man willing to spend three or four thousand pounds on a pair of shoes.'

'Fair enough,' Banks said, with a glance at Gerry and Wilkie Collins.

'It could help us narrow down the search, sir,' Gerry said. 'At least as far as his income bracket is concerned.'

'True, we're hardly looking for someone on the dole or minimum wage,' said Banks. He turned to Kim. 'You did promise us somewhat more.'

'That's what I was coming to,' said Kim. She held up another bag with a T-shaped piece of metal and a tongue of dark, twisted material in it. 'It's this that really clinches it,' she said.

'Clinches what?' Banks asked.

'That your man was wearing a Tom Ford suit, or at least a pair of Tom Ford trousers this belt held up. It's a calfskin belt, thirty-four-inch waist, and the buckle is Ford's signature. The gold T on its side.'

'Tom Ford?' said Banks. 'I've heard the name.'

'Beyond your pay level, Superintendent. Think James Bond.'

'Wasn't that the one he wore in *Spectre*?'

'Was it? I'm no Bond aficionado. Far too macho and sexist for my taste. But I do know that Tom Ford suits are connected with Bond and that your skeleton was wearing one of them.'

'Or the trousers, at least.'

Kim held up an envelope containing two small round objects. 'If I'm not mistaken,' she said, 'these are buttons from a single-breasted jacket. The odds are that it was a part of the same suit this belt belonged to. I'm afraid there's not enough material left to analyse, just the belt buckle and the buttons.'

'You're sure?'

'About the suit?'

'Yes.'

'Unless it was a knock-off, which I think is very unlikely when we have a man we already know paid around three or four thousand pounds for a pair of shoes.'

'And how much would a suit like this one have cost him?'

Kim dipped her croissant in her coffee again and took another bite. 'Hard to say. It depends whether it was ready-to-wear, made to measure or bespoke, though as far as I know, Tom Ford doesn't produce bespoke items. But I could be wrong.'

'I know what ready-to-wear means,' said Banks, 'but what's the difference between the other two?'

'It's fairly complicated,' Kim said. 'Basically, with bespoke you get a different pattern for each suit, multiple fittings, greater fabric selection and no limit on design options, usually all in consultation with the tailor. Made to measure can be as straightforward as one session with a store employee and a limited selection of fabrics and styles.'

'So with bespoke, the sky's the limit?'

'That's about it.'

'Dare I ask the cost of all this?'

'Like the shoes, it depends on who makes it. But you can expect to pay anywhere between three and ten thousand pounds.'

'And this particular suit?'

'I can't really say. If it's a single-breasted Tom Ford, say a Shelton two-piece, maybe three or four thousand.'

'But not bespoke?'

'Unlikely.'

'So there's no point in my sending young DC Collins here down to London to ask around on Savile Row?'

'I'm not saying he didn't buy it through a Savile Row tailor, but I shouldn't think so, no. Maybe Harrods?'

'Hear that, Wilkie? But you can give them a ring. We can't spare the train fare for you to nip down to London for a visit to Harrods.'

'Pity,' said DC Collins, 'I could really do with restocking my charcuterie cupboard.'

Kim smiled. 'Well, that's about it,' she said. 'Sorry I can't be more helpful, but there really wasn't a lot to go on.'

'You've been a great help,' said Banks, with another nod towards Gerry. 'At least now we know he was a relatively slim, perhaps fit, man between fifty-five and sixty with a penchant for good quality, expensive footwear and suits, who disappeared sometime between 2012 and 2016. Maybe also a bit of a ladies' man, if the Bond connection is anything to go by.'

Kim Lee rolled her eyes in disgust.

'It really is great, Kim,' said Gerry. 'It gives us a much clearer idea of who we're looking for.'

Kim Lee gathered her samples. 'Glad to be of help,' she said. 'And thanks for the croissants.'

18 December 1980

I planned my journey so that I could stop off at the funeral on my way down to Portsmouth. It was difficult, the train service being what it is, and Lincoln not exactly being on the way from Leeds to Portsmouth, but I managed to get a morning train to Lincoln, changing at Doncaster and Newark, and took a taxi the rest of the way, expensive though it was. Though I had been to the village before, it had been dark, and Alice's father had picked me up at the station in the car. After the funeral, I planned on taking a train from Doncaster to London, where I had arranged to stay overnight with some old school friends who lived in Fulham, before going home to Portsmouth. How I would get back to Doncaster from the funeral, I had no idea. Another expensive taxi ride, no doubt. But it was all worth it. This was my last goodbye to Alice.

And so I came to be standing in a small village churchyard in deepest Lincolnshire at the appointed time, in a north-east wind I swear came directly from the Arctic Circle. Despite the cold, I found myself thinking of Gray's 'Elegy'. It seemed like that kind of place. The gravestones were covered in lichen and moss, darkened and eroded over centuries by the wind and rain. Many of the names on the tombstones had been erased by time, like the ones I remembered in St Mary's cemetery on the hilltop in Whitby when Alice and I had visited there once, not long after we first met. The wind whistled through the gaps in the low stone wall that surrounded the cemetery and offered about as much protection as the scattering of gnarled yews. I wanted a cigarette, but it didn't seem an appropriate time; besides, I probably wouldn't have been able to get one lit.

The church service hadn't lasted long before we all trooped out to the graveside. It was a family plot, where several generations of Pooles were already buried, and there was plenty of room for a few more. The stones were tasteful, though, not in the least ostentatious or grandiose, and there was only one winged angel standing atop 'Edward Laurence Poole, 1840–1928'. The same dates as Thomas Hardy, I noticed, and remembered thinking when we studied *Jude the Obscure* how much great historical change Hardy had witnessed during his eighty-seven years on earth – from the flowering of the Industrial Revolution to the First World War and its aftermath. I spotted three of Alice's university friends among the mourners, though I hadn't had a chance to talk to them so far. There were a few more young people present, and I guessed they were probably local – old school friends or even childhood ones.

The vicar, who resembled a cleric from an Anthony Trollope novel, read the words, and some people even threw handfuls of earth into the open grave after Alice's coffin had been lowered there. I hadn't been to a traditional funeral service before – both my deceased grandparents having been cremated – so it was quite an eye-opener to find things happened very much as I had been taught to expect from so many films and novels. *Dust to dust*, indeed. It was far more stirring than a cremation, and I found my mind drifting to the Alice I had known alive, excited by life and all its possibilities. Despite everything that had happened between us, I was profoundly glad that I had known her and loved her. I wasn't sentimental enough to con myself into believing she was the only girl I would ever love. I knew, or hoped, that I still had a long life ahead of me, and that I might even marry one day, and have children. But Alice would always be a part of me, as would the cruel, horrible way in which she had been torn from us all.

The wind made my eyes water, so I was glad when the ceremony came to an end. There is something about the way people walk away from a grave – slowly, stooped a little, contemplative, sad, each in their own world of memory or grief, or both.

'Nick, are you coming up to the house?' Mr Poole asked me. 'Please come. We're not far away. I'll give you a lift, if you like.' Joyce Poole stood beside him and smiled through her tears, as if to give her consent. I'm not sure she even recognised me.

I hadn't really thought where I was going to go after the funeral, I realised. All I had was a half-baked plan of finding a village pub I could walk to, ringing for a taxi and staying warm until it arrived. So I jumped at Mr Poole's offer. It would be a buffer between the funeral and the journey to London. Besides, I hadn't eaten all day, and I was very hungry, as well as freezing.

8

5 December 2019

'How exciting,' said Winsome as Banks drove down Blackpool prom past the Central Pier, the South Pier and the Pleasure Beach, closed for the season, on their left. 'I get to go to the seaside twice in two weeks.'

'I hope you didn't bother to bring your bucket and spade,' said Banks.

'Spoilsport.'

'It's December.'

'Gerry and I found a great little fish and chip in Blackpool on our way back last week, not far from here.'

'We'll see what we can do later. Pity the Illuminations have finished.'

'I've never seen Blackpool Illuminations.'

'You've missed a real treat,' said Banks.

'Why do I think you're being sarcastic?'

Banks glanced at her and grinned. 'Because I am. They used to be quite the thing, though, in Blackpool's heyday. Along with the entertainment on the piers, the Tower Ballroom and rides like the Big Dipper and the Ghost Train at the Pleasure Beach. Every summer half the north of England went to Blackpool for their summer holidays, except for Fair Fortnight, in July, when it was full of Glaswegians. It was booming with families on holiday back then, and the Illuminations extended the season.'

'Did you ever go?'

'Once,' said Banks. 'Mostly we went to Skegness or Great Yarmouth, but one year we ventured further afield. I was about twelve, just at that age when I wanted to go off exploring by myself rather than trudging around with my parents. Hang out in coffee bars. Maybe even meet a girl.'

'A girl? At twelve?'

'Why not?'

'You must have been a fast developer. Go on.'

'Not much to say. It was all right. It rained quite a lot, but you expect that on holiday. We went up the Tower, of course, and one night we saw a show on one of the piers. I remember Joe Brown, the Tornados, Johnny Kidd & the Pirates, but that's about all. I do remember I wanted to go and hear Gene Vincent and the Animals and a bunch of other bands on one of the other piers, but my parents weren't having it. And I had a fine time wandering the Golden Mile, or checking out the joke shops on the pier, buying itching powder, Dracula teeth and whoopee cushions.'

'What on earth are they?'

'You don't know what a whoopee cushion is?'

'No.'

'Well, I'll try and put it as delicately as I can. It's a small cushion that you can hide under a real one, and when someone sits on it, it makes a farting sound. Great for shocking grandparents and maiden aunts, not that I had any of the latter.'

Winsome laughed. 'I don't believe it!'

'It's true.'

'And now? Blackpool?'

'Well, I'm sure you know as well as I do that Blackpool's one of the most depressed towns in the country. And a hotbed of crime. Drugs, prostitution, you name it. No more Morecambe and Wise, Billy Fury and Tommy Cooper at the Central Pier.'

'Sad. Whoever they are.'

'Were. Blame the package holidays and cheap trips to Lanzarote, Benidorm and so on. People don't take their holidays in Britain any more.'

'Do you think the weather might have something to do with it?'

'Now *you're* being sarcastic. But yes. Back then we didn't have much choice – it was Blackpool, Morecambe, Scarborough, Bridlington, Great Yarmouth, Skegness, all the seaside resorts – but since those sunny spots down south have become more accessible and less expensive to visit, then . . . what does Blackpool have to offer?'

Beyond Squire's Gate, the landscape metamorphosed from urban to rural, and soon they were driving on Clifton Drive with the nature reserve to their left and the sea on the right. Winsome stared out over the water. At least this time the sun was shining, reflecting on the masts and hulls of ships, on the whitecaps and waves crashing on the sands.

Soon they were through the town of St Annes and past the White Church into Lytham, then Winsome pointed and Banks pulled up outside the flat where Harold Gillespie lived. Winsome heard the dog barking as they approached the door, just like the last time. They hadn't phoned ahead, as Banks had told her he wanted the element of surprise.

Gillespie opened the door, stooping to hold the dog's collar, and expressed surprise at seeing Winsome back again. Banks introduced himself and said, 'Just a few more questions, Mr Gillespie, if that's OK.'

'Yes, of course.' Gillespie stood aside and let them into the front room. A petite woman holding a leash in her hand stood in front of the empty fireplace. 'My wife, Sylvia,' said Gillespie, handing her the dog.

He still didn't look too healthy, Winsome thought. Sylvia was quite a few years younger than her husband. She had a trim figure, wore little make-up and her blonde hair hung loose over her shoulders. When she smiled, her mouth turned up more on one side than the other, giving it a twisted, almost cynical expression.

Gillespie introduced Winsome, and surprised her by remembering her name and rank. Then he turned to Banks, and the muscles of his jaw tightened when Banks mentioned that he was a superintendent.

'I am honoured,' Gillespie said. 'Have there been developments?'

'A few,' said Banks. 'That's why we wanted to talk to you again.'

'Do you need me?' Sylvia Gillespie asked. 'I was just going to take Jasper for a walk.' She stroked the Labrador as it strained to get at Winsome, who remembered the friendly though unwelcome attentions of last time and kept her distance. It wasn't that she disliked dogs, but Jasper was big and frisky, a difficult combination.

'It depends on what you know about Wilveston Farm,' said Banks.

'Nothing, I'm afraid,' said Sylvia. 'Harold and I weren't married until he'd already moved here.'

'Then I won't be needing you,' Banks said.

Winsome felt relief as Sylvia put on the lead and dragged a reluctant Jasper out of the door.

'Sylvia is my second wife,' Gillespie explained. 'Louise, my first wife, died in 2014. After a long illness, as they say. Cancer.'

'Sorry to hear that,' said Banks.

Gillespie shrugged. 'It was a long time ago. Sylvia and I have been together two years now and we've made a good life for ourselves. Please, sit down. Can I make you some tea?'

Winsome fancied something hot and wet after their drive and was pleased to hear Banks accept. Joshua seemed to be coming down with a cold, and he had been especially restless the previous night, so Winsome hadn't got much rest, even though Terry had tended to him most of the time. As a consequence, she felt tired and edgy at the same time. Fortunately for her, Banks always insisted on driving, and she had been happy to leave it all to him, relaxing in the passenger seat listening to the lovely music he was playing – Brahms clarinet sextet and sonatas, he told her – and managing to stay on just the right side of sleep until the excitement of arriving at the coast. Banks's Porsche, inherited from his brother, was definitely road worn, but it still ran smoothly.

The room felt warm and cosy, and Winsome had to make an effort to stop herself drifting off into a slumber while Banks walked around examining framed family photographs on the mantel and sideboard. Then he stopped at the picture window and studied the view for a while.

Gillespie reappeared with the tea after a few minutes, and as soon as it was served sat back in his armchair and crossed his legs. He was wearing jeans and a rust-coloured sweater. He ran his hand over his smooth bald head. 'So what can I do for you this time?' he asked.

'We've got something approaching a description of the victim now,' Winsome said. 'So, first off, we were wondering if it might be someone you recognise.'

'You still think the remains were of someone local?'

'It seems the most logical explanation,' said Banks. 'At least, we're starting out with that assumption, but we're willing to move on if it gets us nowhere.'

'So, what do you have?'

Winsome took out a typed sheet from her briefcase. She didn't need it – she could remember the image Kim Lee had pieced together – but it looked official. 'White male, fifty-five to sixty, slim, healthy and reasonably fit. We think he was wearing a Tom Ford suit and handmade leather shoes. Does any of that ring a bell?'

'I'm afraid not,' said Gillespie. 'Who is this John Ford whose suit he was wearing?'

'Tom Ford,' said Banks. 'It's the name of the designer. John Ford was a movie director. Think the sort of suits James Bond wears. Daniel Craig especially.'

'Sorry. Of course I've heard of John Ford,' Gillespie said. '*The Searchers* is one of my favourite films. I used to love westerns when I was a kid, and I must confess I still indulge on occasion. But I'm afraid I know nothing about James Bond or Daniel Craig. I simply don't pay much attention to popular culture these days. You must think me terribly ignorant.'

'Not at all,' Banks said. 'I use them merely as points of reference. The main point is that this suit and footwear were very expensive. And stylish. So we have a man who made enough money to throw it around on clothes, maybe five thousand pounds on a pair of shoes and up to ten on a suit.'

Gillespie whistled between his teeth. 'Then, no,' he said. 'I can't think of anyone I knew who could afford that kind of money on getting dressed up.'

'We don't even know if he was dressed up for anything special,' said Banks. 'It could have been his regular daily wear.'

'The answer is still no. Most of the people I knew at Wilveston were other farmers, or farm labourers, and I can assure you that none of them would consider spending that much money on a suit. Mostly we wore wellingtons, jeans and waxed jackets.'

'Hardly surprising,' Banks said. 'What about businessmen you dealt with? Buyers, hauliers and so on? The Eastvale Drainage people?'

'I'll admit that some of the office staff wore suits, but I doubt any of them earned enough to go further afield than M & S.'

'Fair enough. So you can't think of anyone you knew during those years who dressed like that?'

'None. Sorry, I can't help. What makes you think the victim was someone I knew?'

'It's just a possibility we have to investigate,' said Banks. 'You should understand that. I gather you used to be a police officer, yourself?'

Gillespie stiffened slightly and frowned. Then he glanced at Winsome. 'Yes. Why? I mean, how did you . . . ?'

'We always do a little background research into people who help us with our inquiries, as I'm sure you used to do,' Winsome said. 'It just came a little late in this case.'

'Well, yes,' Gillespie went on. 'I spent thirty years in the force and then retired. If I may say so, Superintendent Banks, you look like someone who's done his thirty and more.'

Banks smiled. 'Guilty as charged.'

'Can't get enough of it? One of those coppers who has no life outside the job? Dedicated to catching villains for as long as you live?'

'Something like that,' said Banks. 'But why did you retire? Didn't you enjoy the work?'

'I enjoyed it well enough. Most of the time. As I'm sure you know, it can sometimes be dull and sometimes too exciting. My career tended to linger on the dull side. And I did have a full life outside the job. Louise, the kids, my parents, the farm. So, in answer to your question, I left to take over Wilveston Farm. My father became ill and couldn't manage any more. I was only forty-eight, so I felt I still had a bit of life and propensity for hard work left in me yet.'

'And farming was in your blood?'

'Well, yes, it was. Or so it turned out to be.'

'Where did you serve?'

Gillespie glanced at Winsome again. She couldn't interpret his expression – perhaps a hint of betrayal, disappointment, as if it were her fault that they knew about his police past. 'I'm sure you've already researched all about my unexciting career,' he said. 'And quite frankly, I don't see how it has any relevance to the issue at hand.'

'But why didn't you tell us, Mr Gillespie?' Winsome asked. 'Why not mention it to DC Masterson and me when we first came to see you? It would only be natural, after all, something we all had in common.'

'I never thought,' said Gillespie. 'It just didn't come up. I mean, you never asked about what jobs I'd done. And it's so long ago now, almost a quarter of a century. Another life. It would be like talking about being in the Scouts when I was a lad. Well, maybe not that far back, but you know what I mean.'

'But it was your career,' Banks pointed out. 'And it could be relevant. A copper can make a lot of enemies over a thirty-year career. No doubt some of the criminals you put away would think nothing of spending ten grand on a suit.'

Gillespie snorted. 'You know as well as I do that most criminals are thick as two short planks. And I should imagine most of the ones I put away bought their clothes at Woolworths.'

'Petty criminals, true. But there are other levels. Some criminals make a lot of money. The ones at the top.'

'I didn't move among such rarefied circles. Besides, I'm sure most of them were still tasteless losers.'

'You worked at the Met for a while, I believe?'

'Yes.'

'What did you do there?'

'Various jobs. Most of the time I worked at the Yard.'

'What jobs?'

'Desk jobs, mostly. Archives, communications, monitoring. I can't really say more than that. It's classified.'

'Special Branch?'

'Well, I did sign the Official Secrets Act.'

'Counterterrorism?'

'I can't say.'

'If you told me you'd have to kill me?'

'Well, not quite . . . but . . .'

'I'll take that as a yes.'

'Take it any way you like.'

Banks leaned forward. 'I can't understand why you're being so obstructive. After all, as you said yourself, it was a quarter of a century ago.'

'Let's just say I resent your line of questioning.'

'Why is that? What have you got to hide?'

'I'm not stupid, Superintendent. By asking if I knew anyone like the person you think was buried in the field, you're implying that I might have had something to do with his being put there.'

'Did you?'

'Don't be ridiculous. But if you think I knew the person whose skeleton you found – either through my police work or through farming – then you're implying I'm somehow connected with the crime.'

'Well, you are. It was *your* land. Never mind that it was over a mile away from your actual farmhouse. But nobody's suggesting you had anything to do with the murder. Perhaps the victim was a local in dispute with someone else? Another farmer, say, who had something against you. It could even have been someone from your police past, someone who knew your land and wanted to put the blame on you, frame you, cause you problems.'

'So he buried a body on my property? Most unlikely. If that was the case, he did a poor job of it. Until now. I mean, why not at least leak a hint or two when he did it that a body had been buried there, then you could have given me a hard time back then?'

'I'm not giving you a hard time, Mr Gillespie. It's just that we have to consider these things. Surely you know that. And even if you were involved, it might have been an accident, self-defence, and you panicked and buried the body.'

'On my own property?'

'Everyone makes mistakes.'

Gillespie glanced from Banks to Winsome and back. Then he stood up. 'Interview terminated,' he said. 'I think I've been patient enough with the two of you, but I've had enough. I've told you I can't help you with your investigation, and now I must ask you to leave. I'm feeling tired. It's time for my afternoon nap.'

Banks and Winsome exchanged glances, then got up and went back to their car. They saw Sylvia Gillespie bringing Jasper back from his walk, across the swathe of grass, and she waved.

'Methinks the farmer doth protest too much,' Banks said as he drove back towards the coast road. 'Did you notice how annoyed he seemed that we'd found out he used to be a copper? I think we should have a closer look at Mr Gillespie's police record.'

'But it *is* a long time ago,' said Winsome.

'There are more deep, dark secrets in the Met, Winsome, than there are grains of sand on Blackpool beach. And over time, unlike sand, they fester, spread their corruption. If Gillespie was involved in something dodgy back then, there's no reason it shouldn't come back and bite him on the arse ten or more years later. Plenty of prison sentences are that length, for example.'

'So we're after an ex-con, maybe, someone he sent down?'

'Could be. Not necessarily, though. It's a start. I just got the feeling there's a lot Mr Gillespie didn't want to tell us, especially about his days at the Yard, and that makes me want to know what it is.'

'What do you want me to do?'

'Go through his record, these county forces he worked on. See if anything at all stands out. A name, an event, commendation, black mark, any off-the-cuff remark. Anything.'

'Will do.'

'And leave the Met to me for the time being. I have one or two ideas about that hush-hush business at the Yard.'

They passed the Pleasure Beach again, and Blackpool Tower, like a mini-Eiffel, stood not far ahead of them. 'It's getting on for tea time,' Banks said, 'so how about directions to that fish and chip shop?'

18 December 1980

As it turned out, the Poole mansion was neither quite as old nor quite as creepy as I remembered it. Set in extensive walled grounds beyond wrought-iron gates, it was a much more modern pile of light stone, with outbuildings and stables among neatly manicured lawns, flower beds carefully positioned here and there, and an imitation Italian fountain between the gravel drive and the front portico. There were probably no dim, panelled corridors lined with gilt-framed oil paintings, or candelabras that reached out to grab you as you passed by. No suits of armour with swords lurking in nooks waiting to chop off your head, either. Only in my imagination. But it *was* large.

The funeral tea, if that was what it was, had been beautifully catered. Young women in maid outfits were dashing about between the forty or so guests spread through three large, interconnecting drawing rooms, distributing drinks, vol-au-vents, sandwiches and, later, cake. In a kind of daze, I shook hands with uncles, aunts and even, I think, a grandparent. I also chatted with a few of Alice's old friends from the area, most of them attending universities across the country, and all of them shell-shocked by what had happened.

Joyce Poole was far too grief-stricken to do much but sit in a winged armchair and drink G and Ts as people lined up to pay their respects, but Reginald more than made up for her, flitting from guest to guest, a pat on the back here, gentle hand on the arm there. When he came to me, he seemed exhausted, and I saw how much of an effort he must have been putting into life without his beloved daughter all these weeks. I was very glad to discover that smoking was allowed, probably because Mr and Mrs Poole both smoked.

Later, with a second tumbler of very good whisky in one hand and my second roll-up in the other, I found myself talking to Mandy Pembroke, a physics student who had probably been Alice's closest friend at university. I hadn't seen her since the murder and had no idea how much she knew about my tattered reputation. She certainly never mentioned it, which was a tribute either to her good taste or her ignorance. Nor did she act as if she were talking to a suspected murderer. I had always liked Mandy best of Alice's friends. For a while, during our first year, she had been going out with a friend of mine, Barry Hargreaves, and we had double-dated on occasion, mostly just for pub or film nights, curries or concerts at the refectory. We had seen the Ramones, the Pretenders and UB40, among others. I hadn't seen much of Mandy during our second year, when things were beginning to get rocky for Alice and me.

'Nick,' she said, cradling a glass of white wine. 'I wasn't sure if you'd be here. How are you doing?'

'I've been better,' I said. 'You?'

'Same. It's hard. Especially given . . . you know . . . the way it happened.'

I didn't want to talk about Alice's death any more and sensed I would have to head her off at the pass. 'Still, I've got plenty of good memories. You, too, I suppose?'

'Yes, of course. I'm so glad I knew her. Though I must say . . .'

'What?'

'Last year, when the two of you were having a difficult time?'

'Yes.'

'We were in the same boat, you and me. I don't mean . . . Oh dear, I'm not expressing myself very clearly, am I? I mean that our friendship was going through a pretty rocky patch, too. Alice and me. She was getting far more political and judgemental.'

'Tell me about it.'

'I suppose we were just drifting apart – different interests, making different friends and so on. I split up with Barry, but we hadn't been that serious to start with. He was fun, though.'

'We had some good times.'

'We did. Remember the Roy Harper concert?'

'The one where he actually turned up?'

Mandy laughed, then put her hand to her mouth and glanced around, embarrassed. Nobody was looking at her. She lowered her voice. 'Yes, that one. I got so drunk that night . . .'

'I think we all did. It must have been the shock.' I hadn't noticed it before – perhaps because whenever I had met Mandy, Alice had been present too – but she was a very attractive girl. Different from Alice, of course – not quite as tall or coltish – with dark curly hair, olive skin and beautiful loam-brown eyes. She also filled out the black dress she was wearing in all the right places. I felt a sudden stab of guilt, but also of lust, and I realised it was a long time since Alice and I had last slept together, and that there had been no one else since. Perhaps there is something about funerals that brings out desire in the living.

'But I was meaning to say,' Mandy went on, 'that I saw less and less of her that year. As you know, she joined that bloody Marxist Society for a start. I mean, I'd call myself a socialist – I'm certainly not Conservative – but it all got too much for me. The proselytising, the posturing, the inflexibility. They bored me to tears. And some of those people she started hanging around with.'

'I know what you mean. I must admit it contributed to our break-up, too. Did you see much of her this year?'

'No, not a lot. To be honest, I didn't much like that new boyfriend of hers.' She touched my arm gently. 'I'm not just saying that. Honest, Nick. She changed. He changed her.'

'In what way?'

'Despite the politics, Alice had always been pretty open-minded, curious about things, enjoying life. Well, you must know.'

I remembered Alice's smile – the kind that lit up a day – and how she sometimes skipped like a child with mere joy at a new discovery or interesting thought. 'Yes,' I said. 'I do know.'

'Well, it's like she lost all that. I suppose you could say she was no fun any more. She lost her sense of humour, too. And I blame him. It was like when someone gets evangelical about religion, and there's usually some sort of charismatic figure that draws them in and leads them on, takes them away from their family and friends.'

'Mark? It certainly seems he had an influence on her, that's for sure.'

'Yes. And it wasn't just politics. He was manipulative, too. He manipulated her emotions and her thoughts. I think sometimes she even realised it, but didn't know how to rebel. There was once when I thought she was almost ready to talk to me about him – you know, a real girls' heart-to-heart – but it never happened.'

'When was this?'

'Not long before her death. A couple of days.'

'Why didn't it happen, this heart-to-heart?'

'We were in the Fenton one lunchtime. Alice had had a couple of pints, and you know she didn't like to drink too much. We were talking about the Ripper and murder and all that sort of thing and getting along well. It was only when she went on and on about the Marxist stuff that she got on my tits.'

I almost said they were very nice tits, too, but managed to stop myself in time.

'Then he came along and joined us. Mark. That put a damper on things. They left together soon after. I never saw her again. And I swear he gave me a look as they left.'

'What kind of look?'

'Mean. Nasty. A warning. A sort of stay-away-from-her look. Or maybe I'm just imagining things.'

'And you got the impression that she wasn't happy?'

'It's not that. It was just like happiness didn't matter to her any more. It was something for the bourgeoisie. There was only the struggle. It's one thing to help starving children in Africa, but quite another to dedicate your life to overthrowing capitalism.'

'For some people it's one and the same struggle. They don't believe we'll conquer famine and inequality until we get rid of capitalism.'

'I suppose that's it. But there was something on her mind. Oh, that's Jenny over there. Please excuse me. She wants to introduce me to someone. Are you staying long?'

'No. I have to get to Doncaster so I can catch a train down to London tonight.'

'Are you driving?'

'No.'

'I can't take you to London, but I can drop you off at the station in Donny, if you like.'

'You can? What about your friends?'

'We came separately. Jenny's driving Sophie back up to Leeds. I'm heading for my folks' place in Sheffield. Donny's sort of on the way.'

'That's great. I'd be very grateful.'

'OK. Just hang on. I'll come and get you when I'm ready.' She glanced at her watch. 'Half an hour or so, let's say?'

'See you then.'

I watched Mandy wander off and I next found myself talking to one of Alice's old school friends and her husband, a chartered accountant. I had another whisky, a lot more relaxed now I knew I didn't have to worry about taxis and so on. Besides, I was also intrigued to explore further what Mandy had said about Alice having something on her mind shortly before her murder.

6 December 2019

'Come on,' said Banks, sticking his head around the squad room door. 'It's Friday night. Time for a break. Over the road. My treat.' It was after six o'clock, and Gerry and Wilkie Collins had been hard at it all day. Banks waited while they shut down their files, tidied their desks and grabbed their coats. The weather had taken a nasty turn since the previous sunny day at the seaside, and a cold rain was pouring down on Eastvale. Puddles reflected the streetlights and Christmas decorations in the shop windows, and polished cobbles shone wetly as the three of them dashed across the road to the Queen's Arms on the corner of the square and Market Street.

It was that quiet time of evening between the after-work crowd, who had gone home for dinner, and the clubbers, who would arrive about nine or ten for a few pints before venturing off to the Vaults or Zoomers, which had recently opened just off the square. Even so, the Queen's Arms was almost full, with couples and groups of friends who planned on spending a Friday evening there chatting about the week, playing darts or simply enjoying a few pints. Thankfully, Cyril no longer had video games, and had never installed a large-screen TV, so the only soundtrack was his painstakingly assembled and ever-evolving playlist of sixties and seventies oldies: at the moment, Eden Kane's 'Well I Ask You'.

Banks managed to seat the three of them at a table by the window, where the general hum of end-of-the-week chatter was enough to ensure they wouldn't be overheard. 'You're both officially off duty,' he said, 'so I'll take no excuses. Gerry? Pinot Grigio?'

'That'd be lovely,' said Gerry.

'Large?'

'If you insist.'

'And Wilkie – or DC Collins, if you prefer it – Cyril keeps a good pint here.'

'I don't drink, sir,' said Collins.

'Not at all?'

'Well, not alcohol.'

'OK. What's your poison, then?'

Collins pushed back the lock of hair that had flopped over his eye. It promptly flopped back again. Banks felt like suggesting a gob of Brylcreem but he kept quiet. 'Britvic orange is fine with me, sir,' Collins said. 'No ice.'

'So it is. Anything to eat?'

They both declined.

Banks managed to edge his way through the crowd surrounding the bar and get the attention of the barmaid. He didn't recognise her and guessed she was probably new. Cyril seemed to have an endless supply, mostly young women from the Eastvale College trying to make a few extra bob to pay off their fees and loans. He got the drinks in and ordered a cheeseburger and chips for himself, since he had nothing in the fridge at home, as usual.

Banks made his way back to the table with the three drinks and managed to sit down without spilling a drop. He took a long swig of his beer before asking Gerry how they were progressing. She and Wilkie Collins had been hard at work investigating missing persons for almost a week now.

'Still no luck, sir,' said Gerry.

'Are you getting the assistance you need from outside?'

'The NCA have been great. Really helpful. It's just the numbers, and finding people to talk to.'

'Even after you've eliminated so many right off the bat?'

'Even after that. Don't get me wrong, sir. Kim's information helps a lot, but it's sometimes very difficult to get to the point of finding out what kind of suits and shoes a misper wore without asking next of kin. And even if the questions don't upset them, they certainly puzzle them.'

'I can understand that,' Banks said.

'The age group's easy to determine,' added Collins. 'And, of course, it's also easy to exclude women and children. But even with it narrowed down to men between fifty-five and sixty . . .'

'It's quite an eye-opener, too,' said Gerry.

'In what way?'

'The stories. They can get to you. Sometimes you get so you just want to start investigating everyone to find out what happened. There was one chap, right age group, went out to the shop to buy a pint of milk for their breakfast tea and cereal. The minimart was just across the street. Broad daylight. He never came back. Never even got to buy the milk. Nobody saw him or where he went. Left his wife wondering what the hell happened. They'd had no inkling of anything being wrong. No signs of depression or poor health. The marriage was strong. He was popular at work and around the neighbourhood. And that was that. Four years ago, it was. Sometimes I found myself thinking it would be better if they were dead. I know that's a terrible thing to say, but the not-knowing must be even more agonising, especially over the years. The imagination can invent far worse possibilities than anything that happens in reality.'

'Like the *Mary Celeste*,' said Banks. 'A whole ship's crew missing, and to this day nobody knows why. But surely sometimes they do turn up again? They can't all be buried in fields dotted around the country.'

'Oh, yes,' said Gerry. 'But those aren't the ones we're looking at.'

'We'll keep going, of course, sir,' said Collins. 'But it's slow, like DC Masterson says. If we get a possible through sex and age, we have to contact surviving family members or friends to find out how he dressed. The National Missing Persons Bureau can't really help us with that.'

'Sometimes we can write off possibilities by means of line of work and financial situation,' said Gerry. 'A lowly wages clerk or factory worker isn't likely to spend money on Tom Ford suits, for example, so we've only managed to find one or two people in the right income bracket, but even they've turned out to be no-goes for one reason or another.'

'I'm sure it's disheartening,' said Banks. 'But you'll have to stick at it for a while longer.' He finished his pint just as his food arrived. Only Gerry said she'd like a refill, so Banks bought her another Pinot Grigio, a small one this time, and another pint for himself. His last of the evening, though he knew he might indulge in a little wine or whisky when he got home. Drinking alone had never bothered him. Sometimes he preferred it. Johnny Keating's 'Theme From *Z Cars*' was playing as he carried the drinks back. Cyril's sense of humour.

Banks smiled to himself; he was probably the only person in the pub who knew what it was.

'I've got an idea that might help things along,' he said when he returned.

Gerry raised her glass. 'All help is appreciated.'

'You could write up a description sheet, using what we've got so far, the clothes and so on. Then we could ask . . . Oh, shit.'

'What is it, sir?' Gerry asked.

'I was going to say we could ask Ray to sketch us a likeness, to the best of his ability, but . . . Shit, it's the first time I've made the mistake of thinking he's still alive.'

Gerry touched his sleeve. 'We all miss him, sir,' she said. 'And we miss DI Cabbot, too.'

'Annie will be all right,' said Banks. 'She'll work her way through it. We can get someone else to draw one up. You know, slimmish bloke in a posh suit and shiny shoes. Pity we don't know if he had any hair or not.'

'Or what he looked like, sir,' said Collins.

'Thanks for pointing that out. But what we can do is present a figure of a kind. After all, we know his height, his waist measurement, length of leg bones, shape of his skull and so on. It should be possible to build up an image from that information, even if it doesn't have a face and hair. Talk to Drs Galway and Runcorn again, if you can find them, and see if they can give you anything more to go on. Dr Galway should know the length of his arms and legs, for example. OK, so we won't have a face or hair, but it could be enough to get us started.'

'Do we publish this sketch through the media?' Gerry asked.

Banks took a bite of his burger. 'And we also send it out to the national police forces, including the NCA. Someone might know who he was.'

'I agree, sir,' said Gerry. 'I'll get back to the—'

'It can wait until tomorrow. Finish your drink. Then take a break. Relax. Get some sleep. You both look like you could do with some. Much more of this and your eyeballs will start spinning.'

'First thing tomorrow, then,' Gerry said. 'I can get hold of a police sketch artist through HQ.'

'Ah, yes,' said Banks. 'I understand you have a contact there.'

Gerry blushed. 'No secrets around this place, are there?'

'Word gets around. You were trying to keep it a secret that you're seeing Jared Lyall?'

Gerry grinned. 'Not really, sir. We're just good friends.'

'Of course.' Banks noticed from the corner of his eye that Wilkie Collins seemed disappointed to hear of Gerry's 'good friend'.

'So we have a plan,' said Banks. 'I'll just finish this burger, then I'll give you a lift home, Gerry.'

'It's not far, sir. I can walk.' She glanced at her watch. 'Besides, it's nearly time for my cookery class at the college. If I'm not working, I can go. It's spatchcocking chickens tonight.'

'You're studying cookery?'

'Why not?'

'Why not, indeed. I look forward to tasting some of the results one day.'

'You're on, sir.'

'There's no need to walk in this rain. I'll drop you at the college. DC Collins?'

'I've got my car parked in the square, sir. Just as well, as I live in Ripon.'

Banks raised his glass and they all clinked. 'To success,' he said, then gave Gerry a sideways glance. 'And spatchcocking chickens.'

18 December 1980

It was dark by the time we set off for Doncaster. Mandy had a pale green Escort, and she drove well, as far as I could tell. Fast enough, without speeding, and with an eye on the other traffic. Fortunately, she said she enjoyed a cigarette now and then, so smoking was clearly allowed in the car. I rolled myself a cigarette. Mandy turned her nose up at my offer to roll one for her but took out a packet of twenty Benson & Hedges from the glove compartment and slid one out. She had the radio on softly. It must have been Radio 3 because they were playing classical music, a piece for string quartet so quiet and full of silences it got drowned out by the engine noise.

Before we'd got far, she asked, 'Got any gear?'

I was surprised, as I hadn't taken her for a dope smoker, but I said I had and she asked me to roll a joint.

'Will you be OK?' I asked. 'You know . . . the driving and all?'

She gave me a withering glance. 'It wouldn't be the first time. I find it actually helps.'

I'd known a few drinkers who said the same thing about a double scotch for the road, but I let that go by and rolled a joint – with some difficulty given the moving car and the darkness – and we shared it. The musical silences became more interesting.

'Remember what you said earlier about Mark?' I asked after a while.

'That I didn't like him? Didn't trust him?'

'Yes.'

'I remember.'

'Any particular reason?'

'Not really, no. Just a gut feeling. You know?'

'Did he try anything on with you, for example?'

She glanced at me sideways and smiled. 'That would hardly be unusual,' she said. 'And no real reason to dislike someone.'

'So he did?'

'Yes. Once or twice. Subtle, though. Like it could have been accidental, the way his shoulder brushed against my tits. And before you ask, no, I didn't reciprocate and he didn't get anywhere. Alice and I may have been on the outs to some extent, but she was still my best friend, and I wasn't going to sleep with her boyfriend.'

'But you did fancy him?'

'He was attractive enough, and he could be charming. Maybe under different circumstances . . . But . . . well, no, not really. I told you there was something about him that put me off. There was something sort of hollow and just *off* about him.'

'What do you mean?'

'It's hard to describe. You know sometimes when the mouth movements don't match the speaking on TV or at the movies? Out of sync? Sort of like that, but emotional rather than physical.'

'As if he was lying or pretending?'

'Not quite that, but that's the sort of direction. Impersonation. I suppose, to be blunt, I thought there was something fake about him.'

'His political beliefs?'

'No. I didn't pay much attention to them. I'm sure he believed in the revolution and all that. No, I mean, as a person, in himself. Like I said, it's hard to describe.' She paused a moment then gave me another sideways glance. 'I'm not so superficial that I'd sleep with someone just because he was attractive and smooth-talking.'

'But what was it about him that made you think that? Something he said, or did?'

'Like I said, just a gut feeling.' She took a hit on the joint, passed it to me, and held the smoke a while before letting it out slowly. 'Though there was one time . . .'

'What happened?'

'Nothing, really. I just saw him somewhere he shouldn't have been.'

'What do you mean?'

The headlights coming at us sometimes seemed too close, and made dazzling patterns on my eyeballs. I hoped Mandy wasn't experiencing the same distortion. It wasn't particularly strong hash, but we all have different thresholds.

'He'd told Alice he was heading down to London for the weekend,' she said. 'She had a major project due, so she couldn't afford the time to go with him. I was with some other friends, and we decided to go drinking in town rather than around the university, for a change. You get tired of the same old pubs.'

'I know. So what happened?'

'I can't remember what pub we were in. It wasn't anywhere I'd been before.'

'Where was it?'

'I can't really remember. We'd been to a few by then and I was probably a bit pissed. But I think it was down past the station, under the dark arches. Holbeck, somewhere, I suppose.'

'OK. What happened there?'

'The place was full and noisy, but it definitely wasn't a student pub, if you know what I mean. Mostly grumpy old Yorkshiremen slurping their Tetley's and complaining about the younger generation or something or other, and a noisy group of young lads watching football on the telly.'

'Mark was there?'

'Yes. I'm sure he didn't see me. As you can imagine, we didn't stay long, and it was a big place, really crowded. The football lads got too friendly, so we left.'

'What was Mark doing?'

'He was sitting at a table in the far corner, opposite a bloke I didn't recognise.'

'Not a student, then, or member of the Marxist Society?'

'I don't think so. I mean, of course I don't know every student, and I certainly don't know the members of the Marxist Society or Socialist Workers Party, but I hadn't seen him before. Besides, he was older, and a bit rough-looking.'

'How much older?'

'Thirties, I'd guess. And he was . . . well, you know, not the kind of bloke I'd like to find behind me walking home late at night. I know that's a superficial judgement, but even so.'

'Sadly, I think in these times you're more than allowed to make such a judgement about any man walking behind you late at night.'

'Right. Well, that's it, really. As I say, I'm pretty sure Mark didn't see me. We were at the other end of the room and there were lots of tables between us. I only got a glimpse of them every now and then when someone got up to go to the bar or move to another table. Besides, they were deep in conversation. I didn't even see Mark look up, let alone check the place out. Not that it would have mattered. Not to me, at any rate. Thing is, I suppose I thought it might matter to him. Maybe he didn't want to be seen with this bloke. And he was supposed to be in London.'

'Did you tell Alice?'

'No. It's not as if he was with another woman or anything. And he might have been intending to set off down south later that night.'

'What if he was a pouf and this was his boyfriend?'

'Mark? I don't think so. Besides, they didn't give off that kind of vibe.'

'You said this other bloke was rough-looking. Can you describe him?'

'I don't have a clear picture, but he was sort of burly.'

'Fat?'

'No. Just burly. Muscular, I guess. No neck. Shirtsleeves rolled up, a tattoo on one arm. Too far away to see what it was.'

'I get the picture.'

'And he had a sort of skinhead cut, though he didn't look like a skinhead, if you know what I mean. But as I said, he was no oil painting.'

'I understand.' I was definitely intrigued. I knew that Mark pursued strong political interests – and perhaps this was someone he had come into contact with through them – but even so, why the clandestine meeting? And what did he have in common with this thuggish neo-skinhead Mandy had described? Communism attracted all kinds, and there were no doubt plenty who joined looking for trouble. Maybe this was someone from one of those splinter groups who wanted violent revolution NOW. I realised I would probably never find out, but I filed it away with all the other details in my mind about Mark. I was building up quite a dossier on him by now. And a fat lot of good it was doing me.

It turned out that Doncaster was more of a diversion than I had imagined, and we soon found ourselves inching along the outskirts in heavy traffic. Council estates, rows of derelict slums, streets lined with rundown shops and dangerous pubs.

'Don't worry,' Mandy said. 'I know my way about this part of the country. I can hook up with the M18 after I've dropped you off. Be home in a jiffy.'

'If you say so. I'm very grateful.'

She glanced sideways at me. 'Think nothing of it. And thanks for the joint.'

As I got out with the small overnight bag I'd brought, Mandy leaned over and said, 'It was nice spending time with you again, Nick. I never did believe any of those people who told me they thought you murdered Alice. I hope I'll see you again next term.'

'You will,' I said, flabbergasted at her comment. 'You certainly will.'

And I shut the door and watched her rear lights disappear into the traffic flow, then I took a deep breath and headed into the busy station.

6 December 2019

The rain had stopped by half past nine, when Banks was relaxing in the conservatory sipping a glass of Languedoc. He had been listening to the heavy rain spattering against his windows for an hour or so by then, and noticed the slow journey towards silence. When he had first got home, he had fully intended to make a start on sorting out Ray's LP collection but quickly decided it could wait until tomorrow. He had nothing special planned for Saturday. Instead, he made a quick phone call to DCS Burgess, leaving a brief message on his mobile, then settled into his favourite wicker chair to listen to the rain and watch the runnels run down the windows, without thinking about anything much. The case was progressing at its own rate. The world was still a mess. The people he loved seemed safe and happy. His son was working at a recording studio in London and his daughter was teaching History part-time at Northumbria University. He had given up worrying about his future. It would be what it would be.

And it was into this zen-like contemplation of nothing that his phone played its blues riff going on for ten o'clock. Banks recognised the number he had dialled earlier.

'You called, O master,' said Burgess.

'I did,' said Banks. 'Where were you?'

'Having a drink with an old friend.'

'Where are you now?'

'Back in my room. Let me see . . . I think it's a Premier Inn. Southend-on-Sea, for my sins.'

'What on earth are you doing there?'

'Highly secret government inquiry business.'

'I can see they spare no expense for their operatives.'

'It's not as cheap as the Travelodge.'

'That's good to know.'

'So what can I do for you, Banksy?'

'I need some information and I think you might be just the man to get it.'

'Flattery will get you a broken nose.'

'Seriously.'

'Why me?'

'You still have contacts at the Met, I assume, at the Yard and so on?'

'Quite a few, yes. My work takes me there now and then.'

'I'm looking for background information on a copper who worked there from 1975 to 1981.'

'That's going back a bit.'

'Can you help?'

'Depends. What department did he work in? Or departments.'

'That's the problem. I don't know what he did there. Winsome was digging around, but she got stonewalled. Classified.'

'Sounds like the Branch.'

'What I thought.'

'I can try,' said Burgess. 'No promises. They can be tight as a gnat's arse when they want to be. What's this bloke's name?'

'Gillespie. Harold Gillespie. If it helps, he joined the force in 1964, North Riding Constabulary, as it was then.'

'Your neck of the woods.'

'Indeed. After that, he worked out of Dorset and Bournemouth from 1970, as a DS, mostly in Traffic. When he got promoted to DI, he moved to the Met, and when he left there, he transferred to Cumbria.'

Burgess whistled. 'That's a long way from London. The boonies. I wonder what he was running away from?'

'Me, too. Or being moved away from. He was on Traffic for a while. Made superintendent quite soon after, too.'

'Traffic *and* a promotion. That definitely reeks. How does he figure in your case?'

'He retired after he'd done his thirty, in 1994, and went to work the family farm up here near Eastvale until just over two years ago, March 2017. A CPO forced him out to make way for highway and retail development.'

'A new shopping centre, eh? Just what we need.'

'He's the man who owned the land where our skeleton was dug up.'

'And you think he might have had something to do with it?'

'I don't know. I just want to know a bit more about him, that's all. And when I hear something is classified, it always increases my curiosity.'

'You know what that did, I suppose? He'd hardly be likely to bury a body on his own land, would he, even if he didn't know it was going to be dug up? And surely when he found out, he would have had a chance to move it before the mechanical diggers moved in.'

'So I've been telling myself,' said Banks. 'But I'd still like to know more about his background, what he actually did.'

'OK,' said Burgess. 'Leave it with me. I'll see what I can do.'

'Thanks. When will you know?'

'I'm off home for the rest of the weekend tomorrow afternoon. Then I'm in the London office Monday and Tuesday.

After that, I'm not sure. I'll see what I can unearth while I'm down there and give you a call, say, midweek.'

'Excellent. And thanks a lot. Enjoy a good night's sleep.'

Banks heard Burgess's barking laugh as he switched off the mobile. He went into the kitchen and poured another Languedoc then went back to the conservatory and played John McLaughlin's *After the Rain*, which seemed the ideal choice now the rain had stopped.

9

On Saturday morning, Banks spent some time reading his
Seamus Heaney collection and came across a poem that fascinated him called 'The Tollund Man'. There was another poem
on a similar subject, 'The Grauballe Man', which he also read
several times. Then he spent some time online googling the
'bog people', as these remarkably preserved Iron Age bodies
found in peat bogs were known. He found some stunning, and
gruesome, photographs and read some amazing stories. In
some cases, their stomach contents could be analysed. Some
had been murdered: the Grauballe Man's throat had been cut;
there was still a leather noose around the Tollund Man's neck;
the Roum Girl had been decapitated; and then there was the
poor Windeby Girl, only fourteen years old, who had been
drowned in about twenty inches of water. Most of these were
around 2,000 years old. Grace Hutchinson probably knew all
about them. If only he could have got as much trace evidence
from the more recent skeleton in the field, he might have been
able to identify the victim by now. Around noon, Banks turned
off his computer and went into the entertainment room.

Liam, Banks's carpenter friend from the Queen's Arms,
had done a magnificent job on the bookcases. Ideally, Banks
would have liked mahogany, koa or walnut, but they turned
out to be too expensive. Pine was another option, but Liam
said it was too soft for the heavy load of LPs. The last thing
Banks wanted was a sagging shelf. He also hadn't wanted the

unit to be too high because he needed to be able to reach each level without stretching. In the end, he went for four 72-inch-long oak shelves, each fourteen inches apart to accommodate the twelve-inch LPs comfortably, with housed shelf ends and two supports – one at twenty-four inches and the other at forty-eight – for extra strength.

It still cost a small fortune, but they looked spectacular and fitted in well with the room's overall, warm glow. Liam had also arranged a series of tiny lights under each shelf, which were useful not only for identifying titles, but also added aesthetic value.

Now, Banks thought on Saturday afternoon, it was time to get them stocked. The LPs lay spread out in piles over the floor, just as he had carried them from Noel's van the previous Sunday. Zelda's stuff, including Ray's sketches and paintings of her, were upstairs in his spare room. He would deal with them later. He also still had the preliminary sketches of Gerry, which he had forgotten to take in for her.

Banks was no frustrated librarian, but he liked some sort of order to his books and records. Alphabetical usually worked fine, though he also divided his books into fiction and non-fiction and lumped all the genres in together. As far as he was concerned, fiction was fiction, and either good or bad, no matter whether it was a detective novel, horror or classic.

With the records, he had formed a similar plan. He would separate pop and rock from jazz and blues, and should there be any classical in Ray's collection, which he doubted, he would mix them with the few he already owned. A good ninety per cent of the new shelf space, however, would be taken up by pop and rock.

And so he began. Ray had kept his collection mostly in alphabetical order by band or performer's last name, and Banks had tried not to mix them up during transport, so it wasn't too difficult to find batches ready-made for the shelf, from Aardvark, an almost forgotten organ-heavy prog rock band from the late sixties, to early ZZ Top. Compilations were a problem. Ray had owned quite a few of those, especially the excellent Island Records ones: *Bumpers, Nice Enough to Eat* and *You Can All Join In,* which still had its 14/6 price sticker on – a real bargain in those days, when LPs generally cost 32/6. They could come in their own row after 'Z', alphabetised by title. Banks picked out *Bumpers,* a double album with a bright yellow cover and a gigantic pair of orange and yellow trainers – or 'bumpers' – on it and put the disc on. Traffic opened the album with 'Every Mother's Son'. Music while he worked.

By the time Quintessence were belting out 'Jesus, Buddha, Moses, Gauranga' (no Mohammed, Banks noticed) he was up to the 'J's and only going so slowly because every now and then he would take out an album and scan its cover art and track listings, indulging in a lot of nostalgia – Dr Strangely Strange, Foghat, Blue Cheer. By five o'clock, when it was dark, he decided it was time for a glass of wine, so he helped himself. Mostly he sat on the floor as he continued to sort the albums, standing to place them on the shelves. After *Bumpers* he put on *Nice Enough to Eat,* which opened with Fairport Convention's 'Cajun Woman' and zipped along through the usual Island roster – Mott the Hoople, Spooky Tooth, Jethro Tull, Free – until it ended with Heavy Jelly's 'I Keep Singing That Same Old Song'.

He was surprised to discover a number of spoken-word LPs among the collection, including Basil Bunting reading 'Briggflatts', Allen Ginsberg's 'Howl', Ezra Pound reading some 'Cantos', T.S. Eliot's *Four Quartets* and *The Incredible New Liverpool Scene,* with Adrian Henri and Roger McGough. They would get a small section of their own.

Apart from the music, it had been a quiet afternoon so far. No phone calls or visitors. He had picked up a pork pie and salad from the local farm shop for dinner, and later he would probably wander down to the Dog and Gun in Helmthorpe to listen to some folk music. He was up to Tyrannosaurus Rex (Ray had no 'T. Rex') when his mobile went off. He could see it was Gerry's number.

'Sorry it took me so long,' she said, 'but I had a devil of a time getting hold of the sketch artist. Apparently, he plays rugby for the Eastvale HQ team on a Saturday, and they were away to Skipton.'

'No problem,' said Banks. 'What about our two doctors?'

'Dr Galway was in her office at the infirmary. I got Dr Runcorn at home, but he didn't have a great deal to add. It's done, and I wondered if you wanted to see it before I send it out?'

'Sure,' said Banks. 'Can you do it now?'

'I can send the file.'

'Just let me get my desktop fired up,' Banks said. 'I have a hard time seeing anything clearly on this mobile screen.'

Banks walked through to the little study at the front of the cottage and got the Mac booted up and running. When Gerry's email came through with the attachment, he was able to click on it and open it. The drawing was excellent, Banks thought. He had expected something resembling a stick figure or a skeleton in a posh suit, but instead he got a slim man, with arms a little too long and an oval face, though featureless skull, standing in a charcoal-grey Tom Ford suit, like some images he had seen of Daniel Craig online. Perhaps the artist had used those poses as a guide.

'Excellent,' he said. 'I hope you told him he did a great job.'

'We'll have to see about that, won't we, sir,' said Gerry. 'I mean, whether it gets results. But I thanked him profusely.'

'Good.' Banks scanned through the description and saw nothing he wanted to change.

'Wilkie wrote it up,' said Gerry. 'Credit where credit's due, he's very succinct.'

'So I see. Anything new on the mispers search?'

'No, sir,' said Gerry. 'We did have a possible, a fifty-nine-year-old bank manager from Stockport, who went missing five years ago on holiday in Australia.'

'Promising,' said Banks.

'Not really. He never returned to the UK, as far as immigration records show.'

'Pity. Maybe he got bitten by a funnel spider or got lost in the outback or something.'

'Whatever happened, no body's ever turned up.'

'It's getting late. Are you heading for home?'

'Already there, sir. I just wanted to play about with the circular on my own desktop. As a matter of fact, Jared and I are off to see *Knives Out* at the Swainsdale Centre tonight.'

'Enjoy. I've heard it's very good.'

'Well, it does have Daniel Craig playing the detective, sir.'

4 January 1981

When I walked out of Leeds City station after a long and frustrating day of train travel back from Portsmouth – note to self, never travel on a Sunday if you can help it – I was sure I could sense something in the air. And it wasn't only the rain. Perhaps it was the relief of arrival, of being back on what had become my home ground after a boring two weeks of being polite to distant relatives and walking the streets of Portsmouth alone whenever I could get out of the house. Whatever it was, it persisted as I finally boarded a number one bus on Bishopgate and set off.

I went upstairs, took the vacant front seat and rolled a cigarette. It was dark outside, and the city lights were blurred and smudged through the rain-streaked bus windows as we crossed City Square, then the Headrow on our way to Wood-house Lane and home. There were only a few other people upstairs and the conversations I could hear were hushed. But there seemed a sense of excitement in the air, just as I had felt on leaving the station.

When I got to the house and walked up the front steps, I noticed that Geoff's light was on in the ground-floor bay window. One of the basement lights was on, too – Maria's, I thought, not Anton's – but no one else appeared to be back yet. I could hear the low chattering of Geoff's TV as I checked my post on the table by the door, finding nothing of interest either for me or for Alice, then I walked up the stairs to my own first-floor bedsit, turned my key in the door and switched on the light.

Nothing had changed, except the room seemed to have grown colder in my absence. Before even taking off my new leather jacket – a Christmas present from Mum and Dad – I shoved a coin in the meter and turned on the gas fire. It would take a while, but eventually the chill would vanish from the air. I dumped my bag on the bed, turned off the bright overhead light and lit a shaded lamp and a couple of candle stubs, then sat in the armchair closest to the fire. All I wanted, for a short while at least, was peace and quiet, the sound of the gas fire hissing, rain on the window, the occasional creak as ancient beams warmed up, and the odd car passing by the corner with Hyde Park Road, splashing through roadside puddles. After I'd smoked a cigarette and warmed up a little, I put the kettle on for a cup of instant coffee.

Over the holidays, I had picked up a couple of albums with money kindly donated for Christmas by various uncles and grandparents – the Specials' latest, and a second-hand copy of David Bowie's *The Man Who Sold the World*. I put the Bowie on first.

I had also bought Anthony Burgess's *Earthly Powers* with my uncle Vernon's annual book token, and I was hooked from the remarkable opening sentence. I'd been reading it on the train and was about halfway through, so I decided to read until I started to feel tired. I would probably have an early night.

I had hardly got through the first page when I heard footsteps on the stairs and a knock on my door. I hadn't heard the front door, so I assumed it must be Geoff. Or maybe it was Maria deciding to come down off her pedestal and offer her gorgeous body to me at last.

It was Geoff.

'Welcome back, mate,' he said. 'I heard you come in. You've got to come down and see this. You won't believe it. Come on. Hurry up.'

He seemed excited, so I followed him down the stairs and into his room.

The television showed a group of men in suits, almost immediately recognisable as cops, even if you hadn't seen their faces splashed over the TV and newspapers for the last few years. It was the Ripper Squad, and one of them – Ronald Gregory, the chief constable, I think – was saying how delighted they were, how *really* delighted. It took a while to sink in, and a bit of explanation by the presenter, but it appeared they had caught the Yorkshire Ripper at last. At least, they had a man in custody they believed was him, and they obviously believed it enough that they were starting their party already. I didn't catch all the details, but it seemed they had caught him by chance after a couple of patrol officers approached a car parked suspiciously somewhere near Sheffield's red-light district.

'Can you believe it?' Geoff said, reaching for a bottle of Glenfiddich. 'Christmas present,' he explained, then poured two generous glasses, holding his up in the air. 'This calls for a toast.'

11 December 2019

The early part of the week passed uneventfully. Gerry and Wilkie Collins worked at trying to put a name to the skeleton, but to no avail. Leads materialised, then went up in smoke. The closest they came to a breakthrough was on Tuesday morning, when Gerry found that a man the right age went missing from Carlisle around the right time. She drove out there to talk to his surviving family – wife and daughter – only to find out that the man was definitely not the kind to wear 'posh' clothes and had been wearing old corduroy trousers and a blue and white Carlisle United kit shirt when he disappeared during a summer beer festival. Despite this, Gerry added his name to the several others already on the list for possible follow-up, failing all else. After all, someone could have killed him and changed his clothes, unlikely as it seemed.

On the Wednesday lunchtime, Banks nursed his pint in a country inn on the southern edge of the Forest of Bowland, not far from Chipping. On a brighter day he might have taken the scenic route through the Dales National Park, but it was a gloomy December day with intermittent showers, some of them quite heavy. The M62 had been tough going and the M6 not much better, but when he turned off at Preston and drove into the more rural landscape of Grimsargh and Longridge, then into the rolling hills of the forest proper, the traffic thinned dramatically and even the rain eased off.

The location had been the choice of Dirty Dick Burgess, who said he was in the area on business connected with the undercover operations inquiry. Banks found the place easily enough and got there early. According to the certificates on the whitewash and brick walls, the place had won awards for both its beer and its food. The beer was Marston's Pedigree – not too shabby. The menu certainly looked promising, with such items as seared mackerel, French black pudding and roasted king scallops for starters, and pressed, salted pork belly and ballotine of rabbit loin for mains. The prices were commensurate with the names of the dishes.

Apart from a couple of locals chatting at the bar and one elderly couple in the window seat already enjoying their lunch, the place was almost empty on that grey and chilly Wednesday, the day before the general election. It already seemed obvious who would win, and Banks didn't like him. As he waited for Burgess, he tried to think of a prime minister he *had* liked and found it tough going. He got as far back as wondering if anyone had ever really *liked* Harold Wilson or Ted Heath before the door opened and Burgess blustered in. He rubbed his hands together before sitting down and casting a critical eye over the empty lounge, the horse brasses, local landscapes, large fireplace and polished bar rail.

'Don't blame me,' he said. 'One of the lads recommended this place. Used to live not far away. Gargrave, I think.'

'It'll do fine,' said Banks. 'But why here?'

'Bloke I need to talk to. Retired DCI. Lives in Preston.'

'What an exciting life you lead.'

'What can I say? Fast lane all the way. I'll have a pint of lager, by the way. Foster's if they've got it.'

Banks went to the bar, where the bored young man leaned, reading through Twitter feeds on his mobile. He poured the pint then went back to his mobile.

'So where are they putting you up in Preston?' Banks asked when he had sat down.

'Bloody Premier Inn again. It's not so bad, I suppose. Clean. Quiet enough. Nice view of the Poundstretcher and Aldi through the window. It's not as bad as the place I had in Glasgow, a Best Western, if memory serves me well. The view from there was a huge brick wall topped with barbed wire, and beyond it, an abandoned factory with broken windows and no roof. It was like something out of a Cold War landscape.'

Banks laughed. 'As I said, an exciting life.'

Burgess glanced through the menu then announced that he wasn't really hungry so he'd just have the fillet beef burger with blue cheese, beef dripping chips and a chutney, goat's cheese, pea and shallot salad. Banks went for the fisherman's platter.

After he had put in the order, Banks sat down and held up his glass. 'Cheers.'

'Cheers. Voting tomorrow?'

'Nah,' said Banks. 'I probably won't bother. Not much point up where I live. It's a modern version of the "rotten borough". You could parachute in a Hitler, Stalin or Putin, and he'd still get all the votes as long as he wore a blue rosette on his lapel.'

'Methinks you're having me on.'

'Like most things, it's not without a grain of truth,' Banks said. 'You?'

Burgess sighed and scratched his head. 'Well, I think Comrade Corbyn and his lot should be locked up, for a start. But . . . look, Banksy, you've known me a long time. I've always voted Conservative. We've argued about it often enough. I was a keen supporter of Mrs Thatcher. Still far and away the best leader we had in my lifetime, as far as I'm concerned. She had vision, integrity, charisma. But this bloke? What the fuck? The hard hat, high-vis jacket and lab coat, three-word slogans. Is it some sort of a joke?'

'Sadly, I don't think so,' said Banks. 'You know, it's probably the first time I've ever agreed with you on politics. You must be getting soft in your old age. There was a time when you'd have thought his negative qualities made him exactly the right man for the job.'

'Maybe. But there are limits.' Burgess put his index finger to the side of his nose. 'And believe me, I know a thing or two. I lived in London while he was mayor, don't forget. I know where the bodies are buried.'

'Do tell?'

'Maybe someday, when I've had enough to drink. But for now, I've got some of the information you asked for.'

'Some?'

'There are gaps. Plenty. It's hardly surprising, though. Back then, there were more crooks at the Met than you'd find at a shepherds' convention.'

'Then?'

'Fair enough. It hasn't changed that much. But your man did work for the Branch, and he did leave under a cloud. People remember him.'

'This cloud? What was it?'

'Don't know. I couldn't find anyone who admitted to knowing or remembering the specifics. Something to do with an op that went wrong. There was no written evidence in the files. At least not the ones I could gain access to. There are more, of course, hidden away somewhere. Like the Stasi, Special Branch believed in leaving plenty of written evidence of its actions and misdeeds, but it keeps it under stricter security.'

'So how do you manage your inquiry?'

Burgess snorted. 'With difficulty. There's some word of mouth – we depend a lot on whistle-blowers – a few top-secret files we've unearthed, lists of agents and so on. But it's all partial, like doing a thousand-piece jigsaw puzzle of a sunset. And we're understaffed. And with false identities and so on, it's often hard to find out who the original agents were.

I mean, the names they were born with and so on. They all had fabricated identities. Sometimes more than one.'

'There must be some records. When they joined the force, for example?'

'Believe me,' said Burgess, 'we get our hands on everything we can. That's why I'm particularly interested in your case.'

'I'm not even sure I have one yet. No whistle-blowers on Gillespie?'

'Not so far. But I'm thinking he may be something we can tackle at a later point if we can dig up enough.'

'What makes you think that?'

'When you told me Gillespie went from the Branch to work Traffic in Cumbria, then got a promotion, I realised something must have gone wrong, that the wheels must have come off.'

'But come off what?'

'That we don't know. Don't despair, though, Banksy. It's not all bad news. In fact, far from it.'

At that point a young woman came out of the kitchen door carrying a full tray and deposited their full plates on the table. She asked if there was anything else they wanted, but neither did, so she said, 'Enjoy your meals' and walked off. Burgess watched her go.

'Not bad,' he said. 'I wouldn't kick her out of bed, at any rate.'

'Oh, grow up,' said Banks.

'You're no fun.'

Banks looked at his plate and saw an attractive arrangement of seafood, from scallops and prawns to cod and salmon and a little mound of crab meat. 'OK,' he said. 'How about the good stuff?'

Burgess washed down a mouthful of burger then said, 'First off, I found out that Gillespie was indeed working for the Branch around that time. In fact, he was working for the SDS.'

'The Special Demonstration Squad? Isn't that your area of interest?'

'Yes. The Undercover Policing Inquiry. Know much about the SDS?'

'No. Only what we talked about last time we met up, and what I've read in the papers. All that stuff about undercover officers forming relationships with women in the groups they were assigned to penetrate.'

'Unfortunate choice of words there, but that's basically it. And sometimes the women who were duped come forward and tell us their stories. That's given us some of our best leads so far. It all started with a chance discovery. Woman on holiday in Italy with her boyfriend is searching for her sunglasses in the glove compartment, when she finds a passport with her boyfriend's photo next to a different name. Then she finds a mobile with emails from two children, calling her boyfriend "Daddy".'

'Oops,' said Banks. 'Somebody wasn't being very careful.'

'Indeed. The balls-up that started it all. Pin your ears back for a lecture. The SDS was formed in 1968, under the command of Special Branch, with the approval of the Wilson government. A Labour government, note. It started out as a very small unit, only about ten agents for the first few years. Affectionately known as "the hairies" because most of them grew long hair and beards to fit in. They were pretty much a law unto themselves. It was a clandestine operation, too, known only to a few officers in the upper echelons of the Yard. A "black op", you might say. Basically, their brief was to monitor subversive groups by joining them, living among them, to gather information on any individual or group likely to cause problems for the state.'

'So it was political from the outset?'

'Yes. Don't forget the late sixties and early seventies were a hotbed of left-wing terrorism. It's easy to forget these days, with ISIS and Al-Qaeda and your right-wing thugs, but you had your Baader-Meinhofs, your Red Brigade, your Black Panthers, your Weathermen, even your IRA.'

'And these were the organisations the SDS penetrated?'

'Well, not exactly. It wasn't as easy as that. They tended to start out with softer targets – marginal groups like ban the bombers, the make-love-not-war crowd, squatters, free festivals, student societies, the Young Liberals, animal rights, that sort of thing.'

'Generally fairly harmless people who simply wanted a better world.'

Burgess grinned. 'Good to see you haven't lost your sense of humour, Banksy. As far as the Branch was concerned, these were only terrorists in the making. And even later, in the eighties, when your man Gillespie was involved, we had the Militant Tendency, Red Action and Trotskyites infiltrating the Labour party. The work these officers did was seen as necessary to the security of the nation.'

'Who were these men?'

'They were coppers, like you and me. And I'd assume most of them thought they were doing a worthwhile job, helping preserve order. As I suppose you did when you did your undercover spell targeting drug dealers.'

Banks speared a scallop. 'That was different,' he said. 'The ones I was after were scum, and I wasn't targeting them because of their political beliefs. Did these SDS agents all use assumed identities?'

'Yup. Handed in their warrant cards and were given fake passports, driving licences and bank accounts. Often, they'd use the identity of a dead child. They got that idea from *The Day of the Jackal*. It was a pretty complicated process. You'd have to find an identity at St Catherine's House, the registry back then, someone born around the same time as you who died in childhood. Then you'd familiarise yourself with their lives, their families, where they lived. Some officers would even visit the graves of the children whose identities they'd taken. Just to get a feel for it, like.'

'And these operatives had carte blanche?'

'Well, they weren't supposed to commit crimes any more than the next person.'

'In reality?'

'Some had to. In order to maintain their cover, for example.'

'You mean like shooting a traitor to prove you were a genuine gang member?'

'I wouldn't go that far. I'm sure murder was frowned upon, but a touch of burglary or arson never went amiss. Of course, you'd report it to your handler immediately and get retrospective authorisation.'

'Any records of this?'

'They were called the "green files". Code 588. But don't get your hopes up. These are top secret, access denied. As a matter of fact, the impression I got, asking around, was that they'd been destroyed, or "damaged in the move from one building to another". Same thing. As have most records pertaining to the early SDS.'

'So there's nothing left on Gillespie?'

'Not much, no. Certainly not written down. No records of the operations he ran, agents' names, true or invented. And believe it or not, I don't have the magic touch that makes Special Branch want to open up their archives to me at the drop of a hat, even if they existed. Despite the fact that I worked for them on occasion, and I'm officially on the inquiry team.'

'What, then?'

Burgess scratched his temple and took another bite of his burger before answering. 'Well, as you know, I've been around a few years, worked for dozens of different branches, squads and so on.'

'I know.'

'Which means I've got a lot of contacts, some of them now retired and far enough away from the Job to not worry too much about what they let slip.'

'And.'

'Old pal of mine, who shall remain nameless. He worked for the Branch briefly in 1982, just after Gillespie's time there. He wasn't SDS, by the way, but he was one of the few who was in on the secret.'

'A whistle-blower?'

'Not exactly. At least not a very loud and tuneful one.'

'Do tell.'

'When I brought Gillespie's name up, he went quiet for a moment. I asked him what was up, and he just said he'd heard rumours, that's all, if it was the same bloke. The name rang a bell. Someone who'd made enough of a balls-up to have to pull in a few favours and then move on.'

'Gillespie?'

'So he believes.'

'What was the balls-up?'

'He didn't know. Or said he didn't. I believe him. It was a long time ago, and his memory's suffered from years of alcohol abuse. I mean, if you remembered every bit of titillating gossip you heard in your life, there wouldn't be much room left for anything else in your brain, would there, especially if it was already like a Swiss cheese?'

Banks tasted some of the crab meat. It was good. 'Point taken,' he said. 'Did he know anything at all except that this balls-up occurred and that it involved Gillespie?'

'He knew Gillespie was a handler, not an agent.'

'That's a start.'

'And there was a name, only he wasn't sure of the context.'

'What name?'

'A girl's name. Alice Poole. Mean anything to you?'

Banks thought for a moment, then said, 'No. Never heard of her before. Who was she? What did she do?'

'Sorry, that's all I could get out of him. He said he remembered it because her last name was the same as his daughter-in-law's: Poole. Gillespie's downfall had something to do with this Alice Poole. Whether he assaulted her or what, I don't know. All I know is that she figures in this. Another mate told me they didn't employ any women in the SDS, so she can't have been an agent herself. I'd guess . . .'

'What?'

'Well, you know why we're having this inquiry, don't you? What we talked about earlier.'

'Yes. Because a number of undercover agents formed sexual relationships with the women they were spying on. In some cases, even got them pregnant, promised marriage when they already had a wife and kids of their own, then simply disappeared. Either way, they caused the women a great deal of lasting emotional distress.'

'I see you've been reading your *Guardian*,' said Burgess. 'But you're right. Well, it's a start, isn't it? Last time I looked, Alice was a woman's name.'

5 January 1981

Monday swept by in a whirlwind of information and rumour. First, we were told the Ripper's name – Peter Sutcliffe – that he was a thirty-five-year-old lorry driver, that he was married and lived with his wife Sonia in a suburb of Bradford. Photos of the house appeared in that morning's *Daily Mirror*. The two coppers who had arrested Sutcliffe were interviewed. Apparently, they had become suspicious about a parked car and approached it, finding Sutcliffe with a prostitute inside. His answers to their questions had sounded evasive and unlikely. He had also nipped into some nearby bushes to urinate, or so he had said.

Every crime, however minor, involving a man close to a red-light district had to be communicated to the Ripper Incident Room back in Leeds. The Sheffield police had duly done this on Saturday, and after two long days of interrogation, Sutcliffe apparently confessed. The Sheffield police also revisited the scene and found that he had hidden a knife and a hammer when he nipped out of sight 'to urinate'.

Trainloads of journalists rode up to Yorkshire from London to feast on the carnage, all pursuing interviews with Sutcliffe's wife and surviving victims, offering small fortunes for their stories. Chequebook journalism was back with a vengeance, if it had ever been away. There was so much coverage and scrambling for stories that newspaper editors were warned about preserving Sutcliffe's right to a fair trial. Even *The Times* complained that the police shouldn't have held their press conference so soon. They didn't actually *say* they had caught the Ripper, but they didn't have to. I'd watched the broadcast, and it was pretty obvious what they were all ABSOLUTELY DELIGHTED about. Not that the public cared much about all that. They just wanted to know the grisly details and be reassured that the reign of terror was over.

A large angry crowd gathered outside the court, Dewsbury's Victorian Gothic town hall, late on Monday afternoon as Geoff and I watched on TV. Over two thousand people jostled outside the building, shouting death threats when the police van passed by, many holding up banners demanding that Sutcliffe be hanged, others crying that hanging was too good for him. Gangs of skinheads held up homemade nooses. Inside the courtroom, Sutcliffe was charged with the murder of Jacqueline Hill and the theft of two car number plates worth 50p. Some of this I found out from newspapers, some from radio and some from TV.

On Monday night, Geoff and I, along with Anton, who had got back that afternoon and seemed over his John Lennon mourning period, went up to the Hyde Park and had far too much to drink. Everyone was in a celebratory mood, with strangers shaking hands and patting each other on the back; even Jill and her friends gave me a warmer welcome than I'd had in some time, though there was no hint of invitation or flirtation with Jill the way there had been before. I guess at least they all knew by now that I wasn't the Ripper, though perhaps they still harboured a suspicion that I *had* killed Alice.

12 December 2019

Banks sat in DI Ken Blackstone's small cubicle in the modern white concrete and glass Leeds District Police Headquarters nursing a mug of black coffee and gazing out on Elland Road, Leeds United's football stadium, as he tried to explain the situation.

'Alice Poole isn't a terribly common name,' he said. 'And from the information we had, we knew we were looking for someone – probably a young woman – in late 1980 or perhaps early 1981. DCs Gerry Masterson and Wilkie Collins worked out the parameters and spent a day trawling through the various databases and came up with one strong possibility: a newspaper article in the *Yorkshire Evening Post* dated 30 November 1980. An Alice Poole, age twenty, was found murdered in Burley Park, Leeds, on 28 November 1980, at the height of the Yorkshire Ripper's renewed reign of terror. In fact, Jacqueline Hill, a Leeds University student, had fallen victim to Sutcliffe around ten days earlier, and the writer of the newspaper article raised the possibility that this was yet another Ripper victim.'

'And after that?'

'They must have realised pretty quickly that they'd got it wrong, because no more articles on the subject appeared. And the name never appeared in any later pieces or investigations regarding Sutcliffe's victims. Gerry checked thoroughly.'

'So you're assuming the Ripper Squad found forensic evidence or something like that to scupper the theory that she was one of his victims?'

'Something like that, yes.'

'OK,' said Blackstone. 'But I still don't see what this has to do with your case. The skeleton.'

'It's precarious, I admit,' said Banks. 'But it's the only lead we've got so far. The land on which the skeleton – our murder victim – was found belonged to a Harold Gillespie until a CPO forced him out in March 2017. We're pretty sure the body was buried before then. Before he retired to run the family farm, Gillespie was on the force, and back in the late seventies, he worked for a spell as a handler for the SDS, the Special Demonstration Squad, among other things—'

'That lot under investigation at the moment?'

'The very same. They were run by Special Branch, so, according to my contact, getting information out of them is like getting blood out of a stone.'

'This Gillespie never worked for West Yorkshire, did he?'

'Not as far as we know, and Winsome has checked out his career.'

'How is the lovely DS Jackman?'

'Happily married with a new baby and friendly Jack Russell.'

'Do give her my best. But what does all this skeleton business have to do with a murder victim from nearly forty years ago called Alice Poole?'

'I don't know. That's the problem. All I can find out is that when someone remembered Gillespie, he seemed to associate the name with some kind of cock-up, and Gillespie being quietly shoved out to work Traffic in Cumbria. The only other thing he remembered hearing around that time was a girl's name, Alice Poole. He remembered it because it was the same last name as his daughter-in-law: Poole.'

'But he's no idea who she was, what part she played? He didn't remember the context?'

'Not as far as I know. If there was, indeed, a context given. And I trust my source to have done his best on that score.'

Blackstone glanced out of the window and seemed to be turning things over in his mind. 'Well, it was well before my time,' he said, 'and we don't have computerised records going that far back.'

'Paper?'

Blackstone grimaced. 'Dodgy.'

'Don't tell me, lost in the move from Millgarth?'

'Not quite. But there was a fire a few years ago, destroyed a part of our old archives.' He stood up. 'I'm afraid we'll have to start where we did last time we had a case stretching far back in time.'

'Wakefield?'

'The West Yorkshire Archive Service. But it's not in Wakefield any more. They moved. The archive's in Leeds now. Gildersome, as a matter of fact. Much closer.' He glanced at his watch. 'Come on, I'll drive you. It's about a ten-minute drive, depending on the traffic.'

They got there in seven. The archive was housed in the three-storey, flat-roofed red-brick building of Yorkshire

Joint Services. Blackstone negotiated their way past reception to the archive area, where they presented their warrant cards and were shown to the requisite storage shelves, where a matronly woman with the name tag 'Marcia' sat them at a table and went off with the request form Blackstone had filled in.

'I remember last time you told me you had your eye on one of the archivists,' Banks said. 'That doesn't happen to be her, does it?'

'No. That didn't work out. Turned out she was on the verge of getting engaged. Story of my life.'

Banks laughed. Marcia came back carrying a large, bound volume, the police occurrence book for late 1980. Banks flipped through the pages until he got to the entry he was looking for. A woman named Frances Lee had called in to report finding a girl's body in Burley Park at 7.14 a.m. on 28 November 1980, while out walking her dog. A little later, there was another entry indicating that patrol officers had visited the scene and confirmed the woman's original statement. And because it was an occurrence book and not the murder file or a police notebook, that was about it. Banks checked, but there were no further references beyond the identification of the deceased as Alice Victoria Poole, according to her student union card, found in her shoulder bag in the bushes near the body. A file had been opened and an investigation begun.

'Sure there's no chance of the original files?' Banks asked.

'I'll check, but don't get your hopes up. Your best bet now is to see if either of the investigating officers is still alive and have a word, if possible. One of them might remember something. I can help you check human resources to find out where they are now.'

'Thanks, Ken.' Banks copied down the names of the investigating officers: a DI Stuart Glassco and a DC Christopher Marley.

'Why don't you head off and do a bit of shopping while you're in the big city?' Blackstone said. 'I think HMV is still open, though not for much longer. There's a new branch in the St John's Centre, too. And, of course, Waterstones is still with us. We can meet up later at our usual curry restaurant, and I'll try to have some information on Glassco and Marley, and maybe even Alice Poole.'

'Is it still there, too? The cafe. Same place?'

'Yes.'

'OK,' Banks said. 'Six-thirty all right?'

'Want to stay over tonight? I've still got that spare room.'

'Sounds tempting, but I'd better get back. There's a lot going on at the moment.'

'Fair enough,' said Blackstone. 'I'll drop you off in town and head back to Elland Road. You can pick up your car after dinner.'

28 January 1981

By the time the new term began on Wednesday, Sutcliffe was on remand in Armley Jail, not much more than a hefty stone's throw from the university. By then it was hard to separate speculation from truth, rumour from fact. There was plenty of jubilation around the university, but lectures continued as usual. I was more than well aware that this was my penultimate term, and that it would end with my finals, after which I would be loosed upon the world to make a living, honest or otherwise. We had a lot to cover that term, even though the poetry course only went up as far as Hardy and the novels stopped at *Sons and Lovers*. In addition, I had my special options, courses on Coleridge and Shakespearean Tragedy, along with an introduction to American Literature that took in such figures as Poe, Melville and Hawthorne, so there was quite a lot of reading, *Moby Dick* not being the least of it.

Now that Geoff had made his television available to me again on occasion, I was able to watch the last couple of episodes of *To Serve Them All My Days*, which ended as sadly as I knew it would, and then we got into a crazy, hilarious sci-fi series called *The Hitchhiker's Guide to the Galaxy* and a good adaptation of Malcolm Bradbury's *The History Man*. But I spent a lot of my time reading, determined to cut down on the booze and dope and go to see only the bands I *really* wanted to see, which that term would include the Cure, Elvis Costello and Iggy Pop. Despite my workload, I still tried to have a life. Anton was busy studying, too, and we spent fewer evenings together, though I always looked forward to chatting with him about what he'd been reading, and listening to Sun Ra or Alice Coltrane over joints and wine.

Mandy and I saw quite a lot of each other, too, and it wasn't long before we were sleeping together on a regular basis, at either my place or hers. We found that despite the differences in our degree pursuits, we had plenty in common when it came to music and movies. And sex. We regularly attended the university film society, enjoying special seasons of Bergman, Truffaut and Kurosawa (thankfully, there was no Jean-Luc Godard) – and to indulge our baser instincts, we sought out as many horror films as we could.

But I studied hard, and despite the welcome distraction of Mandy, I often thought about Alice. I had heard nothing more from the police, of course, and didn't expect to. I tried once more to get in touch with them after Sutcliffe had been caught, but my message remained unanswered.

12 December 2019

Their usual curry house had bead curtains, sitar music and the scents of cumin, coriander, garlic and ginger wafting through the air. It was as full that night as it had been every other time Banks and Blackstone had eaten there, mostly with students and the occasional professor from the nearby university. Blackstone never had trouble finding them a table, though. They ordered pakoras and samosas to start, then saag gosht, aloo gobi and plenty of naans, along with two pints of lager. Banks would allow himself just the one drink, as he was planning on picking up his car at Elland Road and driving back home to Gratly after dinner. The buzz of conversation ebbed and flowed around them along with the kitchen smells. When their drinks arrived, Blackstone and Banks clinked glasses and each took a gulp.

'We're not very far from where Alice Poole's body was found nearly forty years ago,' Blackstone said, sliding a couple of file folders across the table to Banks, who put them in his briefcase to read later at home.

'Burley Park, wasn't it?'

'That's right. In some bushes off Park View Road.'

'Was she walking home?'

'No idea,' said Blackstone. 'I drew a blank on the Alice Poole case.'

'You found nothing?'

'Nada. Zilch.'

'Isn't that odd?'

'In a way. But it's also very easy for things to get lost over forty years.'

'Even the record of a whole murder investigation?'

'Even that. I'm hoping Christopher Marley will be able to tell you more.'

'He's still around?'

'Yes. He was the DC on the case. His boss, DI Stuart Glassco, died five years ago. Of course, he was long retired by then. Marley's still a relatively youthful sixty-five by all accounts. Lives with his wife in a semi in a little village a few miles north of Harewood, on the Harrogate Road. Outskirts of Harrogate, really. Been retired since 2005.'

'Still a DC?'

'No. Marley made it as far as DI. And Glassco was a detective superintendent when he died.'

'No black marks?'

'Not as far as I could tell from a cursory glance at the personnel files. Back in those days, though, you could get away with . . .'

'Murder?'

'Maybe not quite that, though I'm sure it happened on occasion. No, I mean they might have beaten a confession out of a suspect. That sort of thing.'

The pakoras and samosas turned up, and both men diverted their attention to the food in front of them, dipping each piece in a pungent tamarind sauce then eating.

'Anyway,' Blackstone went on, after quenching the food's heat with a long draught of lager, 'I talked to Chris Marley on the phone and he said he'd be happy to talk to you. Like a lot of retired coppers, I got the impression he's starved of job talk. Said he'll be at home all day tomorrow.'

'I'll pay him a visit,' said Banks. 'I'd like to see how some of these bits and pieces start to add up, if they do. Any connection between Marley or Glassco and Gillespie?'

'If there is, it's not apparent. They never worked out of the same station, or even on the same county force at the same time. Doesn't mean they didn't meet up at a course or a convention or something, but . . .'

'It doesn't mean they did, either.'

'Right. But if Gillespie was somehow connected with the Alice Poole murder when he was working for the Branch, and Marley and Glassco handled it up at this end, their paths might have crossed then. I'll ask around.'

'Anything else?'

'Not really,' said Blackstone. 'There are a lot of gaps in the records from back then, as you no doubt know. Moves, fires, sticky fingers eager to make certain things disappear. It may be harder these days with all the computer technology, backups, passwords and so on, but it still happens. Things get lost.'

'Sounds like one of those laws of nature,' said Banks, then moved his plate away to make way for the main courses. Blackstone ordered a half pint of lager, but Banks went for water. It would be dark when he drove home and there was a chance of patchy ice here and there. Before starting the main, he checked his mobile again to see if any messages had slipped through while he wasn't paying attention, but there was nothing. A quiet day back up at the station, then. He had been hoping for a break in the identification of the skeleton, but Gerry or Winsome would most certainly have let him know immediately if there had been any hint of that. He put his phone away and spooned out portions of saag gosht and aloo gobi on to his plate, picking up a naan almost too hot to hold to eat it with.

As they ate the meal, their talk moved to mutual friends, the election, unworkable government directives and eventually away from work to music. Blackstone was a fan of female jazz singers and was extolling the virtues of Stacey Kent and Cécile McLorin Salvant, both of whom he had discovered only recently. Banks was impressed. He was still stuck on Billie Holiday and Julie London. When it came time for dessert, Blackstone couldn't resist the lassi, but Banks wasn't a fan of Indian sweets, so he plumped for a black coffee, and after that they drifted towards Blackstone's car, parked just around the corner, and set off for Elland Road.

10

13 December 2019

Refreshed after a fairly early night following a single glass of Côtes du Rhone and Billie Holiday's *Lady in Autumn*, Banks was in his office bright and early on Friday morning, listening to *Today* over a cup of strong black coffee and a croissant from the bakery across the square, as he dealt with the previous day's paperwork. Quickly tired and depressed by the boring work and the interminable discussion of the election results, which had turned out as he had expected, he turned the station to Radio 3, which was promising Vaughan Williams's Fifth Symphony, a far more enjoyable alternative.

This case was proving particularly difficult, more so because they didn't even have a handle on the identity of the victim yet. Gerry and Wilkie Collins were just about getting to the end of their tether, and Winsome was fast running out of places to dig for more information on Gillespie. Drs Galway and Runcorn had given their all; Stefan Nowak and his crime scene investigators had done all they could. What more was there?

And so the morning went on until, when Banks was thinking he might as well head out for his chat with retired DC Christopher Marley, Gerry came bursting into his office, waving a sheet of paper, Wilkie Collins in her wake.

'I think we've got him!' she said, dropping the paper on the desk.

'Calm down, Gerry,' said Banks. 'Let's take it slowly. What exactly have we got?'

But Gerry was quivering with excitement. Clearly all those days of no progress had built up to this, and she couldn't contain herself. 'The victim's identity. I think we've got it! And it explains why he never turned up in all our missing persons searches.'

'Let me put some coffee on,' Banks said, 'and we can all sit around that little table over there and talk about it. OK?'

Gerry nodded. Her face was flushed and her eyes a little wild, but she did as Banks suggested and sat down, knees together, arms folded, quivering and clearly anxious to get on. But Banks took his time. He set the coffee machine going and took a couple more mugs from the little cupboard beneath it, then sat. Wilkie Collins seemed more composed than Gerry, though there was a definite flush of excitement on his school-boyish features, too.

'OK, Gerry,' said Banks, sitting opposite her. 'Give.'

Gerry took a deep breath, tucked errant strands of ginger hair behind her ears and leaned forward. 'You know I sent out that sketch the police artist did the other day?'

'Yes.'

'I made sure it went out nationwide. I must say, I didn't expect too much, given it was just a sketch of a skeleton in a fancy suit, but something just came through from South York-shire Police. I got a phone call from a DI Dobson in Sheffield saying he thought he might be able to tell us something about our man and that I should come and talk to him.'

'He didn't tell you anything more?'

'I got the impression that he didn't want to say too much over the phone.'

'Curiouser and curiouser. What did you say?'

'That I'd be happy to pay him a visit as soon as it was convenient.'

'And?'

'Now, sir. I mean as soon as we can get there.'

'Excellent. But he gave you no idea whatsoever over the phone about who it might be?'

'None. And we'd already been through South Yorkshire's missing persons reports for the period in question with a fine-tooth comb. Nothing stood out. Not even a nibble.'

'Off the books, then.'

'Sounds like it, sir.'

'No wonder DI Dobson didn't want to discuss it over the phone. Tread carefully.'

The coffee machine came to the end of its cycle and Banks served both Gerry and Wilkie Collins with mugs then sat down again. 'What do you make of it, DC Collins?' he asked.

'Me, sir?' Collins swallowed and gave Gerry a nervous glance. 'Well, I wasn't on the phone call, sir, but the impression I get is that we're in with a good chance here. Obviously, someone slipped through the cracks, whether he was reported missing incorrectly – I mean, his age or something else that would put him outside our search parameters.'

'Or he wasn't reported missing at all?'

'There is that possibility, sir.'

'Right,' said Banks, standing up. 'Gerry, you and Winsome go talk to this DI Dobson. Find out all you can. I'm afraid you'll have to keep an eye on the shop, DC Collins, as I also have an appointment.'

Collins looked downcast.

'Don't worry, lad, your chance will come,' said Banks. 'They serve who only blah blah blah.'

'Yes, sir.'

But Collins didn't seem much more cheerful as he followed Gerry out of the office. Banks stood by the window and stared down on the market square, where a gentle rain had been falling all morning. Delivery vans came and went, shoppers crossed the cobbled square under umbrellas, and somewhere, in some nearby attic, someone was practising the drums. A group of carollers gathered outside the church and started singing 'Once in Royal David's City'. It reminded Banks of his childhood.

Banks finished his coffee, put the mug on his desk, then grabbed his raincoat and went out. Time for a quick bite to eat before driving down to Harrogate to talk to retired DC Christopher Marley.

April 1981

In the lead-up to the trial, there were all sorts of rumours flying around, many of a most fantastical nature – that Sutcliffe was really an alien, that he was a member of an obscure Satanic cult, that he and his wife had carried out the murders together, or that he was a werewolf or a Jekyll and Hyde figure who went through a physical transformation before he killed. None of this, however, seemed to take into account those of his victims who had survived and who recognised him.

But nowhere in all these rumours was Alice ever mentioned. I kept my eye on the press coverage for any developments, but though lists of the names of more of his victims appeared, Alice's name was never among them. Nor was there even the slightest rumour of her inclusion in all the reports I read. Some argued that the list Sutcliffe gave was complete, others that he kept some names back – that he had committed a number of unsolved murders and assaults – but Alice's name never appeared among these speculations, either, and no evidence supporting this theory ever materialised. If Sutcliffe *had* killed Alice, why hadn't he said so?

There was also much argument over chequebook journalism and the outrageous sums of money being paid to Sutcliffe family members. Some commentators argued that the prospect of so much money might make a witness exaggerate or otherwise embellish upon the way things had really happened. But still it went on. People took the money and told their stories.

I was pretty much certain by then that Alice hadn't been one of Sutcliffe's victims, and that the police had known this all along, because of certain peculiarities in the crimes that hadn't been present in the case of Alice. He had favoured a hammer and screwdriver, for example, and Alice had been strangled, I now knew. And there were no doubt other details they hadn't revealed to the public. I still had my suspicions about Mark – especially after talking to Lucy and Mandy – though sometimes I even found myself believing that the police must have known he couldn't have done it, either, because they lacked forensic evidence, or their evidence pointed elsewhere. Only they didn't know where. And they weren't going to tell me.

So Alice's murder remained unsolved. But just because they hadn't put all the pieces together didn't mean that it couldn't be done. Just because they hadn't gathered enough forensic evidence, that didn't mean the evidence didn't exist somewhere, if only someone were to make an effort and search for it.

In the end, I had to accept that Alice had not been murdered by Peter Sutcliffe. Mark Woodcroft still remained on top of my suspect list. And of Mark Woodcroft there had been not a sign.

13 December 2019

A short distance north of Lord Harewood's stately spread, and some distance off the main Harrogate Road, was the village where Chris Marley and his wife had moved after his retirement. Though the word village often invokes images of duck ponds, thatched cottages and cosy inns, this place had little of that in evidence. True, there was a Victorian hall, mostly used for local council meetings, and an old church – thirteenth century, perhaps – with a squat tower and weathervane, but the rest of the village was definitely mid to late twentieth century, even the pub, a dull, square brick building unimaginatively called the Farmer's Inn. Several streets of red-brick houses, semis or terraces with gardens and hedges, for the most part, ran off a handkerchief-sized village green with one broken bench under its spreading sycamore. The place resembled a sixties council estate far more than it did Cranford, though Banks guessed there would be a few outlying detached mansions and estates not far beyond its borders.

Still, as a place to retire to, it certainly wasn't without charm. Banks found the Marley house near the end of one of these streets. It was a smart semi with a well-trimmed lawn and small garden behind the hedge. The garden was no doubt wonderful in spring and summer, but in December there were only hints remaining as to its former glories. But Banks had enough imagination and had seen enough gardens over the various seasons to know that what he was looking at was a source of great pride. He must remember to mention it to Mrs Marley, or Marley himself, if he turned out to be the gardener. The ornate nameplate fixed to the gate identified the house as CAMELOT.

Banks walked up the stone path and rang the doorbell, which played a snatch of 'Colonel Bogey' just to take one by surprise. In seconds, a sixtyish woman with grey hair and a ruddy complexion opened the door, said she guessed he must be Superintendent Banks and asked him in.

After hanging his raincoat up in the hall, Mrs Marley led him through to the living room, where a two-bar electric fire glowed red and fake coals flickered. It was way too hot, but it clearly suited the Marleys, as she was wearing a yellow cardigan and he a blue pullover. After Banks shook hands with Christopher Marley, he sat in the armchair Mrs Marley directed him to and said yes to the cup of tea she immediately offered.

Marley was a youngish sixty-five, though only a few vestiges of his red hair clung to his scalp. He had virtually no eyebrows and his freckled face was unlined apart from the edges of his mouth and his eyes. He was lean and fit enough, and when he stood up, he stood straight, as if the old training had made its mark. He was wearing slippers, but Banks imagined his shoes would be polished so much he could see his reflection in them. Old police habit. His wife was about six inches shorter than he was and a little plumper, but she also had that youthful glow about her features. Country living? Or was it just that the older Banks got, the younger everyone else looked?

'Good drive?' Marley asked, his voice slightly higher pitched than Banks would have expected.

'Easy enough,' Banks said.

'You came down from Eastvale, is that right?'

'Yes.'

'Lovely part of the world. That's where Olive and I wanted to move when I retired, you know. The Dales. Our dream place.'

'Why didn't you?'

'Prices. Couldn't afford it.'

'True enough, it's expensive if you don't luck into something.'

'Is that what you did?'

'Yes. Typical old Dales cottage, a bit run-down. Not much to look at from the outside. The owner was keen to sell up and go live with her sister in Tadcaster. She hated the idea of holiday cottages, and as soon as I convinced her I intended to live there for ever, she let me have it for about half what she could have got. I told her I thought her price was low, not wanting her to feel I was pulling a fast one, but she was adamant. She knew what it was worth, she said, and she knew what she wanted for it. I was the right person for the place.'

'So what was the problem with it?'

'It's haunted.'

'Really?'

'Well, not so as you'd notice most of the time, but there is a sort of presence, yes. That's about the only way I can describe it. Quite benevolent.'

Marley shook his head slowly, as if he took ghosts in his stride. 'Some luck. A friendly ghost. Whereabouts is it? Eastvale itself?'

'No, it's up the Dale. Little village called Gratly. Up the hill from Helmthorpe.'

'I know that area,' Marley said. 'Olive and I used to go for walks around there. Tetchley Fell, right?'

'That's the one.'

'And the Roman road.'

'Yes.'

'Well, I never.'

When Olive Marley came back in with the tray, her husband told her what Banks had said, and she oohed and aahed.

'Still, it's pretty nice around here, don't you think?' Banks said. 'And your garden's lovely.'

Olive blushed. So *she* was the gardener. Modest, too.

'Oh, yes, don't get me wrong,' Chris Marley said. 'We love it here, don't we, Olive? But the Dales . . .'

Banks glanced out of the window. It wasn't much of a view in the December drizzle, just rolling fields of dark brown earth and clumps of trees here and there, the odd farmhouse, smoke twisting from its chimney. But in spring and summer, he thought, it would be quite lovely, with all the green of the grass dotted with wildflowers, and perhaps a field or two of bright yellow rapeseed, the trees in blossom and leaf. Then in autumn the leaves would turn and fall. Beyond the dark fields spread a broad patch of sky, grey now, but no doubt pretty in good weather, when it would be blue, with perhaps a few fluffy clouds dotted about. The window faced west, so the sunsets would probably be spectacular, too. All in all, not bad for a retired copper.

Marley rubbed his hands together. 'Well, we'd better get down to brass tacks, Mr Banks. Never keep a busy copper waiting, that's what I used to say. It all seems so long ago now.'

'You weren't tempted to stay on over your thirty?'

'No. To be honest, I'd had enough by then. Not that the job didn't have its moments.' He glanced at his wife. 'But Olive here went through a serious illness, so it made sense for me to retire when I could, and care for her.'

'I hope all's well now, Mrs Marley,' Banks said.

'Oh yes. Yes. Fine, thank you. Fit as a fiddle. Anyway, I'd better get out of the way and let you boys talk shop.' She touched her husband's shoulder. 'I'll be in the sewing room if you need me, Chris.'

'Righty-ho, love.'

Banks felt moved by the obvious love between the two of them. And perhaps a little jealous. He had no one in his life who felt that way about him. Or vice versa. They spent holidays in Spain and Portugal, by the looks of the dolls and tiles. Golf trophies stood in a cabinet, framed family photographs on the sideboard and sentimental knick-knacks and prints ornamented the nooks and crannies and walls of the room. The Marleys seemed happy in one another's company, and how many couples could truly say that these days?

'Yes,' said Banks after a sip of tea. 'I'm anxious to talk with you about the Alice Poole case, if you remember it.'

'Oh, I remember it well enough,' said Marley. 'Actually, it was my first murder. You don't forget that in a hurry, you know.'

'You certainly don't,' said Banks, who remembered the naked, mutilated body of a prostitute abandoned in a Soho alley who had become his first murder case. 'Your first dead body, too?'

Marley nodded and swallowed. 'I can still see the poor lass sometimes, when I close my eyes, just as she was, lying there in the rain, pale as . . . white as snow.'

'Had the body been interfered with in any way?'

'Sexually, you mean?'

'Anything.'

'No, not as far as I could see. She was fully clothed, the sort of things you'd expect a student would wear for that weather – black jeans, a light blue puffer jacket, ankle boots. And the pathologist later confirmed there had been no recent sexual activity, consensual or otherwise.' Marley paused. 'What is it that interests you about Alice Poole, after all this time, if I may ask?'

'Do you know, I'm not really sure. The name came up in an unexpected context, that's all, and ever since then, I've been trying to fit it in with the other fragments I've got, but its place has eluded me so far.'

'Yes. That makes sense. It was a strange case. Hardly a case at all.'

'Why was that?'

Marley glanced around the room as if making sure his wife wasn't hiding behind the sofa, then said, 'I don't know about you, but this tea tastes insipid. Would you care for something a bit stronger?'

Banks knew he should probably refuse, but he wanted Marley to feel at ease with him, which wouldn't be the case if he didn't join him in what was apparently going to be an illicit drink.

'Well, if you insist,' he said. 'But just a wee one because I'm driving.'

Marley nipped across the room, opened a walnut cabinet and poured two tumblers of Black Bush. 'Don't need ice, do you?'

'No,' said Banks. 'As it comes is fine.'

'Good man.' Marley handed him the drink, sat down again and took a sip. 'Ah, nectar,' he said. 'It's not that Mrs Marley doesn't approve, you understand, but just that it's probably a bit early in the day as far as she's concerned. But you have to make exceptions for company, I say. It's not every day I get a visit from a colleague.'

'I understand.' Banks held up his glass. 'Sláinte.'

'Sláinte,' said Marley.

'Now, Alice Poole. What time of day was it? Do you remember?'

'Early morning. Around eight. Just after first light. Well, it was probably about nine when we actually got there. First on the scene were the Ripper Squad detectives, of course. You've no idea how insane things were down at Millgarth back then.

The Ripper Squad, the murder room. Do you know they had so many file cards and written statements they had to have the floor reinforced?'

'Were you a part of the squad?'

'No. Not officially. We were all seconded whenever necessary. I took a few statements after the Jacqueline Hill murder, for example. And this was just after that. A week or ten days. So we were all on tenterhooks. It was a terrible business. I know we got a lot of flak over the years for not taking the Ripper seriously enough when he was just attacking prostitutes, and maybe there's some truth in it. I'm not proud to say so, but maybe there is. Still, when it's a young student with her whole life ahead of her, it somehow strikes people different, doesn't it? I'm not saying it should – a human life is a human life – just that it does. Just think how many people in the city at that time could imagine it happening to their own daughters. They wouldn't see it that way if it was a prostitute in Chapeltown, would they?'

'Probably not,' Banks said. He was well aware of the criticisms, the macho culture of the police, the bad crime-scene jokes and sexist, misogynist attitudes. They had been prevalent enough at the Met during his days there, and occasionally raised their ugly head in North Yorkshire, too. Easy enough when the victim was a hard-bitten prostitute, perhaps, but not so much when she was a sweet little student.

'Anyway,' Marley went on, 'so there we were, standing in the freezing rain at nine in the morning, the poor girl at our feet. The scenes-of-crime officers were already at work and it soon became clear to them that she had been killed elsewhere and then dumped. The Ripper didn't usually move the bodies. And she'd been strangled. He didn't usually do that, either. Of course, there could be any number of reasons for a change in MO – the hunt for him heating up, for one thing – but on the whole, the detectives from the Ripper Squad dismissed the idea that it was his work and buggered off sharpish. DI Glassco and I got the case.'

'What was your first move?'

'Well, the team searching the general area found the girl's backpack dumped in some bushes about twenty feet away. There wasn't much in it – just a couple of university textbooks, notebook, pens, tampons, cigarettes, hairbrush, keys, cosmetics, plastic lighter and so on. What you'd expect. But she also had her student union card, and a letter from her parents with her address on it, along with theirs, and that was a great help. We informed the local police in Lincolnshire – that's where she came from – to get in touch with the parents and have them come up as soon as possible to identify the body – then we, that's DI Glassco and me, went to her address, a big old Victorian student house, divided into bedsits, on Kensington Terrace, just opposite Hyde Park. She actually had the top flat, a one bedroom, which probably cost more than the bedsits. We found out later that her mates called it the "Penthouse". Joking, like. It wasn't that palatial. As far as we could tell, her rooms hadn't been disturbed in any way. There were no signs of a struggle and nothing to indicate any motive for an attack. Wherever she had been killed, it most likely wasn't in her flat.'

'What about suspects?'

'None so far. We talked to the other students in the house, and one of them turned out to be an ex-boyfriend of the victim. That's always an interesting avenue to pursue – exes in general – so we probably went at him a bit harder than the others. Nothing out of order, you understand, just rigorous questioning.'

'Good cop, bad cop?'

'That sort of thing was pretty popular back then.'

'Do you remember his name?'

'Nick something. I'm sorry but I can't remember his sur-name. He was an English student. You can probably get it from the university records if you need it.'

'It might come in useful,' said Banks, making a note. 'And she was twenty years old?'

'Yes, just twenty. She was in her final year.'

'So the odds are that Nick would have been about the same age, also in his final year?'

'Makes sense. She'd have been unlikely to go out with someone in a year below her.'

'And Nick became a suspect?'

'Sort of. Yes. I suppose. He was obviously upset about split-ting up with her, and apparently she ran off with another bloke. This Nick told us that the last time he saw her was the night she was killed, and that she was on her way over to the new boyfriend's. I can't remember his name, but he lived on St John's Terrace. Across the park. Nick thought they were heading to London the following morning to attend a demo – she was political, like – but Alice obviously never made it.'

'And the new boyfriend?'

'Gone. Not a whiff. Disappeared into thin air. That was one of the strange things about the case.'

'Did you question his neighbours and check out his flat?'

'We were going to, but the super told us a couple of special-ists had already been sent up from the Yard, and they'd done all that and come up with nothing.'

'Didn't this seem strange to you? I know Scotland Yard send their experts to the provinces in books and movies, but it rarely happens in real life these days. Even in the eighties, I shouldn't think.'

'No, it wasn't common. And it did seem strange.'

'Did anyone explain why?'

'Not to me. But remember, Mr Banks, I was a lowly DC. Who'd bother explaining to me?'

'Who were these specialists?'

'No idea. Never saw them, never met them. They came and went pretty quickly the day the body was discovered, and the boyfriend was pretty much out of play after that.'

'So what happened next?'

'We brought the ex-boyfriend, Nick, into the station for more formal questioning, but it became pretty obvious quite soon that he didn't do it. For a start, he didn't have a car. Couldn't even drive. And there was no way anyone could have carried the girl's body all the way to Burley Park.'

'Did you ever find out exactly where she was killed?'

'No, we never did. While we had this Nick in the station, the Ripper Squad took an interest again and sent one of their lads down to observe.'

'They thought Nick might actually be the Yorkshire Ripper?'

'You have to understand, Mr Banks, we were all desperate to catch him by then. The whole community, the women especially, were living in terror. The team was coming in for a lot of grief and anger from all over the place.'

'So they were desperate enough to consider this Nick?'

'For a while, yes. But it didn't last long. The bloke who sat in with DI Glassco just shook his head and walked out, so I heard. For a start, Nick was way too young to have committed any of the Ripper's earlier murders. In fact, he was a school-boy in Portsmouth at the time of the earliest. Also, as I said, he didn't own a car and couldn't drive, and we know the Ripper drove to various red-light districts around the north to find his victims. In fact, they were even suspicions that he was a van or lorry driver of some sort.'

'Which, indeed, he was,' said Banks.

'So it turned out. They dismissed Nick, and so did we. I did hear he turned up at the station a few days after we'd interviewed him. Wanted to see us. But we were off the case then. We heard from the desk sergeant that he had a postcard he said was from Alice Poole's boyfriend, posted from Paris, shortly after she was killed.'

'What did it say?'

'I never found out. It sort of disappeared in the internal mail system somewhere.'

'Interesting.'

'Like I said, it was a strange case altogether. Mark. That's it. That was his name. The new boyfriend. Mark. I remember now because I thought at the time how it was sort of similar to Nick. You know, a nick and a mark? I do a lot of crossword puzzles.'

'Right,' said Banks. 'Do you know Mark's surname?'

'Afraid not.'

Perhaps if they could track Nick down through university records, he would know Mark's surname. 'Any idea why you were taken off the case?'

'No. It's like it just ceased to exist. That's the best way I can put it. One minute, we're plodding along as usual, asking questions, the next, the rug's been pulled from under us, and we're reassigned to investigate a series of burglaries in city centre shops.'

'Was another team put on the case?'

'Not that I ever heard. The last I knew of it, DI Glassco was called into the super's office. There was some sort of bigwig there, up from London. And the next thing I knew, that was it. Curtains.'

'Did you ever have any idea why?'

'I was pretty green at the time. I just thought it was because we had no real leads and we were sort of marking time, shuffling paper. Maybe they really did hand it over to the Yard, the way they do in books.'

'Did you ever hear about the case again? About Alice Poole?'

Marley tossed back the remains of his Black Bush. 'Not a dicky bird.'

'And this boyfriend of hers, Mark, did you find him?'

'No. And nobody really knew anything much about him. Like I said, he seemed to disappear into thin air. He was older than her. Not a student. On the dole, I think. And she was one of those communist feminists. Member of the university Marxist Society or Socialist Workers Party or some such outfit. Went to demos and all that. Apparently, this new boyfriend was part of that crowd.'

'The politicos? The demo crowd?'

'That's right.'

'Did you talk to other members about him?'

Marley shook his head. 'Never got that far.'

'How long did your investigation last in total, would you say?'

'We were taken off the case around the time John Lennon got shot. I remember that well enough. Olive and I loved the Beatles. Still do. The day after, it would be, when the news broke over here.'

'That would be 9 December 1980,' said Banks, who also remembered the day well.

'Right.'

'So you were on the case just over a week.'

'Sounds about right. Officially. We hadn't really done anything since we interviewed Nick a few days earlier, though. Around the third.'

'So less than a week?'

'That's it.'

'And during that time, had you ever felt like you were making any progress? Getting any closer to finding a killer, or a motive?'

'No. Definitely no motive, that's for certain. Like I said, we suspected the ex at first, but if everyone killed their girlfriend after splitting up, there'd be . . . well, you know what I mean. And we were pretty sure by then that it wasn't him. There was the new boyfriend, Mark, of course, but we never found him, never got to talk to him, and nothing pointed to a motive as far as he was concerned.'

'Except that he vanished,' said Banks. 'Ever wonder where he went?'

'Often. It's not that easy to disappear so completely. There was that postcard from Paris.'

'Did he own a car?'

'Yes. A Morris Marina. That was another reason for suspecting him. Not because he owned a Marina, although . . . well, let me just say I wouldn't have bought one myself, but because he owned a car. Nick told us Alice Poole was going to Mark's flat. I mean, he could have killed her there, then carried her out to the car later that night, when everyone was asleep, driven over to Burley Park, carried her into the bushes and dumped her. Maybe he thought he was making it look like the Ripper.'

'Did you mention that possibility to anyone?'

'DI Glassco and I discussed it briefly. I think he may have presented it to the super, but nobody went anywhere with it as far as I know.'

'And you never heard another thing about this mysterious Mark?'

'Not a thing.'

'Was his car ever found?'

'Not to my knowledge. If it was, nobody told me or DI Glassco.'

In the silence that followed, Banks took a sip of whisky and enjoyed the burning sensation as it went down. He couldn't think of much else to ask Marley. The investigation had clearly been so sloppily handled and so quickly swept under the carpet that he couldn't help but think there had been interference from above. But from whom? And why? Marley clearly didn't know. He had simply been a junior DC following orders to the best of his ability. His not to reason why.

Marley spread his hands. 'And that, Mr Banks, is just about that. Ever had a case like that?'

'Not quite,' said Banks, putting his empty glass aside. 'Just one more thing: did you ever get the impression that there was some sort of cover-up involved?'

'Well, I can't say it didn't cross my mind. But I couldn't for the life of me think why anyone should want to cover up the poor girl's murder. Except the killer, of course. Why wouldn't they want to find and punish whoever killed her?'

'I can't imagine, either,' Banks said, then stood up. 'Many thanks, Mr Marley. You've been a great help. And thanks for the whisky. Please don't bother to see me out.'

'But you must say goodbye to Olive,' said Marley, 'or she'll be most upset.'

'Of course,' Banks said, and he waited while Marley went to fetch his wife. He certainly had a lot to think about after their talk, but whether it helped him or not was hard to know. He glanced at his watch. Perhaps Gerry and Winsome had come up with something from their visit to the Sheffield police. He'd ring them when he got back to his car. Then Olive Marley came through the door and they said their goodbyes.

July 1981

The trial at the Old Bailey, when it came in May, was something of an anticlimax to me, though as far as the media were concerned, it was an excuse for a feeding frenzy. Sutcliffe claimed manslaughter due to paranoid schizophrenia, which the prosecution challenged by arguing that he had conned the police into believing he was mentally disturbed, that he heard voices telling him to kill prostitutes and had hallucinations. This discussion went on for some time and was followed by the grisly details of Sutcliffe's crimes, the things he had actually done to these poor women. I wouldn't say I have no stomach for blood and gore – I love horror movies, after all – but some of the details of what he did with a screwdriver and hammer, and the sexual perversions he carried out afterwards, actually made me feel physically sick, so I tuned out.

I also failed to pay it much attention because the finals were drawing closer, and I still had a great deal of reading to do. I had an extra incentive to do well, as my father had promised to let me have the old family Morris Minor this summer if I came out with a good degree – by which I assumed he meant a first or a two-one. This dream was enough to keep me going through the tough slog of April and May, along with the occasional delightful night spent with Mandy.

When the finals were eventually upon me towards the end of May, I felt prepared, but nervous. I knew there was always more work I could have done, more critics I could have read, more time I could have spent rereading, but time was up, and I was as ready as I was likely to be.

There is nothing quite so daunting as a large examination hall – in this case, the Great Hall, in all its red-brick Gothic Revival glory, with its broad stone staircase and tiled wainscotting. The examination hall itself, with its spaced desks, seemed full of strange echoes as we all dutifully filed in and took our seats. Then, at the precise hour, we were told to turn over our exam papers and begin. This ritual was repeated day after day for a little over a week, with the occasional morning or afternoon off to revise, and though that first time unsettled me, I became used to it and simply got on with my work. I had no sense of how well, or how badly, I had done. Only that I had answered the questions to the best of my ability. Now all I could do was wait.

I hadn't really thought of trying to find a job yet – hadn't thought at all about what I was going to do with my life – but the car beckoned, and with it, freedom. I had hardly any money, and my parents weren't well off, but I could probably work my way around Europe doing casual labour here and there. I knew people who had done that. Still, I also knew times were hard. We were still caught in a world economic recession, mostly because of the fuel crisis. The unemployment rate was at 2.5 million and we'd recently had riots in Handsworth and Brixton. Not a great time to be job-seeking. Margaret Thatcher had seen to that. Of course, I could always follow Norman Tebbit's advice to do as his father did in the depression and get on my bike and look for work. But with any luck, I would have a car.

When the exams were all over, of course, we had a big party in the house. And after that came the sad moment that all university students experience when they've been away from home for three years: that strange, exciting and frightening time between the end of one era and the beginning of another. People started to drift away. Anton went to Liverpool to take a teachers' training course, the gorgeous Maria from the basement went off to Italy with her parents, and Mandy went back to Sheffield. Dave and Sally left their bedsits, too, and in no time, or so it seemed, there was only Geoff and me left. The house had a strange, haunted feel to it. Being old, it creaked a lot, and it was easy to imagine insubstantial figures flitting about during the night. I didn't sleep well, and I even woke up once or twice disoriented from dreams about Alice. The campus, too, was a ghost town, all my friends from lectures, tutorials and the MJ Lounge gone. No more excited chatter about last Saturday's gig, or the one coming up. On a breezy day I could easily imagine tumbleweeds rolling down between the buildings.

We had several spells of beautiful weather, and on his days off, Geoff and I would sit out on top of his bay window, smoke joints, listen to *My Life in the Bush of Ghosts* and watch the world go by. They were lazy, dreamy days for the most part, and I was content to drift along the surface of my life. I had already ditched the idea of doing graduate work. I had had enough of studying for the time being.

I was due to move out of the bedsit at the beginning of July, and my father offered to drive up and help me. There wasn't much stuff, only books, clothes, records and my stereo. They would fit easily in the back of the car. The bedsit was furnished, and the few cups and pots and pans I had picked up at charity shops could stay there for the next tenant.

I wasn't sure what I was going to do next, but I didn't think I could stomach a whole summer with my parents down in Portsmouth. In many ways, that would be even lonelier than Leeds. But there was the car, and before I could do anything with it, I would have to learn how to drive. So I took my father up on his offer, and on a sunny Saturday afternoon I said goodbye to Geoff and to Leeds and got in the passenger seat of the soon-to-be-mine Morris Minor, with all my belongings in the boot or on the back seats, and we set off for the M1.

13 December 2019

Gerry and Winsome hit heavy traffic around Leeds, but after that, they made good time down the M1 to Sheffield.

Gerry felt embarrassed when she remembered her visit to Banks earlier that day. Far too excitable. But it had been a long hard week of getting nowhere fast. The success had sent a rush of blood to her head and . . . well, it was what it was. But now she was going to find out just how close they were to identifying the skeleton found at the Roman excavation. At least, she hoped so. It could turn out to be just another dead end, of course.

The police HQ was quite close to Meadowhall, Sheffield's huge indoor shopping centre, the largest of its kind in York-shire, and for many years, at least, the only one. Everyone went there. You could even take the train from Leeds.

'Maybe we'll have time to go shopping later,' Winsome said.

Gerry, who wasn't a great fan of shopping for its own sake, hoped not. The idea of being stuck in that enormous mall, full of harassed mothers dragging around tired children kicking and screaming, gave her the shudders. Maybe she was a snob, but she always thought there was a touch of the zombie about crowds of shoppers. Perhaps it was a memory of *Dawn of the Dead* she had seen years ago. The original George Romero version. Besides, she was far more excited about the informa-tion she was hoping to get from DI Dobson than the prospect of a visit to Primark or Foot Locker, though a visit to the Apple shop wouldn't be such a bad thing, if she had to. Winsome was the boss, after all.

The police station was a modern building that seemed to be made entirely of glass. A uniformed officer on reception phoned up for DI Dobson, who said he would be right down.

As they waited, Gerry asked about the glass, and the officer told her it wasn't glass at all, but some sort of anodised aluminium powder with an insulating core. It still looked like glass to Gerry. Warm glass.

DI Dobson appeared a couple of minutes later, a slightly paunchy balding man in his mid-forties, shirtsleeves rolled up, tie askew, red braces holding up his trousers, and led them upstairs to an empty office with a long wooden table, ten hard-backed chairs and a large-screen TV on the wall: a meeting room of some sort. Or perhaps it was where they all watched porn after a hard day's thief-catching.

Dobson shuffled some papers on the table before him. Winsome and Gerry sat opposite him, and Gerry opened her binder to take notes. They had agreed that Winsome, being the senior officer, would carry out the interview and Gerry would observe and absorb.

Without preamble or an offer of refreshments, Dobson began. 'I suppose first off you want to know why this person didn't appear on any of your missing persons searches?' he said.

'It would be a start,' said Winsome, 'especially if he fits the criteria we specified.'

'Oh, I can assure you that he does.' Dobson pulled on the fat lobe of his left ear. 'That's what got me interested in the first place. The description, the artist's impression. He always was a snazzy dresser. Expensive suit, handmade Italian shoes, the whole kit and caboodle. He wasn't a show-off, you understand. He kept a low profile, on the whole, but he did like to be seen now and then around the galleries and concert halls with the rich and famous. A man of wealth and taste, you might say, in his trademark Tom Ford suit.'

'Right age bracket?'

'Sixty when he went missing.'

'So why no missing person report?' Winsome asked.

'Nobody reported him missing. Besides, there would have been no point.'

'Why's that?'

'Because the man you are asking about – Michael Wesley was his name, by the way – was a local crime kingpin, and his disappearance was in many ways a foregone conclusion, not to mention a cause for much celebration, around this building in particular. He was either murdered by the opposition, or perhaps by one of his own people in some internal power struggle, and his body was disposed of in such a way, and in such a place, as we'd never have a snowball's chance in hell of finding it. Either that or he simply decided to cut his losses and leg it before someone offed him.'

'Which was it?' Winsome asked.

'We're still not certain. Naturally, we questioned his associates. Also naturally, none of them was able to tell us a bloody thing. Our inquiries and local searches turned up nothing. On the other hand, Wesley's fortune was so well hidden by shell companies and offshore accounts that even our forensic accountants couldn't crack it.'

'So he may have had access to substantial funds abroad?'

'Indeed, he may have. We also checked ports and airports, by the way. Nothing there, either. Or Eurostar.'

'Passport?'

'Word has it that he always carried it with him, along with sufficient cash to make a quick getaway if it became necessary. We also suspect he might have had more than one. Passport, that is.'

'So he remains missing?'

'That's right.'

'But never reported as such.'

'Yes.'

'So how did you find out? I mean, if he wasn't missing, what made you search and ask questions?'

'We wanted to talk to him on another matter, and he couldn't be found.'

'When was this?'

'Maybe a month or so after he disappeared.' Dobson pulled on his ear lobe again. 'To be perfectly honest, we were glad to be rid of Michael Wesley. He'd been a thorn in our sides for over ten years, and we were just glad that he was gone. Wherever. The ninth circle of hell or somewhere. Nobody officially reported him missing because he just drove off under his own steam one evening, and no report was recorded. As I said, we carried on an investigation when we couldn't find him a month later – I won't vouch for its thoroughness – and I've already told you our conclusions.'

'What about his car?'

'No sign.'

'What make was it?'

'It was a Porsche. Expensive, but not a flashy model. Like I said, he tended to keep a fairly low profile, despite the posh clobber.'

Same as Banks's car, Gerry thought, though she had heard he inherited it from his brother.

'So you wouldn't be surprised if this Wesley's body turned up buried in a field by the A1 up in North Yorkshire?' Winsome said.

'Not in the least.'

'What exactly was his criminal enterprise?'

'Bit of everything, really. Mostly it was clubs. He owned quite a few of them in Sheffield and the surrounding area, along with a part interest in a casino. Not on paper, of course. Not officially. And with the clubs came the usual – girls, sometimes trafficked from overseas, strippers, drugs, money-laundering, enforcement, a touch of larceny, murder. He was also suspected of being behind a few bank and jewellery robberies in the area, but again, we've no evidence to prove it. One of Wesley's greatest skills was staying a few steps ahead of us and an ability always to find a viable hiding place or an unbreakable alibi.'

'Did he have a record?'

'No. Nothing. Not even a parking ticket.'

'Did he have someone on the inside to slip him useful information?'

'It's possible.'

'Did you investigate it?'

Dobson nodded. 'Inconclusive. Wesley was clever, and a canny judge of people. He was also ruthless. We suspected him of being behind at least three murders, for example, but we had no evidence.'

'So, all in all, he was a thorn in your side, as you put it, and you were glad to be shot of him?'

Dobson folded his arms and grinned. 'That's about the long and the short of it.'

'Any chance one of his henchmen might have done it? Not a contender. I mean a foot soldier.'

'Why would they? He paid them handsomely.'

'Someone else offered them more, perhaps? Or maybe it was a concerned citizen, someone who thought the city would be better off without him.'

'You mean someone took the law into their own hands?'

'It happens.'

Dobson pursed his lips. 'I'm not saying it didn't happen that way, but running off while the going was good was just as likely.'

'Had you penetrated his organisation? Did you have anyone on the inside, undercover?'

'Not that I know of.'

'Was Wesley facing any particular challenge to his authority that you knew of at the time of his disappearance?'

'A man like Wesley is always facing problems and challenges. It's the law of the jungle. There was nothing specific. One of his captains was getting too big for his boots. We went at him quite hard after the disappearance, but he didn't crack.'

'Do you think he did it?'

'He was certainly a person of interest.'

'Is he running the show now?'

'No. He died in an unfortunate accident involving a tree and a long rope a few weeks after Wesley disappeared. The new man's called Calum Logan. From Manchester. But he wasn't even on the scene here when Wesley disappeared.'

'When exactly was that?' Winsome asked.

Dobson shuffled his papers. 'He was last seen driving away from the Underground Village club on the evening of 21 May 2015, at about nine o'clock, shortly before the club had opened, like. At least, that's the information we have. The place had a reputation for drugs. It's gone now. Turned into a cheap shoe shop, I think.'

'Who saw him go?'

'An employee. Wesley had an interest in the place, so it didn't seem at all odd that he should be there. And the date was verified by his wife – common law – Veronica Holden. At least she told us she hadn't seen him since that night.'

'But she didn't officially report him missing?'

Dobson gave a harsh laugh. 'The last thing she would want was us all over the place, going through their papers, asking questions, turning the house over. Besides, she was probably glad to be shot of him, too.'

'There were problems?'

'Aren't there always? Rumours, mostly. Affairs and so on. Maybe the occasional flare-up of domestic violence.'

'Was she a suspect?'

'There wasn't anything to suspect anyone of, DS Jackman. Besides, she had a good alibi.'

'She could have hired someone.'

'Indeed she could. You'd better ask her about that.'

'It doesn't sound as if your accountants got very far investigating Wesley's business affairs.'

Dobson shrugged. 'I guess he could afford better accountants. Besides, when we questioned the wife, she said she was quite used to Wesley disappearing for days, even weeks at a time. It never seemed to bother her. It's true he travelled quite a lot. Here and abroad. Hence the passports.'

'She knew what he was?'

'She liked to pretend he was just a businessman who did the occasional dodgy deal, but I think she knew. It didn't seem to bother her. She liked the life.'

'Was she in it with him?'

'We didn't think so. She just enjoyed the trappings and ignored how they came about. Some rumours had it that they lived pretty much separate lives, though they shared a large house.'

'She still around?' Winsome asked.

'Aye. She might be able to tell you more than I can, if you can get her to open up. I'll give you the address.' He wrote on a sheet of paper and slipped it over the table to Winsome.

'We'll give her a try,' Winsome said. 'Just a couple of minor points before we head off. Have you ever heard of a man called Harold Gillespie?'

'In connection with Wesley?'

'That would be best, but any connection would do.'

'No, afraid not.' He paused. 'Hang on a minute. I vaguely remember someone by that name. Harry Gillespie, was it?'

'That's right.'

'He was here. Well, the old building. But he was with South Yorkshire. Before my time, of course. I can't say as I ever met him, but I know the name.'

'What about Alice Poole?'

'Sorry, no. Doesn't ring any bells.'

'Any DNA from Wesley on record?' Gerry asked, without much hope.

'Like I said, we never got close enough to him for that.'

'So he was your local crime kingpin, and he has no criminal record?'

'Actually, now I think of it, that is one other odd thing about him.'

'What is?'

'Well, not only does he have no criminal record, he has no record at all.'

'What do you mean?'

'Exactly what I say. One of our best trackers tried a thorough check early on in Wesley's criminal career in Sheffield, and he came up with nothing at all. Before Michael Wesley turned up here in June 2005, it was just as if he didn't exist.'

Winsome glanced at Gerry, who put away her pen and binder. They both stood up, thanked DI Dobson, shook hands and left.

II

September 1981

When the exam results came out a little later in July, I discovered I had got a two-one. I was slightly disappointed that I hadn't got a first, but that didn't last. A two-one was pretty damn good, and more important, my father was pleased with it. As promised, he passed on the old family car to me and bought a second-hand Vauxhall, in which we all drove up to Leeds and back for the graduation ceremony later that month. Also in July, I started driving lessons and passed my test on my second try towards the end of August, having messed up parallel parking the first time. In September, I drove the old Morris Minor around Portsmouth first, getting a feel for the gears, brakes and steering. It was in pretty good condition, considering my father had been driving it for years. Soon, I plucked up the courage to drive as far as Weymouth and Dorchester. Then I spent my days motoring around Hardy country, all rolling hills, tiny villages and thatched cottages separated by occasional stretches of drear, lonely moorland, just like I imagined Egdon Heath.

The trips inspired me to read some of the Hardy novels we hadn't done at university, which was all of them except *Jude the Obscure*. I even visited the cottage in Higher Bockhampton where he had lived for his first thirty years, saw the bedroom where he had been born and cast aside as dead, the casement window where he sat writing *Far From the Madding Crowd* and gazing out over the woods and surrounding countryside.

It was all very romantic, and it rekindled in me the desire to write that I seemed to have lost over my final year at university. I bought a notebook at WHSmith back in Portsmouth and started jotting down thoughts and ideas as they came. That's how the idea for this hodgepodge of journal and memoir came to me. I wanted to tell my story, especially how my life was so entangled with what happened to Alice.

Somehow, I never got across the Channel, but I was quite happy tootling along from Piddlehinton to Lulworth, Puddleham to Bere Regis. It was beautiful countryside, and I was enjoying Hardy's books far more than I thought I would. Some days I took sandwiches and had picnics by rivers or streams. I even found myself a girlfriend in Bournemouth, and we drove around together seeking out isolated spots to make love. But once in a while the spectre of my future rose to haunt me. I even reconsidered applying for a master's degree or a PhD somewhere. Maybe I could become a university lecturer myself. But that dream, like all the others, soon lost its appeal.

It was in the last week of September, and I was starting to worry about money, when it hit me. I loved writing. For years before I went to university, I had written poems, short stories and even attempted a couple of one-act plays. None of them were very good, but I had enjoyed writing them, and practice makes perfect, as they say. I couldn't simply get a paying job as a writer, or could I . . . ?

13 December 2019

Gerry could see by the packages that Winsome had been to Kenji and Levi's. Gerry herself had visited the Apple store, where she had finally caved in and bought the little gold-coloured MacBook she'd had her eyes on for a while. It was one thing checking them out online, but quite another to touch one, hold it in her hands. It weighed practically nothing, would fit in just about any sort of bag she saw fit to carry and it did pretty much everything she wanted. No contest. It was a bit pricey, but she had been saving up for a while.

'So what do you think about DI Dobson?' she asked.

'I think we've got to take him seriously,' Winsome said. 'It's the only real lead we've got so far.'

'Possible lead,' said Gerry.

They were eating lunch in the Handmade Burger Company in Meadowhall, Winsome munching on a peanut butter and bacon burger she said she had developed a taste for while she was pregnant, and Gerry nibbling on a Brie and cranberry chicken burger.

'You don't believe Dobson?' Winsome dabbed at a spot of sauce on her lip.

'It's not that. I was watching him pretty closely, and his body language was mostly in line with what he was saying.'

'What, then?'

'I said "mostly". The interesting times were when it wasn't.'

'And when was that?'

'When he was talking about the possibility of an inside man.'

'You think he was lying?'

'I think he wasn't telling us the full truth. I just don't think they tried very hard. You heard what he said. Wesley was a pain in the neck. He got away with murder and laughed at them. They were well shot of him. Good riddance to bad rubbish. And don't tell me the local police didn't have an undercover officer in Wesley's organisation. It wouldn't surprise me to find out that one of them had helped him on his way, either. Stranger things happen at sea, as they say. Maybe they know damn well who did it, that he's probably one of theirs, and maybe they couldn't give him a medal, but they could at least manage a "get out of jail free" pass – or "do not go to jail at all", in this case. Especially if their man didn't blow his cover and managed to remain in the organisation. Much easier to keep him there, where he might come in useful, rather than drag him in for questioning and involve the IOPC, the CPS and the rest of the rigmarole.'

'You think Dobson knows who did it?'

'I think he has some strong suspicions.'

'So how does this affect our case?' Winsome asked.

'You probably know better than I do, sarge, but I'd say if one of their officers killed Wesley and dumped the body on our patch, then it creates a strong possibility of a major shit-storm ahead.'

'But we've no way of proving it,' said Winsome. 'Especially now, what, nearly five years since he disappeared? And we can't go throwing around accusations without any evidence to back them up. It's just as likely he sensed some sort of threat and took off somewhere. Dobson said Wesley always carried his passport, and he had enough cash for a quick getaway, with no doubt access to plenty more in those shady overseas accounts once he'd got out of harm's way. He was also seen driving off *alone*.'

'By one of his employees, remember. Employees can be got at.'

'True. Or bribed. But we don't even know if Wesley's our man yet. He *might* have simply disappeared. After all, according to Dobson, Wesley didn't even officially exist before he landed in Sheffield in 2005.'

'We might have a hell of a job proving whether he's our skeleton, too, without DNA,' Gerry said. 'A Tom Ford suit does not an identification make.'

Winsome sighed. 'OK,' she said. 'Let's put theories aside for the moment and see if we can find out more about Wesley from Veronica Holden.' She took another bite of her burger, then put the last quarter aside. 'I'd forgotten these things always give me heartburn,' she said, rubbing her chest.

October 1981

Dick Ockham, editor of the *Ossett Observer*, wasn't wearing a visor, but he might as well have been. His grey hair was unruly, his complexion ashen, his eyes glaucous and his white moustache stained with nicotine, like dog piss in the snow, from the Senior Service that always seemed to be hanging from his lips and just about burned to the end. His shirtsleeves were rolled up, held in place by black sleeve garters, revealing his thick, hairy forearms. In fact, he was one of the hairiest men I've ever seen. It grew out of his nose, out of his ears and I even thought it was growing out of his eyes until I realised it was just his bushy eyebrows. His egg-stained tie hung askew, and the top button of his shirt was undone. On his desk, amid an array of discarded pencil stubs and scribbled notes, sat an overflowing ashtray and a framed photograph of a matronly woman with two small children. The tiny office was a mess; shelves packed with stacks of paper, box files and loose-leaf binders everywhere.

I shifted in my chair opposite him. It was my first job interview, and I was nervous as hell. So far, he had asked nothing, merely glanced over my CV and a sample of my writing, grunting every now and then.

'I see you have a degree in English Litter-a-chewer,' he said finally, putting heavily sarcastic emphasis on the last word.

I swallowed. 'Yes.'

'Hmm. We'll soon cure you of that. Know anything about reporting?'

'Well, I've read newspapers. I mean, I read them. Still do.'

'So I suppose you think it's all charging around breaking big stories, don't you?'

'Well . . . er . . . no. I never really thought much about it that way at all.'

'Why do you want to be a reporter?'

'I want to write.'

'At least you can spell, and you seem to know what a sentence is. Know the area at all?'

'Around here?'

'Where else?'

'Well, not really. I was at Leeds University, though, as you know. It's not far away.'

'Geographically, perhaps. But we serve a number of small, very tight communities. Mining communities, to a large extent. Industrial. Our readers are not a particularly cultured lot, but they're no philistines either. And they know their way of life is under threat right now. They don't like to be patronised. Get on well with people, do you?'

'Most people. I mean, I've never had any complaints.'

'Lucky you.' Ockham lit another cigarette and leaned back so far in his chair I feared it might fall backwards. I'd been thinking of lighting one, myself, but the room was so full of smoke I didn't think I'd be able to breathe if I added to it. 'I suppose I could take a chance on you,' he said. 'But I'm warning you, it won't be a walk in the park. You'll be covering a bit of everything: weddings and funerals, local sports, brass band concerts, village fêtes, council meetings and a little am-dram here and there to lighten things up.'

'I'm ready to learn.'

'You are, are you? Well, there won't be much time for that, I'm afraid. You'll simply have to learn on the job. By doing. There's only you, me and young Hattersley, and we won't have time to teach you the ropes. There's Mary, of course, who takes care of everything else, but she won't be able to teach you what you need to know.' He coughed and rubbed his chin. 'And we don't pay very much.'

'I don't need a lot,' I said.

He grunted again. 'Well, that makes a change from some, I suppose. Got a car?'

'Yes.'

'All right. See Mary about your National Insurance Card and so on.' He glanced at his watch. 'And after that, head down to the council chambers and have a listen to the debate on those new traffic lights for the high street. Two hundred and fifty words by five o'clock. OK?'

'Got it,' I said and stood up. 'Er . . . I . . .'

He had already gone back to reading some copy and looked up irritably. 'What is it now?'

'Well, I mean, I don't have a notebook, sir.'

For the first time, Ockham laughed, then went into a fit of coughing. After that, he said, 'We can't have an intrepid reporter without a notebook, can we? Ask Mary. She takes care of stationery supplies, too.'

'And . . . er . . .'

'Yes. Spit it out.'

'Where are the council chambers, sir?'

13 December 2019

Gerry drove in silence and Winsome watched the landscape go by, changing slowly from urban through suburban to rural. She thought about her shopping at Meadowhall. At Levi's, she had bought the first pair of jeans she had felt brave enough to wear after giving birth, and at Kenji, some supplies for her Japanese calligraphy. She found *shodō* a relaxing and refreshing pastime, a sort of meditation. Terry had got interested in Japan and its aesthetics, and had become a very good sushi chef in the process, and Winsome had picked up on his interest in Japanese art. She had grown up near Spring Mount, in Jamaica's Cockpit Mountains above Montego Bay, and there had been quite a few Chinese-Jamaican families in the community. Winsome had become friendly with Hope, a young girl from such a family, and had watched as her friend painstakingly drew hieroglyphs with a brush and ink. It was this memory perhaps, as well as Terry's interest, that had started her on Japanese calligraphy, even though she knew Chinese was different in many ways. The *kanji*, or Japanese characters, were taken from Chinese scripts in the first place. So now she had some more special paper, a new brush and some very black ink to play with.

She directed her thoughts closer to the problem at hand: Michael Wesley. Was it his skeleton that the young archaeologist had found on her dig? And if so, who was responsible for his death? He had been hit twice on the side of his head, she remembered, perhaps with a poker, so there was little doubt that it was murder. Which meant there was a murderer walking free out there. Maybe even a police officer. The odds against finding out exactly who had done it were about as good as those of bringing one of Wesley's competitors or partners in crime to justice. And Winsome reminded herself that the culprit might even be the very woman they were going to speak to now. Never rule out a spouse in a murder case.

Veronica Holden lived in the Hope Valley, not far from the Derwent Dam, where the famous Dam Busters did practice runs in the Second World War. It was in the Peak District a few miles west of Sheffield, a beautiful national park not unlike the Dales, but Winsome found it bleaker, more forbidding, perhaps because of the December weather.

After circumventing Sheffield to the north, they headed west on the A6101 past squat, dark stone hamlets and open countryside and found the house at the end of a terrace block in the village of Bamford. It was small, not much more than an old farmworker's cottage, Winsome thought, built of lime-stone and the darker millstone grit. Hardly the sort of place for a gangster's moll, but perhaps Veronica Holden wasn't your typical gangster's moll.

Their first clue that she wasn't came when she opened the door. Not only was she beautiful, probably to be expected, but she was also Black. Well, not really *black*, Winsome thought, though a white man might call her so, but what they called a *browning* back in Jamaica, a light-skinned Black woman. Winsome guessed that one of her parents was white. She wore little obvious make-up and was dressed comfortably in baggy jeans and a grey sweatshirt with the logo of an American uni-versity emblazoned on its front, but even in that casual outfit she seemed effortlessly elegant. They introduced themselves, not having called ahead, because Winsome had assumed a gangster's widow would probably not want to talk to the police, given the chance to refuse. But Veronica's manner was welcoming. She opened the door wide and bade them enter.

'Come in, come in. I don't get many visitors out here.'

'I can imagine that,' Winsome said.

Veronica studied her. 'Jamaica?' she said.

'Yes. Some years back.'

'Barbados,' Veronica said, then sang a snatch of 'Don't Trust Jamaican Man'.

Winsome laughed. 'Mighty Sparrow. I haven't heard that for years. And, yes, he's probably right.'

Veronica got them seated in comfortable armchairs and went into the kitchen to fuss about with tea. Winsome glanced around the room. It was tastefully decorated, and she noticed a woman's touch in the pastels and quilts and crocheted throws. There were also a number of sculptures, mostly dark, smooth wood carved in abstract shapes, polished to a bright shine. Several paintings hung on the walls, not quite abstract – there were identifiable human figures and landscapes – but definitely scrambled through an artist's remarkable imagination and a palette of bright colours.

'I suppose you were expecting a stripper or a retired prostitute,' she said as she stood leaning in the kitchen doorway, arms folded, while the kettle came to a boil. 'Sorry to disappoint you. I never was a stripper, though a number of my male colleagues at work seemed to think I should have been.'

'We had no preconceptions whatsoever,' Winsome said, though it wasn't entirely true. Everyone had his or her own image of what a gangster's moll should look like, and Veronica Holden certainly didn't match Winsome's identikit image, which was more like Kim Basinger in *L.A. Confidential*. She also noticed that Veronica had a posh southern accent, even posher than Gerry's, definitely not Yorkshire like her own.

The tea made, Veronica sat down opposite them, leaned back, crossed her long legs and folded her hands on her lap. 'So what is it about?' she said. 'New developments in my husband's disappearance?'

'Possibly,' Winsome said, 'but before we go into that, I'd like some background on Mr Wesley. We've talked to the local police, but they weren't able to tell us a great deal.'

'I'm not surprised,' she said. 'Mike did his best to keep them at bay. And they were for ever yapping at his heels like those annoying little dogs. Some of them. The rest were standing in back alleys with their hands out.'

'So your husband had police officers on his payroll?'

'Naturally. They were just a nuisance, that's all. Like wasps at a picnic.'

'Corrupt?'

'Rotten to the core. But that's South Yorkshire. Maybe North Yorkshire's different. I'll keep an open mind.'

'We're not corrupt, Ms Holden,' said Gerry. 'And we're not here to yap at your heels or hold our hands out.'

Veronica laughed. 'I'm glad to hear it. And it's Ronnie, please. You want background? Well, Mike wasn't much of a one for talking about the past, so I can't really tell you a thing about his childhood or early career. As far as I know, he grew up in Colchester, and he did once say it was where he unspent his childhood, and that nothing can happen anywhere. He was misquoting Philip Larkin, I think.'

'So you know nothing about his background, his early years?'

'No. He seemed well educated and well read, but he never mentioned uni, and I got the impression that whatever jobs he might have had in the past had either displeased him or merely formed the foundation for what he was doing then.'

'Which was?' Winsome asked.

'Property management, investment, the entertainment business.'

'The clubs and the trafficked hookers?'

Veronica waved a long tapered finger in the air. 'Now, now,' she said. 'We're not going to go there. As far as I was concerned, Mike was an adventurous businessman, who may have occasionally stepped over the boundaries of what was acceptable, but not into the land of the illegal. There's plenty of toys around for kiddies. Adults deserve their own entertainments, too.'

'That must be comforting to believe,' Gerry muttered.

Veronica gave her a sharp glance.

'Why didn't you report him missing?' Winsome asked.

'And involve the police? Now why would I do that?'

'It's the natural thing to do, isn't it? What about when he didn't come back? Weren't you worried?'

'Even if I had been, I would hardly have gone to the police for succour and comfort. Mike often disappeared without explanation. But when a couple of weeks had passed without a word, naturally I became curious.'

'Not worried?'

'Mike wasn't someone you worried about. Besides, we were pretty much living separate lives by then. Oh, we were civilised about it. We had dinner together sometimes, went to galas or the opera together. I mean, there were no blazing rows or anything.'

'Why did you split?'

'The usual reasons.'

'So what *did* you do?'

'I asked around. One of Mike's colleagues used to be a private investigator. He helped me.'

'And?'

'Nothing. No leads, nothing. Except he was last seen leaving one of his clubs. The Underground Village, I think it was. Bit of a dump, to be honest.'

'Nobody had any idea where he was going?'

'As far as we could discover, he didn't tell anyone.'

'Was that unusual?'

'Not at all. Mike could be very secretive when he wanted to, which was most of the time.'

Winsome paused. This line of questioning was getting her nowhere. 'When the police were made aware of Mr Wesley's disappearance,' she said, 'did they interview you?'

'Of course. Several times. Once under caution. The first suspect is always the spouse. Surely you know that.'

'And?'

'And nothing. I had nothing to do with Mike's disappearance, and they had no proof to the contrary.'

'How did you first meet?' Winsome asked.

Veronica poured tea and resumed her relaxed position. 'London,' she said. 'Before we met, I was working in the City, in finance. That's my background. And in case you're interested, my father was an international financier and travelled the world a lot. He met my mother while he was at university in Toronto, Canada, and took her back to live in Barbados. It was all quite exotic to her. That's where I was born. And, yes, I suppose you could say I had a silver spoon in my mouth. We moved here for my father's work when I was six and from then on, it was the best schools, the LSE, apprenticeship at Goldman Sachs. I met Mike at a bankers' party, one of those champagne and caviar affairs you probably read about in the papers. We started going out and . . . well, the rest is history.'

'Still in London?'

'For a while, yes.'

'What was Mr Wesley doing then?'

'Mike was working down there, too. I'm not sure at what. He was very cagey about it. But he had plenty of money, and he seemed to know everybody who counted. He already had connections up north, and he was building towards a move. I must admit that almost put me off the whole thing. I mean, all I knew about Sheffield was that they used to make steel and had a football team called Wednesday.'

'When did you make the move?'

'Around 2005. It'd have been about fifteen years ago now.'

'And Mr Wesley went straight into his property management role?'

'It took longer than that, but not much. Even though he'd been spending most of his time in London, for a year or so he had been building up his northern portfolio. By then, he owned several clubs, but he had little or nothing to do with the day-to-day running of them. We're not talking about the bada bing. He also owned some apartment buildings and a wine import business. We lived the life, mixed with the elite: footballers, pop stars, bishops, chief constables, politicians, Russian oligarchs. Mike was handsome, ambitious, creative, charismatic. We travelled – lunch in Paris or Rome, winter breaks on the Australian Gold Coast or down on the Cape Peninsula, a little hideaway in Taormina, on Sicily. They were good times.' She gave Winsome a direct, serious look.

'So what went wrong?' Winsome asked.

'Like I said before, the usual. He couldn't keep his dick in his pants, for a start.'

'Did you help him run his businesses, given your background in finance?' Gerry asked.

'Are you married?'

'No.'

'Then you probably haven't learned yet that it's best to keep some distance between your business and your husband's. There's nothing more likely to bring about marital discord than mixing the business and domestic. It's one thing arguing over who's going to do the dishes and another about how you mislaid that cheque for fifty thousand pounds.'

'So that's a no?'

'It is.'

'And what was your business after you teamed up with Mr Wesley?'

'I was a lady of leisure, and I enjoyed it very much. Still am, as a matter of fact.'

'You inherited?'

'I was always well provided for, despite our differences. Mike was never mean or stingy. But as I'm sure you know, because my husband is simply missing, there's been no probate or legal settlement. Not until he's been gone seven years.'

'Or a body is found?' Gerry said.

Veronica leaned forward. '*Have* you found a body?' she asked. 'Is that why you're here?'

That explained to Winsome why Veronica had been keen enough to welcome the police into her home, despite her problems with them in the past. Possibly they were coming to give her the good news that her husband's body had been found and everything was hers. At least everything legitimate – the laundered money, everything she could find.

'We have an unidentified body,' Winsome said, 'and we're making inquiries. There's also the question of who was responsible for his death.'

Veronica touched her throat. 'You mean murder?'

'I'm afraid so.'

'But you're still not certain it's my husband?'

Winsome didn't want to tell her that all they had was a skeleton. 'No,' she said. 'That's why we have to ask so many questions.'

'I see. Go on.'

'Have you ever heard of someone called Gillespie, Harold Gillespie?'

'Yes.'

Her response stunned Winsome, who could only utter, 'When?'

'It was shortly before Mike disappeared. I answered the phone sometimes – the landline – when he was out, and the man on the other end said to tell him Harold Gillespie had called, that he would know who it was.'

'Had you talked to him before?'

'Never. Why?'

'And did he call back?'

'I have no idea. I went out with a friend that evening. I suppose they must have talked at some point.'

'How long before your husband's disappearance was this?'

'Just a matter of days, I think. Why? Is it important? Is Gillespie the man you think is responsible for my husband's murder?'

'We don't know, Mrs Holden,' said Winsome. 'We're still just casting around in the dark.'

But every little piece builds a bigger picture, she thought. And it was certainly enough to bring Harold Gillespie in again and have a good long chat.

'Did you ever meet him?' Gerry asked.

'No. As I said, I only spoke to him on the phone once.'

'Do you know what his relationship with Harold Gillespie was? What linked them?'

'When I gave Mike the message, he had a strange expression on his face, and I asked who this Gillespie was. He just told me it was a voice from the past, and we left it at that. Like I said, secretive.'

'What about the name Alice Poole?' she asked.

'No,' said Veronica, shaking her head. 'That one I've never heard of. What did she have to do with Mike? One of his floozies?'

'No, she wasn't a floozie. And we don't know if she ever did have anything to do with your husband. We're just looking for connections.'

'How long do you think it will be before you find out for certain it's him?'

'It depends,' Winsome said. 'We still have a lot of pieces to fit in first. Do you have a photograph? It might be helpful.'

Veronica went over to a sideboard drawer, rummaged around for a while and came back with a snapshot of a smiling, handsome man in an expensive suit with an open-neck white shirt. 'That was taken about six years ago,' she said.

'How old was Michael when he disappeared?'

'He'd just turned sixty. But a very young sixty.'

Winsome put the photo aside. 'Do you mind if I ask you how long you've been living here?'

'About two and a half years now. Eighteen months after Michael disappeared.'

'Where did you live before?'

'Just outside Sheffield. A place called Dore. It's a bit coun-trified. Posh. But we had a flat in town we used quite often. A penthouse apartment. Mike liked theatre and concerts and galleries and so on.'

'So why the move?'

'I don't know, really,' Veronica said. 'The Dore house was just too big. It was OK when we were both living there, even separately, but not when I was on my own. And the flat was OK, but I didn't want to live in the city centre. For a while, it seemed like several of his colleagues were queuing up to find who was going to succeed him in my bed. Maybe they were even taking bets. I got tired of the lot of them and did a bunk. Sold the house and the flat. Luckily they were in my name. Michael didn't like his name on things. Got a good price. Fetched up here. I'd grown used to living in the country. And town isn't far away, if I need it. So, I looked around and bought this place.'

'But why stay in an area that must have so many memories for you?'

'You mean up north?'

'I suppose so. Why not go back to London?'

'Why would I? I tired of city life. And—' They heard a car pull up and a door slam, then noise in the hall, the front door banging shut. Then, 'Mummy!'

A big grin split Veronica's face. 'Well,' she said, as the living-room door burst open. 'This is the main reason Michael and I stayed together as long as we did.'

And in walked a schoolboy. Aged about eight or nine.

'Meet my son, Robert,' Veronica said. 'Back from school right on time.'

Gerry and Winsome looked at one another and smiled.

16 December 2019

'So now we can put a name to our skeleton,' Banks said on Monday morning, standing in front of the whiteboard, which was covered in pictures, scrawled names and arrows linking the various people involved. 'Veronica Holden was more than willing to let Winsome take a saliva sample from her son, Robert, who she assured us was also Michael Wesley's son, and Jazz here tells us there is a familial DNA connection. Veronica was also able to name Wesley's dentist, so we compared dental records, too. Our skeleton was Michael Wesley. The problem now,' he went on, 'is who was Michael Wesley?'

'There's nothing,' Gerry said. 'I've scoured the records, but there's no trace of a Michael Wesley before March 2005. It's exactly as DI Dobson said.'

'Which makes me think he must have stolen his identity around that time,' Banks said. He turned to the board and tapped the photograph of Wesley. 'But one thing we do have now is a connection between Michael Wesley and Harold Gillespie. We don't know what it is, but they obviously knew one another, and if Veronica Holden is right, they had known one another for a long time, even if they hadn't been in touch for ages. Gillespie phoned Wesley in May 2015, shortly before he disappeared. One other thing we know is that Wesley was a criminal and Gillespie is a retired police officer. Anything come to mind?'

'Gillespie was working for South Yorkshire Police at the time of his retirement,' Gerry said. 'Sheffield. So whatever it is, it's probably something bent.'

'True enough,' Banks agreed. 'Though Gillespie was gone by 1994. Even as far as your man Dobson was concerned, he was nothing but a vaguely familiar name. And Wesley wasn't known to the Sheffield police until around 2005, when he came up from London and became a major player in the club scene. That's ten years. But let's start looking for any time Wesley and Gillespie might have intersected. How did they meet, how did they get to know one another? Was it during Gillespie's Sheffield days or even earlier? And here's another theory to consider: we know that Gillespie worked for Special Branch in the late seventies and early eighties, managing undercover agents in the Special Demonstration Squad. Now, I don't think it's unreasonable to assume that this "Mark", who disappeared, apparently never to be seen again, after the murder of Alice Poole in Leeds in November 1980, was a member of that squad. As we're hearing recently, a number of undercover officers abused their positions by indulging in relationships with women in the groups they were assigned to infiltrate. Perhaps we have a case of that in Mark and Alice Poole. Chris Marley, the retired detective who worked on that case, also told me that the investigation into Alice's death was shut down in a matter of days, which absolutely reeks of Special Branch desperate to hide some faux pas. There was also a boyfriend called Nick, who might be able to tell us something if we can find him. Gerry?'

'Nicholas Hartley. I checked with the university alumni office. Born in Portsmouth, 15 April 1960. He got a BA in English Literature from the University of Leeds in 1981, then went into journalism. Apparently, he worked as an investigative journalist for the *Guardian*. He's technically freelance now, but most of his assignments still come from there. He's won a couple of awards, worked on the cash-for-questions story, the Hutton Inquiry, the phone hacking scandal.'

'He shouldn't be too hard to find, then,' said Banks. 'Political journalist?'

'Mostly. A touch of crime, too. Controversial, like the Stephen Lawrence case. And now, believe it or not, he's working on the Pickford Inquiry into undercover policing.'

'Interesting how that topic seems to keep coming up,' said Banks. 'Too much of a coincidence.'

'What about Gillespie?' asked Winsome.

'Let's see if we can dig up a little more before we haul him in,' Banks said. 'I'd like a bit more ammo when I'm interviewing an ex-cop. Check out his finances, too. But let's not forget – the skeleton was found on what was Gillespie's land at the time of burial. It's a suspicious connection, and along with Michael Wesley, Special Branch, the Special Demonstration Squad and the Alice Poole murder, it becomes even more so. What about the wife, Winsome? Veronica Holden. Do you think she could have done it?'

'She could have,' Winsome answered. 'I mean, they'd drifted apart, were living separate lives. He had a taste for other women. Plenty of motives there.'

'And the money.'

'And the money. She could have done it. Or paid to have it done, more likely. There is one thing, though.'

'Yes?'

'If Veronica Holden had her husband murdered for the money, wouldn't she want to make sure his body was found, rather than wait seven years for a settlement?'

'Good point,' Banks said. 'Unless she had a different motive. Woman scorned and all that. But you're right. Even then she would have probably had the money somewhere in her thoughts. Maybe we should check with DI Dobson again, see how hard they went at her?'

'She said she was interviewed under caution. I should imagine they did a fairly thorough job, but I'll give him a call.'

'What do you think happened, sir?' Gerry asked.

'If I were to guess,' said Banks, 'I'd say that Alice Poole found out her boyfriend Mark was an undercover police officer infiltrating the Marxist group she belonged to. She naturally felt betrayed, they argued, and he killed her, then dumped the body thinking it would look like a Ripper murder. Then he hightailed it down to London and went running to his handler Harold Gillespie and told him what happened. Gillespie then packed Mark off abroad and managed to stall the investigation into Alice's murder.'

'And Michael Wesley's death?'

'That, I don't know. Maybe Veronica Holden was behind it, or an ally of hers in the gang. Or maybe it was something to do with Wesley's and Gillespie's past. Remember, Wesley had no recorded life before 2005. Maybe he was one of Gillespie's agents. Maybe he was even Mark, the boyfriend. The ages fit. If Wesley was sixty when he died, in 2015, he would have been born in 1955 and twenty-five or maybe twenty-six in 1980. Young enough to infiltrate a student political group, but also young enough to be inexperienced in real police work.'

'It's all a bit of a stretch, though, isn't it, sir?' said Winsome.

'I suppose so,' Banks admitted. 'I mean, without any real facts or evidence to back up any of these theories, that's all they are: theories. But you know as well as I do that sometimes you don't get anywhere in a complicated investigation unless you use your imagination and make the occasional leap. I'm not saying I know any of the details or all the whys and where-fores, but I think I might have given a reasonable precis of what could have happened.'

'So where do we go from here?'

'Right,' Banks said. 'We have quite a few tasks ahead. First off, Gerry. Now you know Nick Hartley's profession, I'd like you to track him down and pay him a visit. There's no reason to be heavy-handed yet. Remember, his ex-girlfriend was murdered, possibly by Mark. But you can use my theory of what happened if you think it'll shake him up. And find out more about who Mark was. We need to know.'

12

'I want to ask you a few questions,' said Gerry.

'That makes a change,' said Nick Hartley. 'I'm usually the one asking the questions.'

Gerry laughed. 'Nice place you've got here, by the way,' she said.

'Thanks. I used to have a flat in London, but I got tired of big city life.'

It was the second time Gerry had heard this in a week, the first being from Veronica Holden. 'Didn't Dr Johnson say—'

Hartley laughed. 'Yes, I know. Everyone tells me that. But Dr Johnson didn't have to live in twenty-first-century Camberwell. Besides, I like the north.'

From what Gerry knew of history, she imagined living in Johnson's London was far more of a challenge than living there today. They were sitting at a black-tiled island in the kitchen of Hartley's Victorian terrace house in Otley. The windows framed a view of the back garden, a broad lawn surrounded by tall shrubbery to shield it from the neighbours, flower beds around the edges. One gnarled old oak stood off to the left, a rope hanging from its sturdy lowest branch, and beside it stood a swing and a red slide.

'Children?' Gerry asked.

'For the children I never had,' Hartley said. 'Of course, it might have been different if I'd ever got married. They were here when I bought the house, and I still thought I might marry and have children one day. Still, I don't mind a quick turn on the swings and slide every now and then. Takes me back to my childhood.' Hartley was in his late fifties but still had a full head of dark brown hair and the slender torso of someone who worked out regularly, or ran marathons. He also had a goatee beard and wore black-rimmed glasses. His clothes were casual, but expensive casual – not Primark. He had welcomed Gerry amicably enough, but she sensed an edge to him that was perhaps part nervousness and part fear. She remembered that he was a journalist with a major national newspaper. She would have to tread carefully.

'These questions,' she said. 'They're about Alice Poole.'

Hartley said nothing for a moment, seemed to be staring into the distance, then he gave a quick shake of his head and said, 'I was in love with Alice, but she left me for someone else.'

'I know,' said Gerry. 'Mark.'

Hartley raised an eyebrow. 'Always come prepared, eh? Anyway, I harboured hopes that we might get back together, then she was snatched from me.'

'And did you blame Mark for that?' Gerry asked.

'I'm pretty sure he killed her, if that's what you mean.'

'Why?'

'Because she was on her way to his flat the last time I saw her, and because he disappeared that same evening she was killed. He ran off, or drove off, and after that he was nowhere to be found. Why do that?' He paused, then added, 'If anyone even bothered looking for him. Why are you so interested? It all happened a long time ago. Have you found Mark or something?'

'Or something,' Gerry said. 'I agree the circumstances you mention are suspicious, but there could be other explanations.'

'Like what?'

'He could have been worried that he would be a suspect, or they could have had a row and he could have stormed out, then stayed away after he heard she was dead.'

'Pah,' said Nick.

Gerry thought his response was probably the right one. She didn't believe it herself, either. Neither of her explanations had the ring of truth. 'OK,' she said, 'fair enough. Let's assume for the sake of argument that Mark killed Alice. Why would he do that? Wasn't he supposed to be her new boyfriend?'

'I've no idea. Something went wrong between the two of them, obviously. I mean, I wasn't privy to their life together. Maybe he was a psycho-killer for all I know.'

'Not much of a theory, is it?' Gerry said. 'What's his surname, by the way?'

'Woodcroft. Mark Woodcroft.'

'And you never saw him again?'

'No.'

'How about this for a theory? Mark was an undercover police officer infiltrating left-wing political groups, and Alice discovered his true identity. He killed her to silence her, to protect his cover, and his boss helped squash the investigation into her murder.'

Gerry's version of Banks's theory seemed to make Nick even more nervous. 'But that doesn't make sense. What did he gain? He never came back, so his cover didn't really matter any more, did it? If Alice's murder was meant as a cover-up, it was a pretty unsuccessful one.' He paused, and Gerry could see the journalist take over. 'But I can certainly believe that about the police squashing the investigation. If you've got proof that's what happened, I'd be interested in seeing it. Or hearing more.'

'Just a theory,' said Gerry. 'But let's assume Mark got away with it scot-free and lived to deceive another day. Maybe he did come back. With a different identity.'

'Perhaps . . . There's an inquiry into undercover policing going on right now – you probably know I've been covering it.'

'We know.'

'But nobody's mentioned murder so far. It would make a great—'

'Nick, I'm merely advancing theories, speculations. What do *you* think happened with the police investigation into Alice's murder?'

'They were bloody useless, if you want my opinion. No offence. And someone definitely put the kibosh on it. Glassco and Marley seemed stuck on me as their main suspect, but when I started coming up with evidence that it might have been Mark, they weren't interested. I think it's entirely possible they were warned off by higher-ups, which means your theory might make some sense.'

'What evidence?' Gerry asked.

'Well, maybe not hard evidence, but a girl who lived in the same house as Mark said she heard him and Alice rowing that evening, and somebody came down the stairs and drove off around two in the morning.'

'Did she see who?'

'No. But she definitely heard someone. Heavy footsteps, she said. It could have been them, couldn't it? It could have been him carrying her body to dispose of it. She also said the police hadn't even been around asking questions, but she'd seen two plainclothes officers search Mark's room. At least, she assumed they were police.'

'Anything else?'

'The postcard.'

'We know about that, too. Do you remember what it said?'

'"I'm sorry." That was it. And his signature.'

'Doesn't that indicate that he didn't know she was dead?'

'Or perhaps it was an attempt to convince the police that he didn't know she was dead.'

'How did you get hold of it?'

'All the mail for the tenants in the house got dumped on a table by the front door in the morning.'

'So you took someone else's mail?'

'Well, Alice wasn't going to pick it up, was she?'

'What did you do with this postcard?'

'I took it to the police station. Millgarth. The officer on the front desk told me that Marley and Glassco were no longer on the case but he'd take care of it.'

'So he took the postcard from you?'

'Yes. And the other bloke appeared for another good look at me.'

'Which other bloke?'

'He was in the room for a while when Glassco interviewed me at Millgarth a few days earlier. Then he lost interest, just shook his head and left. I'm pretty sure he was from the Ripper Squad, checking me out.'

'They thought *you* were the Yorkshire Ripper?'

'I'm sure it passed through their minds, before they found out I was too young. Don't forget, they were desperate then. A university student had been murdered by the Ripper just days before Alice was killed. The whole city was on edge.'

'Can you think of anything else unusual that happened around that time? Anything to do with Alice?'

Nick went silent for a while. Gerry glanced around the kitchen. It was bright and airy, with a brushed-steel fridge and freezer unit, cooker and dishwashing machine, along with hanging copper pots, a large spice rack and plenty of cupboard space. A row of cookbooks stood on one shelf and a small TV sat on the countertop. A fat crow landed briefly on the swing, then cawed loudly and took off.

'No,' Nick said finally. 'Everything just sort of wound down after that. Real anticlimax. There was nothing in the papers.

The police never came back. No sign of Mark. I rang Millgarth once or twice but got the runaround. It was like there never was any Mark or Alice or murder case in the first place.'

'What was Mark like?'

'Do you know, I can't say. I never really knew him. In fact, I don't think I ever spoke to him, except maybe once to say hello at a party.'

'Have you ever heard of a man called Harold Gillespie?'

Nick shook his head.

'You haven't come across his name in your coverage of the undercover policing inquiry?'

'I can't say as I have. But it's early days yet. I'm still working on background.'

'Michael Wesley?'

'No.' He glanced down as he answered and stroked his goatee.

Gerry wasn't sure she believed him about not knowing either name and made a mental note of her reservations. Lies could often be even more illuminating than the truth. 'Thank you, Nick,' she said. 'I think that's just about all.'

She could sense the relief in his body language. He was probably torn between his journalistic instinct to pump her for information and the desire to be rid of her as quickly as possible.

'What's all this about?' he asked. 'You never did tell me. Like I said, I mean, that was all years ago. Nobody cared about Alice then. What's changed? What's the story?'

'We found a body,' Gerry said. 'A skeleton, actually. We've identified it and connected it with someone we think was involved in Alice's murder.'

She told him because she thought it might jar him into telling her more. She could swear he turned a shade paler, but he said nothing. She handed him her card. 'If you think of anything else,' she said, 'or if you come across the names Harold Gillespie or Michael Wesley, don't hesitate to get in touch.'

He'd been telling her just what he wanted her to know, of course, and holding a fair bit back. But what, and why? Was it simply his journalistic training, or did he have something to hide?

June 1982

Astounding as it may sound, I not only enjoyed the job, but I seemed to fit in quite well at the *Ossett Observer*. I rented a cosy little flat just outside the town centre and threw myself into my work. Even old Ockham gave up berating me after the first few months, during which it seemed I could do nothing right and made every rookie reporter mistake, from missing an angle, burying the lead and forgetting to describe the brides-maids' dresses at a wedding. Fortunately, I was never tempted to make up a story. I later heard that was a firing offence.

Jack Hattersley and I got on pretty well, too. He was in his mid-forties and had been on the paper since he left school at sixteen, so there wasn't much he didn't know about the kind of thing Ockham wanted, and how he wanted it done. In the few spare moments he had, Jack was quite willing to pass on a few useful tips. Most of it was fairly dull work – cats stuck up trees, competition winners, school plays, new Belisha bea-cons, school sports days – but I managed to tackle them all and even, I like to think, put my own little spin on each story. Even the Belisha beacons. If I ever got too clever for my own good, which I admit I did on occasion, Ockham was only too happy to let me know.

Ockham didn't encourage us to go out and seek stories, but I thought that might be a useful skill for a reporter, so

I tried it on my own initiative. The first few times he held up the resulting sheets of paper between his thumb and nicotine-stained index finger, looked at me as one would at a cat presenting its owner with a dead mouse, and dropped them in the wastepaper bin. But then along came April 1982, and the Falklands War.

Of course, a little weekly like the *Ossett Observer* was hardly going to send me over the Atlantic as a war correspondent, but there were repercussions at home, and when one of our local lads was wounded during the Exocet attack on HMS *Sheffield*, on 4 May, I was assigned to get his story after his return a month later. 'Dig deeper' became my mantra. Find the real story. And that was what I tried to do.

I had no time for the present mood of jingoism, flag-waving and nationalistic sentiments, but of course, I put my own feelings about the matter aside and determined to approach the story without bias. If the lad was a hero, it would be a story about a hero, but if he had just been a scared kid used as cannon fodder, then that would be the story I would tell.

Derek Younis was a slight young lad of nineteen who'd been in the navy since he left school. The Falklands conflict, of course, was his first taste of real war, and it hadn't lasted very long. All my preliminary research suggested that he was no hero, but no coward either. He had an exemplary record and had handled himself well thus far in the war.

I was sent to get the basic details of what happened, and perhaps a little stirring patriotic message from the lad, but when I started talking to him, I knew that would be difficult. I sensed something very wrong. To say he was distracted would have been an understatement. His attention was all over the place except on me, and the last thing he wanted to talk about was the war. His wound, as it turned out, was more serious than a minor scratch or burn; he had suffered from smoke inhalation that left him wheezing, and he had lost an arm. He had spilled so much blood that he would have died if they hadn't got him out of the burning cabin and into a helicopter fast and shipped him to the nearest field hospital. He also didn't want to stay inside while we talked – he said he felt claustrophobic – so we sat in the back garden of his parents' house. Luckily, it was a mild, sunny spring day.

After several minutes of getting nowhere, I asked him if he was all right, if there was anything I could do for him. He brought his eyes back from whatever internal horror he had been fixated on and looked at me as if seeing me for the first time. 'All right?' he said scornfully. 'No. I'm not fucking all right.'

'What is it, Derek?' I asked, as gently as I could. 'What's bothering you?' *A missing bloody arm, you idiot*, I told myself as soon as I'd asked the question, but that wasn't his response.

Instead, he collapsed back in his chair, as if suddenly deflated, gasped for breath and searched for words. 'I don't know where to start. I can't talk about it,' he said. 'I can't give you what you want. I can't even see a photo of a fucking naval ship without nearly throwing up. You should just go away.'

'Do you have nightmares?'

'Do I? Every fucking night. That's if I can even get to sleep to have them. Mostly I just toss and turn. It's running through my mind all the time, like one of those old cinema loops. The explosion, the small cabin, the sudden, over-whelming smell and the smoke, the fire and . . .' He stopped and shut his eyes 'The noise!'

'Calm down, Derek,' I said. 'You're safe now. You're back home. You don't have to talk about it if you don't want. When did you start feeling this way?'

'Just after I got back. I was in hospital for ages, then they shipped me home. It was all right at first. I was relieved to be here, thankful to be alive. You know. But then the nightmares started. I was jumping at shadows. I couldn't stand being indoors. And I couldn't seem to tell anyone what was happening.'

'Why are you telling me?'

'I don't know. You're a stranger. Maybe I feel I have to tell someone or I'll go mad. I've even thought of killing myself.'

As a student of literature, I had developed an interest in psychology and psychiatry, and a couple of years ago I had read an article about something called post-traumatic stress disorder. Apparently, it had been recognised during the 1970s in American veterans returning from Vietnam, and had just recently been added to the *DSM-II*, that huge encyclopaedia of psychiatric conditions. General opinion held that it was very much the same thing they used to call shell shock in the First World War and battle fatigue in the Second. The symptoms were exactly what Derek was describing. As we talked, I discovered that he also felt distanced from all his old friends, and even from his parents. He didn't enjoy going out or socialising because he always stumbled across something that took him back to the traumatic event – maybe a car backfiring or a certain smell, even the sight of smoke curling into the air. It was unpredictable, he said, and it made him too anxious to take the risk.

I asked him if he had sought any help, and he said he hadn't, that he didn't know where to go. His own GP had simply recommended plenty of rest and a positive attitude. I suggested he see another doctor, and when I left, I gave him my number at the office in case he needed to get in touch. He seemed grateful, but I doubted very much that he would. I doubted he would even remember our meeting, so overwhelmed was he by the trauma of the past.

I wrote the story concentrating not on Derek's war experience – though I tried to describe the attack as graphically as I could – but on the emotional scars that the experience had left on him: the sleepless nights, anxiety, nightmares, flashbacks. Ockham gave me his usual expression of distaste after the first paragraph, but he read it through, then said it wasn't the kind of thing the *Observer* usually printed, and that he didn't appreciate what he saw as a 'slight anti-war bias' but that I should leave it with him. He would think about it.

I guessed that was probably it, and my hard-won tale of woe would end up in the wastepaper bin, but the following morning Ockham had me in his office, gave me a bollocking for going off-piste and rambling on for too long, but he said he would publish it.

The story appeared in the following week's edition. Ockham had edited it, as he usually did – after all, he was the editor – and made plenty of cuts, but not to the point of distorting my original in any serious way, except to make it appear a little less anti-war and less rambling.

To my joy, the piece was picked up by one of the national dailies. Of course, I was thrilled to bits. This was exactly the kind of thing I was eager for, recognition beyond the narrow parochial barriers of the *Ossett Observer*.

And not only that – the story also brought forth a response from a local psychiatrist who eventually began to treat Derek Younis for his condition. So I became not only the writer of the story, but the subject of another story about how my work had helped someone. These were heady days, and I thank Ockham and Hattersley for constantly taking the piss to make sure I didn't get too big for my boots.

But successful as it was, Derek Younis's story didn't provide my ticket to the big time. That only came over two years later.

19 December 2019

'Sorry to keep you waiting, Mr Gillespie,' said Banks as he entered the interview room with Winsome.

'What's this all about?'

'A voluntary interview under caution, but if you feel you need a solicitor, we can get one for you.'

'I have my own, thank you very much,' grumbled Gillespie. 'And I'll bring her in if I feel I need her. I've got nothing to hide, so let's just get this over with as quickly as possible. I'm not feeling terribly well.'

He looked dignified, Banks thought, but awfully pale and drawn. His head and brow were filmed with a sheen of sweat. He wore a tweed jacket over his V-neck sweater and shirt, though it was warm in the interview room. They went through the formalities, then Banks said, 'First of all, we were hoping you could give us a bit more information about your role at the Met in 1980.'

'What more?'

'We know, for example, that you worked for Special Branch as a handler of agents on the Special Demonstration Squad. Is that correct?'

Gillespie sighed. 'You know I can't talk about that. It's classified. I signed the Official Secrets Act.'

'I can't imagine it's as classified as all that to tell us about a job you had nearly forty years ago. Especially as it's now the subject of a government inquiry. It doesn't matter. We already know. I was just seeking confirmation from you.'

'How did you—'

'We have our sources. I take it you do know about the undercover policing inquiry Theresa May announced back in March 2015, when she was Home Secretary?'

'Of course.'

'Then you know they'll eventually get around to you and the agents you supervised. There will be documentation. Even classified documents will probably come to light.'

'There's nothing I can tell them. Everything was pretty much par for the course.'

'I believe you handled an agent called Mark Woodcroft. Not his real name, of course. Is that right?'

Gillespie folded his arms.

'No matter,' Banks went on. 'We know it's true. What I'd really like you to tell me, though, is whether Mark Woodcroft later became Michael Wesley.'

'Who?'

'Michael Wesley. The Sheffield crime kingpin. The man you telephoned in May 2015, a few weeks after the under-cover inquiry was announced, and just a week before he disappeared.'

'What's your question?'

'Did you ring Michael Wesley in May 2015?'

'So what if I did? He called me first and I missed it, so I called him back later.'

'So you did know him? How long?'

Gillespie paused, then said, 'Since he worked for me as Mark Woodcroft. But I hadn't seen him since.'

'Now we're getting somewhere,' Banks said. 'Why did he phone you in May 2015?'

'He'd heard about the inquiry and wanted to know what I was going to say. He was worried I would give him away.'

'Was that because you were united by a common secret?'

'What secret?'

'That Mark Woodcroft murdered Alice Poole and you covered for him. Hard for either of you to admit it without incriminating yourself, though.'

Gillespie tensed and tugged at his shirt collar as if he were having trouble breathing. 'This is getting a little too accusatory.'

'What happened?' Banks asked. 'What happened on the night Alice Poole was murdered in Leeds?'

'I don't know. I wasn't in Leeds at the time. I'm not so sure where I was, it was so long ago, but no doubt I could come up with an alibi if necessary.'

'We're not accusing you of murdering her.'

Gillespie had a brief coughing fit. 'What *are* you accusing me of? I'm confused.'

'Nothing, as yet. As I said, this is a voluntary interview.'

'About what?'

'OK. Let's move on. When did you last see Mark Woodcroft, or Michael Wesley?'

'I don't remember exactly when.'

'Are you sure you didn't see him in May 2015 to synchronise your stories for the coming inquiry?'

'I've already told you. We talked on the phone.'

'Then what,' Banks said, 'was Michael Wesley's body doing buried on your land with the side of his head bashed in?'

Gillespie said nothing for a moment, then he slumped forward and rested his hands on the desk. 'I think I'd like to talk to my solicitor now,' he said.

November 1984

I was still working at the *Ossett Observer*, still covering cats up trees, school concerts, weddings and council meetings, when the miners' strike hit South Yorkshire badly in March 1984, and lasted an entire year. It was a complex affair, a titanic struggle between the NUM and NCB, which in itself was only one battle in the bigger war between Margaret Thatcher and the trade unions, especially Arthur Scargill. Obviously, the *Observer* wasn't interested in the political ramifications of the strike to any great extent, only the local consequences. In fact, when it all started, Ockham had both me and Jack Hattersley in his office, unprecedented in itself, and warned us about taking political sides in anything we wrote about the matter.

I found it perhaps even harder to be neutral about the strike than I had been about the Falklands War, especially after the Battle of Orgreave in June, when the police on horseback and with truncheons drawn charged into the picketing miners. Later on, when I had covered one or two local picket lines and the often violent police response and seen what the threat of closure of a local colliery did to a community, I felt even less neutral. But by then, I had developed enough journalistic skill to put aside my own feelings on issues and find the story.

In this case, there were so many stories, spreading over a long period. Even so, the running battle took me right back to my university days, and Alice's conversion to the Marxist cause – our arguments about workers and unions, relatively civilised at first, ultimately becoming toxic and forming a wedge between us. It wasn't that I was on Thatcher's side – even before her time, as far back as the Winter of Discontent, I spoke up for the unions – but I wanted to see more dialogue and less ideology, more compromise and less dialectic. However much I argued, it didn't make me very popular with Alice and her friends, who remained firmly on the side of the workers, no matter what they did or demanded.

About halfway through the strike, I had the idea of running a series of weekly vignettes focusing on individuals affected by the strikes, whether it be striking miners themselves, or their wives and families, local shopkeepers, landlords, politicians, barmaids, postmen, strike-breakers, union officials, pit managers and police. The range of responses and engagement was astounding, and the power of the emotions unleashed even more so. Naturally, there was a lot of anger, but there was also sadness, nostalgia, fear and a palpable sense of loss as pits were scheduled for closure, and the communities that depended on them knew they were about to die. Mining was a hard life, and certainly not one I had ever wanted to try, but it brought communities together in a way nothing else did, except perhaps war. I tried to capture all this, at least express it through the words of those I spoke to about it, and the series became so popular that it was also picked up by a national daily. So once again I had my name up there along with the big boys.

And this time it paid off. When the strike was over, and my series came to a natural end – though I posted a series of follow-up interviews at various intervals – I had enough credibility that when a vacancy came up at the *Yorkshire Post* in the summer of 1986, I knew I was in with a chance.

19 December 2019

Banks felt tired when he got home on Thursday evening, after he had watched Harold Gillespie walk out of the interview room to go and telephone his solicitor. As it would be a couple of hours before they could meet, and no doubt Gillespie would require a lengthy meeting, Banks decided to postpone the interview until the following day. He knew it would give Gillespie time to come up with the sort of story his solicitor felt he could sell to the police – or the courts, if it came to that – without causing her client a great deal of discomfort or distress, let alone jail time. A story everyone could live with. After all, some of the events under discussion took place close to forty years ago, and others four. Evidence withers and blows away, people forget, things change. Banks knew there was little chance of convicting Gillespie of anything, but he wanted to know what happened, if only for his own peace of mind. He also knew that Gillespie had been testing him in the voluntary interview, trying to gauge how much they already knew and match it with what he would then have to tell them.

A new issue of *Gramophone* magazine awaited him on the carpet inside the front door, along with a couple of Christmas cards. He didn't get much post these days, as he paid most of his bills through direct debit. He had even thought of switching to the online version of *Gramophone*, but decided he liked the look and feel of the actual magazine too much, so why bother?

After polishing off the fish and chips he'd picked up in Helmthorpe on his way home, Banks poured a glass of Malbec and carried it through to the conservatory. He streamed Chausson's 'Poème de l'amour et de la mer' through and settled down in his favourite wicker chair to think. Wind swept the rain almost horizontally across his windows, and the hills beyond, already dark against the sky, were full of threat and foreboding. Eliot had it wrong, he thought. April wasn't the cruellest month; that was December. Or maybe February. Either way, it wasn't April.

He thought over Gerry's phone report of her conversation with Nicholas Hartley. She had thought it a wasted journey at first, but realised that sometimes *not* finding out anything could only make you more certain that something was there. It was the same feeling Banks had after his talk with Harold Gillespie. Now he was sure both were hiding something. He was even beginning to think there was some sort of conspiracy going on, and he wanted to get to the bottom of it. Hartley was a journalist, far more interested in getting a story than telling one. It was hardly surprising that he had denied knowing Harold Gillespie or Michael Wesley. If he had come across Gillespie in the role of handler, perhaps through his researches into the inquiry, then he might have somehow got himself involved. Good journalists have sources at all levels, in all areas, and it wasn't beyond the bounds of reason that someone had pointed Hartley in the right direction. A whistle-blower, perhaps. Especially if he suspected Mark Woodcroft of Alice's murder and knew that Woodcroft was an undercover cop at the time. Maybe he had wanted revenge. But did he know? And if so, how?

All this talk recently of undercover cops depressed Banks, because it made him think of his own time, back in the mid-seventies. *Bella.* The memory had troubled him during his conversation on the subject with Burgess. It was something he deeply regretted, but hadn't been able to tell anyone, not even Sandra, his wife at the time.

Of course, he wasn't a member of SDS, so had no knowledge of Gillespie, Woodcroft and their ilk. He had been working under orders from his super, infiltrating a drug operation in Notting Hill. It was quite a network of importing and distributing, right down to street selling, sometimes as simple as a dealer on a bike riding around the neighbourhood ringing his bell like an ice cream van. Only it wasn't ice cream he was selling. The head honcho, the one suspected of connections with overseas manufacturers and exporters, was called Larry Fletcher, and he had a girlfriend called Bella, a fragile beauty with the smile of an angel who drifted about in long flowing dresses as if her feet weren't touching the ground. Which they probably weren't.

They lived in a flat on Powys Terrace, and Banks became a frequent visitor after striking up a conversation with Fletcher in the Duke of Wellington. It started, as these things often do, with music. Both were big fans of John Coltrane and Miles Davis, then went on to find out they also had a great deal of late sixties music in common – Captain Beefheart, Kevin Ayers, Soft Machine, Family, Incredible String Band. Fletcher was better read than Banks and kept quoting Ginsberg, Kerouac and Burroughs, as well as Sartre and Camus, so Banks gave himself a crash course in the Beats and existentialists in what little spare time he had. Fletcher was also a man who liked the sound of his own voice, which meant he didn't demand much except that people listened, and Bella was totally in thrall to him. She hung on his every word, did his every bidding.

On the one or two occasions when Banks had been alone with her, he had found her to be a timid but intelligent young woman from a difficult background – a mother who neglected her and stepfather who abused her. She had taken to drugs and the streets at about fifteen and was now in her late teens, still using, but at least sleeping under a roof. Much of the time, though, she was on the nod. It seemed to be the place she wanted to be as often as possible, the place where nothing and nobody could touch her. A lot of it was down to her past, Banks knew, but Fletcher also had a great deal to answer for. He knew her weaknesses and played upon them. What they call these days coercive control, but didn't really have a term for back then.

Banks only saw him hit her once, but it was so swift and brutal he had to work hard to stop himself from blowing his cover and leaping to her defence. Afterwards, of course, Fletcher was apologetic, said he loved her and smoothed it all over with a needle and a spoon. Banks knew that he hit her on other occasions, too, saw the results. It was a terribly destructive relationship, and Banks started to think of ways he could wean Bella away from Fletcher without revealing that he was a cop. But he couldn't. Fletcher had such a strong hold over her, and she had so little self-esteem and confidence that she just took it all as long as there was a fix at the end. There was no way she would run away. Where would she go?

Then the inevitable happened. Banks went to Fletcher's flat one day, found Fletcher out, heard the cat wailing and saw Bella on the floor, dead from an overdose, the needle still in her vein, a dark bruise by the side of her left eye. He felt sick with guilt. If only he had done something, got her away somehow, got her in rehab, whatever. But he hadn't. He had just watched from the corner of his eye while he ingratiated himself further with the abominable Fletcher. Even then, finding her, he didn't think he could call the police or an ambulance without it appearing suspicious, so he simply left her there. Let Fletcher deal with the problem whenever he got back. In the end, the operation was a success, and Fletcher was caught with a large enough haul to put him away for a long time. But sweet, frail, lovely Bella was dead. And it was Banks's fault. He had felt nothing but loathing for undercover work after that and had never done it again.

He poured himself another glass of wine and switched to the Grateful Dead's *Europe '72*. He had seen them at Lyceum on that tour, and it had been a terrific show. Maybe now it would shake him out of his low mood. He was just getting into 'Mr Charlie' when his mobile went off. He was surprised to find that the call was from Annie Cabbot.

He turned the music down and said, 'Annie, how are you?'

'I'm fine,' she said.

'*Where* are you?'

'I'm in Cornwall.'

'Laying a few ghosts?'

'I still have friends down here. Friends of Ray, too. Everyone in the St Ives artistic community knew Ray.'

'Zelda, too?'

There was a short pause. 'Some of them. The consensus is that she genuinely loved him.'

'I could have told you that. In fact, I think I did.'

'So I made a mistake. OK? I . . . I jumped to conclusions, judged too harshly. But that doesn't give you the right to get off one of your "told you so" shots.'

Banks laughed. 'Sorry. Seriously, though, how are you doing?'

'I'm OK. Really. I just wanted to let you know I'm sorry for acting a bit silly lately.'

'You weren't silly. You were hurting.'

'Well, whatever . . . But I'm coming to terms with things. I know Ray's gone, and Zelda . . . Well, if I ever see her again, I'll behave differently.'

'I'm glad to hear you're getting things together. Do you know what you're going to do?'

'I'll be back at work soon. And I've decided to move into the house. Enough of living in a bijou inside a labyrinth. It's isolated, but I think I can deal with that.'

'Anything I can do?'

'Well, while I'm away, if you like, you can tidy up, splash a lick of paint here and there. And the toilet in the bathroom needs—'

'You want me to get some workmen in to fix the place up?'

Annie laughed. It was a sound he'd almost forgotten. 'Real Mr Handyman, aren't you? No, it's OK. Don't bother. How's the case?'

'The skeleton? We're getting there. At least we know who it is now. But we still have a few loose ends to tie up.'

'Excellent. Believe it or not, I'm looking forward to getting back, and returning to work again. How's Winsome?'

'She's good. Gerry, too. And young Wilkie Collins seems to be turning out OK. He's a bit nervous and shy still, I think, but when he gets over that, he might make a good copper.'

'Right then. I'd better get back to my friends. Talk to you again soon.'

'Yes. And, Annie?'

'What?'

'Thanks for calling and letting me know, you know. I was worried.'

'Oh, get on with you, you big softie.'

Banks felt a lot better after the conversation, so much so that he refilled his wine glass for a third time and turned up the volume on 'Black-Throated Wind'.

13

September 1995

Five years after I thought I had left the city for good, I found
myself back in Leeds again. Needless to say, one of my first
stops was the old house where I used to live. Geoff was still
there, still working at the central library, and we went out for
a curry and a few pints. He was engaged to a young woman
from work called Rebecca, he told me, and they were looking
for a house. Nothing else had changed very much. Students
came and students went, and he didn't really know the present bunch very well at all. There were no rooms free, so no
chance of my moving back in, but I managed to find a decent-
sized flat further up in Headingley, off Cardigan Road, not
far from the cricket ground. It was furnished – barely – which
suited me fine, and more spacious than the place I'd had in
Ossett, with a living room, one bedroom, a small kitchen and
my own bathroom and toilet. But I could afford it. After all,
more money had come along with the new job. I could even
see the cricket ground from my window, but unfortunately
not well enough to sit there and enjoy a game.

The *Yorkshire Post* building stood at the corner of
Wellington Road and Wellington Street, its tall square clock
tower already famous among the locals. The atmosphere was
a lot more charged than the offices of the old *Ossett Observer*,
and my duties far more wide-ranging and challenging, my
editors more demanding and less polite than old Ockham.
Though the paper's main concern was Yorkshire, it did have

a broader reach and described itself on its masthead as 'Yorkshire's National Newspaper'. There was plenty happening in Leeds itself, of course, but we liked to think we could also have our say on national events, especially political issues, as they would often have an effect up north. There was a lot going on in the newspaper business, too; this was the period when Rupert Murdoch was busy smashing the print unions and getting rid of the NUJ. There was also a strong sense of competition at the *Post*, which had not been the case at the *Observer*, unless I counted the occasional race against Jack Hattersley for the latest update on the pit closures. I soon learned who to cultivate and who to avoid, though, and once I knew that, life became far more bearable – competition and back-stabbing, dictatorial editors and all.

And the *Yorkshire Post* was where I started to specialise. I didn't actually have a 'beat', but I tended to work mostly on politics and crime, which, as I soon discovered, often went hand in hand, and on social issues, which were often the result of the aforementioned alliance. I still got to do the occasional concert or theatre review and local interest story, but now I also got to work on such national issues as the homes-for-votes scandal, in which the homeless were removed from marginal wards, often to condemned accommodation, and the council houses sold off to people more likely to vote Conservative.

I didn't have a great deal of spare time, and I spent most of it in my flat, reading and sometimes writing stories and poems for my own entertainment. I still didn't own a television – I thought it would be too much of a distraction – so now and then I'd go over to Geoff's to watch something, just like the old days, and of course, we'd have the occasional curry and drinks together. Though I saw Anton infrequently, as he was now teaching in Shrewsbury, we kept up a regular correspondence and found we were still like-minded on most issues, though we tended to write mostly about books and music we'd been enjoying rather than politics. I also met a girl in the Original Oak, and we started seeing one another. Monica was a grad student writing her thesis on Elizabeth Bishop. Both of us were consumed by our work to a large degree, but when we did manage to get together, we had some good times.

All in all, life was good. I'm not saying there weren't dark moments, especially those times when I found myself thinking about Alice, remembering her slightly crooked smile, that look in her eyes when she thought she was being teased, and the passion with which we made love. Perhaps it was because of her that I couldn't seem to commit myself fully to any new relationship. It suited me that Monica was as busy as I was and that we never had any talk of marriage or even of living together. Things were fine just the way they were, or so I thought. I was still young, in my late twenties those first few years at the *Yorkshire Post*, and my career had moved far more quickly than I had expected. I had thought I would probably have to spend seven or eight years at the *Ossett Observer* before being considered for a job on a prestigious paper like the *Post*, but I managed it in almost half that time, thanks to the miners' strike.

And so life went on, into the nineties. Then, in September 1995, after almost ten years, I finally left the *Yorkshire Post* to work for the *Guardian* and set about the arduous task of finding myself an affordable flat in London. There was no particular event that brought this move about, though I had won one or two awards during my time in Yorkshire. I heard from a colleague that there was an opening, and I applied, went down for an interview, and eventually I was accepted. I was sad to leave the *Yorkshire Post*. I had made some good friends over the years there, though I still had no steady girlfriend – Monica having moved on by then – and my living quarters hadn't changed. I had been feeling a kind of stasis for some time, and it felt right to move on. A new chapter was opening up, and it was soon to prove the most important and life-altering chapter of my life.

20 December 2019

Late that Friday morning, less than a week before Christmas, Harold Gillespie and his solicitor, Kathleen Bryant, turned up at Eastvale Police HQ for the interview. Banks had already discovered from his team that there was nothing suspicious about Gillespie's finances. The CPO payment for Wilveston Farm had covered the cost of his new home in Lytham. His lifestyle was hardly excessive and more than manageable on his police pension, his wife's teacher's pension and their investments.

So the odds were that Harold Gillespie had not been on the take, or at least not since his retirement.

Gerry had also managed to find out that Gillespie had recently finished a course of chemotherapy for pancreatic cancer, which probably explained his paleness and fragility. The doctor wouldn't give up much, of course, but Gerry had gathered that the prognosis was not good.

She had also phoned DI Dobson in Sheffield and learned that Veronica Holden had an ironclad alibi for the night her husband disappeared – she was on a trip to Prague with a couple of friends. Also, her finances showed no unusual transactions around that time, though that didn't rule out a wad of cash she might have put aside somewhere to pay for her husband's murder. On the whole, though, Dobson was inclined to believe that she hadn't been involved.

The more he thought about it, the more Banks came to believe that the previous day's interview had really been a fishing expedition on Gillespie's part. He had wanted to know how much they knew before he decided what to tell them. Banks had possibly surprised him with the identification of the skeleton as Michael Wesley, and unearthing his connection with Wesley through what Veronica Holden had told them. He had been shaken enough to confirm that Wesley and Woodcroft were one and the same, but there were still many questions to be answered.

When the four of them sat down in the bare interview room – Banks, Winsome, Gillespie and Kathleen Bryant – Banks ran through the formalities and caution before Kathleen Bryant announced that her client was acting against her advice in the statement he was about to give, and that she felt she was there primarily as a referee to make sure there was no dirty play on the police's part.

'Decided to come clean, Mr Gillespie?' said Banks.

'I've decided to tell the truth, if that's what you mean.'

'I'm glad to hear it. Can you start with what happened on the night of 27 November 1980?'

'It was the morning of the 28th, early. I was asleep in bed when my telephone rang. I answered and heard Mark Woodcroft, one of my agents, on the line. He'd been having problems with his girlfriend, he said, and while he was out, she had been searching his flat for evidence of infidelity and had found his genuine passport under his own name – Melvyn Williams – hidden in the back of a drawer. His cover was blown. They rowed, she went ballistic at the betrayal and he ended up strangling her.'

'How did he sound? Was he distraught?'

'He was pretty calm, I'd say. He stressed that he couldn't risk her telling everyone who he was because it would scupper the IRA operation. He said she was beyond reasoning.'

'Where was he when he told you this?'

'London. He'd driven down through the night. He wanted to know what to do.'

'What did you tell him?'

'I told him to meet at our usual safe house, then I phoned my boss and invited him along. I'd never had anything of this magnitude happen before. This wasn't a situation I wanted to handle alone.'

'What happened when you got to the house?'

'Mark told us that he'd dumped the body in a park in Leeds, was sure nobody had seen him, then driven straight down and reported to me.'

'What did you suggest he do?'

'Nothing at first. There were extenuating circumstances, you see.'

'Oh? And what were those?'

'I'm afraid this is where the Official Secrets Act does become relevant, Superintendent. I can only give you the bare bones.'

'Go ahead.'

'Melvyn Williams was one of our best officers. He had recently come off an op infiltrating an eco-terrorist organisation, which had resulted in a number of arrests and no bloodshed. Always a good outcome. Next, he was sent to infiltrate the Socialist Workers Party up in Leeds, which he got to through the university's Marxist Society, because we'd had a tip-off there was an IRA cell setting up there. You might remember this was a time of many terrorist threats from across the Irish Sea. Everyone remembers the M62 coach bombing and the Birmingham pub bombings, but maybe forgets the dozens of other bombings they executed during the seventies – London, of course, Bristol, Guildford, Manchester, Glasgow. The list goes on. So this incipient new cell was of great interest to Special Branch at the time.'

'But the IRA weren't Marxists,' Banks said. 'Far from it.'

'A student Marxist organisation is a lot easier to infiltrate than the IRA,' said Gillespie. 'And they also had close links to the Socialist Workers Party. You're right about the Marxists, course, but there was some connection between left-wing groups and violent terrorist organisations. The left had an interest in Irish republicanism, Irish nationalism, anything to destabilise the union. Red Action, for example, were a violent left-wing group, and they supported the IRA paramilitary. To cut a long story short, Mark had succeeded and met with IRA members and he had got wind of a plot to assassinate a government minister during a visit to the north in the near future.'

'And that was worth Alice Poole's life?'

'We're not here to make moral judgements, Superintendent Banks. Please keep such remarks to yourself,' said Bryant.

'If morality isn't one of the reasons we are here, then what the hell are we doing?' Banks replied.

'We're here to make sure the law is followed in all respects. Please continue with your questions and keep your opinions to yourself.'

'We're talking about a terrorist plot against the government,' Gillespie said. 'And if Mark's cover had been blown, his life would have been in serious danger. These people didn't mess around.'

'But didn't killing his girlfriend and running off make him look suspicious to the terrorists, anyway?'

'Not necessarily,' said Gillespie. 'It wasn't unusual for people to travel in the course of the revolution. And there was no proof that Mark had killed Alice. We tried to put the lid on the whole thing and deflect from that conclusion.'

'Successfully, so it seems,' said Banks.

Bryant gave him a nasty look but said nothing.

'My boss decided we had to get Mark out of the country fast, which we did. We also sent a couple of men up to Leeds immediately to go through his flat, make sure there was nothing incriminating there. Then he had a word with the local police. They already had enough on their plates with the Yorkshire Ripper, so I must say they weren't too unhappy to give up on poor Alice Poole. And before you play the morality card again, do I regret it? Yes. I've regretted it every day of my life. But do I think we did the right thing? I do. We didn't kill the girl. That was Mark's doing. Yes, we covered it up, let a murderer go free. But that wouldn't bring Alice back. We had to preserve the information we had gleaned from Mark's work. He'd risked his life for it. As far as he was concerned, if the IRA found out he'd informed on them, he'd be a marked man. If there was an assassination plot, surely you can understand we had to do something?'

'So what *did* you do?'

'We had details, names, places. We got men up there, covered all the angles.'

'And what happened?'

'Nothing.'

'There was no plot?'

'Or they found out we knew about it somehow and cancelled it.'

'So Alice died for nothing?'

Gillespie stared down at the table. 'We didn't know that at the time. As I said, there's not a day goes by I don't think of what happened.'

'What did you do next?'

'I did what any handler would do. I bundled Mark off to France and told him to lie low.'

'Whose idea was the postcard?'

'You know about that?'

'We know a lot, as you're probably discovering.'

'It was my idea. Agents often did it when they broke off relationships. It had the benefit of making it appear that Mark hadn't killed Alice, didn't know she was dead.'

'Nobody was even bothering to investigate that possibility by then. You and your superiors saw to that.'

Gillespie just shrugged. 'Call it insurance, then.'

'What happened next to Mark Woodcroft? Did you see him again?'

'Not for five years,' Gillespie said. 'Then he turned up in Cumbria, when I was living in Carlisle. He was finished on the squad, of course, and I couldn't have helped him, even if I'd still been with the Branch. They cut me out of the loop pretty early on.'

'What do you mean?'

'One of the things bothering him was why I hadn't answered any of his letters. It seemed he had written to me on numerous occasions asking when it would be possible, and safe, for him to come back to England. He knew his police career was over, of course, and I certainly didn't get the impression that he either expected or wanted it back. He'd moved on. He wasn't even Mark Woodcroft any more; he was Murray Wilson. Funny, he always kept the same initials, no matter what identity he assumed. Superstition, I suppose. I told him that I hadn't even received any of his letters. Clearly, they had been intercepted at a higher level and either filed or destroyed, most likely the latter.'

'How did he seem to you?'

'Different. Oh, he looked much the same – he always was a fussy dresser – but there was a hard edge to him I hadn't noticed before. Maybe it had always been there. And I think he was on drugs. Cocaine most likely, judging by the way he was so jumpy and fidgety, pacing about as he talked. He said what happened up in Leeds and afterwards had made him realise how pointless his job had been, that down in Marseille he had learned to use his skills in other ways. He wasn't worried about a career. He said he had plenty of new opportunities and it would be no problem for him to make a packet.'

'Drugs?'

'That's what I suspected, especially given his erratic behaviour. But he never came right out with it. I guess he couldn't forget that I was still a copper. Apparently, after a while in Paris, he'd drifted down to Marseille and infiltrated the club scene, or so he told me. Real *French Connection* stuff. There are some remarkably tough crims down in Marseille, I've heard. He travelled a lot, made a lot of contacts, and again I assumed it was to do with drugs and perhaps the clubs – gambling, prostitution and so on. Remember, he was freelance now, no longer a police officer, and I imagine pretty soon there was a shift in his way of seeing the world. He was working for himself now. No rules. No boundaries. He'd already broken the law once in a serious way, killing Alice Poole, and after that, I think he started unravelling morally, and became the opposite of what he'd been. It happens to coppers more often than we think, and I think it happens even more to undercover officers with a very unstable sense of who they are to start with. He's not the only one I've seen turn to the dark side over the years. In the end, he wanted to come home and put his new skills to use over here, along with old ones, such as infiltrating criminal groups, pretending to be someone he wasn't. Only this time he wouldn't be doing it on the right side of the law. He didn't come right out and say all this, you understand, but it wasn't hard to infer it from what he did say. And I had an old mate on the Marseille force I'd met at a conference, Ron Maisonville, so I phoned him and he told me an Englishman very much resembling my description of "Murray Wilson" was connected with some of the big and nasty guys in the Marseille crime scene. So he served his apprenticeship in Marseille and came back here to reap the benefits. We parted badly, and he warned me that I'd better never reveal anything about what he'd done because he'd drag me down with him. I told him I had no interest in revealing what he'd done. And my part in it was something I'd have to live with for the rest of my life. He sneered at that and left.'

'What did he do after he came back? Do you know?'

'Not really. We didn't keep in touch. I heard things from time to time. For example, once, towards the end of my time in Cumbria, I came across a description of someone very much like Melvyn suspected of working with the Colombians. It was a request for information from West Midlands, so it seems as if he got around.'

'But you knew he was Wesley?'

'Yes. I knew that he was going under the name Michael Wesley, and that he was a big player on Sheffield's crime scene.'

'How did you know that? You'd retired by then, surely?'

'By chance. You probably know I ended my illustrious career at South Yorkshire. It's true I retired in 1994, but I still had some mates left down there. One in particular. We'd meet up every now and then for a meal – he was a bit of a gourmet – and at one of the restaurants we went to he pointed out Michael Wesley to me. He'd mentioned him before, of course, and the initials MW should have clued me in, but when I saw him, I recognised him immediately. I don't think he saw me.'

'So you knew Woodcroft was Wesley before he phoned you in May 2015?'

'Yes, it was probably about 2012 when I saw him in the restaurant.'

'Why didn't you report him?'

'Again, I would have thought that was obvious. He kept my secret, my part in covering up a murder, and he made it clear that if anything happened to him, he'd let everyone know. And there would have been no evidence of his misdeeds. He was very careful that way.'

'But everyone will know now. You're telling me.'

'It doesn't matter any more. I'm dying, Mr Banks. I don't care what happens to me. I'd like to spend my final days with my wife, but that's all.' He coughed. 'Could I please have a glass of water?'

Banks glanced at Winsome, who left the room to fetch a glass of water. Gillespie sipped it slowly, his hand shaking.

'Do you want to take a break?' Banks asked.

Gillespie shook his head. 'No. I've come this far, I'd rather finish it, if that's all right.'

'Fine with me. But let me know if you're too tired to carry on.'

'Thank you. I will.' He put the glass down.

July 2012

I became familiar with the *News of the World* hacking scandal after about ten years at the *Guardian*, in 2005, by which time I was considered senior and talented enough to be let loose on it as part of a team of investigative reporters. I had already built up a substantial network of sources in all areas over my time on the paper, and was able to dig up a great deal of background information when it was discovered that a private investigator working for a *News of the World* reporter had intercepted a voicemail relating to the royal family. Our team soon discovered that the hacking had spread much further than the royal family, to include government ministers, MPs in general, footballers, celebrities, the military and others. Over the following few years, we also found out that the police, so it appeared, knew about this but did nothing, perhaps because they themselves had been supplying the papers with information for money.

We continued to report on these matters on and off over the next few years, and in July 2011, the shit hit the fan when it was revealed that the voicemail of murdered schoolgirl Milly Dowling had been hacked shortly after her disappearance, along with the phones of victims of the July 2005 London bombings. This all led to multiple high-level resignations and, ultimately, to the closure of the *News of the World*. Not a great loss, as far as the *Guardian* was concerned. David Cameron announced the Leveson inquiry into the whole affair, and like greyhounds let out of the starting gates, reporters from all over the country were off chasing the hare down the course.

This was, of course, a case of journalists reporting on other journalists, and I must say how glad I was that the *Guardian* was owned by a trust rather than a greedy Australian media mogul. The trust made most of its money elsewhere, which meant that though the paper was still a business and always tried to make a profit, we weren't reliant on the political whims of our owners and the parties they supported.

It was when I was still working on the hacking scandal in 2012 that I came across Gary Kirk again. By then, the erstwhile secretary of the Leeds University Marxist Society was a Labour MP, whose phone had been hacked when he was on a government committee dealing with the MPs' second-home expenses.

It was nothing earth-shattering, but some damaging information about his homosexuality had found its way into the *News of the World*, and after trying various methods to identify the leak, it was discovered that the only way it could have been done was through the hacking of telephones and voicemail.

When I came across Kirk's name, I remembered him from the old university days, so thought I would take it upon myself to go and interview him, both to see if what he had to say about the hacking business would make a good story and because, well, I suppose because he was a link with Alice, who still consumed my thoughts when I least expected her to.

We met in a crowded pub close to the Houses of Parliament and settled down in a corner with a couple of pints. Some journalists avoid meetings in pubs and cafes because they fear someone might overhear, but I had never found it a problem. I was wary, of course, and cast an eye around for suspicious characters every now and then, especially reporters from rival newspapers, but in my experience, most people were far more interested in their own conversations than anyone else's. And the noise level was usually so high you couldn't hear what anyone at the next table was saying. Over the years, I had developed my own form of shorthand and used a notebook for interviews instead of the mini tape recorders preferred by others. It sometimes made transcribing a little harder – mostly because of my terrible handwriting – but that was a small price to pay for the convenience.

'Well, I never,' said Kirk as he leaned back in his chair and took stock of me. 'If it isn't *the* Nick Hartley. Done all right for yourself, haven't you?'

'I can't complain.'

'I always wondered what happened to you. You haven't changed all that much, I must say.'

'On the other hand, you've lost a bit of hair and put on a few pounds. The high life?'

'I wish. You were an arrogant little prick back then. Maybe some things don't change.'

'And you were a narrow-minded apparatchik who walked around as if he had a stick up his arse. Have you changed?'

'Touché. Well, it's a good thing we've both grown up a lot since then, isn't it? What was it, thirty years ago? Married?'

'I never seem to have met the right woman.'

'Still stuck on that young lass you went out with back then? The one who got herself killed?'

'Alice.'

'That's the one.'

'I still think of her, yes.'

'I'm sorry. I didn't mean to be so blunt.'

'And I thought it was a common trait of Labour MPs.'

Kirk shrugged. 'She was a bright lass, and her heart was in the right place. I liked her.'

I nodded.

'Did you ever find out what happened?'

'No. All I know is it wasn't the Yorkshire Ripper.'

'But you have your suspicions?'

'Always.'

'The new boyfriend?'

'Mark Woodcroft. Yes.'

Kirk took a long pull on his pint. I did likewise. 'Woodcroft,' he repeated. 'That was the one.'

'Another of your members.'

Kirk raised an eyebrow. 'Woodcroft wasn't a fully signed-up member,' he said. 'Just a sort of hanger-on. He was actually a member of the Socialist Workers Party.'

'Did he have a job?'

'No. But that didn't matter to them. Don't forget, these were the Thatcher years. Quite a lot of workers were without work.'

'But you mixed socially? The two societies?'

'We had a lot in common, yes, though our methods were different. The SWP was always more inclined to use violence to achieve its ends.'

'Do you know what happened to Woodcroft?' I asked.

'I never saw him again after Alice's murder. Nobody did, as far as I know.' Kirk paused. 'I might know something, but you mustn't make too much of it. I'm taking a risk talking to a journalist about it.'

'Well, as anything you know about Alice and Mark is nothing to do with the main reason for our meeting, I don't think you need to worry about that.'

'Word of honour?'

'Yes.'

Kirk slugged back the rest of his pint. 'Another?' he asked.

'Please.'

Kirk went to the bar and as I waited, I wondered what on earth it was he had to tell me. Though I had thought about Alice a lot, I hadn't really given Mark Woodcroft much consideration for some time. As far as I knew, he might also be dead. But if Kirk knew something about the circumstances of his disappearance, it might help me fill in a few blank spots from the past.

He came back and plonked the drinks down on the scratched and scarred table. 'It was around that time,' he said.

'What time?'

'The time Alice was killed.'

'OK. Go on.'

'Well, as I'm sure you know, we were a pretty harmless bunch of theoretical Marxists. I mean, we never did much but attend lectures and read books. Went on the occasional peaceful demo. We talked a good revolution, perhaps, but mostly we were a bunch of middle-class kids with our heads up our arses.'

'What I always thought,' I said.

Kirk grinned. 'But once in a while we rubbed shoulders with far less harmless, less savoury people at international conferences and so on. It was inevitable, sharing the same basic ideology, to a degree, and differing only on the way to achieve the changes we wanted.'

'Like the Socialist Workers Party?'

'Oh, they weren't that much different from us, really. True, there were a few thugs in the organisation looking for an excuse for a punch-up, but that didn't happen very often. No. I'm talking about serious threats. Baader-Meinhof, the ETA – the Basques – the Red Brigade, the Red Army Faction, Black September and, of course, the Provisional IRA and its more violent offshoot, the Irish National Liberation Army.'

'Sounds like that Monty Python movie with all the different fronts,' I said.

'Very much. Except these were far more deadly.'

'What happened?'

'In Leeds at the time, we had some active members of the IRA. Now it's true it wasn't usual for Marxists to have anything to do with the IRA, especially a student Marxist society, but some factions of the left wing were becoming more violent – even our group – talking about forming a party called Red Action, and some Marxists were already supporting the IRA paramilitary wing, the INLA. That may be what Woodcroft had been sent to find out about. He couldn't go direct to the source, but by hanging out on the fringes – the Marxist Society, the Socialist Workers Party – he might be able to find a way into the more serious combatants. Especially if he expressed a willingness to embrace violence. But he was conned.'

'Hang on. What do you mean, he was sent to find out? By whom? When?'

'Sorry, I'm jumping ahead. Of course, you don't know. Bear with me a while longer, please. I happened to get to know one of the Irish crowd, a bloke called Kevin O'Leary. Sounds like a cliché, I know, but that was his name. My mother's Irish, and it turns out he came from the same village, so we chatted every now and then. He was very cagey. He was interested in Marxism and came to a couple of our lectures, but there was never any talk of practical politics or official business, you understand, just a pint and a chat about the old country. I'd say we met maybe three times in all. One of those times, I saw Mark Woodcroft just leaving his table as I arrived. It was in a pub just out of the city centre, off the beaten track, actually, so it surprised me to see him there.'

I remembered what Mandy had told me about seeing Mark with a rough-looking man in a pub in Leeds and wondered if this could have been the same occasion, the same person. 'Go on. I'm interested.'

'I mentioned this to Kevin, but he said nothing at first, just looked thoughtful. A few days later – this was not long after the murder and Woodcroft's disappearance – I saw Kevin again and he took me aside.' Kirk glanced around. 'It was a crowded pub, much like this one. First, he asked me how I knew Woodcroft, and how well, then, when he was satisfied, he told me a story. It seems Woodcroft had been sniffing around the IRA for a while now and one or two people were getting quite suspicious of him and his questions. According to Kevin, they came up with a plan. Basically, they set him up. They took him into their confidence about an assassination attempt on an important cabinet minister who was supposed to be visiting Leeds in a few days' time. It was all pure rubbish, of course. They were stringing him along, testing him out. But they obviously managed to convince him with carefully planned details and so on. When the day came, one or two of the IRA members set themselves up at viewpoints on the route and they saw armed police breaking into the very places they had told Woodcroft their assassins would be waiting. There was even one place they said they had as a back-up, with a bomb planted there, and the bomb squad went straight in. Well, it was pretty obvious to everyone by then what was going on. The cabinet minister never turned up, by the way.'

'Mark Woodcroft was a police informant,' I said, half whispering. Why had I never thought of that before?

'Exactly. But you didn't really know him, did you? And the only context you saw him in was as the man who you thought had stolen your girlfriend. He'd disappeared days before the sting operation. I asked Kevin if they'd ever seen or heard of him again and he said no. I believed him. If he had still been around . . . well, I wouldn't have given much for his chances. As it happened, that was also the beginning of the end for me as far as radical groups were concerned. I started to edge away from the Marxist Society and the rest, became more interested in working through the system to change it from the inside. But that's about the long and the short of it. Mark Woodcroft was an undercover police officer posing as a young radical.'

'Christ,' I said. 'Did Alice know?'

'Not as far as I could tell,' said Kirk.

'Do you think they could have . . . ?'

'Who? The IRA? Alice?'

'Why not, if they found out about Woodcroft? They were hardly known for showing mercy.'

'There's no reason they would have even known about Alice. Alice had nothing to do with Mark Woodcroft's other life.'

'As far as you know. OK. But what if she found out who he really was somehow? Confronted him. Knowing Alice, she had a temper on her, she'd have hit the roof at being conned that way, feeling betrayed by someone she trusted and cared for.'

'It's not for me to say,' said Kirk, 'but Woodcroft would no doubt have had a very clear idea of what would happen to him if his cover was blown.'

'Enough to . . .'

'Kill Alice? Possibly,' Kirk said. 'But we can't possibly know that she discovered his true identity and confronted him with it.'

'Perhaps not, but it would have given him one hell of a motive. Others in the house heard them arguing on the night Alice died, though they didn't hear about what. They also heard heavy footsteps going downstairs in the middle of the night, and a car driving off. Woodcroft was never seen again, at least not around those parts.'

'I wouldn't jump to too many conclusions, Nick,' said Kirk. 'Besides, it was over thirty years ago. There's not much you can do about it now.'

I drank some beer. 'Perhaps not. But there's plenty of food for thought.'

'You haven't forgotten why we're here, have you?'

'No.' I took my notebook out. 'How and when did you first become aware your phone was being tapped?' I asked, but my heart wasn't really in it. All the time I talked to him I was thinking about Alice, imagining that final confrontation between her and Mark, his hands around her throat.

20 December 2019

'Perhaps we can move ahead now and talk about what happened after the phone conversation in May 2015?'

Gillespie rubbed a hand across his brow. 'A couple of things happened shortly after the news about the inquiry into undercover policing was announced that March. First off, I had a journalist from the *Guardian* come buzzing around asking questions. He'd already been nosing about around the Yard – you know how these reporters always have their sources – and he'd picked up a few hints that something was amiss in the programme.'

'What was his name?'

'Nicholas Hartley. Anyway, the long and the short of it is, I gave him a quote. Just to get rid of him, you understand, but . . .'

'What did you say?'

'That we should welcome such an inquiry. That there were a lot of secrets that might come out as a result.'

'That was pretty foolish, wasn't it?'

'I'm not saying it wasn't. But don't tell me you've never screwed up with a bloody journalist. Like wasps, they just won't go away.'

'So let me guess: Michael Wesley read this article with the quote and it got him worried?'

'Right. It's not hard to find me. I'm in the phone directory, for a start. I missed his call, and he left a message, and that's the one I was replying to, the one you found out about. Naturally, he was pissed off and concerned I was going to speak out of turn, despite our shared secret. He suggested I arrange a meeting between the three of us, preferably at my place, and that he and I should meet first and work out a strategy.'

'Did you tell Wesley the journalist's name?'

'No. It didn't seem relevant. These inquiries take a long time to get up to speed, and we were pretty certain that there was no existing documentation. Believe me, nobody at the Met or the Home Office wanted it to be known that one of our undercover agents had got away with murder. But a prying journalist can stir things up and cause trouble, especially one from the *Guardian*. There were still a few people around the Met who'd heard rumours of the Alice Poole murder and the involvement of an SDS officer. And you can't silence everyone. But, on the whole, we were pretty sure things would turn out all right. I couldn't put him off, so I thought Michael

Wesley and I together could give him a convincing story.
Something that would satisfy him, at least. Maybe give him a
couple of juicy titbits about the undercover operations to send
him off in other directions. That was the plan, anyway.'

'Might Wesley have recognised Nick Hartley's name from
the byline on the story?'

'That's hardly likely,' said Gillespie. 'How often do you look
to see what the writer's name is when you're reading a newspaper? Besides, who'd remember the name of a girlfriend's
ex-boyfriend from thirty-five years ago?'

Banks tried to think. He'd been going out with Emily Hargreaves when he was Hartley's age back then, and she'd just
split up with someone. Could he remember the name? No
way. 'Well, maybe if the girlfriend had been murdered,' he said.

'Even so . . .'

'Did it not cross your mind that Wesley might have been
trying to arrange the meeting so he could get rid of you
both? That that was his reason for suggesting he come out to
Wilveston Farm that night?'

'No. But OK, let's say you're right. Maybe I'm being stupid.
Maybe he did remember Hartley's name and thought he'd get
rid of us both. But it didn't seem that way to me at the time.
It doesn't matter now, anyway. Whatever he had planned, it
didn't work out for him.'

'And you had no idea that Nick Hartley and Michael
Wesley, or Mark Woodcroft as was, knew each other?'

'Not at that time. None at all. How could I? I know now that
Hartley was Alice Poole's ex-boyfriend, and that he blamed
Woodcroft for her murder, but I didn't know it at that time.
I may have heard his name, thirty years ago or more, when
I was dealing with Mark, but if I did, I didn't remember it.
Nick Hartley was nothing at all to do with our operation up
in Leeds.'

Gerry had told Banks that Nick Hartley denied knowing either Gillespie or Wesley, but she had sensed he was possibly lying. Now it was clear he had wanted to distance himself from what had happened at Wilveston Farm that evening in May 2015.

'So what happened that night?' Banks asked.

'Wesley suggested a particular evening, a Thursday, I think, and I said OK. I invited the reporter. I really thought we could put this thing to rest, put him off the scent. Wesley arrived first, as planned, and we went through what we were going to tell the reporter, what we could say to convince him there was nothing untoward, and so on. We could give him a few juicy stories – not concerning us, of course – but something that would sell papers, and send him on his way. Then he arrived.'

'What happened?'

'Like particles colliding. It took the two of them only a short while to recognise one another, then they were at it. Shouting, shoving. I got between them and tried to calm them down, but Wesley was having none of it. He was strong, stronger than both of us, and he knocked Hartley to the ground and tied him up with some electrical cord. He said we should kill him, that it was the only way. I argued that someone was bound to know where he'd gone, that he'd be missed and there would be others to follow. But Wesley was used to making people disappear, he said. He also had a gun, and he was waving it around like a madman. I had realised all those years ago what he was, how he'd changed when he came back from the Continent. But right then, when Hartley was lying on the floor struggling with his bonds and Wesley was walking up and down with the gun in his hand and spouting about what he was going to do to him, I just snapped and told him no: I wasn't going to stand for Hartley's murder, that I'd rather stand trial for my past actions if

I had to. I meant it. I'd been carrying the guilt around with me for years, and the thought of atonement was taking more of a hold. Then he came at me, turned the gun on me. I knew then it wouldn't matter to him if he killed us both. I was close to the fireplace, so I picked up the poker and hit him. He stopped and dropped the gun, then I hit him again, and he fell. After I checked and found he was dead, I untied Hartley. I wasn't sure what to do with him. After all, he'd seen me kill Wesley, but it was in self-defence, and in defence of *his* life. He could go to the police, I supposed, but after we'd talked a long while and I'd told him much of what I've just told you, I didn't think he would do that.'

'You even told him about covering up Alice's murder?'

'Yes. Everything. I think he believed me that I was genuinely gutted by the whole thing. I'm not saying he condoned it or anything, but at least I'd just killed the man who did it. Wesley was a monster I had helped to create, and now I had destroyed it. That was some sort of justice, I suppose.'

'What did you do with the gun?'

'There's a flooded quarry about two miles from the farm. I dropped it in there the next day.'

'What kind of gun was it?'

'I've no idea. I never worked with firearms. A small, black snub-nosed sort of thing.'

'So what happened next?'

'I just told Hartley to go, do what his conscience told him was best, but that I'd take care of everything. I maybe felt deep down that it wouldn't be so bad even if he did go to the police. I deserved it. If not for Michael Wesley, then for Alice Poole. But time passed and nothing happened. No stories in the press about errant undercover agents – well, plenty of those, but none about them turning to murder – then the CPO came in, and I moved to Lytham, met Sylvia and . . . well, we've been living there quite happily until the diagnosis.'

'Why did you bury Wesley on your own land?'

'To be honest, I didn't think too much about it. It was very much an on-the-spot decision. I didn't have far to go, and the field was pretty much abandoned. It was a lonely spot, so I was unlikely to be disturbed, and even if I was, it was my land. Why shouldn't I be digging there?'

'In the middle of the night?'

'That might have been harder to explain, but nobody came.'

'And when the CPO came through? You could have moved him then.'

'I didn't really have the heart for it. And I hadn't got the stomach to dig up his corpse and move it. Whatever you think I am, I'm not a monster. Besides, where would I move it to? I didn't think I had anything to fear. If they did concrete the field over for a road or a forecourt, so what? An archaeological dig never entered my mind. Not until DS Jackman here mentioned it when she first came to talk to me.'

'What about Wesley's car?'

'One of the perks of my job was that I built up a number of useful contacts over the years, not all of them above board. There was a chop shop in York that would have had it a different colour and number plate and in Saudi Arabia in the blink of an eye. There wasn't much else to clear up except the blood on the flagstone floor.' He drank some more water. His hand was still shaking. 'Are we nearly finished now? I'm really very tired.'

Banks glanced over at Kathleen Bryant and nodded. 'I think we can call it a day for now, Mr Gillespie,' he said. 'You know the drill. In a short while, you'll be charged and placed in the cells until you face a magistrate. Do you have anything more to say?'

Gillespie shook his head. 'No,' he said. 'Nothing more. It's all been said.'

14

20 December 2019

The celebration in the Queen's Arms that evening was about as joyous as you'd expect when you've just consigned a dying man to prison. Not that Harold Gillespie was ever likely to see the inside of a jail cell. The following day, Nicholas Hartley would be called in to corroborate Gillespie's story and make an official statement.

But it felt as if the hard work was over, and the team met up after work. As per tradition, Banks bought the first round – white wine spritzers for Winsome and Gerry, orange juice for Wilkie Collins and a pint of Timothy Taylor for himself. They found an empty table and sat around sipping their drinks, looking glum. Cyril seemed to have jumped forward in time with his playlist that evening. Linda Ronstadt was singing 'Dark End of the Street'. Banks was only thankful he wasn't playing Christmas music like everywhere else. He had put the decorations up, though, and a large tree festooned with tinsel and blinking red, green and blue lights stood in one corner.

'Look,' said Banks. 'We did our jobs, that's all. It's a shit deal. I'm not making excuses. But we didn't kill anyone, we didn't cover up a murder, and no matter how bad Gillespie felt about what he did, he still did it.'

'So what will happen now?' Wilkie Collins asked.

'Surely you remember your legal training? The CPS will step in and decide whether we've got a case. With a confession, it's usually a shoo-in. Then the lawyers descend, bargain, haggle, whatever it is they do.'

'Will he go on trial?'

'I doubt it. In the first place, he confessed. He's not pleading not guilty, so he won't go in front of a jury. Like I said, the lawyers will thrash it out and reduce the charge and the judge will rubber-stamp it. But if you ask me, I don't think Gillespie will live long enough even to get that far. There's such a backlog these days, he'll be dead before he gets to court.'

'No jail time then?'

'I very much doubt it. He's hardly a flight risk, so he'll stay on bail until they've worked out the charges and so on. At least he'll probably get his wish to spend his final days with his wife. Even if he did plead not guilty – or extenuating circumstances – he'd probably get off. His boss basically told him to get Mark Woodcroft out of the country and erase all traces of what he'd done. And any competent barrister could argue self-defence in the killing of Michael Wesley. The fact that Wesley was a nasty piece of work would also count in Gillespie's favour.'

'What about Nicholas Hartley?' Gerry asked.

'Failing to report a crime? I don't know,' said Banks. 'I suppose we'll have to charge him. It's a serious crime, but perhaps in this case his lawyer, or his newspaper's lawyers, will also be able to bargain down. Let's face it, Wesley *was* going to kill him.'

'According to Gillespie,' said Winsome.

'You don't believe him?'

'Yes. It's not that. But you have to admit his confession had a kind of "processed" element to it. I'm not saying it was manufactured, but it certainly felt well worked out, as if he'd examined it from every angle and made sure he'd got it all covered. Hartley in jeopardy, Wesley turning on Gillespie, the handy poker. Then there's burying the body. Did it really not enter Gillespie's mind that it might be found on his land? And why not move it when he heard about the CPO? Surely he knew then they'd be digging up the land? That story about him not having the stomach for it sounds a bit weak to me.'

'It's no weaker than anything else,' said Banks. 'Woodcroft killed somebody on *his* watch. Gillespie was party to covering it up. That meant they shared a guilty secret from then on. Neither one could get out of it without putting himself in jeopardy. But Woodcroft underwent his sea change in Marseille, went to the dark side. Gillespie was the only one who actually *felt* guilty, the only one with a conscience. It ate away at him over the years.'

'I suppose so,' said Winsome. 'But it still sounds weird to me.'

'It is weird,' said Banks. 'But then, so are a lot of things. And people. Confessions often sound weird, too.'

'I know. I suppose I'm just pointing that out.'

'So, basically, nothing's going to happen to Gillespie?' Wilkie Collins said.

'Well, Gillespie's going to die of cancer very soon, if you call that nothing.'

'I mean legally.'

'No. That's just the way it happens sometimes. You'll have to get used to it.'

'It's not that I want him to go to jail,' Collins said. 'I'm not one of those "hanging's too good for him" types. As a matter of fact, I'm against it. Hanging, that is. I feel sorry for the poor sod. I just wanted to know how the process works from here on. It's my first murder.'

Gerry touched his shoulder. 'Don't worry, Wilkie,' she said. 'We'll make sure you're involved in all the paperwork on it from now on.'

Collins blushed. Winsome winked at Banks. Eventually the others wandered in – Jazz Singh, Stefan Nowak, even Kim Lee and Dr Karen Galway. They pulled over another table and spread out. Banks bought more drinks. With the influx of new people, the mood shifted and Gillespie and his fate were more or less forgotten in the general buzz of conversation and laughter.

But Banks had heard Winsome's doubts, and he wasn't without his own. In a way, she was right; it was all too pat. It was, of course, quite possible that Gillespie had planned this murder from the start, luring Wesley to his isolated farmhouse after the announcement of the inquiry. Perhaps he and Hartley had been in cahoots and planned it between them? That would explain why Hartley had lied about knowing Gillespie or Wesley. As an investigative reporter, Hartley could have found out about Gillespie from the same source Burgess found out about Alice Poole, only 'Alice Poole' would have meant a hell of a lot more to him than it had to Burgess or Banks. Maybe it was even Hartley who had dealt the final blow. But it was nearly five years ago, and there was no forensic evidence – the farmhouse had been flattened – and no witnesses except Gillespie and Hartley themselves.

The Alice Poole murder was even more remote – forty years – and it was only through Burgess's intricate network of old mates that Banks had been made aware of the case. Gillespie's old boss was long dead, and there was no one to gainsay his explanation – the IRA plot against the government, the decision to cut Woodcroft loose and get the locals in Leeds to back off. It was all so believable,

especially in the light of some of the things that were coming out of the inquiry already, about the SDS undercover
cops forming sexual relationships with vulnerable women
and so on. Perhaps the inquiry would dig up something
on Gillespie, Woodcroft and Alice Poole. Maybe it would
make the headlines, and Nicholas Hartley would write the
story. But it wouldn't have much effect on Gillespie, who
would most likely be dead by then, or on Woodcroft, who
had been dead for years already. *Cui bono*. Nobody, that's
who. But all this, he told himself, was pure speculation,
imagination.

The music changed. He hadn't been listening for a while,
but suddenly Fleetwood Mac's 'Man of the World' was playing, one of the saddest songs Banks knew. Somehow, the
Christmas tree and colourful decorations made it seem even
sadder. He looked up to see his boss AC Catherine Gervaise
walk in and offer drinks all round. He got up and went to the
bar with her, helped her get the order in and carry the drinks
over to the table.

'How's it all going?' she asked on the way.

'Fine,' said Banks. 'Everything's going just fine.'

'Got your man again, I see.'

'So it seems.'

Gervaise frowned. 'What do you mean? Nothing wrong
with the confession, is there?'

'No, it's not that,' Banks said, putting the drinks he was carrying before Winsome and Gerry. 'I can't quite put my finger
on it, but something just doesn't feel quite right.'

'We all have doubts, Alan. We second-guess ourselves all
the time. If I were you, I'd put it out of my mind and get that
there pint down you.' She held the drink out to him.

Banks took it and sat down. 'You're probably right,' he said.
And began to work at getting that there pint down him.

13 May 2015

Over the next few years, the hacking scandal managed to keep us busy much of the time. The gift that keeps on giving. In addition, there were plenty of other stories to entertain and amuse us: cash for access, offshore tax havens, various lobbying and corruption scandals and the daily run-of-the-mill escapades of the usual parliamentary suspects. But through all that, I didn't forget my discussion with Gary Kirk, and I didn't forget Alice.

One of the things I learned early on in my journalistic career was the importance of reliable sources. It helped to know people in the know, such as cops, councillors, politicians and those who worked on their fringes, such as cleaners, secretaries, aides and manicurists, who might just overhear the odd gem every once in a while. It had to be a strong reciprocal relationship based on mutual trust, and I liked to think I had achieved that all along the line. Your source had not only to have impeccable qualifications, but also complete faith that you wouldn't reveal his or her identity. Of course, to publish anything important, you had to have two sources or more, but you didn't need two sources to put you on to a story in the first place, which was the other important thing I learned.

Also, a good journalist doesn't simply do as he's told: he goes out and finds stories, or sources and whistle-blowers phone him with tips because they trust he can get something done. Then he goes to an editor and sometimes gets approval, sometimes not. But he must always be hungry for a new story, not content merely to write up the latest council meeting or am-dram production, which was of course where I started back in Ossett.

So over those years, whenever I could take the opportunity, I would do a little more research into the world of undercover police officers, and when Theresa May announced the inquiry into undercover policing in March 2015, I was already at the front of the queue as one of the most qualified to tackle the story, armed with the necessary sources and leads.

It was a source in Scotland Yard who nudged me towards my first breakthrough, a retired officer who had worked on the Special Demonstration Squad in its early days. I tracked him down to a seaside cottage in Whitby, on the North Yorkshire coast. I didn't have to work too hard to convince him that his identity would remain anonymous and any information he gave me would be sacrosanct. As it turned out, he didn't know much, but to my elation, he did remember some trouble over a woman called Alice Poole. He knew no details, but said he assumed the woman had made some complaint about being deceived into a relationship with an undercover police officer. Apparently, it happened all the time, and nobody really took much notice of it. He didn't remember the officer's name, but he did remember that the handler was Harold Gillespie, an old friend, now himself also long retired. He said he thought Gillespie lived on a farm in Yorkshire, though he couldn't remember exactly where, but I knew I could find him easily enough through the usual means – mostly likely the phone book.

Shortly after the inquiry was announced, I rang Harold Gillespie. He said he didn't remember anything about an Alice Poole, or Mark Woodcroft, and that as far as he was concerned, none of his agents had affairs with the people they were sent to spy on. But he knew what was coming with the inquiry, so he agreed to see me and discuss various issues of his old job. And he did give me a good quote about secrets coming out. Perhaps he hoped to head off any trouble at the pass, but he said he would need to contact a few others first, and for me to hang on until I heard from him. If I was patient, and lucky, I might even get to meet an ex-undercover officer.

Then, in the second week of May 2015, Gillespie invited me to come over to his farm on the following Thursday.

21 December 2019

Banks couldn't sleep the night of the celebration, and it wasn't because of the beer, or the Highland Park he had enjoyed with Love's *Forever Changes* when he got home. It was the case. Something felt wrong, as Winsome had said, and he couldn't put his finger on what it was. There were all kinds of little things – Winsome's suspicions to do with Gillespie not moving the body when he received the CPO, or even burying it on his own land, to begin with. And her sense that the whole confession had a sort of manufactured air about it.

He got up well before first light and made a pot of coffee, then listened to *Today* as he drank it and mulled over his ideas. It was over a week after the election, but it was close to Christmas, and things were fairly quiet on the political front. After half a pot of coffee and two slices of toast and marmalade, he set off for the station. It was a Saturday, and he didn't have to go in, but there were things he wanted to check. It was a chilly morning and what light there was seemed thin and weak.

Up in his office, he turned on the desk lamp and set about reading statements and notes. There was Gillespie's confession, all neat and tidy, answering all the questions that had been put to him. There was really nothing to be faulted. They had a solid case, motive, means, confession, so what was wrong? Gillespie had been Wesley's handler back when he was Mark Woodcroft, an undercover police officer in the Special Demonstration Squad. Woodcroft had killed Nick Hartley's ex-girlfriend, Alice Poole, because she had uncovered his true identity, and if she told her political friends who and what he really was, it would risk the operation with the IRA group he was infiltrating. So far so good.

Jump forward to 21 May 2015, a couple of months after Theresa May had ordered an inquiry into the SDS. Fearing they might be brought to task for their crime, Gillespie and Wesley get together, on Wesley's initiative, to get their stories right. A *Guardian* reporter called Nicholas Hartley starts buzzing around Gillespie, who thinks it would be a good idea to invite him to this meeting with Wesley. With any luck, they can give him enough to put him off the trail. Then it all goes tits up. It turns out Wesley and Hartley know one another from way back, and Hartley suspects Wesley of killing Alice Poole, his ex-girlfriend. A fracas ensues, Wesley pulls a gun and Gillespie wallops him with a poker, then sends Hartley on his way, buries the body on the far side of his land, dumps the car in a chop shop and tosses the gun in a flooded quarry. End of story. Or is it?

Things could have happened differently. Of course they could. People lie, misremember. But there seemed no reason for any of that in this case. Unless . . .

It wasn't a road-to-Damascus moment, more like the slow glimmer of an old radio valve lighting up, but it was a possibility, and there were things Banks could do to check it out and make sure he was on the right path.

21 May 2015

It was dark when I pulled up outside the farmhouse in North Yorkshire. There were already two cars outside in the yard, a Land Rover I assumed to be Gillespie's and an old-model Porsche. If Harold Gillespie had persuaded a retired undercover police officer to talk to me, he was clearly someone who had done well for himself.

Gillespie opened the door when I knocked and led me through to a large living room. Though it was mid-May, it was a chilly evening, and there was a fire burning in the large fireplace. Another man stood warming his backside by the fire. He seemed vaguely familiar, but it took me a moment to recognise him. His hair was different, of course, and he was wearing an expensive suit, but after a short while, there was no doubt in my mind that I was looking at Mark Woodcroft.

I glanced towards Gillespie. 'What the fuck?' I said.

'It's Hartley, isn't it?' Woodcroft sneered, moving towards me. Somehow, I got the impression he was on drugs, most likely cocaine. His movements were jerky, and his eyes were wild. 'Tell me, which rock have you crawled out from under? Reporter for the *Guardian* now, are you? My, my, how we've gone up in the world.'

'You bastard. You—'

'Oh, save it,' he said.

'What's going on?' Gillespie cut in. 'Do you two know each other?'

'I wouldn't say that,' Woodcroft said, 'but we had a girl-friend in common back in uni days. Alice, wasn't it?'

'You know damn well.'

'Yes. Alice. Thick as two short planks, but a bloody good fuck. Talk about a screamer. She told me all about you, you know. How useless you were in bed. How you could hardly get it up half the time. How you—'

I couldn't help myself, but I punched him. It was only a glancing blow, but it brought a speck of blood to his lip. Gillespie tried to hold me back with one arm while keeping Woodcroft at bay with the other. 'Let's be civilised about this!' he cried.

'He killed her,' I said. 'This man murdered Alice Poole.'

Gillespie let go of me, but Woodcroft was having none of it. He was breathing fast and reddening, his eyes turning to nar-row slits. 'So what if I did?' he said. 'The interfering cunt was ready to blow the whole operation, just because she found my old passport, the one in my real name. I tried to tell her I was James Bond on a secret mission, but she wasn't having any of it. She was fucking hysterical by then.'

'You bastard.'

Woodcroft pulled out a gun from his waistband and turned to Gillespie. 'What are we going to do with him, Harry?' he said. 'I say we kill him now. He's a fucking journo. We can't trust him.'

'This isn't a story he can tell,' said Gillespie. 'Besides, he'll be missed. You can be sure his people know where he is. They'll come looking.'

'So what? You might be here, but I won't be. And you won't be telling them anything without incriminating yourself, will you? Or should I kill the two of you?'

'My God. Is that what you planned to do from the start?'

While Woodcroft was glaring at Gillespie, I spotted the poker in its stand beside the fire and grabbed it. He turned back to me, still pointing the gun, and in one smooth motion I swung it as hard as I could at Woodcroft's head. It made contact with his temple, and he stopped mid-sentence, dropped his gun and put his hand to his head, then brought it away wet with blood. He looked disbelieving, surprised, as if no one could ever do such a thing to him. I hit him again, perhaps even harder that time; his legs buckled and he crumpled to the floor.

'My God,' said Gillespie, kneeling beside him and feeling for a pulse. Woodcroft's eyes were open, and I could tell that he was dead. I'd seen dead eyes before. 'You've killed him,' he said, standing again.

I dropped the poker. 'What are you going to do? What the hell did you think you were doing, inviting the two of us like that?'

'I didn't know,' he said. 'I knew Mark from the old days, of course, but I had no idea you knew him. How could I have?'

'He never mentioned me back then?'

'Why would he? You weren't on his brief.'

'Christ.' I slumped on to a sagging armchair. 'What a mess. So what are we going to do about your friend?'

'He's no friend of mine,' Gillespie said. 'Sure, I was his handler. I helped him out when he was in trouble.'

'You mean when he killed Alice?'

'It was my *job*! And if you want to know the truth, there's not a day gone by when I haven't regretted it.'

'Good for you. What's he doing here?'

'He got in touch with me when he heard about the inquiry. He read the article you wrote after we first talked. Said we should meet up and get our stories synchronised. Then you turned up.'

'And look how that worked out,' I said. 'What *are* we going to do? We should probably call the police right away.'

'No,' said Gillespie. 'Think of the questions. It's way too complicated. It'll all come out. The past. Everything. They'll know you had a motive because he killed your ex-girlfriend. They won't believe it was self-defence. As for me, that whole business of thirty-five years ago will come out. I'll be ruined, if not sent to jail.'

'Then what?'

'We'll tidy up. Make it look like nothing happened, like he wasn't even here.'

'Won't he have friends who know where he is?'

'I very much doubt he'd have told anyone in his immediate circle. He's a wealthy career criminal now. He probably won't even be missed. I'll bet the police will certainly be glad to be shot of him.'

'So what do we do?'

'You take the body and get rid of it as far away from here as possible. There's a shovel in the yard you can take if you want to bury it. That's probably best.'

I swallowed. 'I don't know if I can do that.'

'Your future depends on it, so you'd better try.'

'And you?'

'I'll clean up the blood, get rid of the car. And the gun.'

'How will you do that?'

'I have my contacts.'

'And nobody will be any the wiser?'

'If we're lucky.'

Then we talked for a long time, Woodcroft's body still lying on the floor in front of us. I was ready to hate Gillespie for condoning and covering up Alice's murder, and I still found it hard to forgive him. But I understood the position he had found himself in. He didn't know Alice. And, besides, it was Woodcroft who had actually strangled her, not Gillespie. So we parted, if not as friends, at least as enemies who understood and perhaps respected one another.

It seemed a reasonable division of labour. Gillespie helped me get the body in the boot of my car, wrapped in a cotton bedsheet, and threw the shovel in after him. Then he told me to get on my way and never look back.

It was late by then, well after midnight in the quiet countryside where most farm folks are in bed by dark. But I felt sick with anxiety. I couldn't get the image of the body in the boot out of my head. What if he wasn't dead when I opened the boot? I was even flashing on that gruesome scene at the beginning of *Goodfellas*. And before I'd driven very far, maybe just a mile or so, I came across a field beside a rough country lane, with no houses in sight. First, I put the car out of the way, in a passing place. Then I managed to get the body over the drystone wall, which was by far the hardest part. The soil was hard at first, but softer after I'd dug a few inches, and it didn't take long. When I thought it was deep enough, I rolled the body in and, trying not to look, covered it up again. I patted down the earth, threw on a few sods and set off for home.

23 December 2019

Nick Hartley made a lonely and anxious figure sitting across the interview-room table from Banks and Winsome. His newspaper hadn't supplied him with a solicitor, as the reason he was there was nothing to do with his immediate assignment. Instead, he had managed to engage a local solicitor from one of Eastvale's most prominent firms. Banks had worked with, and against, Lindsay Chalmers a few times before, and knew her to be both fair and conscientious.

In the time since his minor epiphany the previous day, Banks had managed to accomplish a number of things: he had talked to both Gerry and Winsome again about the interviews they had conducted; he had got in touch with a mobile phone company; and he had talked to Drs Galway and Runcorn again extensively. A police frogman had also recovered Michael Wesley's gun from the quarry, under Gillespie's directions, which at least confirmed Gillespie's contention that Wesley had been armed – unless it was his own gun, of course, which seemed most unlikely, given the circumstances. It was a .38 snub-nosed Colt revolver, American in origin, and it still had all six bullets in its chamber. It would probably be impossible to trace back to Michael Wesley, as it had no doubt been acquired illegally.

First, Banks got Hartley to sign a consent form, which his solicitor read over first and OK'd. Then, after reciting the caution and turning on the tape machine, he asked Hartley if he would describe what happened at Harold Gillespie's farm on the night of 21 May 2015. Hartley didn't even bother denying that he'd been there but began by apologising for not mentioning this on his previous interview, with Gerry, but said he was nervous about Gillespie implicating him. As a seasoned journalist – for the *Guardian,* no less – he didn't fully trust the police. Banks was with him on that, though he was careful not to admit as much. But now they had Gillespie's signed confession, he said, there was no reason why Hartley couldn't corroborate his story, was there?

'Not at all,' Hartley said, and proceeded to give them, in almost exactly the same words, the story that Gillespie had told of the events at Wilveston Farm on 21 May 2015.

When he had finished, Banks let the silence stretch a moment, then said, 'Are you sure it was Harold Gillespie who struck the fatal blows?'

'Gillespie hit him with the poker, if that's what you mean.'

'Twice?'

'Yes. Twice.'

'On the side of his head?'

'Yes. Here.' Hartley pointed to the spot.

'When did you first meet Gillespie?'

'That same night. May 21st. We'd only spoken on the phone before then.'

'And he had no idea who you were?'

'You mean that I was Alice's ex-boyfriend? No. All he knew was that I was an investigative journalist.'

'Have you seen or spoken with him since that night?'

'No. Why would I?'

Winsome slid over a sheet of paper, which the solicitor scanned first.

'This is a list of Harold Gillespie's phone calls on the evening after his first interview, after he left the station.'

There were only two numbers listed, and Hartley swallowed as he looked at them.

'That one,' Banks pointed, 'is Gillespie's wife, Sylvia. No doubt he was informing her he would be staying in Eastvale overnight and wouldn't be home. But this one, here, is yours, if I'm not mistaken.'

Hartley said nothing.

'Am I right?' Banks asked.

Hartley glanced at his solicitor, who nodded.

'I suppose there's no point denying it,' he said. 'Yes, it's mine.'

'What did Mr Gillespie want to say to you?'

'Just to tell me that he'd been interviewed about that evening at the farmhouse and he was OK. That he'd told you what happened, made a full confession.'

'And that made you feel relieved?'

'I don't know if relief is the word, really. I mean, I felt sorry for him. Like he said, it was self-defence.'

'Oh, I shouldn't worry,' Banks said. 'We take things like that into account. We found the gun, by the way. Michael Wesley's gun. That goes a long way towards corroborating the self-defence plea. Besides, given his condition, I don't think Mr Gillespie will be seeing the inside of a cell any time soon.'

Hartley frowned. 'His condition?'

'Didn't he tell you? He's a dying man. Terminal cancer.'

'I . . . oh . . . I didn't know. I'm very sorry to hear it.'

'Yes. He's got nothing to lose by confessing. He told me he probably wouldn't even live long enough to go to court.'

'That's sad.'

'Yes. Something bothering you, Nick?'

Hartley tugged on his goatee. 'No. Why do you say that?'

'Well, let's say I have a suspicious mind – I'm a typical copper – but I find it interesting that we have a man who gives us a comprehensive confession to a crime and then phones the other person who was at the scene with him. Someone who previously never even mentioned that fact to my DC.'

'I've told you about that. I apologised.'

'And that makes it all right, does it?'

'I'm sorry.'

'Are you sure Harold Gillespie didn't call you to tell you what he'd told us so that you could repeat that same version of events, if asked? To get your stories straight?'

'But that's what happened. Why would he lie?'

'Why, indeed? In addition to being a sick man, Harold Gillespie was consumed by guilt. Guilt over something he did a long time ago. He helped a man get away with murder. The murder of your ex-girlfriend, Alice Poole. And I think he had a very good motive for his confession: atonement. To his mind, saving you was the only thing he could do to atone for what happened to Alice on his watch.'

Hartley put his head in his hands.

'What are you suggesting, Superintendent?' Lindsay Chalmers asked.

'I'm getting to it,' Banks said. 'Please be patient. Well, Nick? I'm waiting.'

Hartley looked up. 'Waiting for what?'

'Your answer. Don't you think it likely Gillespie confessed to the crime out of a sense of atonement, and because he has nothing to lose? You, on the other hand, still have a fairly reasonable length of time ahead of you.'

'But I didn't do it. Yes, I was there, and I didn't report the crime, but I didn't kill Mark Woodcroft.'

'I think you did. Shall I tell you why?'

'Why?'

'When I got to thinking about things, I realised we'd probably never solve this case satisfactorily because we didn't have any solid forensic evidence. After all, Gillespie's farm has been flattened, and Woodcroft, or Wesley, was a skeleton when he was dug up. But skeletons also have their stories to tell, Nick. I went back over the reports and talked again to the scientists who handled the post-mortem – a forensic anthropologist and a forensic pathologist. I could list their qualifications, but I don't think I need to. Not yet.' Banks glanced at Ms Chalmers, who didn't react.

'I don't understand,' Nick said.

'According to the experts, Mark Woodcroft was killed by the two distinct blows to the side of the head – the temple, in fact, near the front, where the bones are most fragile. Exactly where you pointed just now. The weapon was a heavy rod, a poker, perhaps. It also broke the eye socket.'

'So? That's what Mr Gillespie said.'

'Yes. He said Woodcroft was walking towards him pointing the gun, and he hit him twice with a poker.'

'That's how it happened.'

'No, it's not, Nick. The blows were struck from the front, to the right side of Woodcroft's head. Had to be. Do you know what that means?'

'I . . . no . . .'

'It means the killer was left-handed. Harold Gillespie is right-handed. I've checked. But you are left-handed. My DC remembered from her little chat with you. And you proved it just now, when I put the pen on the table for you to sign the sheet of paper. You picked it up and signed it with your left hand. Then again, when you pointed to the spot on your head.'

'But that's . . . preposterous. It's . . . no jury would ever convict anyone on such weak evidence as that.' He glanced at Lindsay Chalmers. 'Would they?'

'Not for me to say what a jury would do,' said Ms Chalmers. 'But I think you should try to answer the superintendent's questions as truthfully and as fully as you can.'

'Are you really sure, Nick?' Banks went on. 'It's a scientific fact, solid forensic evidence. The blows were struck by a left-handed person. Of the two people left alive in that room at that time, one is right-handed, and the other left-handed. You are the left-handed one. Harold Gillespie took the fall for you because he felt guilty for the death of your ex-girlfriend, even though he'd never met her – or even you, before that fatal night at the farmhouse. He'd certainly heard of Alice Poole from Mark Woodcroft, and he'd been partly responsible for shutting down the police investigation into her murder over forty years ago.'

'It was still self-defence,' Nick said. 'Woodcroft had a gun. He was going to shoot me.'

'OK,' said Banks. 'I'll accept that. I'm not saying there weren't extenuating circumstances. I'm sure Ms Chalmers here will do her very best to make sure the circumstances are clear to all. But what I want from you is the truth. I don't like being lied to. And I don't like the idea of someone going to jail – or even just being charged with – a crime he didn't commit because he's covering for someone else. That reeks of cowardice. I think Harold Gillespie told you he was terminally ill and that he had confessed to the crime you committed, and you let him do it. Neither of you thought it would ever come to this, and when it did, you thought you were home free. Well, you're not, so you'd better start telling us the full story – the true story – right now.'

Hartley rubbed his eyes and sipped water from the glass in front of him. Then he glanced at Lindsay Chalmers, who gave him a nod, turned to Banks and said, 'Let me start at the beginning.'